THE MAN
BURNED BY
WINTER

THE MAN BURNED BY WINTER

WINTER

A ROOKER LINDSTRÖM THRILLER

PETE ZACHARIAS

THOMAS & MERCER

Published by Thomas & Mercer, Seattle

www.apub.com

Amazon, the Amazon logo, and Thomas & Mercer are trademarks of Amazon.com, Inc., or its affiliates.

ISBN-13: 9781542039659
ISBN-10: 1542039657

Cover design by Zoe Norvell

Printed in the United States of America

For my mother, Lorna.
And for anyone with a dream.

Prologue

Snowfall

She would be the third one, another piece waiting to be finished. He imagined the brushstrokes, the wand flourishes, and that gentle wisp sound on the cotton fabric. With his eyes closed, he could see the eighteen-by-thirty-six canvas. They were always done in neutrals: whites, grays, and blacks, like a perfect photograph.

The only splash of color, a signature in the bottom right-hand corner, like a velvet bead of water—or a drop of blood trickling down.

The flurries fell against her skin. Her face was bare, chalky and pale aside from the mascara tears frozen like charcoal at her cheeks. She was lovely, a perfectly blossomed rose. Eyes like blue glass stared up at the starless night sky. Cotton speckles drifted to the banks of snow below. Their mist lit the trees, leafless and withering through a light fog. Through their naked branches, he made out the semi's high beams: two watchful eyes, milky white and intrusive. From a quarter mile away on the expressway, the semi looked like a Hot Wheels car. With a whistle of wind, the 18-wheeler's squeal vanished around a bend, and it was gone.

He was left alone again with her.

He peered up at the powder that glazed the alder and oak branches; every now and then a faint crackle would signal one's crash to the ground. The trees survived the brutal winter by going dormant, everything within slowing down.

She lay with her back up against the tree, her breasts as porcelain as the snow surrounding her. She wasn't dormant. She was dead. He'd made the perfect snow angel. A flake danced from the sky and fell gently on her cheek; he caressed it with the knuckle of his gloved hand until it was gone. Broken twigs and dead earth had tangled and matted in clumps on her ash-blonde hair. Despite the size of the hole in her chest, the bleeding had finally stopped. The sea of white had begun to slither over her bare legs; by the time she was found, they'd be swallowed whole.

She was the third body the police would find, and they'd be further from catching him than when they'd found the first. There would be traces of lubricant from the prophylactic in her mouth, but they wouldn't match it to that found on any of the previous victims. They would look for foreign hair, blood, fingerprints, semen—but they'd find nothing. They were trying to solve an intricate puzzle without so much as a single piece. He'd leave them something, but they wouldn't know what it was. He had folded the photo in quarters, zipped it inside a plastic bag, and stuffed it into her mouth. It was only a copy. He'd send them the real one soon enough.

While she lay there, now looking up at him, he brushed the hair from the front of her shoulder to her back. He left her tears frozen like icicles on her fair skin.

She was light. He'd carried her from the ice-fishing shed nearby. It was small, but large enough for his needs. The hut was invisible in the night, obsidian siding with a bloodred metal roof and warped wood floors. Two tiny windows were on opposite ends; no chance she'd be able to fit through. The nearest road was a quarter mile away, and Route 169 was nearly a half mile to the east. He'd studied every way in and out, who came and went, for a week. After seeing no one, he'd decided it was the perfect place.

He'd been watching her longer. The lying-in-wait, the stalking, blending in with the darkness—he loved it. It made him feel invisible. Powerful. Sweat dampened his hair beneath the brim of his dark baseball cap, the perspiration in the pits of his underarms soaking through his T-shirt, the bulge growing in his pants.

He seemed ordinary. That was his gift. He didn't struggle to be social. He hadn't been a bed-wetting, animal-carving, Oedipus-complex youth. Sure, he'd been drawn to violence early on, but what boy wasn't? They were always out playing cops and robbers, cowboys and Indians— or whatever they were supposed to call it now. He'd never forget holding his father's gun for the first time at age nine. The rifle was hidden high out of sight on the dining room hutch, a Winchester Model 70. He marveled at it, the weapon heavy and glistening in his little hands. He'd also never forget the way his mother screamed at him to never touch it again. He learned later the reason she was so angry: the rifle was loaded.

Even now, he thought back to the night that changed everything. There'd been a murder not far from home; he'd eavesdropped while his mother and father spoke in hushed voices over supper. When it came on the nightly news, his parents shut off the television. But it was the talk of the town, so he soon learned. A girl had been raped and beaten to death by her ex-boyfriend. Everyone knew Marcy Knight for her double Ds and they knew Billy Simms for being a low-life piece of shit. Only a few miles away, he couldn't resist the urge to sneak out. He slipped out late that evening when everyone was asleep and rode his seven-speed Mongoose Switchback two miles, cloaked in black to blend in with the night. Grouse Creek Road was surrounded by wide-open land, mostly wild grass, tall weeds, and barley fields. There were some houses and barns spaced out, but at night it was capsuled in blackness.

The bike was still a little big for him, the seat like a horse saddle, high and stiff, digging into his bony ass. He slowed in front of the house, sweat starting to bead down the messy haircut his mother had given him. He dropped his bike to the curb. The house was still sur-rounded in yellow tape, which he ducked under.

The door was locked. He should've known it would be. But he thought one of the windows might be open to get some of the smell out. He moved fast, pulling at each one. Luckily enough, toward the back of the house, one window budged. He slid it open and climbed inside. The windowsill dug into his rib cage. Red lines, maybe even bruises, would linger, but he didn't care. He flicked the switch on the hefty Maglite he'd stolen from beneath the sink at home. After a blink, the room was illuminated in a dim phlegm yellow. He crept into the bedroom and saw the blood splattered on the wall and king bed. He shined the light there, mesmerized by all of it. The mattress had sunken in the center. *Marcy Knight*, he thought while he admired her blood.

The room had soured. Still, the musty darkness and dead-body smell didn't faze him. In the harsh light, the ceiling warped and cur-dled until it was lost in the shadows. The rug was an ugly gray and old. Numbered yellow markers perched on the floor. He shined the beam over them, at the red lines and blotches on the carpet and the rigid imprint of a large sneaker sole. While he backed away to take it all in, he bumped into the mirrored vanity, where the bitterness of hair spray and mint lingered.

He heard a rattle of keys, thought he heard someone coming to the door. He flicked off the flashlight, ran to the window, and hopped down to the ground, his pants catching and tearing as he climbed over the sill. He slid the window shut behind him as quietly as he could, made his way back to the bike, and pedaled off at light speed for home. With sweat trickling down his forehead, the cool breeze tugging at his damp hair, he imagined himself as Billy Simms while Marcy Knight died under him.

The next morning, his mother woke him. He'd be late for the bus if he didn't get up. He hopped out of bed, felt a mess in his underwear, and saw a small, dark stain in the flannel sheets. When his mother went to make the bed, she saw it too. And he lied.

He told her that he wet the bed, that the murder on the news scared him. She kissed him on the forehead and told him it was fine, that she wouldn't tell his father. She started pulling the sheets, and he got changed for school. He went on like nothing changed, but everything had. From then on, he'd sit in the classroom daydreaming about how Billy killed Marcy. He found himself wondering about pain and blood.

Over the years, he had studied people like himself. He was more than aware how murder cases were run. He'd studied criminal defense and criminal justice, analyzed how serial killers worked and why some got caught. He read everything he could find on psychological profiling. With four kills and counting, his hat was in the ring. He was one of them, even if he wasn't crazy about the term *serial killer*. He was different from them. He was *better*, he told himself. He wondered when the police would finally let the public in on his—*their*—secret. That the bodies were connected. That there was a serial killer, and the Land of 10,000 Lakes was his hunting ground.

He wondered what they would call him when his work was done.

His eyes were closed. He could feel her there before him, cold and dead. And as he lifted the radio, he pinched the volume knob and turned it up. Crackling static and droning voices rang out, followed by a female dispatcher's voice and some sort of whirred chatter coming from a different channel's frequency. As he listened, he could feel the snow splash wet and cold against his warm skin. An icy wind spread goose pimples all over his body.

. . . 10-83 . . . Hick's Bar . . . Repeat, disturbance at Hick's Bar. Something about . . .

He listened for a few minutes before he opened his eyes and looked down at her—and nearly smiled. He powered the radio off, turned on his back foot, and left her there. By the time the police showed up, his tracks would be long gone, erased from this world, as was she. His boots sank ankle-deep in the vast ocean of white. They plunged deeper and deeper as if he were walking through quicksand. The cold snaked up his ankles and into his socks. Though the muscles in his back and calves were screaming, the pain was refreshing.

The police needed to hurry. If they waited too long, the picture wouldn't be perfect anymore. A spell of warm fall weather was on the way; the pristine snow would turn gray and slushy, and she would turn purple and blue and attract the crows. He was angered by the thought of their batting wings and shrieking caws. The vision of them pecking at her eyes and pulling at her flesh, ruining his masterpiece.

PART I

Chapter 1

WHAT HAVE YOU DONE?

The voice sent Detective Tess Harlow bolt upright in bed. Her eyes snapped open so fast, the vein in her head pulsed. The night table handle rattled. The drawer whisked outward. Her hand fell over the SIG Sauer P226. There was no one. *Another nightmare.*

For a long time, that voice had reminded her of melt-in-your-mouth chocolate brownies, fresh out of the oven. Before they went in, as a little girl, she always got to lick the batter off the wooden spoon. Now the voice—*you'll see for yourself*—that's what she told Dad.

She had slept her usual toss-turning nights up until a month ago. She'd lain there, eyes closed, listening to the whoosh of the toilet valve around midnight. The snapping creak of Mrs. Crawford sleepwalking on the floor above hers between one and two. But they didn't keep her up all night. Neither did the homicides or missing persons.

But ever since this case landed on her desk, she felt the shadows on the walls watching her.

It started after they found the first body. *That gruesome cut across the victim's throat . . .*

The feeling only worsened after the second and third victims. Dread hung there in the dark. She could sense it crackling in the air. While she lay in bed trying desperately to sleep, her pulse racing, there was something ominous haunting her. She thought she knew the culprit.

Fear.

She changed out of an oversize shirt and into plain clothes. She brushed her hair and tied it in a ponytail, holstered her gun, put a pot of coffee on, and ripped into a protein bar.

◆ ◆ ◆

Tess scribbled her name and the time on the clipboard and sauntered to room 6B. *9:12 a.m.* She rubbed at the hammering ache behind her eyes before her knuckles rapped delicately on the nameplate for Janice Harlow. One lone flower petal fell to the floor before she turned the handle.

Seeing that name always made Tess grimace. After all, Janice Harlow didn't exist anymore, not really. Her mother hadn't spoken—hadn't *really* spoken since the incident. Shortly after, Tess had gone over to the house one afternoon. Her mother was still wearing the same pajamas she had on the last time she'd seen her. Fruit flies swarmed everywhere. Bananas had sunk, jet-black. Tess's dad was gone. With the craze of her work schedule, there was no other option than assisted living.

The room was nothing fancy. The bed was made. A cheap flat-screen played Janice's soaps. There was a kitchenette and an empty table with dead flowers in a vase. There in a flannel checked pajama set sat Janice Harlow, stiff as a board on the seaweed sofa with an old news-paper in her lap.

Tess walked over to the crystal vase, pulled the dead roses out, and replaced them. "Hi, Mom," she said.

Her mother stared at her with a blank smile. She wasn't dying. She wasn't old. But after the incident, she wouldn't take care of herself. And she wouldn't speak. Not even to her only daughter.

Tess had been there when her mother identified the two men who were now back on the streets. Janice Harlow only nodded and muttered one word. *Snowflake.*

Weeks later, her mother already a recluse, Tess Harlow was the next of kin called in to identify her father. The last time she'd seen him alive was the first time she'd seen him cry—*really* cry. He said he failed. When she asked what he meant, he said, "To protect and to serve." And she understood. Joe Harlow was buried in Itasca Calvary Cemetery. This time of the year in Minnesota, the earth wasn't particularly ripe for digging a grave plot. She remembered driving on the 169 past the cemetery and seeing Tommy-John Michaels—ironically, he played football instead of baseball. All-state lineman—bundled up, operating the backhoe.

With her mother staring mutely at the TV, Tess unfolded the paper printout from her pocket. It was an article from the *Valley Chronicle.* She studied the title and byline.

THE BATTLE OF ANGELS AND DEMONS
By Rooker Lindström

Before she could read long, she heard her mother's grumble. She lifted her head to see Janice staring at the same newspaper article as last time. Her fingers curled around the paper arthritically. And that was when the words left her lips chillingly, in the same voice that haunted Tess's dreams, a voice that wasn't *Mom.* This woman sounded possessed, like a different voice said it from over her shoulder.

"WHAT HAVE YOU DONE?"

For a split second, she looked at her mother gravely. Tess turned her head away from the vacant stare as fast as she could, but her hands couldn't wipe the tears away faster than they fell. She hurried to the door without another word and shut it with her back to the room. Her face trembled. She sniveled, the way she'd cried when she was a little girl.

And as she slowly stopped shaking, she sniffled hard, cleared the shaky rasp from her throat, and pinched the ash-white scar on her fingertip.

While she signed out on the visitor log, the heavyset orderly behind the desk tried to console her. "She'll be okay, hon."

Tess looked down at the name tag on her shirt. "Margery, just get her out of the fucking pajamas."

She walked away thinking about demons.

◆ ◆ ◆

Thin ice, Harlow. Pretty soon it's going to collapse beneath you.

On the drive to the station, she replayed Chief Larsson's thinly veiled threat in her mind. She was weeks, maybe days away from transfer or demotion. This from a chief who was the prototypical deadbeat—Jim Larsson hadn't been in the office in more than a month. When he graced them with his presence, he puttered along and appeared half-asleep doing it. And yet he had given her extraordinarily little time to catch a serial killer, and so far, they had nothing. Nothing aside from three bodies, two killed identically, but all three left with a calling card. Each one was a black-and-white photo print—the location where the body was staged—with a bloodred droplet in the bottom right-hand corner.

As she walked past the bullpen, Tess was surprised to see the whole team was already at their desks: Detectives Vic Sterling, Xander Whitlock, and Martin Keene were clustered in the center of the room, with Detectives Elias Cole and Millie Langston at opposite ends. Tess's old desk used to be right across from Martin's before she was promoted to lead the team.

"Tess," Detective Vic Sterling implored with a half-eaten hoagie sandwiched between his hands.

"How can you eat that shit before noon, Sterling? And when you argue with me, it's 'boss.'"

"Boss." He saluted her with the sandwich still in hand, oil or vinegar or some liquid substance running down his palm. "Keene just filled us in on the Lindström plan. What the hell are you on about with that nut? You want to bring our lead—hell, our *only*—suspect into our investigation?"

"It's my call."

Whitlock pulled the Styrofoam cup from his lips. "Not a good one," he uttered.

"What was that?" she said.

He went on slurping his coffee loudly, his lips wet with foam. He gave a whatever-you-say shrug and wiped his mouth with the back of his hand.

"Look." She sat on the edge of an empty desk. "He'll be a consultant with limitations. I just want to see if he can help us out."

"The guy's a pencil pusher. How's he going to help us—by writing a column on the killer? Just save us all the time, slap the cuffs on him, or . . ." Xander raised a finger in the air like the greatest epiphany in the world landed, wings fluttering in his lap. "Just shoot him."

"Did you want to leave, *Alexander*?" Tess said.

His brow furrowed. "Need I remind you he's the son of Gunner Lindström? Just sayin'—this guy shows up here out of the fucking blue, and bodies start popping up like herpes sores."

Sterling took another colossal bite from his hoagie, lettuce and pickle falling out the other end. "Experience in that arena?" he asked with a mouthful of food. Crumbs flew from his mouth, and he brushed them from his desk to the floor. Tess saw Millie Langston's nose wrinkle in disgust.

"Fuck off." Whitlock's lip curled. "It's him. We're idiots to think it isn't."

"Well," said Keene. "Innocent until proven guilty."

"He's not a columnist, by the way," Tess said. "He's a journalist. He's covered crime for a decade. He's published articles on serial killers, deep profiles. And yes, *Xander*, he was raised by one. He was the victim of the Madman, Tate Meachum—*who he caught*. At the end of the day, maybe he can give us a different perspective."

"I still don't think that makes him any more qualified than one of us," said Cole. "Your call, though."

Tess rubbed her caffeinated eyes and stood. "Look, I'm not saying he's more qualified. But he has some experience in this realm. How many serial murder cases have any of us worked?" The silence spoke volumes. "Let's go over what we do have."

"Three women," Sterling spoke up. "Midtwenties to early thirties. All three white, blonde, between five feet three inches and five feet eight inches. Weight between one hundred twenty and one hundred sixty pounds."

Cole chimed in next. "No DNA from our killer left on the victims or the calling card. Bruising to the face, body, and buttocks. Nonfatal knife wounds on the torso and abdomen. Fatal knife incision—possibly a hunting knife—to the sternum. Damage to the vaginal wall."

"The hotline?" Tess asked.

"Just a few wackjobs—phony confessions and pranks here and there," Keene said. "Looks like he's right-handed. The blow to the right side of the face is nearly identical to the last two victims."

"We have three bodies," Tess said. "Keene, Cole, and Whitlock—I want each of you recanvassing the areas where the victims were last seen."

Whitlock tilted the last bit of liquid into his mouth and tapped the bottom of the cup until it was dry. "No one saw a thing. We have no eyewit—"

"*I know.* Believe me, I know. But we can't wait for another body. Just try again. Take your pick. Follow up with the families, best friends, significant others. Let me know what you find. Langston—" Millie Langston was sitting with diplomatic posture, jabbing the point of her pen against a pad. "Keep looking for commonalities among the vics—physical features, job, schooling, anything. Maybe you can narrow down the grid of where they were last seen or taken. Maybe we find his hunting ground."

Langston was already clicking away on the keyboard at light speed. "On it, boss."

Xander crushed the cup in his fist. "Where will you be?"

"Paying a visit to Mr. Lindström. I want us to keep our eyes on him. There's still no telling if he'll help us—he doesn't like police, not after what happened to his son—but I'm willing to try." She started to walk away.

"What about the chief?" Keene asked.

Tess grabbed her coat from her chair and spoke over her shoulder. "Fuck Larsson. Let's go, Martin."

Tess pushed through the double doors and winced when the air nipped at her neck and plunged into her jacket. She zipped it up to her throat. The cold only seemed to submerge deeper into the depths of the coat's lining. A quick shudder forced its way out of her. The parking garage's fluorescent lights burned dim overhead. They flickered like a quiet flame, some smelling like singed hair.

Tess pressed the button on the fob, and the car doors clicked open. She slid inside and shut the door fast, a breath of cold air leaving her lips just as quickly. A short-chained badge hung from the rearview mirror. She touched a finger to it—the one with the scar in the shape of a snowflake—breathed in, and started the car.

Chapter 2

He woke up to a dripping sound. His gaze slowly rolled up to the ceiling. *Shit.* Overhead, the old boards were damp and sagging, only a few rusted nails holding them in place. The split-level wood cottage was splitting at the seams. *Condemned* and *not fit for human habitation* were the inspector's citations. Foundation issues riddled the cottage, maybe termites or dry rot; he hoped there wasn't asbestos, but he knew there probably was.

His father had left the place to him when he died. It was one of the few things he'd ever given Rooker—unless you counted a good beating or two, or twenty, or some unwanted advice on being a man. Even back then, the place was barely standing.

In the early nineties, the tabloids coined the cabin's one thousand square feet *Lindström Manor*.

If the walls could talk, they wouldn't. They would scream.

But to someone unaware of what had happened in the house all those years ago, they'd see a fixer-upper on a private half-acre lot, where cracks of warm sunlight bled through the old hickory trees onto a yard plenty big enough for little ones to run around, not to mention a sweeping, million-dollar view of Deer Lake. Rooker's best memories of the place were from childhood, especially the warm, impenetrable darkness of the woods. The kind of dark where you can't see your hand in front of your face unless there were clouds of fireflies or the gentlest flashes of lightning over the lake.

On a summer night, they looked like a hundred light bulbs a hundred feet away, all switching on and off. He never cared to catch them. Sitting far away from his father, he'd watch them, dozens of tiny amber glows brightening and dimming. While he listened to the sporadic chirps and rattles from the wet earth, the fermata of buzzing in the trees, he grew envious of them. Even as one tiny beetle landed on his forearm, its belly lit like a harbor light, the wings and antennae fluttered, and in an instant, he couldn't tell if it was still there. They could vanish. Why couldn't he?

Returning to the present, Rooker scratched his bed head, his fingers tangled in an unruly knot the shade of milk chocolate. His eyes shut. Gone was the prospect of drifting back into a fitful, insomniac sleep, of returning to the fireflies. For all the quiet of his remote home, Rooker's sleep was fragile as ever. So often, when his son, Britton, was still a baby, Rooker would wake at all hours of any black, still morning just to check on him: 1:43, 2:35, 3:49, 5:01. Sometimes he'd just lie hopelessly awake in the merciless silence—that awful, heightened ringing—listening for any sound just to go to him.

He hoisted himself up and surveyed the room. The sheets were balled on the floor; he'd never bothered to put them on the mattress. Only a blanket underneath him and a heavier blanket on top. The Minnesota winter crept in through the walls, the windows, and the wood. Even inside, it was enough to haze his vision and burn the bristles in his nose. Outside, he knew gray clouds flooded the skies, looming over him like a headstone.

The dripping sound continued, the roof water leaking through to the five-gallon plastic bucket beside his bed. He'd found it outside filled with webs and creatures and feces, but after a quick rinse, it seemed up to the job. It was just about full to the brim.

There was a banging on the door that matched the thumping in his skull. As more pounding erupted from the door, he blinked at the sandy residue mizzling from the ceiling. He stood up and looked out between the two-by-twelve wood planks that boarded the windows. They were still sturdy, the wood and nails much newer than the ones holding the roof together. While he scratched at three days' beard, he gave a glance at the vehicle and the plates through the narrow slit. A shadow-gray Ford Taurus parked in the fresh powder. Unmarked with blacked-out windows. Two telltale lights behind the front license plate. The ones hidden in the front grill. He found both. A detective.

It wasn't the first time he'd seen the car; the vehicle had been following him only days ago when he'd trekked into town for some essentials. He could still see the homeless man outside the market. Tethered by a red string to a shopping cart full of junk. A mangy gray beard, silver hair spilling out beneath a dirty beanie cap, and an old Vietnam War field jacket. He watched over the vet's shoulder, looking for any movement near the Taurus. Rooker noticed his feet, corned and split and raw. Without thinking, he slid his heels out of his boots, took off a pair of holey socks, and handed them to him.

"Hey, thanks," the man said in a low, broken rasp. But his next words were like an icy grip around Rooker's wrist. "You that Lindström boy, ain'tcha?"

"Nope," he said as his bare feet sank into the cold depths of his boots. "Wrong guy."

When the banging continued, Rooker accepted his fate; he'd have to face the detective sooner or later. From the shallow top drawer, he pulled a T-shirt and wrestled it on while he tiptoed down the stairs. Each step of old wood bawled. He didn't bother with pants, only adjusted the crotch of his boxers so nothing was too visible. On his way toward the door, he grabbed a bottle of cheap vodka off the end table and took a swig. It burned going down, but it woke him up ever so slightly. The door put up a fight, but after a few jerks it budged. He opened it just enough to see part of her face and to eye her petite but sturdy frame.

"Detective."

"How did you—"

"I'm not an idiot." He gestured past her. "Who else is in the car?"

"My partner, Detective Martin Keene. I'm Detective Tess Harlow."

"Why isn't he up here with you?"

"Because I wanted a word with you, and I didn't want you to feel threatened."

"Please," he said. "I can see his gut from here. What do you want from me?"

She gave a curt nod to the crack of room she could see behind him. "Mind if I come in?"

He stared down into her stormy eyes, overcast gray with shekel-gold flecks around her pupils. "Am I in trouble?"

"No."

He moved aside to let her in. She slid past him and into the living room, where there was a threadbare plaid sofa with sinking cushions; a coffee table splintered in areas, warped in others; and a depressing-blue recliner chair, which was where he typically sat. Aside from the books on the mantel, the only other things in the room were a fuzzy blanket folded over the back of the chair and a cheap flat-screen. As she slipped by him, he smelled what he was sure was men's cologne. Maybe she'd been trying to be more masculine on the job. At least 75 percent of her colleagues were male. He noticed her eyes scanning the cottage, taking in any scenery that was the least bit scenic. He knew what she was doing. He even knew why she was here.

"Mr. Lindström, is there any chance you can put some pants on?"

"You invite yourself into my house, then you tell me what to wear?"

"Fair enough . . . So, this is it, huh?" She hesitated and crossed her arms, hands burrowed deep beneath her elbows. Was she trying to look more imposing or attempting to stay warm? He figured the latter.

Beneath a steel-gray hooded jacket zipped halfway, she wore a navy fisherman sweater and a pair of dark wool gloves. "I like what you've done with the place." She said it as if she'd been there before. Of course, she'd probably gone through the crime scene photos. "They say you're a recluse now, bedsores and fangs and the works."

He watched her size him up, probably expecting a haggard skeleton. "Think that's a vampire. Wrong coffin."

"Right." He caught the edge of a smile before her head turned again, her eyes probably buzzing at gnat speeds around the room.

He sighed. "So, who is it you found dead? That's why you're here, right? You think I'm some wizard who catches killers?"

She turned back to him. "You were a crime reporter. You know I can't disclose that to a civilian. And for the last part—"

"What makes you think I can catch someone you can't?" He knew what he was, and he knew what he wasn't. And he wasn't someone who could help her. He'd been hitting the bottle daily, not only stopped working out but stopped living, and now he was seeing things—things that weren't there. Not only did he not want to help her, he thought, but he was in no condition to.

"You've done it before."

Scratching at the phantom pain in his shoulder, he scoffed. "Does that count as catching someone?" he said with a crude roll of his eyes. "A man eating free meals in a cozy prison cell, when he should be dead."

"Serial killers aren't exactly common here . . ." Her voice trailed off for a moment, but then she pressed harder. "How familiar are you with your father's case?"

A snicker flared from his nostrils. *Familiar?* Hell, he probably knew that case better than the detectives who worked it two decades ago. Despite the hardened numbness he'd built up toward his father, the morphine-like euphoria was fading. Now as he balanced his weight more so on one leg, he chalked up the judder in his hand to a lack of sleep. And though the mention of his father put his brain on high alert, the lethargic feeling overpowering him made him feel like a salted slug.

Sleep, he thought. *I just want sleep.*

But instead, he took the detective's bait. "Is that a serious question?"

"You know how he killed his victims?"

Suffocation. Then decapitation. Hunting knife.

She continued: "Suffocation. Then he cut their heads off clean. With a hunting knife. Not multiple slashes or lacerations but a pristine cut. The victim we just found—"

"You want my alibi?"

"I wouldn't be here if I didn't already have one. I want to bring you into my investigation. I read some of your crime beat articles and a few of your profiles. 'Master of Arts and Killing.'" She let that last phrase hang there. It was an article he'd written, a title he'd been pleased with at the time—thinking the pun clever. Now it made him wince. "You detailed several killers, BTK being one. And another one, the Madman . . . You investigated whether their impulse to create art was innate or developmental. You referred to them as artists in their own right."

He said nothing.

She has an alibi . . . How? What does that mean?

"You said that in killing, they 'fulfill their craving, like a vampiric bloodthirst' to create art. Do you really believe that?"

Now he scratched his arm nervously. "I believe that I can't help you."

He followed her eyes to the heavy bag on the other side of the room, barely held together by different lines and lengths of tape chained to the ceiling. The bag was rigged up over a wooden beam and held in place by a thick, rusted S-hook. An old weight sat beside it. All that was left from the Everlast logo were the *E*, partial *v*, and *t*. The rest camouflaged well, faded into the black leather material of the heavy bag. Dull-silver strips of industrial-grade tape plugged a few holes. He thought about taking a big swing at it but decided against it. He'd dismissed the weight set too. The one time he'd gone to work on his chest, the barbell sounded like it was cracking down the middle.

"We have a gym at the station. And food, coffee, even a shower."

"Insult after insult. You have a funny way of asking for help."

She walked over to the end table, reached to touch the picture frame that was facedown.

"Don't."

She stopped. "More people will end up like your son if you don't help us."

"Get out."

"Mr. Linds—"

"You have the nerve to come here throwing my son's murder in my face? And *the Madman*," he mocked, then bit down hard on his lip. "If you want to bait me with my son's killer, have the balls to say his name, not that bullshit. *Madman*. Tate Meachum is nothing more than a *man*, a vile one. And as far as your investigation goes, I sure as shit don't owe you people anything." His voice had grown louder, his hand rattling down at his side. "Don't come back."

She let out a deep sigh. "I'm sorry I upset you, and sorry that I used your son. But we may have a copycat . . . The first victim . . . Look, you were too young to do anything about your father. I'm giving you a chance—we could use your help." She took her card out of her pocket and slid it on the windowsill for him to see. When the door shut behind her and he heard the engine fade away, the dense silence of the woods returned.

He walked over to the photo. He never turned it over. Instead, he'd lie beneath the small glass table and look up at his son, happy as can be, smiling at him as if he were up in heaven. Not that Rooker was ever a believer. He'd seen bad things happen to good people, good things happen to the bad. But still, he had a morsel of hope. He couldn't bring himself to look at him now, though. Not today.

Chapter 3

For most of her life, Detective Tess Harlow hated the very idea of being a cop. Joe Harlow never wanted this life for his daughter. Her father was a man of few words, but he made it abundantly clear that he wanted her to be a doctor, schoolteacher, accountant—or anything else for that matter. She could hear the tenderness in that grizzly tone even now. *Anything but a cop.*

Her dad worked the graveyard shift: midnight to ten a.m. He was up all hours of the night, responding mostly to bar fights and domestics. Some nights—after she'd pretend to be asleep when he'd check on her before his shift—she'd sit up, wondering if her father would make it home. On the weekends, she'd hear him come through the front door and watch his body sprawl out on the couch with a cold plate of leftovers from the fridge. It was rare that she'd get to eat breakfast or lunch with him.

She never spent a New Year's Eve with him. Christmas was always on a different day. She hated that.

No little girl should understand police codes by the age of ten. But she did. When you grow up as a cop's kid, you're taught to see the world differently—more to assess it and prepare for it. Maybe it had prepped her for the life she chose: the caffeine withdrawals, the frozen dinners and takeout, for-the-drive protein bars, the meal-replacement smoothies.

Now she was at the gun range—Crossbones Firing Range—loading three spare magazines with 9mm Luger rounds. Ten lanes made up the room, each one no bigger than a bowling lane. There was a man at the desk wearing a blue flannel shirt tucked into the waist of his denim jeans, with curls of hair spilling out beneath a forest-green camouflage trucker hat.

The room was pungent. The smells of metal, coal, and charred black steak filled her sinuses. The concoction lodged in the back of her throat. Truth be told, she loved it. But today, she was distracted.

"What's going on up there?" Martin gestured to Tess's head with his own.

She looked down. A few stray hairs that hadn't made it into her ponytail fell in front of her face. She stood frozen in the next stall over from Martin. The man beside her didn't share her blood, but he'd become a brother to her. Windswept golden hair distracted from his unshaven blond face. He was husky at five foot eleven, but there was a deceptive brawn behind the white oxford shirt, black dress pants, and derby shoes. A bulletproof glass insert separated the two of them.

Snap out of it. "I just haven't been sleeping . . ." *Click*—the chamber snapped into place. "I don't think he's on board."

But really, there was a fire there, raging, burning steadily in her chest. *Crackling. Popping.* Her mind had the ability to compartmentalize, but in her heart—she stared down at the scar on her fingertip—there was anger. She couldn't help but think about the two men who tore her family apart.

Snowflake.

Martin rolled up his sleeves. "Melatonin. Sheila snores—it works wonders for me. And are you still on about Lindström?"

She pictured him all over again: six foot two, two hundred pounds give or take, handsome in a disheveled way. Messy dark hair and stubble beard, arms folded across his chest, standing there in a T-shirt and boxers. She remembered a small tremor in his hand—and the disdain he had for her, for the police. And the way he bounced on his toes the slightest bit. In the past, these were nervous tics she'd picked up on with suspects. But after being inside the infamous cottage that was Lindström Manor, she knew it wasn't nerves. The place could induce hypothermia.

Blistering cold.

The thought of being back inside made her teeth chatter.

The magazine clicked into the well. She turned her head to Martin. "He's clever—and stubborn. I think too much of both to jump at the bait."

"You can't get hung up on that, Tess. You tried. If he wants to rot in that cabin, so be it. We don't need him."

But we do need him, she thought. And then she wondered if she'd tried hard enough—whether she had gone about it the right way.

"Yeah, well, the clock's ticking." She tapped at the empty space on her wrist. "It's not your ass if we don't catch this guy."

"*What?* You mean the chief's—"

"Yeah, Martin. If we don't catch this guy soon—I'll be done. Maybe things will go back to the way they were, and I'll scoot my old desk across from yours. Or worse—you can help me pack up my office."

"Christ . . . Larsson . . . that old prick."

"*That he is.* And at the moment, we don't have a whole helluva lot to go on, do we?" When she turned toward him again, his head was hanging down like he was at her funeral. "Same as usual? Best shot wins . . . loser pays up?"

"You're on." Martin riffled through his wallet, unfolded a crisp ten-dollar bill, and slapped it hard on the table.

Tess put on safety glasses and a pair of padded over-the-head taxi-cab-yellow earmuffs. The lane went back seventy-five feet. She sent the target—a human silhouette with white circles and a red center of mass—as far back as it went.

She took a high grip on the pistol in the web of her hand. Posturing forward in a slightly lowered stance, Tess took aim down the sight—focused on the center dot—and pulled the trigger straight back.

Crack. Crack crack.

She fired a gun the way her father had taught her. She was taught that if she had to shoot at something—*someone*—to plant her feet, lean forward to balance out the recoil, and fire more than once.

Remember, if it's you or them going six feet under, it has to be them.

One by one, the cartridges ejected from the gun down to the right of her feet.

When she emptied her clip, she set the pistol down on the table and pressed a button that brought the silhouette toward her. When it stopped, she stared at the tight grouping—and then she turned to look at Martin's slightly wider pattern.

She smiled at him.

Martin shook his head, pulled his wallet out, and opened it. "Double or nothin'?"

26

Chapter 4

November 28

Rooker bounced on his toes. Rubbed vigorously at the goose pimples sprouting on his forearms. Lumbering into the bathroom, he stared at his reflection through the murky glass hung cockeyed above the sink. He looked more tired than he felt—which he didn't think possible. He'd aged considerably in the last year. Lines had formed in places on his face; he couldn't remember when he first noticed them. He'd broken a section of the mirror one night when he'd drunk himself mad. A right straight cracked it, and a chunk of mirror shattered to the floor. That night, he'd poured vodka over his bloody knuckles, hoping some would seep into his bloodstream, and wrapped the wound in duct tape.

Two months had crawled by since he had sentenced himself to die in this hellhole—his father's house of horror.

But even in the busted mirror, he could see shades of his father: a strong jawline and dark bags under his eyes. Rooker's California tan was long gone, his skin a sickly pale. For most of his life, he'd looked more like his mother. He had a thinner nose than his father's and eyebrows that weren't as bushy. He had eyelashes most women would kill for. Growing up, girls always told him he had pretty eyes. His face would pinken. His mother had told him he was far more handsome than his father ever was.

His finger outlined the date on his shoulder the way he used to trace the San Diego skyline from Centennial Park. The numbers were no longer etched permanently into his skin, but he could still feel them in his mind. Now there was only a scar from where his son's birthday had been tattooed. He couldn't bear to face it anymore, so he'd taken a knife to it, carving the skin as if filleting a fish. He could remember the blood dripping down his hand, pooling around the rusted sink drain. Infection and pain were the least of his worries. He'd needed the numbers to go away.

Now, as he looked in the mirror, he saw it all again. The date was there. He was digging away with the knife, his blood dripping. He saw his skin starting to decompose, maggots climbing out of the folds. The blood had curdled, turned to clumps and streams of black spew. It dripped down to the sink, down his forearm, down his legs to the tile floor. He shut his eyes. His heart thrashed. *No. It's not real.*

He went to the mirrored medicine cabinet. The blood and rot were gone, and his only tattoo was the one on his shoulder blade, the rook. His mother had a fascination with birds. The two of them spent hours on the porch watching them. The rook, a bird in the Corvidae family, had been her favorite. For her, it wasn't about all the flare and colors and feathers; it was about the intelligence. She told him how smart they were, how they could solve puzzles; she told him she had known he would turn out smart the second she laid eyes on him, and that's why she named him after them. She always called him Rook; she was the only one. And he loved that. She said the name sounded masculine, American. She didn't want him to be teased in the States, in a classroom with some proper Swedish name his father had wanted to give him, something she'd struggled even to pronounce. His father hated the name. He'd called him *boy* instead, with that harsh, grizzly tone.

After she passed, he got the tattoo. The design was traditional black and gray with a hint of white in places, so it popped against his skin. It incorporated the bird and the chess piece of the same name, the tower hanging wormlike in its beak. It was an exceptionally good tattoo by a well-established Russian artist in Orange County. He was tough to book and charged a flat rate of $1,500. That part Rooker was fine with. But he needed the man to *want* to do the tattoo; it had to be a concept that made him interested. The artist, bald and skinny with a long teardrop goatee, looked like a mural himself, covered in full sleeves of fresh and faded tattoos that crept up his shoulders and neck.

Rooker had sat still to the point that even the artist was impressed by his tolerance for pain. He'd listened to the loud buzzing of the tattoo gun for just under five hours while the needle dug into him—a thousand wasps, all stinging him in unison.

Rooker turned what was left of the corroded cross handle of the water pump; one of the ends had broken off. The water hissed, and a sad, clumpy stream poured from the faucet into his hands. He splashed water onto his face, turned the nozzle hard until the droplets completely stopped, then walked back and sat in the old reclining chair. He booted up his PC, and it took him only a minute to find a recent article on the murder. As he gazed at the image of the tree where they had found the girl's body, his breath caught. It was strange. He felt like he knew the place, but he wasn't sure why.

Charlotte Johnson. Twenty-seven years of age, social worker at the Itasca Resource Center. A second photo showed her alive and well, smiling for the camera. Her body was found in Itasca County. She was tortured, raped, and stabbed.

The killer has good taste, he thought. The girl was young and beautiful. Her eyes were bright with youth and hope, her hair a silky grayish blonde. His eyes moved like a typewriter, reading the words like he'd been typing them himself. Every now and then, the journalist in him would question word choice or phrasing, his hand itching to make a correction. Nonetheless, he had to admit, while it wasn't how he'd write the story, it was good.

Back in California, Rooker had been a journalist—and a good one. He'd been writing for the *Valley Chronicle* in Riverside County for nearly ten years. Ten years of journalism and crime reporting. It really hadn't flown by. And it wasn't a rush like it once was. But now that he left and would never be going back, it felt like a past life, a life he drank to forget.

Rooker wondered how much truth was hidden behind the article's words. How many bodies did they have that were connected; how many leads did they have to go on? There was no sketch of a man someone had seen near the crime, no mention of a person who seemed suspicious or out of place. These articles always tried to instill some sort of hope at the end. Whether it was a promise of a quick arrest or that the police were doing everything in their power, that the killer would be brought to justice. It was all bullshit. He knew from experience.

Rooker didn't have all the facts. He could, maybe, if he helped the police. He held the card between his forefinger and middle. Detective Tess Harlow. He read it once more before he tossed the card across the room like he was a croupier. The thin corner hooked beneath a nail head jutting out from the floor.

Rooker was handy enough to fix the place up, but that wasn't why he'd come here. He told himself it was to escape, to get away from the bright lights and commotion of California, the mutilation of his boy, the end of his marriage. He even wanted to think he was hiding, long enough for the pain to go away. When it refused to go away, the booze did the trick, at least temporarily. But sometimes the sounds of California still haunted him. They were the shadows that raised the hairs on his arms. Chilled his spine. The bustling city traffic and the ocean swells. The Valley girl accents and beach-blonde surfer slang. They were sounds he couldn't bear to hear again.

He often thought about the detective, Eduardo Arroyave, who had put him in the crosshairs of his son's killer. Rooker would have to close his eyes and breathe in for five seconds, breathe out the same. It was the only thing he could do not to break something else. He had already broken the California detective's jaw when he'd come to apologize. He could still hear the snap when his knuckles had connected like a rock on a windshield. As the detective went down, Rooker was still throttling him. If four officers hadn't pinned him down, the man would be dead. Rooker resisted the entire time, but they let him go, and the cop didn't press charges. He heard the guy resigned, probably couldn't live with getting a little boy killed.

He went to the narrow fridge, an outdated white-top freezer-refrigerator that went up to his chest. There had been a freezer box decades ago—a lighter outline on the floorboards shadowed where it had been—but the police had taken it when they discovered the women's heads stored inside. Rooker remembered seeing it the few times he was here; the bulky padlock that secured it shut must've weighed ten pounds.

He once told himself he'd never buy a fridge that couldn't fit a large pizza box. Thankfully, the fridge came with the place because it could maybe squeeze a small pie. He opened the door and reached behind the beer to find the deli meat he'd pushed to the back to keep it colder. It had spoiled. Green mold had worked its way toward the center of sliced sausage and meatballs. It was traditional Swedish food that took him back to his childhood. A loaf of black bread for open sandwiches and gravlax he'd intended as a treat—all of it had spoiled. He grabbed the milk instead, started to bring it up to his mouth but smelled the spoils of that too the moment the cap twisted. When he turned the gallon jug over, he could see the chunks and curdles inside. From the doorway, he launched it outside as far from the cottage as he could.

He went to the old stainless-steel kitchen sink, a dented farmhouse model. The cold-water handle spun fast in his hand. He knew there was probably air in the line if not something worse wrong with it. After a few seconds, the water sprayed, then ran down in a normal stream. He cupped the water in his hands and threw the first handful on his face, the second down his throat.

He powered on the coffee maker, the one luxury he allowed himself. It was a standard five-cup coffee maker. Nothing fancy. All he needed was the hot liquid to wake him up. Not that there were many things he needed to be awake for. Each morning, he woke up with a dull flame in his heart, resenting death for not having taken him in the middle of the night.

There were a few other cottages spaced out on his section of the lake, all of them in much better shape than his. The nearest cottage was a couple of hundred feet away and occupied. Evelyn Holmberg was in her midfifties and widowed, still pretty. She owned the cottage back when his father would make his trips here from California. When Rooker was younger, he had thought about her. Now he tried to imagine what Evelyn must have thought of his father in those dark days. It had been clear that he was an adulterer; he'd brought a different woman home with him nearly every visit back. What she didn't know was far darker: each night Gunner Lindström brought a woman home, he had hacked her head clean off while Evelyn was fast asleep next door.

Chapter 5

November 29

Rooker's head was splitting in half. It felt like a knife were sawing through the center of his skull. There was no sleeping it off. He opened his eyes. Wavy lines distorted his peripherals. A pulsing pain above his eyelids felt like needles pricking him. He wasn't sure how he'd made it upstairs to the bed, but he had. For a moment, he was proud of that. He looked over to the bucket of water. It was nearly half-full again. He couldn't tell if it had been snow that melted on the roof or if it rained last night. He stumbled his way toward it like he was walking on a rocky ship, hovered over it, knelt down, and threw up. Some of it dripped down the side of the bucket; some hung from his chin. When he suspected he was done, he scratched at his groin, wiped his mouth with the back of his hand, and threw himself onto the bed face-first. He groaned into the blanketed mattress. There wasn't a pillow.

He woke up again an hour later. The screams of the women his father had killed rang in his ears. Rooker had never been in Minnesota at the time of the murders, but he was sure they haunted the place. Back then, the news outlets called them the Damned of Deer Lake, sometimes the Damsels of Deer Lake. Sometimes he'd hear incoherent screams or muttered cries, the kind with snot running and words slurring. Sometimes they sounded like hushed sobs muffled by tape tight across their mouths.

After he gathered himself, Rooker made his way down the stairs. Each step mewled beneath his weight, telling him he should get back in bed. He went to the sink and turned the handle, waited for the hiss and spray, and put his hands under the cold stream. The splash intended for his face soaked the neck of yesterday's shirt. The switch for the coffee maker prompted a gurgling, clanging noise he hadn't heard before. It seemed that all he had heard since coming back here were strange noises. Everything had a sound. This was a new one. He didn't want to have to wash himself and dress to go purchase a replacement.

The freezer opened before him to glacier walls and a twist-tied package of frozen waffles. He dumped one from the clear package, tossed it onto a plate, and nuked it for thirty seconds, before yanking the front door open, putting the plate on the porch, and leaving it.

He sank into the recliner but left the bottom closed, brooding childishly over what he'd do about his coffee and food situation.

He could walk over or call Evelyn. She was one of a few people who didn't look at him like he was the son of a killer. Since her husband died, she was lonely. She'd love some company. He thought enough on it to where it sounded like he was doing a good deed. Then he thought of calling the detective; she'd bring him food if it meant getting him to help her. She was desperate, grasping at straws, clinging to the idea of him as a catcher of killers. He knew which one would require more of him. He picked up the receiver and dialed his neighbor.

"Mrs. Holmberg," she said. She'd always answered that way, even after Harold passed away. It lacked a bit of its former cheerfulness.

"Evelyn, it's Rooker."

"Ahhh, Rooker! How are you?" The pep that he remembered in her voice when he was a boy came back. "You never come and visit anymore."

"I know, I'm sorry. I was actually going to ask something of you if it isn't too much trouble."

"Sure, what can I do?"

"Is there any chance you have some coffee? I think my machine just broke."

"Of course!"

"I think there's something wrong with the fridge here too. Everything spoiled. Is there any chance you have something to eat?" The refrigerator was perfectly fine. It was one of the only things in the cottage that still worked.

"Of course. When should I expect you?"

"Actually"—he scratched his aching head—"I'm so sorry, Evelyn, is there any chance you can bring it over? I'm not feeling too well." He wasn't entirely dishonest. To him, hungover was a stage of "sick."

Fifteen minutes later, Evelyn nudged the door open with a large dinner plate wrapped in cellophane in one hand and a steaming cup of coffee in the other. A folded newspaper stuck out from her jeans like a gray thong. She swung the door shut with her foot. Her eyes fell on the handle of vodka on the end table before she noticed him sitting there.

"Long night?"

"Something like that."

"You ought to get that door fixed, dear. I thought I was going to throw my hip out trying to get it to open."

"You aren't that old, Evelyn."

"Well, next time maybe offer me a drink. Otherwise, you can walk yourself over when you need food."

"I'm sorry."

"Still feeding that stray?"

"Geralt likes his Eggos."

Geralt was a big snowy-white cat, fluffy with a grim face, burning pyrotechnic yellow eyes, and a meaty puffer-fish neck. Rooker had named him after Geralt of Rivia.

"Damn cat bites me every time I try to pet it. Never lets me feed it."
Evelyn began to wander through the cabin, stopped at the bookshelf,
and wiped a finger over the lid of a drooping cardboard box. Turning
to face the dense layer of gray filth, she said, "Rooker . . ."

"I know. I'll get around to it."

While she wiped the grime on her pants, she said, "I see you've had
some visitors lately. Police?"

"You noticed?"

"What else does an old widow do during the day?"

"Oh please, stop with that. You aren't old. And you're rather obser-
vant," he said as he unwrapped the plastic from the dish. "Maybe they
should be asking you for help."

"What did they want?"

With the mug pressed to his lips, he said with hostility, "Can't catch
a killer and they seem to think I can." The hot liquid poured down his
throat, loud gulps bellowing as if he hadn't drunk in days.

"Can you?"

"Who knows." He wiped his mouth. "Probably not. This isn't
Scooby-Doo. Not every killer is attention seeking and wants to be
caught. And maybe I don't want to. I should have that much say in the
matter, shouldn't I?"

"Yes and no."

"Sorry?"

"Yes, you should be able to say yes or no. You've dealt with more
pain than most do in a lifetime. But you caught Tate Meachum, whether
you think—"

"I didn't catch anyone. I did the *work*—the work the cops and the
bureau *should've* done. Talking to the families of his victims, canvassing
the crime scenes, narrowing down a grid, thinking like him—or like
my father would have, even."

"Meachum is locked away. He can't hurt anyone ever again. How
isn't that catching him?"

"Because he's *alive*. Isn't he? Living and breathing."

"Well, you've done it all before—"

"And I lost everything. Everything I had left."

"Take a look around, Rooker. What left do you have to lose? All I'm saying is if it would save lives, I think it's a pretty simple answer."

He brooded over that thought. He was stubborn. He only did what he wanted to do, or at least he would now that he was divorced.

"Will you survive without me? I've got to run into town for a bit."

"I think so. Thanks again. I owe you."

"Try not to drink your demons away."

"Trust me, my demons aren't going anywhere."

"And maybe . . . you can wash the vomit off that shirt."

He watched her walk out the door and back to her cottage. It was a split-level like his, only nice. Sometimes he'd see smoke billowing out of her chimney at night and was overcome simultaneously with his boyhood yearnings and his desire for a comforting presence. He heard the squealing of her Volvo, a relic he couldn't believe was still running. Out of the window, he could see the tan four-door sedan with rubber side paneling that had all peeled off. Rooker looked at the newspaper she'd left and read the headline. The font hung large and bold, daunting in the center of the light-gray background. **University Student Found Brutally Murdered.**

He unwrapped what was left of the plastic from the dish, smelling the *isterband* and lingonberry jam immediately. Along with it were some potatoes and pickled beets. He guessed it was last night's dinner. He grabbed a fork from the drawer—it was stuck, but after a few pulls left and right toward him, it pried loose. He returned to his chair, took a few big bites of food and a sip of coffee, and started reading.

LAKE COUNTY, Minn. — A 25-year-old University of Minnesota student was found dead at the end of a Fifth Falls hiking trail Monday morning.

Lake County Sheriff's Department responded to the scene after receiving a call of an unresponsive woman covered in snowfall.

Officials later identified the victim as 25-year-old Rebecca Weiss.

Weiss was reported missing Sunday evening by her college roommate after failing to return to her dormitory.

According to her roommate, Weiss frequently ran trails in Gooseberry Falls State Park, 13 miles north of Two Harbors.

Investigators say she was dead hours prior, but cause of death has not been released.

Police ask that anyone who saw Rebecca Weiss in the days leading to her death contact them.

He took another sip from the warm cup. While he read parts of the story over, he took a pen to the margins and to the writer's name, this time giving in to the urge to edit. The version of the story he'd read on his laptop was much better.

He looked at the image of the trees and the snowfall again. There was something wrong about it. Or something right? He wasn't sure. Whatever it was, it made him do something he told himself he wouldn't do. He walked over to the card he'd flung to the floor earlier, struggling to pick it up until the edge caught beneath his chewed fingernails. Once he retrieved the card, he plopped back down in his chair, picked up the receiver, and dialed.

"Harlow," she answered.

"How many bodies have you found?" he blurted.

There was a brief pause on her end. "Who is this?"

"You searched my cottage without a warrant. I wanted to file a complaint."

"Ah, white-and-gray boxer briefs. I take it you read this morning's paper. Does this mean you're ready to help us?"

"No, it doesn't. How many?"

Silence. He waited. She wouldn't hang up; she needed him.

"Four. Rebecca Weiss makes four."

"Where were the other three found?"

"Coleraine, Grand Rapids, Oslund, now Silver Creek Township, just north of Two Harbors in Lake County."

"All of them found in parks?" No answer. "Can I see the case files?"

"Not without coming down here. I can be there in twenty to bring you in."

This time, he was the one who went silent. He thought about what Evelyn said. She was right. He had nothing left to lose. Maybe he could save someone. And while he stared at the photo that seemed oddly familiar, Detective Harlow's words about his father became louder. She was right too. Rooker had been far too small and young to do anything about his father all those years ago. But maybe now, in a strange way, was his chance to catch him. And still, he wasn't ready to give in.

"Let me sleep on it."

He hung up.

◆ ◆ ◆

Rooker's eyelids flickered like those of a sleeping dog. He had dozed off in his chair, startled half-conscious by his son tugging on his shirtsleeve. Rooker saw him. Tousled brown hair, the gold pendant dangling from his neck, his small hand reaching to put the glass bottle back on the table. He must have fallen asleep with it in his hand; maybe it had slid down to the corner of the chair. He could hear it *clink* against the end table, the stains and rings imprinted against it. In his drunken stupor, his arms fumbled numbly, his fingers clawing at the hem of his son's shirt.

"Why did you let me die, Daddy?"

His heart thrashed. *The numbers. 11:37.* The hairs on the nape of his neck grew legs and crawled—that abhorrent red. Frozen stiff in the shadows, the ringing haunted him like a monster under the bed.

"I'm so sorry."

"You have to save them now. The women."

Rooker clung to the shirt for dear life. His hands were turning white as the snowfall, white as the bodies that were turning up. He clutched the cloth at his son's waist, dragging the boy closer to him.

"It's okay, Daddy, let go."

Chapter 6

November 30

Rooker awakened to the ringing in his ear. Unsure whether he was dreaming it, he cracked an eyelid open and realized it was the landline. His body was curled forward, his chin pressed against his chest, the chair not even reclined. His eyes were damp, his hand closed like a clamp, but he was holding nothing. Slime filled the corner of his mouth and dampened his chin. When he looked down, a dark circle of drool spotted his shirt. He looked at the digital numbers on the cable box. If he stared at them long enough, he'd be able to watch 4:30 a.m. hemorrhage into the blinding darkness. He took a few seconds and pulled the receiver from the hook.

Rooker wiped his face with the shoulder of his shirtsleeve. "Ms. Harlow, it's too early," he groaned.

"How did you know it was me? You don't have caller ID with that dinosaur phone."

"The only people who call me either want to buy my land and rebuild"—he yawned long and loud—"or tell me that the house is unsafe to be lived in. Maybe my neighbor. None call this early. And I don't know if I've slept on it long enough. I'm going back to sleep." He was still torn between selling the estate or lighting a match to it, but he leaned toward watching the fire take shape with a mind of its own. In some scenarios, he was inside while it did.

"We found another one."

He paused. His eyes closed, imagining the victim. He'd seen enough of them, hadn't he? He'd seen the bodies when he was writing pieces for the *Valley Chronicle*. The murder-suicide up on Valle Vista or that hit-and-run on Sanderson Street, the white-haired woman lying in the crosswalk with her head split open like a pistachio. There was a local gang shooting in the cliffs, the body of a boy in a storm drain tunnel in the valley, a domestic violence stabbing in Juniper Springs, an arson case—a mentally ill man constructed gasoline bombs and set a dwelling and parked cars on fire—in San Jacinto off Ramona Boulevard. The list went on. He'd seen his mother too. He'd always kept professionally detached. Until he saw his boy.

"Rooker, the exit is coming up. I need to know now."

This time, his silence wasn't meant to provoke her. He suddenly saw his son again. He wondered if it was just a dream or if his son had really come to him somehow. Or maybe Rooker was just too drunk; maybe he was starting to go mad. He'd almost swear he still felt the soft cotton in his fingertips, smelled the cold weather crawling on his boy's skin. *You have to save them now.* He could hear his son's voice playing over in his mind. *The women.*

His brain flashed back to how it had been after his father was apprehended. The insults, the seclusion—*the son of a killer*. It was an invisible marking he wore like skin. It was a struggle just to carry the household name. *Lindström.* Now it felt as if he were being given a chance to catch his father. Rooker knew that even if he was cleared of the murders, if the killer wasn't found, the public would still think it was him. And even though his boy was gone, he didn't want that for him, to be branded the son of a killer. For people to say what they did about Rooker himself, that he shared evil blood, that he deserved to die.

"Fuck it. Why not?"

"Get dressed. I'll be there soon."

He rose from the chair and reached up to the wooden ceiling beams, pressing his palms against them to stretch his back. His legs and arms shook; a yawn fought its way out of his mouth and gave him a cramp in his lower jaw. While he stretched his legs, two loud cracks erupted, though he didn't feel anything pop. He made his way to the corner shower, which looked more like a narrow closet. He couldn't stretch his arms inside if he tried. He took his clothes off and tossed them to the floor, turned the water on, and heard the same hiss he heard from the kitchen sink. He stepped in and washed quickly, before the hot water had a chance to run cold.

After five minutes, he turned the water off and threw a towel over his head. He rubbed at it until he saw his disheveled hair in the broken mirror. He patted it down, and it looked better. He toweled off and went back to his bedroom, pulled a pair of dark jeans from a drawer, along with underwear, thick wool socks, a T-shirt, and a heavy merino-wool sweater. It gave him a European look, a waterfowl neck with a leather zipper and a slightly darker-gray line pattern on the material. He started putting clothing on, piece by piece. In the seconds his skin was bare, winter's hypothermic chill invaded his body, chattered his teeth, numbed his mouth.

He heard the purr of the Taurus as it pulled into the drive. Halfway out the door, he reached back for the jacket hanging on the hook inside and threw it over his shoulder. The door launched shut. It was the only way it would stay closed.

He'd never owned a heavy jacket until he came to this frozen land; even as a boy, he was only here once during a winter, the rest during warmer months. It was a thick military-green coat, olive drab with a shirt collar and buttons that could close down the front, but he always wore it open. The closed buttons made him feel claustrophobic. The inside was thickly insulated—the lady told him—and it kept him warm. He'd paid $200 for it shortly after arriving and discovering just how bitter cold it could be in Minnesota even in fall. At first, he'd felt heavy when he'd worn it, but it was growing on him, mostly because the alternative was freezing his balls off.

He walked out to Harlow's vehicle, snow and frost casting a shine on the paint and rims. It looked like a sparkling car advertisement except for the gray slush-laced tires.

As he settled into the passenger seat, she handed him a thermos, and the smell of coffee hit him like a punch in the face. "Thanks. Where are we going?"

"She was found at a factory out in Bowstring, about twenty-five minutes."

He took a sip, then another until he felt her looking sideways at him, and he realized he was gulping loud enough for her to hear. The coffee was waking him, the hot liquid coursing through his veins, the icy weather slithering inside his loose jacket. She drove past the wrought iron gate that once blocked off the unpaved drive. The hinges had snapped off years ago, spikes of rusted black iron missing too, shaping something sinister—a few teeth shy of a jack-o-lantern grin. Now the gate was wide open like casted broken arms—chillingly grim, even under the kindest light.

As they drove farther away from his uninhabitable bachelor paradise, he felt oddly warm and calm.

The sky was still dark, another forty-five minutes before there would be signs of life under the cold sun. There were barely any cars on the road. She flicked the siren on anyhow.

Rooker assessed her eyes in his peripheral vision as she drove.

"So, what brings you back here, really?" she asked him.

The question gave him pause. "I'm sorry, is this a therapy session?"

"Okay, why do you live in the house where your father committed murder?"

"The view is beautiful."

"I'm sure the views in California were just as nice. And it had to be a hell of a lot warmer." She cracked a sarcastic smile, but Rooker didn't mirror it.

"Detective Harlow, I know you've done your homework. That cabin is where my father fucked and decapitated women. You remember the headlines? A lot of D's. Dreadful. Disturbed. Drunkard. What they all seemed to say: the devil lived there. The walls deserve to come crashing down after all the things they've seen. There was nothing left for me in California. Most of me died there, and I figured I'd let the rest freeze to death. Seemed like a peaceful way to go."

"Do you think you should be inside when the house finally falls down?"

He didn't answer, but perhaps he did think that. It was something worth considering. A man not able to protect his son. Did the exact opposite, really. He had put his son in danger, placed him in the sights of a psychopath. Rooker may not have been the murderer, but he was the one who killed him. They drove on in silence until her questions ate away at him like fire ants.

"Your dad was a cop."

Now she turned toward him. "Is that a question?"

"No."

"So you did your research too," she said.

He had. He knew she was unmarried, graduated from the police academy in Moorhead, and she had been the lead detective in Itasca County for only a couple of years. "Hit by a driver during a routine stop. He had someone pulled over; then a car drove right into him, slammed into the front of the other car, but both drivers survived."

"Yep."

"His body was found almost twenty feet away; he was killed on impact."

"Yep."

"Is he the reason you became a cop?"

She paused, looked at him, and turned back to the road. "Yep."

She eased off the gas pedal and turned onto a side road, toward the flashing lights in the distance. A few Crown Victorias blocked off the road. She pulled up on the shoulder next to a white Ford Police Interceptor with black-and-gold markings, the Taurus's headlights punching two large tunnels of light through the dense gray fog. Blue lights flickered atop the SUV, which was sitting idle. When Rooker opened the door, his foot sank into gray slush. He pushed off the seat and found his footing before the door thundered shut behind him.

"Detective Harlow." Tess flashed her badge and moved toward the yellow tape. "He's with me."

"Yes, ma'am," the beat cop said and lifted it for the two of them. Rooker ducked beneath the tape after her.

The silver crescent moon hung grim over the lot. Rooker followed Tess's steps across a path where the snow was tire packed. The steel gate was down like a drawbridge, shining like pearly milk under the lunar rock. The factory turned midnight blue in the dark. To Rooker, it looked like a massive barge beached on the curbed lot. Ropes, chains, and wires ran everywhere like a trapeze course.

"What do we have so far?" Tess asked a heavyset man just inside the doorway.

"Our boy is back . . . boss. Same MO . . . Haven't checked her mouth for the calling card yet . . . but make it five."

The man was panting, most likely triggered by the sight of the body. Rooker had seen it happen before, mostly to rookie cops. His belly overlapped his pants and was almost hidden by his thick wool jacket. Almost. The peacoat appeared to be new with a few gray fibers standing up like loose blanket stitching. It looked itchy. Rooker assumed it was a present from his wife, something out of a men's catalog that a more handsome and fit person was wearing. She probably thought it would make her look at her husband differently, with new desire. Rooker was sure it didn't have the intended effect.

"Rooker, this is Martin Keene. He's my partner on the investigation team."

"I like the jacket," Rooker said as he shook the man's thick, hairy hand.

"Thanks, it's new. Wife got it for me."

Rooker smirked.

"So, this is your guy," he said to Tess while appraising Rooker.

"This is him."

Rooker gazed back at Keene. He had soft, friendly blue eyes that squinted when he smiled; blond, medium-length windswept hair; and glasses that barely fit his large head. His eyebrows were bushy, and he needed a shave: blond, orange, and white whiskers made for a patchy beard that traveled down to the collar of his peacoat. If anyone was going to give Rooker trouble or have an issue with his being there, it probably wouldn't be this guy.

The water was just beyond them. Beautiful shades of gray and white made the water look like fogged glass. Lightning-bolt cracks rippled in different directions throughout. He thought back to the only time he'd skated the ice on Deer Lake. He hadn't put skates on in more than twenty years, not since his high school hockey days. Now, while he peered out at the ice, predawn-gray burning cinders in the sky, he wondered how many bodies would fit below.

"Sorry," Rooker said. "You said same MO?"

"Yeah," Keene said. "All of them in their midtwenties or early thirties. Ligature marks on the wrists, bruising and slashing done to maim. Rape. And a kill wound, knife to the center of the sternum."

"And his calling card?" Rooker asked.

Keene raked his fingernails through his beard. "You'll see."

"All right," Harlow said. "Let's see what we've got."

Keene walked them toward the body. He went on talking, but Rooker no longer heard the words. In a daze, he was walking, but he couldn't feel the sludge splashing beneath his feet, couldn't feel his legs moving. Even the cold was no longer raw and piercing.

He followed the two of them up a rust-flaking metal staircase. He didn't hold the railing when he saw that part of it was missing, the parts intact a tetanus nightmare. As they climbed the steps, he started to feel a heavy vibration in his feet. Maybe the three of them shouldn't be going up at the same time.

At the top, a detective was holding a large graffitied steel door open for them. Rooker looked past him to the blue cursive paint. But as he stepped into the room, his eyes went right to the small body lying still on the table. One hand was dangling over the side. A dark-purple ring colored the skin of his thin wrist. His eyes were empty, aimed at the ceiling. Rooker gave one look at the bleach-white skin and felt sick. He closed his eyes. *No, it isn't him. Not again.*

"Rooker?" He heard Harlow's voice, but he didn't want to open his eyes and see his boy again. After a few deep breaths, he forced them open and found the dead woman where his son had been. She'd been butchered, gutted like a fish. The irony of it in a fish factory, the killer had a sadistic sense of humor, a sadistic outlook on women. Rooker walked over to the window and examined the room behind the glass, filled with empty conveyor belts and stools and controls.

He stood next to the woman, staring down at her face. She was pretty, aside from the fear permanent in her expression. Mascara lines ran down both cheeks. Her mouth was unlatched, her jaw probably broken from force. Deep purple colored the swelling along her jawline. Her left lateral incisor was missing. Rooker had a strong feeling that when the killer forced her mouth open, he'd broken her tooth and jaw in the process.

From her clothing, he guessed the victim was a high-end escort. There was a black set of lingerie torn to shreds on the floor beneath her: a black lace brassiere, garter straps that attached to matching black stockings, and sheer panties. The killer probably thought of it all as garbage, the woman as well as her shredded garments. She looked the part of an aspiring model prescribed drugs and cigarettes to stay skinny. Judging by her white teeth, probably not cigarettes. He couldn't see any needle markings, nothing between her fingers or toes, probably not heroin. Her light-blonde hair had some darker roots, yellow waves running off toward the bottom. Rooker imagined how she looked all dolled up beforehand. There was nothing cheap about her makeup beneath the scrapes and bruises.

The killer could have presented himself as a John. He could have tempted her with the promise of a modeling gig. He could have offered her sex or drugs, maybe both. It was impossible to tell. Rooker could see a butterfly tattoo on her hip, the red line beside it where the killer had torn off her underwear. She had another tattoo on her wrist—a half heart with the initials N.P. above it. Ligature marks were just below the tattoo. Rooker suspected the initials belonged to the victim's child: this woman must've known the risks in her job, what men were like.

Harlow was talking to Keene and another man. "Rooker, this is Detective Alexander Whitlock."

"Xander," he corrected.

Whitlock looked thirtysomething, with a stubble anchor goatee along a chiseled jaw and dark, fiery eyes that made him look both tired and angry. He wore his dark hair messily and donned a dark bomber jacket over a light-gray hoodie with dark jeans.

"Where's her purse?" Rooker asked.

Xander shrugged. "Didn't find one on the body, so no ID either."

"You didn't know it was missing, so how would you know where to look?"

Xander's cheeks turned bright red. "What the fuck is this?" He directed the question at Harlow.

"Don't start. You know why he's here. Tell us about the body."

"Why doesn't he? He's your expert, right?"

"He's here to help. He doesn't need to prove shit to you."

"He sure as shit does. He thinks he can do my job better than me."

The lingerie set . . . the makeup . . .

"Call girl," Rooker spoke up.

"What?"

"I'm pretty sure she's an escort."

"How would you know she's a hooker?"

"Escort," Rooker corrected him. "Your mother's a hooker. There's a difference."

Xander's face froze. He lunged toward Rooker, but Tess stepped in.

"That's enough!"

"No, let the Cali boy say one more thing. *Fucking killer.* One more thing and I break his face."

Xander's face was a caricature—the bully who'd peaked in high school, resorting to petty hallway fistfights to feel cool and young. It made Rooker smile knowing how easy it was to set him off. He turned his attention back to the dead woman.

"Her underwear, her tattoos, I mean, maybe a single mother doing her best to provide for her kid, maybe kids. I covered a similar homicide case a few years back. Modeling probably didn't work out; this did. Based on her clothing and those heels, I'd bet she was making a better living than a detective's salary."

Rooker looked at the heap of clothing again. A thought came to him. "Check the underwear. She might have taped over the tags so she could return everything. Or maybe we can narrow down where she bought the set at least."

"That's a wild fucking goose chase," Whitlock snapped.

Tess said, "Sometimes that's detective work for you. Let's get it out there and search the area for the purse. At least we know it isn't dumped out there in the water."

"Did he take trophies from any of the other victims?" Rooker asked.

"Not that we can tell," Keene said. "Finding the purse might be key. A woman's life is in her purse. At least that's what the wife says when she's fumbling through hers for the keys."

"What about the tooth?" Rooker said. "Maybe he took it, or maybe she swallowed it?"

"Maybe," Tess agreed. "The ME should be able to tell us. But a call girl's purse . . . if she is a call girl, you're talking about survival. Protection, whether a Taser or Mace, a small handgun, an ICE, condoms, lube."

Keene examined the body closely. Rooker watched his slow, meticulous methods. His gloved fingers pulled down gently on her bottom lip and lifted her tongue. Martin Keene pulled what looked like a piece of paper from her mouth and unfolded it. Rooker stood beside him and read over his shoulder.

Isn't she lovely?

"What's the other side say?" Rooker asked. Martin turned the paper over in his thick hand.

Ring a bell yet?

Keene bagged the note. Then he took another look inside the victim's mouth. He reached in under her tongue again and, with the precision of a doctor, pulled out another item: a key. Keene held the key out in his upturned palm while Harlow shone her flashlight on it and they all leaned in for a closer look. The key bore a small logo that matched the one on the factory's sign. Rooker surveyed the room, looked past the table to the glassed-in factory floor. He thought he knew the answer. But he suddenly felt afraid.

Just outside the doorway to the factory floor was a control panel with dials and monitors and a master key override for complete start-up or shutdown functions. Rooker pointed at the panel, and Keene looked at Harlow. She narrowed her eyes and nodded, and when Keene walked over, put the key in the override panel, and turned it, the large room behind the glass lit up. A conveyor belt came to life. Rooker cringed at the loud metal churning. He walked down the steps to the center of the belt as a metal tray came out, then another, another, followed by two more. Each tray held a black-and-white photo splattered with red.

Paint? Or is it . . . blood?

Five trays, five bodies. And then one more tray came out—empty. There was another girl dead somewhere they hadn't found yet.

Harlow yelled to her team to shut it down. All the trays had splatters of red on them, red covering the majority of the photographs. Rooker could see the shape of the trees beneath the crimson color.

As the team came in to bag the photos, Rooker made his way back down the rusted staircase and out into the cold. For Harlow, the ice was an ally, the thing that kept the victim's purse from the water. It kept evidence accessible. But for Rooker, the ice was something else. He watched a gale lift the white powder, sending it dancing over the ice. It came over him like a pang, a sick feeling metastasizing all over his body like a cancer. He felt cold and hot. Nauseous. He stood there, looking out at one of his father's photographs.

As soon as the trays had slid down the conveyor belt, and he again saw the trees from the Charlotte Johnson crime scene, he realized why they'd seemed familiar.

His father had been an amateur photographer; he'd taken a small collection of landscapes that he thought someday, someone would treasure and pay handsomely for. Rooker remembered the darkroom his father had made, with heavy blankets over the windows and duct tape to block any light from coming in. He clearly remembered a few of the prints, the collection that his father was so proud of, until he wasn't. The few offers he received, he'd taken as insults.

Harlow appeared beside him now, but Rooker had too many thoughts racing in his mind to speak. Someone knew about the photographs or had them in their possession. But how, after all these years? And why? The killer was re-creating his father's photographs, paying homage to him, celebrating his psychopathy, maybe one-upping him. He'd found a lead, but it was one he didn't want to uncover, something he didn't want to know. And he didn't want to tell Tess. It was one more thing that would haunt him, follow him, drag him back to a place he didn't want to go. *Only me,* he thought. *This could only happen to me.*

"You okay?" she asked.

"Fine," he hissed.

"I'm going to the station. Do you want to head back with me or should I drop you off? You can look at the files if you come back."

"I want to look at the files."

As they walked back to the car, Rooker was in a cold sweat. He needed a drink. He got in the passenger seat. As Harlow slid into the driver's side, she let out a deep sigh. It had been a long night. The sun would be up soon.

Tess pulled onto the main road and sighed again. "I know Xander's an asshole, but you can't say things like that. I brought you here to help, not to piss off the investigation team."

"Sorry."

"Don't let it happen again, please."

He didn't answer. He didn't like being told what to do, like he was a boy being scolded. But that wasn't even it. He didn't want to talk to her. If he talked to her, he would have to tell her about the photographs. He would have to tell her that someone knew he was here and that the message had been left for him.

They spent the ride in silence. The car took the curves and corners so well that Rooker barely shifted in his seat. He'd owned a white Range Rover in California, probably $50,000 more expensive than her Ford, and it never drove this smoothly. When he left for Minnesota, he couldn't have cared less about the car. When his wife tried to contact him, he broke his mobile phone and heaved it into the lake. There was only one person in sight at the time—a boy who launched the newspaper at Evelyn's cottage every morning. Rooker had looked him dead in the eyes, and the boy fled like a gazelle, legs too long for his body kicking up pebbled snow. Rooker then felt a flicker of shame: his wife was better off without him.

His mind wandered to memories of his father. A cold man: icelike, a cold-blooded killer of women for close to a decade. He was the one thing Rooker hated most in this world.

"Are you going to tell me what's wrong?"

"I don't know if I can." His heart jackhammered. His voice nearly broke. There was a runaway freight train throbbing between his temples. How ironic that he'd run from his life in California, and now he wanted to run once again. He'd traveled across the country to die, not be involved in another case or be reminded of how lost he'd become the last time around, be reminded of his son. His mouth went dry. "Can you pull over?"

She eased up on the gas pedal and slowed to a stop to the right of the road. His door was open, and he was out of the car before she even put it in park.

He leaned against the side of the Taurus, hyperventilating. Closing his eyes, he tried to let his mind go blank until he could regain his composure and breathe. It felt like someone was holding a plastic bag over his head. *Come on. Breathe.* He thought about the pill bottle in the medicine cabinet. He squeezed his eyes shut so hard that they hurt. He didn't hear her get out of the car or walk toward him, but he felt her hand on his back, heard her saying it would be okay.

It took him a few minutes in the cold air before he could talk.

"I'm not sure it will be."

"What?"

His breath was shaky, and his lips felt like they were ready to freeze together if he didn't open his mouth. "*Okay.* I'm not sure it will be okay."

"I think okay is all we can ask for right now. There's pure evil in the world; we're doing our best to stop it."

"This evil . . ." The words caught in Rooker's throat. If he didn't tell her, he could find a way out. But he decided he wouldn't take it. "That message was meant for me."

Her eyes narrowed. "What?"

"The photographs. They're my father's." A long breath billowed white in the early-morning light. If there was anything he didn't like to talk about, it was his father. He'd spent years speaking to school psychiatrists, people poking and prodding at his mind, probably to see if he'd inherited his father's sick brain. "He had a collection of photographs he'd taken that he thought were masterpieces. They were nice enough, but they never made him rich. The trays . . . those photos were exactly like the ones in his collection. Someone has the originals or has copies, I can't be sure."

He watched her muddle over it as he took a few more deep breaths.

"*Ring a bell yet?* That was for you?"

"I don't know. I think so. It seems the killer is paying tribute to my father, or maybe he's saying he's a better version. Maybe he knew him; maybe he was involved in my father's case years ago. Maybe he was a fan or a supporter. That's all I've been able to think."

"I'll get some guys together to watch you around the clock. If this guy really—"

"I can handle myself. Look, I didn't ask for this. I came here to escape everything. Instead, I came back to a serial killer . . . making dead women the subject of my father's photographs. I come back to some sick fuck leaving messages for me." '

"But we have a lead now."

"Not much of one."

"It'll help." He heard hope in her voice laced with a bit of excitement. He knew hope was a drug. Once it's taken away, it's damn near impossible to feel that high again. He wondered if it was the first time she'd felt hope with this case.

Chapter 7

December 1

Rooker dozed fitfully until Harlow pulled off the exit. It wasn't long before they were at the station, a sand-colored, flat-roofed building with narrow tinted windows and the American flag waving out front. Concrete and glass traveled up maybe two or three floors. Cars were parallel parked beside the building, early commuters sinking ankle-deep into the snow beneath the streetlamps. She drove over the tracks for the trolley and turned in to the parking garage. Everything sounded so hollow; there were barely any cars parked inside.

Tess walked him through heavy double doors and down a corridor, past cubicles and a sad ficus tree, and into her office. She excused herself, telling him to get comfortable. Rooker looked around the room at the mismatched filing cabinets topped with binders. Case file boxes were stacked against the wall. There was a detailed chart there: pins, photos, newspaper clippings, locations, all of it fastened to a massive bulletin board. Lines of yarn stretched across a map indicating the locations of the murders, all in northern Minnesota. Rooker eyed the pinned-up crime scene photos of the dead women. He felt sorrow and also guilt, like he was partially responsible for their deaths. In a way, he was.

He turned his attention to Harlow's desk. Papers were scattered across the top of it. He fingered a sheet that outlined the statistics of serial killers, the common age ranges and professions, their possible motives. He spotted his own byline. "Masters of Art and Killing" was stapled, and the corners were folded over. He pushed the papers aside to reveal a file with his name on it, his own face staring back from within the folder. A yellow note with a handwritten question mark stuck to it. Was he still a suspect? He didn't care if he was. He was sifting lazily through the file when he saw a picture of his son and closed it.

"I'm sorry," Harlow said, standing in the doorway. "I should've put it away. I forgot it was sitting there."

"It's fine," he lied. He knew he'd been the lead suspect at one point; he had to be. The murders started a month after he showed up to the cottage. And he barely left his house. What possible alibi could he have? The word of a neighbor?

Harlow dropped a packet of paper on the worn mahogany. "We have a missing person's report, Sofia Persson, age twenty-eight. Her photo matches our victim. She's been gone since Monday."

It was Friday.

"Who called it in?" Rooker asked.

She handed him a yellow Post-it with the name and address in scribbled handwriting. "The mother. I'm headed there now. You can come with or you can catch up on the files. Millie Langston is the researcher of the team. If you need anything, she can help. There's also some food in the conference room."

He badly wanted to read the reports on the victims; at the same time, this was a possible break in the case.

"I'll come with you."

On their way out, Rooker peeked into the conference room. On the table was a plate with a basic ham and cheese sandwich, a cup of coffee, and a stack of files. He walked in, grabbed the coffee and half the sandwich, and hurried to catch up with Harlow.

He watched the back of her head, her ponytail swaying left and right as she moved. They stepped into another large room where each victim's dead face was taped to a monstrous whiteboard. For the most part, Harlow's team kept working, though Rooker noticed two sets of eyes on him. One was Xander's, his face sleepless and full of contempt. The other set belonged to an unknown man who was sizing up Rooker, an unimpressed dullness in his eyes.

Rooker surveyed the room. It was what he'd expect: file cabinets, standard gray cubby-like cubicles, nearly matching gray desks inside of each. A few desks were empty. Two flat-screen televisions that looked like they were from the early 2000s were mounted in the corner. They were off, and Rooker couldn't help but wonder if they even turned on.

"Everyone, this is Rooker Lindström. He's helping us on this case." He noticed Martin Keene nod his big, round head. Rooker was starting to like the guy. "Cole found the missing person's report, and we're going to see the mother now. I want everyone to keep working this. We'll be back in a bit, so we'll skip the introductions for now."

They made their way down the corridor, and Rooker could feel a few people from Harlow's team watching them walk out the double doors.

"Is there anything I should know?"

"About what?"

He wondered if he should ask about his file on her desk and decided not to. "You brought a civilian and a suspect into an official investigation. Your team can't be too pleased."

"That's my call. You have nothing to worry about. Xander might throw a punch at you, but the rest should be fine. Just know that I brought you in to consult; you aren't a detective. You follow my lead. You don't make waves. You don't make me regret this."

The drive took maybe twenty minutes. The sky was turning a pale blue behind swirling dark clouds, like rippling waves frozen still. Just beneath, it looked like a nuclear blast. The sun a broken egg yolk, surrounded by a gray and orange mist. In areas, the orange was like warm honey drizzled atop the trees—what looked like shadow giants. The grays like tobacco smoke his father would exhale, only circulating with the car's air-conditioning. There were cars on the road now, but Harlow drove with the flow of traffic. Rooker didn't envy her. She was about to tell a mother that her daughter was dead. He hadn't been lucky enough to see an officer at the door. Instead he'd stumbled into a crime scene and found him. He wondered how much information Harlow would share with the family.

Tess pulled up at the address written on the note. The neighborhood wasn't the nicest. The house was an old two-story with two peaks in the roof bordered by a corroded chain-link fence. Beyond it was a small, flat yard of snow and a recently shoveled broken concrete walkway. The gate wasn't latched, but Tess had to yank up one end to swing it open. The staggered siding was different shades of dirt white. There was clearly roof damage. Rooker would know. He imagined buckets inside, strategically placed, like the ones he had in his home, catching the rain and melted snow. A section of the roof shingles was warped and possibly rotted.

Harlow pulled out her badge. Rooker waited for her to get in front of him. Thin black wires dangled from an empty square where the doorbell should've been. She knocked three times, fragments of the paint-chipped surface crumbling to the ground. There was a moment before they saw the curtains move, but no one came.

This time, as she knocked, Harlow said, "Police, please open the door."

They heard the chain unlock as the door opened a crack. Rooker saw two blue puppy-dog eyes glancing up at him. The boy looked nervous, afraid of them.

"Is Mommy dead?"

Rooker looked down at him and thought, *Yes, kid, she is.* Tess seemed stunned. Rooker felt for the kid. His dad had likely taken off a long time ago. His mother probably loved him but spent most of her time with clients. No matter how much kids love their grandparents, they want their parents around. It wasn't like when Britton was taken from him. Rooker and his ex-wife had loved that kid more than anything, would have done anything in the world for him. Rooker would take off from work just so he and Britton could spend the day together throwing a ball in the yard or watching superhero films from the couch.

"Can we talk to your grandma, please?" Tess asked the boy.

"Who are you talking to . . ." They heard a soft voice and the sound of someone shuffling toward them. A woman about sixty pulled the boy away from the door.

"Yes?"

"Greta Persson? I'm Detective Tess Harlow"—she flashed her badge through the cracked door—"may we come in?"

"Oh God," she said. Her hand went to cover her mouth, then her eyes. Her hand was shaking, feeble and white. "I always feared this day would come . . . Noah, hurry upstairs." The boy didn't move at first. "Hurry along. Now."

She opened the door, and Rooker watched the boy leap the stairs in twos. The boy was thin and bony like Rooker had been growing up. When he was out of earshot, the woman ushered them over to an old sofa that screamed *nineties floral*. The room groaned, creaking beneath them, as if to say that their news, the burden they were placing on this woman, wasn't welcome. A matching floral chair with pirate peg-leg feet sat beside the couch, a cushioned stool in front of it. Folded immaculately over nearly every piece of furniture was an afghan blanket, shielding the room from a perpetual cold. Faded and gold antique picture frames hung from nails scattered on the wall. A chunk of floor bubbled where a strand of sunlight crept through the window.

"I'm sorry, Mrs. Persson, but can you tell us if these were hers?" Harlow pulled a sheet of paper with photos of the victim's tattoos. Mrs. Persson nodded. "We located your daughter's body early this morning. She didn't have any ID on her, but one of our detectives found your missing person's report."

"Was it the drugs or was she killed?" Mrs. Persson picked up a half-empty cup of tea and took a gulp.

"We've ruled it a homicide, ma'am," Tess answered.

Rooker asked, point-blank, "How long has your daughter been an escort?"

Mrs. Persson looked down into her cup of tea, searching for the right words. "I knew for a long time. But I could never bring myself to say anything." She paused, looked at the top of the staircase. Then whispered, "I raised her. I'm too old to raise another one."

Harlow jumped in. "When's the last time you saw or spoke to her?"

"A week ago. I assumed that any time she came around, she had a . . ."

"Client?" Rooker said.

"Yes. And needed to drop Noah off."

Tess shifted in her sinking cushion. "What do you know about her clients?"

"Nothing. I don't want to know any of it; a mother shouldn't have to."

"Was she on her own, or was someone or an agency . . . representing her?"

"I wouldn't have a clue."

"What does her purse look like?" Rooker cut in.

"Her purse?"

Tess shot him a look. "It was missing." She turned back to Mrs. Persson. "There wasn't one where we found her."

"I think it was black," she said, closing her eyes, trying to remember it, "with a chain strap."

Tess pulled a pad out of her jacket pocket and jotted something down quickly with a black pen. "Silver or gold, the chain?"

"Silver."

She scribbled that down. "Did she ever spend several days with someone?" Tess tried.

"Sometimes. Sometimes she'd be gone for a weekend."

"What made you so sure something was wrong enough to report her missing?"

"If she was going to be gone a few days, she'd still call and check in on Noah. She loved him, and he loves her; she was a good mother to him."

"Did she have a husband or a boyfriend?"

"Noah's father ran out on her not long after she had him. She hasn't been dating anyone as far as I know."

"Did she have any friends we could reach out to?"

"None who I can think of."

The interview left a sour taste in Rooker's mouth. They'd come all this way for nothing. This woman didn't know a thing. All she could do was describe a purse they might never find, filled with objects that would probably have no significance. He rubbed at his temples.

"What did you say your name was?" Mrs. Persson said.

"Tess Harlow." Harlow clicked the pen and pocketed it.

"No, I mean you."

Rooker looked up at her, his lips pout-pressed together in a line. She was studying his face with a peculiar intensity, like she recognized him.

"Rooker."

"Lindström?" Her voice turned jarring and raspy. She cleared her throat, her eyes intent on him.

"Yes . . ."

"I dated your father."

Chapter 8

"I'm sorry, what?"

Mrs. Persson's words couldn't have been any clearer, but Rooker still had to ask. He almost thought he'd imagined her revelation.

"Gunner Lindström. We had a love affair. Well, he never told me he was still married, just that he had a boy called Rooker. He showed me a photo of you."

Rooker felt the wind knocked out of him. His mind raced. His throat latched. This was one of his father's women. But how, and why, was she alive? He'd researched his father's case for years, and he never found anything about this woman. He felt like he was stuck in a bad dream, and the nightmare wasn't ending anytime soon.

"Ma'am, you do mean Gunner Lindström the serial killer?" Tess asked.

"He was always sweet as can be with me."

Tess looked over at Rooker. He was searching the woman's face for answers, but she was no one to him. A stranger with age lines over what was still a pretty face.

"Wait one moment." Mrs. Persson was up on her feet and leaving the room.

Rooker sank even deeper into the couch. He was racking his brain, searching for any memory that had to do with this woman and his father, but there was nothing.

Harlow turned to him and whispered, "What the hell is going on here?"

"I think he knew. I have no idea how, but I think the killer knew about Mrs. Persson."

"And what, he went after her daughter? Don't you think he would've gone after her instead?"

"I don't really know what to think. I don't even know how it's possible. But this woman is saying she had a relationship with my father. I don't think choosing her daughter could be random. I think he targeted her."

They could hear the halting steps as she came back down the stairs. When she returned to the living room, she handed Rooker three Polaroids. Time had left its mark; the photos were distressed and a little faded, but he could see his father clearly. They looked to be in love; Gunner's chiseled jaw, the smirk that dimpled his cheek looked so foreign to Rooker. Mrs. Persson, young and beautiful with dark wavy hair, was staring back at him. Even though he loathed his father, it was like a spit in the face to him and the memory of Rooker's mother to see Gunner with another woman. He had always known his father was a charmer; he was probably putting on a show until he could end Mrs. Persson's life like the others. So why was she here in front of him, alive to talk about it? He passed the photographs to Harlow.

"Did you ever show these to the police?" Tess asked.

"Many years ago. After he was caught, my sister told me I had to talk to them. She said if I didn't, I'd put myself in a bad light. Maybe I'd be considered an accomplice."

Rooker suddenly had a thought that made him want to dig his fingernails into his palm until the skin was raw. "Who knew that you were seeing each other, other than your sister?"

"Oh jeez, I wouldn't remember. We're talking more than twenty years ago."

"Do you remember the police you spoke to, their names?"

"Rooker." Tess looked at him to let him know to cool it, but he couldn't. He knew what was about to come out of his mouth, knew it would hurt the woman, but he couldn't stop.

"Have you read the newspaper lately?" he asked her.

Harlow stood up. "Rooker, you need to—"

"Do you remember my father's photographs, the landscapes?"

"Yes," Mrs. Persson said. "They were excellent; I still—"

"The killer is murdering young women and putting their bodies at the scenes of his old photos. The collection that he had." He was rambling now. Tess was pulling on his arm. "Your daughter was one of them."

For a moment, it was like time stopped. He hadn't only dropped a bomb on her. He'd made her watch him light the dynamite wick, toss it into her hands like a gift-wrapped trinket, and let it detonate. Looks of shock, anger, horror—all of it spread across her face. She stared into Rooker's eyes, the son of the killer she had been in love with. Her wounded eyes sought confirmation from Detective Harlow that it was the truth, and she got it.

"I'm sorry, Mrs. Persson . . . we'll be leaving." But the woman's eyes went back to Rooker.

"Was she in pain?" She knew the answer, but she asked anyway.

"She was."

"We're leaving now," Tess declared. "If you think of anything, Mrs. Persson, here's where you can reach me." She left her card on the ancient coffee table.

Rooker found himself in a staring contest with the woman. He wondered what she was feeling. Was she repulsed by the son of a killer whom she'd lain with or flooded with familiarity for his father? Maybe she thought he'd come back to do his father's bidding, making his father proud.

"I still have one of the photos if you'd like it."

"What?" Tess froze. "From his collection?"

"Yes, he gave it to me for free. Well, not for free." The round wrinkles at her cheeks pinkened.

"Can you show us, please?"

This time, Rooker and Tess followed her upstairs, impatient to see the photo. The very touch of the wood railing caked his palm in a cold grime. Once he felt the railing wiggle, he let go and wiped his hand on his pants leg. This case was bringing him back to his darkest place, to the time when long obsessive nights fueled his insomnia and alcohol addiction. To the latter, he was still in the denial stage. Nights locked in his son's bedroom in total darkness: that's how it began. He drank and cried as quietly as he could. Until one night, he decided to start his investigation. He spent hours locked away in there, drinking, refusing to eat, not even bathing. Now he felt frighteningly similar. Tragedy tended to follow him, and this felt no different. He couldn't help but think that these bodies were piling up because he had returned to his father's home. And now there was a killer who somehow knew more about a life his father had hidden than he ever had.

When they reached the top of the stairs, Rooker saw Noah peeking out from what he assumed was a spare bedroom. The room lacked any sort of personal touch, though it would probably serve as the kid's bedroom now. As they passed what looked to be Mrs. Persson's bedroom, Rooker looked in and saw photographs framed on the bedside table, a heavy-looking duvet, and a quilt folded on top of it. She led them to a small storage area that was tucked away at the end of the dingy hall space, then unblocked the tiny door and unfastened the latch. It was jammed at first, but after a loud *click*, she pulled it open. The space was tight. She began to kneel, but Tess stopped her and went in.

"You should find it there on the wall to the right."

Rooker had a thought. If she loved the man behind the camera lens, even loved the photograph, why was she hiding it here? About a minute later, Tess reemerged, holding a photograph. She and Rooker scrutinized it, standing side by side.

Mrs. Persson gave it a quick glance, and her eyes grew misty. "Chippewa National Forest. We parked for the night, watched the sunset. He took his camera out and photographed it."

The sun hovered like a fireball above the trees. They towered over water so still, its reflection resembled a mirror's. The photo seemed to be taken from a hundred yards away.

"It's the first place we made love."

"In the park?"

"In the lot. It was a small car . . . I sat in the car watching him position himself and snap the photo. Afterward, he sat back inside and looked me in the eyes and kissed me like I'll never forget."

Tess turned the photo over, hoping for a message, maybe a handwritten time stamp, but there was nothing there. "May we keep this for now? We'll return it as soon as we can."

"Of course."

The three of them passed what would surely be Noah's bedroom as they headed back down the stairs to the entryway.

"Thank you for your time, ma'am. Again, I'm sorry for your loss."

The words seemed to bring her back to the present. Her posture appeared heavy and in need of sleep that she probably wouldn't get.

"You're handsome like he was," she said, and Rooker turned around. "You don't look *too* much like him, but something about you reminds me of Gunner."

We're nothing alike, he thought.

Rooker turned back to the door and walked out with Tess. When they got to the car, she stopped before she unlocked it.

"I know this isn't easy, your father's murders coming back to haunt you and a killer sending you a message. But that stunt you pulled back there will not fly with me."

"I apologize."

"You aren't a detective. Understood? I run lead. I don't need people filing complaints. *Not now.*"

"I said I apologize."

"I've heard empty apologies before. I need to know I can trust you."

She clicked the button on her key ring, and the doors unlocked. She opened hers, but Rooker did not open his.

"Are you coming or not?" she said.

"The park or the department?"

"Department. I'll send some people to search the park. If anything comes up, we'll go."

"Part of me thinks if the killer knew about Persson, he would've left her daughter at the park. But the other part of me thinks we're being deceived. He's unpredictable."

"You might be giving him too much credit."

"I think you don't give him enough."

Chapter 9

December 2

The moonlight bled lunar white through a small glass pane in the top of the door. Through it, he studied the rolling hills and steep dives of the mountain between the trees, the ski lift's black steel cables hanging high above the ground.

Dust particles and rust coated the room like a layer of frost. Shelves of cloudy mason jars full of old screws and nails and nuts lined the cabin wall: saws, bent screwdrivers and mismatched wrenches, and two axes hung beside an ancient chain saw, the metal covered in corroded orange. A bear trap hung in the center. An old Remington 700 BDL .17-caliber rifle rested on long screws in the wall by the door; he'd already checked to make sure it was loaded. Thick checkerboard curtains darkened the room. And there she was, on the worktable, another girl the world would soon forget. The knife rose and fell, flat on the light hairs of her stomach, to the unsteady rhythm of her breathing.

The resort lodging was temporarily closed for renovations. The cabin—more a maintenance shack—was secluded. They had the mountain to themselves.

He admired the tremble in her face. Two iridescent emerald circles peered up at him with fright. Though her mouth finally finished squawking beneath the cloth, her cheeks blubbered. Before she could whimper like a dog, the way the others had, he put a finger to his lips for her to be silent. Everything happened in this moment. She knew there was no escape. She gave up hope. She knew she was going to die. It was the moment that made him hard. He reached down his pants and closed his eyes. A shaky breath left his lips. When his eyelids rose, he showed her the outline of what she'd created.

While her eyes followed his fingers down the zipper of his black jeans, her whole body trembled. He grew more aroused as she watched him take his pants down. She was already half-naked, her bare butt red and exposed from where he'd slapped her over and over. She quivered, not in the mountain cold but beneath his touch.

He walked beside her and pulled his underwear down. He wanted more from her, but he knew she couldn't be trusted. She was one of them, one of these women who never looked his way, never wanted him. He strutted over to her with his ankles bound by his underwear. When she didn't move to do as he wanted, he slapped her. He squeezed her face by her cheeks, cinching his hand as tight as he could. She cried out, and her head flailed. Anger forced his nostrils open. His eyes closed.

Tears were rolling down her cheeks to the oak wood floor. Her eyes weren't important to him. Not yet. *Soon,* he thought. Soon, his knife would carve into her. Pierce the center of the sternum bone, through to the heart. He'd watch her eyes turn to two empty pits, the life gone, like it had with the rest.

All of a sudden, her eyes bulged wide. A muted scream caught behind the cloth in her throat. He looked down at her, ready to inflict more pain. She started fighting the restraints. He looked at her face, followed her gaze. And that's when he saw him. A boy about twelve or thirteen peering through the glass pane in the door. When the two locked eyes, the boy disappeared, followed by the frantic crunch of footsteps in the snow.

In a swift motion, he pulled his pants up and ran to the door, grabbing the Remington before he flung the door open. The kid was maybe sixty feet away. Then seventy. He took off the safety, shouldered the rifle, and aimed. The rifle led the slightest bit in front of him, and at about one hundred feet, he fired. The boy collapsed into the snow face-first. But it wasn't the bullet that had downed him. It was the piercing whip crack that echoed—it was fear that had sent him to the ground. He ejected the round and pushed the slide forward for a new one. Checking quickly for witnesses, he moved toward the boy, the earth crinkling like broken potato chips beneath him. He watched the boy scramble to his feet. One of the boy's hands was clutching the arm he'd landed on. His other hand was digging into the snow, trying to help him get upright.

The boy looked over his shoulder, up at him. Tried to bolt and fell but scrambled again. He could hear the boy crying, panting. The boy was proving more trouble than he was worth. Come tomorrow, they would all know what he had done—his next piece of art would be complete. And he knew the boy hadn't caught a good view of his face. He would be hiding, worried he'd be hunted down. Fuck it.

He headed back toward the cabin and scoured the ground for the casing. It took him about a minute, sifting through snow, skimming and brushing it like a paleontologist. He found it there beneath the doorway. He picked it up and rolled it in his hand. Once he stepped inside, the second he noticed the empty table, a sharp pain hit him square in the right side of his chest.

His hand closed around her wrist. She was trying hard to pull the knife out, desperate, he was sure, to stab him again. It didn't budge. He leaned back. Drove the heel of his foot into her stomach. The force knocked her backward. Unexpectedly, the knife tore right out of his body.

It was botched. This one was done—no saving it. He took aim and fired. A deafening blast silenced the cabin, but it left a ringing in his head. A red hole tunneled through her skull. He looked down at her,

her eyes empty, the terror gone. He ran to her pile of clothing, threw items aside until he found her shirt in the middle of the heap. He pulled it out, separated his shirt from his blood-soaked skin, pressed the shirt hard against the gash in his chest. It was bad but manageable, he thought. Maybe two inches deep—if the serrated part had punctured him, he'd have a much lower chance of surviving. His hands were still gloved, and he made sure none of his blood touched them, since he still had to finish up.

He dragged her by the ankle through the snow. The moment he started pulling, the sharp pain in his chest was like another knife carving into his flesh. Through a deep groan and gritted teeth, he dragged her about eighty to ninety feet, back toward the ski lift. He dumped her there. He no longer cared how she was positioned. All that mattered was that she was there, at the forefront of one of Gunner Lindström's photos. Rooker would be there soon enough. He would know it was a replica of his father's work. He took the photo from his pocket, rolled it up, and stuffed it down the woman's throat. He rushed back to the cabin. He had one thing left to do.

Thirty minutes later, he keyed the door—metal ticks until it caught—turned the handle, and shoved it open. He hurried around the room and drew the blinds closed. Dust particles soared into the air each time he snatched one of them closed. Just as the room breathed him in, he took a breath, his mouth cotton. Each time he yanked one shut, he peered outside, but there was nothing there except trees and snowy earth.

He shambled past the large sectional couch—one he'd purchased with cash off Craigslist—to the small wood-burning stove and threw in a log. He slipped the knife out of his jacket and tossed it into the sink; it made a scratchy clunk and settled in the center of the drain.

Crouched below the sink, he swung the cabinet door open and pulled out a small medical kit. Beads of sweat poured from his head. The tabs on the box snapped open beneath his shaky fingers. It hurt his chest to move anything on his right side, but he fingered a pair of surgical scissors, set them down, then pulled off his jacket. He lifted the scissors and cut the long way down the collar of his shirt to the hem. He pulled it off and threw it into the sink as well. Taking the kit, he made his way over to the stove.

He sat down in front of the fire, sweat dripping even faster from greasy wet hair. He took out a disinfectant and dabbed at it with a pad, then touched it to his skin. The burn felt like it went right through his chest. An excruciating spasm shot up his spine. He screamed through grinding teeth, his mouth tight, lips sealed shut. He glanced down at the wound. It didn't look particularly good, that was for sure. But he could fix it.

He took out the surgical sutures, a pair of tweezers, and the scissors. He put the sutures close to the fire, let them sit for a few seconds, and got to work. Carefully, he lifted the skin, punctured it, and pushed the wire through to the other side of the gash. A tear-shaped blotch of red raced down his white skin like a water droplet on a window. He pulled it tight until it closed, the pain blistering. He looked down at his chest in the little mirror, knew it would take at least another eight, maybe ten stitches if he played it safe, to close it. He took his time weaving the black through his skin, the wire fine like a strand of hair. Every now and then, a bit of red would drool down from it.

After about ten minutes, he finished with a large white nonstick bandage. He sat up and went to the fridge. It was old, an odd creamy beige with bizarre metal handles, but it worked like new. He opened the door, pulled out a plate of food, and tossed it into the microwave. After a minute, he pulled it out, took off the plastic wrap, and set it on the table by the sofa. He sat by the fire and started digging in. Every time he moved wrong, the stiffness in his wound felt like it was set ablaze, a fire in his chest as hot as the one in front of him. He forced himself to be still and wait for the fire to run its course.

The property was hidden entirely off the grid. He'd paid cash for it, and no one knew it was his. The older man had looked up at him gravely when he offered cash but took it and never looked back. The place wasn't worth much, let alone what he'd paid the man. It was a run-down two-level dump in the middle of nothing, but it was only two levels if you counted the unfinished excuse for a basement. The only way it could be considered nice was if he compared it to the Lindström cottage. The roof was intact. Things weren't in danger of falling apart at any moment, decaying before the eye. There were no neighbors, just a boy who sometimes wandered too far from home into the woods. He'd watch the boy swing a stick, taking golf-driver cuts at the ground, sending dead leaves flying and snow crystals soaring. He'd see something dark, lifted from the snow flying a few feet. One day when the boy was gone, he went out and followed the bloody-feather trail, found the dead bird the boy had all but dismembered.

After he finished the plate, he set it on the table and gulped down a glass of tap water. A week after Lilly Anderson, he'd gone to the doctor because he couldn't sleep. Well, it was more of what was keeping him awake. He'd lie in his queen-size bed, the flannel sheets loose but covering him, tucked just below his jaw. The doctor had prescribed a sedative-hypnotic, a blue-and-pink pill. It was a temporary fix, but it was doing its job. He unscrewed the cap, popped a large pill in his mouth, and swallowed hard. Finally, he kicked off his shoes, put his feet up, and went to sleep.

Chapter 10

Rooker opened his eyes to the rustling of trees. There was a hollowness to it—a whirring hiss silenced by the occasional snap, like a crackle of flame. For a moment, he imagined ocean waves, their swells sweeping the beach. It reminded him of where he wasn't: home.

He expected to see light creeping in through the cracks of wood boarding the windows, but it was still pitch-black. He thought that maybe he hadn't slept at all. But when his bleary vision focused on the bright digital display, the neon-green 8:30 p.m. blinding him, he threw the sheets off him and went down the creaky staircase to the phone. One day he'd end up falling right through them, but when he made it to the bottom, he thought, *Not today*. He sat down in the chair, pressed the pulsing red button indicating there were two voice mails. The first was from the people who told him his house wasn't fit to be lived in. He deleted it. The second message was from Tess. She'd called a few hours ago with news about the case. He decided he'd call her while he looked over the copies of the files she'd given him.

But first, he needed coffee. He got up, started making his way to the kitchen—*fuck*. He'd forgotten it was broken. He picked up the phone and dialed his neighbor.

After a few rings, the syrupy sweetness in her voice came over the receiver.

"Mrs. Holmberg."

"Evelyn, it's Rooker."

"Ah, did you clean the dishes I left there?"

"I've been a bit busy."

"Well, I'm not taking them until they're clean."

"I was actually going to ask you a favor," he said, shame in his voice.

"Of course, why else do you call me?"

"Oh, stop it."

"What do you need?"

He could hear the longing in her voice. "Coffee . . . maybe food? If you would be so kind." His eyes scrunched. He smiled at his own coyness. He sounded like the kiss ass in the classroom, but it would do the trick. He liked to think he still had some of his charm.

"Clean the dish and come over; I'll have it ready."

"Actually . . ." He closed his eyes. "I just sat down with the files. I need to take a look at these." He'd say anything to keep reading deeper and deeper into the darkness.

"You're really something."

"I know—I'm sorry. I'll share some of my top-shelf liquor." He pronounced it *lih-core*. "Very high-end."

She hung up.

Rooker opened the box and started pulling files, reading in chronological order. The first kill, a graduate student, twenty-three, Lilly Anderson. He knew that with serial murderers, often the first kill was personal in some way. But he had a gut feeling this one might not be. He read the report, some sentences he reread, looking for anything hidden in the details. Nothing jumped off the pages at him. She seemed like your pretty-but-average student, reported missing by her roommate. They found her body in Coleraine, propped against an old stone bridge. A deep gash dug along the side of her neck, red and jagged from a blade's teeth sawing back and forth. The killer had begun to sever her head but stopped. He looked down at the photo of her grizzled flesh. Blood spatter was everywhere. Her skin looked plastic, stiff and pale as candle wax. Why did he try to do it to her and no one else? Why did he stop? Was it because it was his first? And then Rooker thought of something else. It's almost as if the killer had tried to emulate Gunner but then changed his mind. Gunner was history. This was his story.

It seemed meticulous and theatrical. He laughed at himself. His father had decapitated women and kept their heads in a freezer, dumped the bodies. So why was this so different?

Her body was found early in the morning. She'd been killed the night before, as most of the victims had been. The scene matched one of the photos found on the factory's conveyor belt. It also matched one of the photos in Gunner's collection, only now the water below the bridge was frozen. The report stated that she had injuries to the back of her skull and her upper back consistent with whiplash or being struck by a large blunt object multiple times. Harlow had left a brief of her own; she believed the killer had slammed the victim down against the ice, using her as a crude ice pick, before drowning her.

There was no mention of rape, no mutilation other than the failed attempt at decapitation postmortem. She was found dressed, her clothing frozen to her skin. He reached for his laptop and made some notes, clicking away on the keyboard.

Why was she different??

Not raped . . . Not enough time?? Worried about a witness??

Rooker looked at the photo of her alive. She was pretty. Long platinum-blonde hair with darker roots, dimpled cheeks, a smile that would make most men believe in love at first sight. Her eyes were bright and dark blue, her lips full beneath a delicate nose.

The shift key flattened beneath his pinkie finger, his index down on the key to the left. After a few lines filled with question marks, he clicked the backspace over and over until there was only one. Leaning back, he tried to put himself in the killer's shoes. But then a bang on the door made him jump and knock one of the files from the arm of the chair. After two nudges, the door opened a crack, and Evelyn used her hip to push it the rest of the way.

"Working yourself mad?"

"You scared the shit out of me."

Her smile turned to a laugh. "I'm sorry?"

"The smile and laugh say otherwise."

She walked over and handed him a thermos filled with coffee. She took the computer off his lap and replaced it with a plate of food.

"Thank you."

He glanced into her eyes; they weren't young, but they were as bright as any of the women in the files beside him. At least in the photos of them while they were alive. It gave him one last thought that he needed to type.

"Let me see that, please, just one second."

She passed him the laptop back, and he typed, *Drowned facedown or faceup?? Eyes?*

It was the first moment he started to feel like he had a sliver of understanding of the killer. After Gunner had been caught, Rooker researched others like his father. Jack the Ripper. Jeffrey Dahmer. Ted Bundy. Charles Manson. Dennis Rader. He read the stories of the Zodiac Killer. He read *Helter Skelter* and the works of Thomas Harris. At first, he wanted only to delve inside his father's mind. Why did he kill? Did he feel remorse? Was he able to see what his actions would do to his family? He wanted to know if his father was incapable of loving him or just never did. Did he ever love Rooker's mother? But aside from diagnosing his father as a sadistic bastard, he surmised his father's murders correlated to his desire for fame in photography. Gunner wanted attention, to be seen, to be noticed.

Rooker became utterly fascinated. Now he would have to find out what the pattern was in this case.

He set the laptop aside. Evelyn lifted it from the sagging arm of the chair and put it on a table across the room.

"Eat before it gets cold."

He sank his teeth into a meat and dill potato dish with cream sauce and a side of lingonberries. She spoiled him absolutely rotten. She smiled as he ate her food. Maybe it was one of the last things that gave her joy, watching someone eat her home cooking.

"Seems like you listened to me after all." She grinned, perusing the large box and the files inside.

"It isn't this noble gesture like you think. I'm doing it for me."

"Just because you say it out loud doesn't make it true."

"The killer is using my father's murders as inspiration. I want to put it all right there where it belongs. In the past."

"I think you want to catch your father."

"Oh, please." He pinched the rigid bridge of his nose. "My father is long dead. His bones rotted away in the same prison he was sentenced to for life."

"Tell me this has nothing to do with him, then."

But it had everything to do with him. He was a monster dressed in a man's skin. He didn't love his son, probably never loved his wife. He'd forced Rooker down into the basement to clean out rat traps or put his boxing gloves on and come at him. There were times when Gunner hit Rooker so hard, he thought he was going to die. At the age of eleven, Rooker was made to drink whiskey until he puked, then forced to clean it up. He made "business trips" out to his Minnesota cottage to sleep with women, kill them, remove their heads, and store them in the freezer, and then he'd go right back home. Evelyn watched his hesitation, perhaps seeing the storm cloud over his head, the expression changing in his face. She was right.

"It's also about the women. You want to save them from a man like your father. Maybe it has to do with saving your mother too."

"He never killed her."

"In a way, maybe he did."

"I didn't know you were a shrink."

His tone bittered. Rooker was talking about things he'd bottled up for a long time. He never spoke about them. He wouldn't now. His mother was a sore subject. He didn't feel like anyone deserved to hear about how amazing she was. Even when she got sick and was falling apart, forgetting people, she never forgot him. She was more spectacular than anyone else he'd ever known.

He wanted to hurl the plate of food across the room.

"Well, I'm glad you're helping the police. It's nice to see you doing some good instead of hitting the liquor so hard."

"Oh right, did you want that drink?"

"No, I'm okay."

He kept eating, chasing every couple of bites with warm coffee. Though Evelyn was taking care of him, he was dying for her to leave so he could get back to his date with the files. The last murder, the conversation with Mrs. Persson, it was all getting in his way. He would scour the pages looking for everything and anything that remotely stood out to him. If it raised the slightest question in his mind, he'd circle it, underline it, type something on his computer. He assumed he wouldn't be going to sleep anytime soon.

"Remember when you would sneak over to the window when you were a teen, and you'd try to catch me undressing?"

Rooker felt the warmth climb from his chest to his cheeks; his forehead felt feverish.

"What?" He played dumb.

"Oh please, don't pretend you didn't."

He smiled. "Of course I did. I was a curious boy."

"Well, you're a man now. Still want to see?"

Rooker led her up the stairs to the bedroom. A dim stream of indigo capered in through the window. The night was starless. Her back was to the side of the bed, the back of her legs pressed against the frame.

She faced him and unbuttoned her flannel shirt herself. Goose pimples spotted her upper chest.

"It's freezing up here."

He laughed. "Maybe I've gotten a little more used to it. Here." His hands went from her chest to her neck; he kissed her hard on the mouth and pushed her down onto the bed. He got on top of her and fumbled around at the clasp to her pants. She lifted his shirt, her hands like ice against his stomach and chest.

"*Jesus* Christ!"

She let out a mirthful chuckle and pulled the shirt off the rest of the way. After a few minutes, it was over.

"Sorry," he said breathily beside her. "I've been a little out of practice."

"It's okay."

Rooker watched her naked form as she walked out of the room down the stairs. He listened anxiously, making sure one of the steps wouldn't finally give out. Then he heard the sputter of the faucet in the bathroom, and he lay there naked, partially under a blanket. The cool air felt good on the places that were bare; the blanket felt even better on the places that weren't.

He stayed there, just staring, feeling as if he could actually see the wood rotting overhead. A few minutes later, he heard the phone ring. He forced himself to get up, hurried downstairs, and lifted the receiver. He heard deep, low breathing on the other end. He didn't say a word; he just listened to it. Out of the corner of his eye, he saw Evelyn standing there wrapped in a sheet that he kept on the couch. He looked up at the clock, saw the numbers that he'd woken up to for several months straight: *11:37.* The caller hung up. He listened to the dial tone. His eyes squeezed shut. His teeth gritted.

In a football spike, the phone launched from his hand to the floor. The battery cover exploded off and ricocheted upward, the batteries soaring in different directions.

"Im-fucking-possible."

"What is it?" Her face was a mixed drink of confusion and empathy.

"How? How the *fuck* is this possible?"

"Rooker?"

"It was never reported; we kept it out of the papers . . ." He didn't know what was going on. How could this happen? Did they let him out? "The killer . . . not this one. The one who killed my . . . my boy. He would call me every night. It was the time my boy was pronounced dead. Every night I'd wake up and see the fucking digital numbers or the hands on the clock. It was always him. Torturing me, reminding me that some fuck . . . murdered my son."

"I think you'd better call the police. The people you're helping, maybe they can help."

"It doesn't make sense. How could someone know about it?"

"I think I'd better be leaving." She started up the stairs to get her clothes.

He felt absolutely gutted. *How could this be happening?*

He needed a drink. He needed to call Tess. But the phone looked destroyed far beyond saving. He heard the creaking stairs and saw Evelyn descending, buttoning her flannel shirt. "Um, can I use your phone?"

Rooker and Evelyn walked to her home in silence. He stood in the small foyer. The place was quaint with cream-colored furniture and rustic touches. The ceiling had a slight peak, with wood beams that resembled cork. He glanced at an old portrait photo of Harold, young and smiling in a military coat and dress cap; Rooker turned away. When Evelyn handed him the phone, he dug out Tess's card from his pocket and dialed.

"Harlow," she answered.

"It's Rooker."

"Hey . . ." Her voice lifted in surprise. "Did you have a chance to look over the files?"

"Some of them. That isn't why I called you."

"What is it?"

"The killer called me. But I'm not sure which one."

"What?"

"I'll tell you when I see you. Can you pick me up?"

"I can be there in twenty-five minutes."

"Oh, and I need a new phone." He hung up. His night with Evelyn ended the way one-night stands usually do: in awkward silence.

Chapter 11

Tess pulled up in the dead of night. The Interceptor splashed through the wet slush surrounding the lake house. Rooker pulled on his jacket and walked out to the car. He opened the passenger door and saw a burner phone still in its packaging. He picked it up, sat down, and closed the door behind him.

"Thanks."

"No worries—we had a few to spare. So you want to tell me what's going on?"

"I need an update on Tate Meachum." The name leaving his lips felt like a knife to the carotid. It made him feel sick; he needed to remind himself to breathe. "I need to know if he's been released or has access to a phone . . . maybe he got one into his cell somehow."

"I'll find out. What does that have to do with anything?"

"I got a call tonight, at 11:37 p.m. I haven't gotten that call in more than a year. It's the time my son was pronounced dead. The killer called me every night at that time, starting with the night after he killed him. I had the same phone call every night for close to a year, until the day I finally caught him. And then it stopped. But all of this was never released. It was kept out of the newspapers. Only a handful of people should know about it. But tonight someone called me, at 11:37, breathing hard on the other line, then hung up."

"What if Meachum told someone, told them to call you to mess with you?"

His face hardened. "I don't think he would," he said. "It was something between the killer and his intended victim. It was personal. He thought it was a bond that we shared, a nightly call where the silence spoke more than any words ever could."

"Well, if it isn't him, he must have told someone. Or it's someone involved in the case who knew he called you."

"I don't think it's that easy. How does the killer know about my father's collection and now this?"

"So he didn't say anything?"

"Nothing."

"Well, maybe we can trace it if he calls again."

"It'll never work."

"Okay. What do you suggest?"

"Tell me about the first one, Lilly Anderson."

"She was a graduate student. Was still dating her high school sweetheart. All her friends said she was harmless, kinder than anyone they'd ever met. A person who would go out of her way to do anything for anyone."

"I read your report. You thought she was slammed down on the ice, some of it had broken and split, and she was drowned."

"That's right."

"Why?"

"She sustained trauma to the back of her skull that was a bit unusual. It wasn't something a fist could do, and no weapon was found in the search. But this didn't look like baseball bat swings to the head. More like she was possibly lifted off her feet and slammed hard against something even harder. When I saw the ice broken apart in sections where she was found, and the body soaked, it seemed clear to me."

"Would you guess that she was facedown or faceup?"

She looked at him, apparently perplexed.

He tried again.

"Was she pulled from the water by him or by the witness or by the police? I didn't have a chance to read the rest of the report; do we know which way she was facing when the body was found?"

Her gaze sharpened with understanding. "I don't know. We assume she was dragged from the water. Her boyfriend found her propped up against the bridge. When she didn't turn up, he tracked her phone through GPS. He said she looked like a porcelain doll, frozen stiff. Why are you so worried about which way she was facing?"

"It's not how she was facing; it's how he faced her. And it's just a theory right now."

"Well, let's hear it."

"It may sound crazy, but I think there's something about their eyes."

"Then why wouldn't he take them as trophies?"

He'd already thought of that. "I don't know. But there are power and control killers; they're the psychopaths who need to assert their dominance over the victim. It's the whole 'eyes are the window to the soul' bullshit.

"The eyes convey everything—every emotion, and so far, each victim's eyes have been open when you've found them. I think he likes staring at them or into them. I think pain and fear are how he gets his rocks off. He takes these girls, binds them. They're defenseless. Maybe at some point they accept their fate. That could do it. Maybe it's when the life leaves their eyes . . . ?" He paused. "I don't know. I have a feeling the first one was his own experimenting, figuring it all out. But I think he was caught off guard somehow. He didn't rape the first girl. Instead he slammed her into the ice and drowned her. He watched her die, and that became his MO."

Tess's phone rang. She pressed the green button and put the phone close to her ear. Rooker was able to hear the words, soft but clear as day.

"Boss, we've got another one."

Chapter 12

Tess footed the pedal harder up the mountain. Under different circumstances, the climb wasn't perilous. But the never-ending ascent only gave them time, and time only left Rooker with unnerving thoughts of the scene awaiting them. Rooker closed the window when he felt the drive playing tricks on him. They hadn't climbed high enough for it to be altitude sickness, but his vision was starting to cloud, and it was getting harder to chamber air into his lungs.

He could smell winter in the air. It was eye-widening, like smelling salts broken beneath his nose. The weight of winter had taken its toll on the road. Cold gray conquered the pavement, matching the twisting steel barricade that turned with the road. Twigs and dead shrubs reached out from the earth like hands. Closer to the top, a couple of abandoned cars were partially visible, buried beneath several feet of snow. The resort was closed.

When they reached the top of the mountain, a baker's dozen marked patrol cars were parked. A cluster of gingerbread-house cabins, each of them with their own snow-glazed front porch, was blocked off. Rooker was greeted passenger side by Martin Keene's robust belly at the window. He was wearing the same jacket, the present from his wife. Perhaps it was growing on her. Rooker doubted it.

Rooker and Tess got out of the car and fell in step with Keene.

"They have the perimeter blocked off."

Rooker nodded toward the police standing by, then at a detective he'd remembered seeing in the station.

"Told 'em we'd wait for you to get here. Mountain's closed until we say so."

"Very good." Tess's voice was all business. "Get most of these guys out of here. I don't want my crime scene contaminated. The techs?"

"They're wrapping up shortly." Keene bounced on his toes.

"First officer on scene?"

"Clay Carver." Keene nodded over at an older cop.

"Great name," Rooker said. "'Like I'm living in a Western."

"Find out what he's touched or where he's walked. Who is that?" Tess pointed to the weeping woman, her sobs loud enough to strike an avalanche. She screamed something at the police who were huddled around more yellow tape.

"A kid's mom. She said her son likes to wander around here, but he didn't come home last night. Walk with me." Keene led the way, Tess following him surveying the scene, and Rooker trailed behind her like her lost puppy. "So this is the mindfuck. You see here—" Keene leaned forward and pointed to a trail of footprints. "Someone fell forward into the snow. We have handprints where someone dragged themselves. They're small, and it looks like the kid was running from someone. It could be the woman's son."

Their feet sank into the snow. Rooker knew his calves would be sore in the morning. Powder kicked up when he lifted his boot; then it buried again in the white. They made their way to the opposite side of the screaming woman. Rooker knew Tess would have to talk to her at some point, but she probably wanted to see the scene without so much distraction.

He tried to distance himself from the woman, but it was no use. When he looked at her, he saw himself, saw the way his world had shattered. You could try to kneel down, try to pick up the pieces one by one, glue them together, but they'd never fit like they had before.

When they passed the officers, three people were walking toward them in what looked like white helmet-less space suits, their heads hooded, part of their faces covered by surgical masks. They approached Harlow.

"Detective," one of them said low behind the mask. He pulled it from his face. "All yours. We'll put a rush on the evidence for you, bag the body once you're done, and get the victim to the ME."

"Thanks, guys."

And they were gone.

Tess turned to Keene. "What else do you have?"

"Not much to go on. Looks like our guy was in the middle of his routine inside." Keene pointed over to the open cabin. "Someone must have seen and ran—could be the missing boy."

Now Rooker wanted to speak to the mother—if her son *was* out here, Rooker wanted to know what the boy was doing wandering around here at night. But he was a boy; that's what boys did. *Boys will be boys.*

Rooker and Tess trudged the rest of the way to the cabin. The door was blocked off with tape. The older cop was standing beside it. Clay Carver's hair was newspaper-gray and white. He scowled as he observed Rooker. He looked about retirement age and sported an eighties Burt Reynolds mustache, salt-and-pepper above his chapped lip. Rooker had never seen him before but guessed he wasn't a fan of Rooker being there. When they reached the tape, the man lifted it so Tess and Rooker could duck and walk through.

"Clay Carver?" Tess asked.

"Yes, ma'am." His eyes were still on Rooker.

"He's with me. Good?"

He made a De Niro face, scrunched like he understood but didn't like it.

"What did you find, Carver?"

"The mother phoned it in this evening that the kid was missing. She said he likes to explore here, poke around the empty cabins." The deep rasp in his voice reminded Rooker of cigarettes and whiskey. "I was nearby, so I got the call. Don't have the best eyes anymore, but this cabin door was wide open, saw that from pretty far away. I came to check it out and found the drag marks . . . and then I found the woman. I phoned it in. It's in my notes." He held a black leather pad in the air that looked like a wallet.

"Sterling," she called over. "Copy his notes down. Once you're done, Carver, you're free to leave. Thank you."

"Got it."

◆　◆　◆

Once inside, Rooker tried to imagine the chain of events.

He looked over his shoulder at the windows and the door. The curtains were a hideous plaid, drawn tight. He checked to see if they were sheer, but he couldn't see through them. The room smelled like metal and sawdust, maybe freshly split cedar. He looked at the door and saw cops moving through the glass pane in the top of it. The boy would have had to be on his tippy-toes to catch a glance of anything. Either the victim saw him and screamed for help, or the killer was on the other side of the table and saw the kid. Rooker figured he'd be too focused to have noticed the boy standing there, so she must have seen him. And then the boy took off running.

Rusted tools lined the cabin wall. If he'd used them, they would have made a mess. Cutting through her with rusty saws or whatever he picked would be like cutting a steak with a butter knife, hell, maybe even a plastic picnic knife. The worktable attached to it was clearly old and hand built. Areas of it looked to have warped either due to heat or tools slamming against it. Rooker glanced at the rifle hanging from old bent nails. There was an odd gap there beside it. Something was missing. He wondered what it was.

His eyes drifted to the ground, where he saw the two zip ties. There weren't any where they found Sofia Persson's body. He hadn't seen any mention of them in the reports. He asked, "Zip ties weren't used on any of the other victims, right?"

"No." Keene gloved up. "Never."

The two of them bent down for a closer look. When Rooker saw slashes in the zip ties, he knew there was something strange. The killer had been thrown off—that much was certain. He had to rush. So either his hands were shaking while he cut the ties from her wrists or she found a way to cut them when he went for the boy. Rooker saw the mist of blood from where he'd shot her.

"Where is she?"

"Out by the ski lift."

Rooker and Tess were told where they could step. They had to walk beside the trail where the killer had dragged her body. Rooker could see her from a distance. As he closed in, he noticed the large hole in her head. She was positioned upright beneath the lift. He looked up at the cables the ski lift traveled on. He wondered if the killer's plan had been to put her on one of them.

"Shit. This is a mess," Tess said.

They stood over the body. Her underwear was missing, but she was still wearing a white bra. Her hair was twisting and blonde. She had an angular face like a diamond and piercing green eyes that made her look alive. But there was the red hole in her head with crusted blood around it.

"Do we have an ID?" Tess asked.

Keene shook his head. "Not yet. No license or anything found inside."

"That might help us." Tess pointed to the dead girl's knee. She had three, maybe four different lines, all different lengths of scarring.

Rooker caught on. "Maybe an athlete. ACL repair."

"Good eye," Keene said.

Rooker studied her left hand and didn't see what he was looking for. He had a feeling the ligature marks would be there. But they weren't. He walked over to her opposite side, bent down, and scrutinized her right hand. "Can you turn the hand over?"

Tess pulled a glove out and turned her wrist over so that the palm was faceup. Rooker saw it. There was a small but deep incision in the upper portion of her palm.

A look of shock fell over Tess's face. "How did she get ahold of a knife?"

"If he was interrupted by the boy, she might have had enough time to get ahold of his. The zip ties had cuts in them," Keene said. "My guess is her hands were bound in front of her—she was able to grab his knife and cut at the zip ties to free them. When he came back, I think she stabbed him."

"Please tell me we have a knife somewhere here," Tess said.

Martin answered, "No weapon turned up yet, only the rifle. We found the calling card in her mouth—it matches with the mountain and the ski lift. We'll test the blood, see if it isn't hers."

"It's hers," Rooker spat.

"You can't rule it out."

"We can't catch a fucking break here," Rooker said.

"A break?" Tess said. "He was caught in the act. If that boy turns up and he saw the killer, maybe we'll get a description. The killer's probably hurt and taking care of himself right now. Who knows, maybe the son of a bitch will die from it."

Rooker looked back to the place she was murdered. "Do you see that?" he said. It wasn't really a question, but it made her look to the trail in the snow, all the way back to the cabin. "How far would you say that is, one hundred feet? Maybe more? Do you think a man who can do that, after being stabbed, is just going to die?"

He watched a series of emotions wash over her before she regained control. Her face shifted into neutral, stayed there, but her voice was as raw as the elevation in the air. "Look, I'm not saying someone's going to go for a stroll and see a guy with a knife hanging out of him. But he's becoming careless: he lost control of the victim, and he might have left a witness. Maybe he's starting to feel invincible."

"Right now, this gives us time," she said. "So far, he's been several steps ahead, but now he's injured. We don't know how badly, but hopefully he's too hurt to go out and pick another woman."

"Detective Harlow," a local cop yelled to her and was hurrying over as best he could through the deep snow. "Think we got something. This kid was watching from the tree line—"

His feet looked like they were sinking deeper and deeper each time they buried in the snow. All of a sudden, Rooker leaped back from the blasting metal crack. It was like a medieval hammer swing, a blacksmith driving metal into a steel anvil. It was blink-of-the-eye fast. The cop let out a shriek of pain and fell forward into the snow.

"What happened?" Keene yelled.

It was the single loudest "fuck" Rooker had heard in his life. The man let out a guttural shriek—Rooker had heard similar screams at nightfall, when the animals roamed and the world was black.

The cop's legs went stiff. His torso flailed like a fish washed up on the shore. He grasped and pried at something near his leg. Everyone moved toward the cop at once. Rooker saw the steel jaws of the bear trap digging deep into his skin and flesh, his shin caved in. Blood leaked down his pants leg and over the tongue of his boot.

Two of the other officers pulled on the trap until it released while another helped him ease his foot out. Tears ran down his face. He looked at his bloody leg, which was shaking like an addict's fiendish hand. Stammered curse words flew along with webbed spittle from his lips.

Tess's face was ghastly, filled with horror and exhaustion. "Get him to an ambulance. Follow the prints in the snow—we don't know what else is out here."

She watched in silence as the group carried their colleague away. When they got him far enough, two men met them with a gurney. They transferred him carefully onto the stretcher and carried him to where he was no longer in sight.

Her hands were on her hips. A deep breath fogged before her face, while her blank stare met that of the dead woman's. "So, where do we go from here?"

Rooker heard her, though the question was purely reflexive. It was only the two of them now. Keene had gone to talk to the kid. When she'd come to Rooker's home that first day and asked for his help, there was a quiet confidence in her. Now he could see the doubt festering, sprouting up in the cracks.

She spoke once again. "Let's bring the team together and get to work. We've been breaking down how he chooses women, where he chooses them, what we think he might look like. But there has to be more we can do." She stopped. "How did you catch your son's killer?"

"It took time. But I was persistent; I followed every lead and question I had until I got him."

"I don't know if we have that kind of time. There're too many bodies."

She turned her head to the dead woman, though every now and then her eyes would fall to the ground.

"Ask yourself what's really wrong," Rooker said.

"What's wrong?" She looked ready to start counting on her fingers but stopped. "Women are dying. And I can't stop it."

"You will," he told her, and continued, "stop it. They do that to you—cases like this. I'm no expert, but I lost everything I had left. I had someone who still cared about me, and I gave up on it. I came here broken and had no intention of fixing it. Somehow, I have you to thank; you gave me a reason to put the vodka down for a little bit and put on pants."

She almost smiled, but it wasn't quite there. Her eyes were heavy, unfocused, sad.

"Boss," Keene hollered. "You'll want to hear this."

Rooker and Tess staggered back through the snow. He knew the cuff of his pants leg was riding up when he felt the cold, wet sensation filling his boot. But there was a nagging feeling that Rooker couldn't scrap. Someone might've been visiting Meachum in prison. His ex-fiancée detested him after she found out his secret; she'd never go and see him. So who? And then there was the killer, who had more information than anyone should about his father.

Rooker and Harlow rounded a corner and saw the crying mother wrap a boy of about twelve in a crushing hug. His skin was fair, and his hair was a dirty-blond mess.

"Where have you been? I've been worried sick!"

"Excuse me, ma'am." Harlow walked over. "What's your name?"

"Kat," she said.

"Full name?"

"Kathryn Hanson."

"This is your son?"

"Jack."

"Do you mind if I ask Jack a few questions?"

The woman nodded.

"Hi, Jack. My name's Tess Harlow. I'm a detective."

"Hi."

"How old are you, Jack?"

"Twelve."

"When's your birthday?"

"July fifteenth."

"Are you hungry? Thirsty?"

"No."

"Your mom's been worried about you. She said you didn't come home last night. Is that right?"

"Yeah."

"Where did you sleep?"

"I stayed at Bobby's. He said he wouldn't tell his parents I was there."

"Why didn't you want his parents to know?"

He didn't answer.

"Why didn't you go home?"

"I didn't want *him* to follow me."

She paused. "Where were you last night, Jack?"

Again, he didn't answer.

"Were you here?"

"Yeah."

"What time were you here?"

He looked over at his mom.

"It's okay; you can tell me."

"After ten."

"What were you doing out here at night?"

"I don't know."

"Were you alone?"

"Yeah."

"Bobby didn't come with you?"

"No."

"So tell me, Jack. Are those your shoeprints?"

"Yeah."

"You were running?"

"Yeah."

"Why were you running?"

"From the man."

"Okay," she said. "Why? Did he scare you?"

"What he did to the lady."

She paused. "Was he hurting her?"

"Yeah."

"Okay, Jack. You're doing great. Can you tell me what the bad man looked like?"

"I didn't get a good look."

"That's okay. Anything at all. Was he tall?"

"Yeah."

"Taller than me?"

"Yeah."

"Taller than him?" She pointed to Martin Keene.

"Maybe a little bit. Skinnier, though."

"What about his hair?"

"It looked dark. He had a black cap on."

"But his hair was dark?"

"Yeah."

"What about his clothing?"

"Dark."

"Was his skin like mine?"

"Yeah."

"Can you remember anything about his face?"

"No. It was too dark."

"Okay. What made you run?"

"He saw me. And when I ran, he shot at me."

"Okay," she said. "Thank you, Jack. I'm going to get—"

"Is she dead?" he asked.

Tess put a hand on the boy's shoulder. "I'm going to get you some food and something to drink. And I'm going to have a sketch artist come out, so I want you to really think about the man you saw."

"What if he comes after us?"

"That's what I'm here for. Don't worry."

98

Rooker fell into step with her as they trudged back to the car. "Dark hair, around six feet tall, black cap, and black clothes?"

"Mm-hmm. The kid is scared. Maybe he remembers more, but we'll have to wait and see."

"You were very good back there," Rooker said. "Let me buy you some breakfast. You look like you need to eat."

He found himself on the scenic route, stomach gurgling beside Detective Harlow. She drove past something that seemed like a church but made Rooker think of the Hogwarts castle. He'd forced the Harry Potter books on his son a few years back. Thirty minutes later, she pulled into a large, newly built complex lined with apartments and identical balconies. The windows, the lines in the buildings, it all looked so modern, symmetrical. She took a turn, drove down a string of cars, and parked in a reserved spot. They got out, and Rooker followed her as she made her way between two apartment buildings into a large glass door and straight toward an elevator. They stepped in, and she pressed the button for the fourth floor. He listened to the low hum as the lift carried them to a stop. The elevator doors opened. Tess turned right and made her way to the apartment on the left. She unlocked the door and opened it, and Rooker was surprised at how nice it was.

He'd expected it to be new, but the room was immaculate. They walked in, and to the left was the kitchen, a very modern, classic white set of upper and lower cabinets with built-in chrome appliances. The backsplash was a dark-gray tile and matched the top of the small island fixed in the corner of the room. The base of the island was a sparkly black and matched the four chairs surrounding a round table. The rest of the open floor plan revealed a living room with a comfy-looking sofa on the left wall and a table in front of it and a stand with a flat-screen television on the right wall. On the far side of the room was a large window and glass-paneled door that led out to a balcony with a view outside. Rooker noticed two chairs and a small table between, and he wondered if the other seat on the balcony had ever been occupied. Her bedroom door was large and open to the right of the television, her bed unmade, probably from waking up at all hours to dead women. Rooker looked at the built-ins and saw few family photos.

There was one of a young girl with straight dark hair. Harlow's face really hadn't changed all that much. She was in the front seat of the squad car, sitting beside a man he imagined was her father.

The next one was her and, he assumed, her mother. It was clear whom she took after, aside from the hair. Her mother's was lighter. Rooker wondered where she was, if she were still alive. He wouldn't ask.

And then the next one made him smile. He couldn't tell how old the photo was, but there she was, younger, alongside a slightly slimmer Martin Keene, desks positioned across from one another.

"That's when I made detective," she said. "Martin became family. They'd invite me over for dinner every week."

It was strange to him. Rooker had felt as if he'd been invading her privacy when he was in her office. Now that he was in her home, aside from a few framed photographs, he felt nothing. There was nothing really telling about the apartment. Even the art on the walls seemed simplistic, possibly even came with the apartment.

"You know, I thought we were getting breakfast."

"You wanted breakfast. I have eggs, bacon, potatoes in the fridge. Bread if you want to do french toast. I'll make the coffee. You make the food." She laughed at him.

"I would have much preferred to go somewhere and pay."

"Of course you would."

Rooker slaved over the stove, peeling potatoes and dicing them. Tess found two frying pans for him, and before long he had the potatoes and eggs scrambling in one pan, bacon sizzling and popping in the other, grease burning his hand. Tess pressed a button on the coffee maker and smiled as he worked.

"We need to follow up with the prison, see if Meachum had any visitors. Maybe another inmate has been talking his ear off or a guard," he said.

"You think this goes that far?"

"We can't rule anything out. Whoever this guy is, he has more information than anyone should. It doesn't make sense yet. How can he know all about my father, know about the phone calls from my son's killer, know about Mrs. Persson dating Gunner? How does he have the photos in his possession?"

"Well, if anything, that should rule out a lot of people. Our suspect list should be small."

"So why isn't it?"

That was the question. Why didn't they have a list of suspects, or at least a list of professions who might have access to this information? It didn't add up yet.

"We'll get to work on it this afternoon, come up with a list. See where to go from there. But right now, I'm starving, so could you pick up the pace?"

When everything was finished, Rooker turned off the stove tops and fished for plates in the cupboards. After a few tries, he found them, with no help from Tess. He dumped most of the food on her plate and took what was left on his, carried them to the table, and sat across from her.

It was the first time in more than a year that he'd made breakfast for someone. Some mornings he would make eggs or chocolate-chip pancakes for his family, but that seemed like a decade ago now. He missed his son like hell. He'd do anything in this world to get him back. He tried to tell himself that he didn't miss Laura. But self-delusion was never very effective.

Rooker finished his plate before Tess had eaten even half of hers. He sipped his coffee and watched her enjoy his cooking.

"I have to say, this isn't bad. I'm surprised you can cook."

"We don't all eat avocado toast in California."

"Really?" She smiled.

A few minutes later, Tess gave up. "I can't finish this. Here." She pushed the plate across the table to Rooker, who had already put his in the sink. He took her fork and inhaled what was left.

"If you were so hungry, why didn't you take more?"

"Chivalry," he said through a mouthful of food and went on chewing.

Chapter 13

December 4

Rooker sat in the passenger seat while Tess drove back to the department. Harlow called the station on the way to make sure everyone would be there when they arrived.

Rooker was again struck by how empty the building was—almost a soundstage compared to the bustling precincts to which he was accustomed.

Since it would be a while before the briefing started, he wandered around. After a few minutes, he found the gym. He stared through the glass at the square box filled with equipment, a wall lined with dumbbells and a heavy bag with several pairs of sparring gloves on a table. It was a hell of a lot nicer than the setup in his home. And he didn't have to worry about the ceiling caving in on him. He opened the door and walked inside, roaming around the room. He slipped one of the large gloves onto his hand and wrapped the Velcro tight around his wrist. He pushed his palm down against it, making sure his hand fit snugly inside. He pulled the other glove on, hardly able to contain his excitement.

He loosened up by twisting his torso and rotating his hips, rolling his shoulders, and making circles with his arms. He kept his shoulders turning, his hips rotating, his hands up. That was one thing his father had drilled into him. *Hands up!* He needed to avoid being clocked by his father's heavy hands. On bad days, it didn't matter how well Rooker covered up. Gunner would just swing for his head, try to force his fist between his gloves, or deliver a big shot to the body. One time he left his son curled up in a ball, walked back upstairs, and shut the door. Rooker cried into his gloves, took them off, and hurled them at the webbed cinder-block wall.

When he felt warm enough, Rooker threw a jab straight into the bag. *Pop.* The bag groaned. The chain swayed above it, rattled low and venomous. The smell of leather filled his nostrils as his punches landed. He threw a straight and double hook to the same spot. *Pop. POP. POP.* It would be a good liver shot right under the ribs. The liver shot was the most underused punch in boxing. Everyone wanted to land the highlight-reel punch to the head, watch their opponent fall toddler-flat on his back, his head bouncing like a ball off the canvas. But a good shot to the liver, the largest internal organ in the body, was like instant paralysis. He remembered Johnny Whitmore cornering him in middle school. Rooker had hit him with two punches, one to the head, the second meant for the liver. He broke two of Johnny's ribs and was scolded by his father later that night.

"You hit him too high on the ribs." His dad had shut the freezer door and unfolded the butcher-paper-wrapped steak. He tossed the meat to Rooker for his hand. Three knuckles sponged and purpled. "A little lower and you would have had him."

Rooker kept punching, throwing combinations that his father had taught him or that he'd learned from watching fights on television. He was always a fan of the guys who were technically sound, combination punchers, could measure you with the jab and stay out of reach. He grew up watching guys like Sugar Ray Leonard, Pernell Whitaker, Wilfredo Gómez, highlights of Ali and Sonny Liston. Rooker kept his head moving, his shoulders turning. He tried to punch through the bag; that was how he had been taught to hit someone. You don't just connect with them. You try to punch your fist through and get your hand back before the counter.

He looked up to see Tess standing behind the glass. She opened the door and told him everyone was there.

"You look pretty good—have to be the best boxer who's gone at that bag."

"Thanks. My dad made me take it up as a kid." His words came out a little winded. He took a deep breath. "Said his boy wouldn't be the pussy on the playground getting bullied."

"Sounds like father of the year."

"As you may have noticed."

Rooker undid the Velcro straps on the gloves. Tess pulled the first one off and Rooker the second.

He followed her back down the hall, wishing he could stay in the gym until he was too tired to think. When he turned the corner and entered the large room, the whole team was clustered around the desks, some sitting, some standing beside them.

"Okay, everyone, the chief is with us today. Chief Larsson, good to see you," Tess said, and an old, hunched man nodded. Larsson looked to be sixty-five going on eighty, with a face nearly as wrinkled as a sharpei, fine strands of white combed across his scalp and daydreaming spectacled eyes. "We have our senior detective, Martin Keene; detectives Vic Sterling, Elias Cole, Xander Whitlock, and Millie Langston; and our medical examiner, Walter Erickson." She pointed each of them out for Rooker. The next part, she said for the chief. "And as you all know, I've brought in Rooker Lindström. He has experience catching a serial killer. He's published informative articles on them as well, which is why I've brought him in."

"He caught one. That doesn't make him an expert," Xander spat.

"How many have you caught?" Tess spat back, and Xander looked away. She continued. "We have reason to believe the killer is currently injured, possibly holed up somewhere. So we have a few days to a week, maybe two if we're lucky, before he strikes again. So call your families and tell them you might not be home for dinner. Let's get to work."

"Why are we so certain we have a few days before he's back out there?" It was Vic Sterling. With olive skin winter-fair this morning, patches shadowed his jaw and upper lip. He scratched just above brows that hung over his eyes like he was perpetually in thought. Sterling tilted back in the chair, his dark hair stiff and his lean arms folded across a cashmere sweater.

"We believe he was stabbed," said Keene, no longer wearing the jacket from his wife. "At first, we thought the cut on the victim's hand was from cutting the zip ties. But the cut on the victim's hand is more consistent with a stabbing, when the blade impales a victim but the force brings the blade edge back toward the aggressor. He probably fought her off, then shot her in the head. Forensics aren't back, but they're identifying the blood found in the cabin as we speak. Our specialist said the bullet looks like an AccuTip-V 17 Remington; mostly used for small game, it would be the caliber that goes with the rifle. The casings weren't recovered; we believe he took them along with the knife."

"Unless there're two different sets of blood in that cabin, there's no proof he was stabbed." Elias Cole's voice was low like rain on a bedroom window. It was calming, but there was something mechanical there too, like the storm played on a loop. Fidgeting with the comb-over part in his widow's-peak hair, Cole was twirling a vintage pen in his fingers to a tune in his head. With a movie-star jaw but without the movie-star face, he had eyebrows like two gluttonous caterpillars.

"So his MO changed because he was interrupted, potentially even injured. Also, a piece of the victim's clothing was taken; there was no top found at the scene. Yes, he could have brought her without one, but he could have taken it to stop the bleeding."

"So far, I think there're too many 'could haves' and 'ifs' for us to decide he'll be MIA for a couple of days," Sterling said.

Rooker took a long, hard look at Chief Larsson, who wore a dark turtleneck beneath a winter fur ruff coat still fully buttoned and zipped. Rooker figured he would somehow make an early escape from the briefing.

Harlow had Keene brief the team on the statement from Jack Hanson, and then Sterling and Cole went over what they found recanvassing and speaking to the victim's families. There wasn't much. No eyewitnesses. No cameras anywhere near the dumping sites.

"I think we need to take another crack at Lilly Anderson's boyfriend, Patrick Meyer," Cole said, his pen still twisting in his fingers. "I think he knows something. He said he remembers seeing a dark sedan multiple times only nights before Lilly was murdered. He said he couldn't get a make or model, that it was dark out. I don't know that I buy it. And more than half of female murders are committed by an intimate partner or family member."

"You got Miles Davis stuck in that big ol' head of yours again?" Sterling nodded at the twirling pen and laughed.

"Shut it." Cole gave a pleasant smile and looked at Rooker. "Not a jazz fan, I take it?"

"No," Rooker shot back. "Gunner was. It's not for me."

"Let's pay Patrick Meyer a visit, then," Tess interrupted. "Dr. Erickson, what can you tell us about the bodies?"

"All of them, with the exception of the first and most recent, are notably similar. He binds them, tortures them, rapes them—we know by the damage to the vaginal wall—and seems to kill them at the same time he's finished with the rape. There is no evidence that he continues postmortem, so we believe he does it while they're alive, up until the moment they die. There's always one fatal stab wound meant to kill the victim, while the rest are to maim and wound. The first victim's death was due to asphyxiation by drowning, immediately following a hard blow, blunt-force trauma to the back of the head. The most recent, as we know, was a gunshot to the head."

Rooker listened to everything, but when the examiner mentioned the kill and rape ending at the same time, he thought he knew what got the killer off.

"Is it the same knife used on every victim?" Tess asked.

"Yes—with the exception of, again, Lilly Anderson. The wounds on the victims, the serration marks where he cuts the body, it all looks consistent with the same knife or at least the same kind of knife. We don't have a make and model yet, but it looks like a hunting knife. You can tell by one side of the blade being curved, the other side straight. The curve is for skinning game; the straight part is for cutting meat."

"I think it's the eyes." They all turned to Rooker. "Dr. Erickson just said the rape and kill likely end at the same time. I think the eyes are what gets him off. He rapes them, and when the knife goes in and he watches the life leave their eyes, I think that's his MO. In Tess's report, she said that she thought the killer slammed the first victim, Lilly Anderson, against the ice, and it broke. She took a nasty blow to the back of her head, so she was still facing the killer. I think he drowned her faceup, and he looked into her eyes when she died. The sick fuck probably came in his pants right then."

"Not a bad theory, but we can't prove it." Vic Sterling seemed honest to a fault, but it was something Rooker admired. He figured Vic to be the kind of guy who, if a woman asked if her outfit made her look fat, he'd say yes.

Whitlock smacked his hand on his desk. "So now we're listening to this guy? It was only a few weeks ago that he was a photo on the wall. He was our prime suspect."

"Xander. One more thing and you're out."

"He shows up here and bodies start piling up. Do we really think it isn't hi—"

"I said that's enough. If I have to tell you again, you're off this team."

"Tell me why you don't think it's him and—"

"Because I've been watching him since he got here!" A pin dropping would sound like a nuclear blast. Everyone looked stunned. Everyone except Martin Keene, who Rooker figured already knew. "When we found Charlotte Johnson, the third victim, he was at the cottage. I've been keeping tabs on him ever since we found Lilly Anderson."

Whitlock's eyes were like ice, cold and frozen on Rooker. But Rooker didn't back down. He never did. That was one of his issues. He stared right back into the two shit-brown pools for eyes in a shithead filled with shit for brains.

Rooker didn't want to look at Harlow. Instead, he glanced over to the chief, whose wrinkles were in a frown. Rooker didn't know if it was the circus act playing out in front of him, the lack of results, or if the old man was just useless.

Keene's voice brought everyone back to the investigation. "Five of the six victims have turned up in Itasca County. Do we think he's from here?"

Cole's head was down. He massaged his forehead. "I don't think that necessarily means anything. Rooker's father traveled back and forth from California. Thanks to Rooker, now we know the killer has Gunner's photographs. That could be the main reason they've ended up here."

"Gunner Lindström kills fourteen women, leaves the heads on ice in his cottage like the catch of the day. Like freshly caught fish." Sterling tapped his finger on his desk. Then: "What does that have to do with this guy? How does he know so much?"

Finally, Rooker thought. Finally someone asked the right question. It was the question he needed the answer to.

Keene cut in. "According to Tess, our killer has access to information that only Rooker, maybe a handful of LA law enforcement, a select few people in his son's case, and his son's killer have. And he knows more about Gunner Lindström than we do. How could the killer have known that Greta Persson dated Gunner at one point? We have to consider some different scenarios. Maybe Gunner confided in someone before he died, or maybe Rooker's son's killer did."

Xander Whitlock halted his time-out. "You're talking about suspects in California and us crossing them off. And don't forget, Greta Persson spoke to police all those years ago. They could have reported that she and Gunner dated, so there's even more suspects for your list right there."

"I think you may be right about Greta Persson, but not about California. I don't think this is someone from the *Golden State*," Sterling said, "but we do have to look into it."

"Why don't you think so?" Now Rooker was curious.

"The thing that made us consider California was the phone call. 11:37. Tess informed us it's the time your boy died and the time your son's killer called you every night. But I don't think that's where we need to be looking," Sterling said.

"What are you saying?" Rooker asked.

"I feel like we're putting too much stake in Gunner's case. Anyone who worked that case would be, at the very least, about fifty years old now. You think someone in their fifties is running around out there in the cold, dragging bodies through the snow? Alone? I'm not saying it's impossible; I just don't buy it. I think someone here knows a helluva lot about Gunner Lindström—maybe some crazed fanatic was able to find out about him and Mrs. Persson. I think somehow, they have the photos in their possession."

"But then explain the phone call," Whitlock chirped.

"I can't. Yet. But I think you need to speak to your son's killer," Sterling said to Rooker. "Where is he?"

"In solitary, a supermax in Crescent City. Pelican Bay State Prison," Rooker said.

Sterling scratched the prickly shadow at his jaw. "I think we should give them a call. I think they need to toss his cell."

Chapter 14

December 4

Rooker's stomach was at a bathroom-race gurgle. He paced. He felt sick. His last sleep was more than twenty-four hours ago. He was faced with two options: fly back to California and look his son's killer in the eye or speak to him on the phone. He chose the second. When he thought of California, it felt like warm bile was crawling out of his intestines, climbing his stomach, seeping into his mouth. His memory of the place was rotten, maggot-ridden. He had vowed to never go back.

Now he saw only the negative. He looked for the bad in everyone, saw only the evil in the world. He walked by people, wondering what secrets they hid behind closed doors. He saw them for what they were capable of, for what plenty of them were: pathological liars living double lives. He'd read some of the articles in the *Valley Chronicle*. The beloved community priest offering blow jobs to truckers at a highway rest stop. The mother who carried the trash out one night, but really abandoned her one-year-old daughter in the neighbor's bin. The incredible father whose personal computer was filled with child pornography. Monsters dressed in the skin of men and women. Darkness was there, alive and breathing inside them all.

But the phone call had to be made. Tess had spoken to the warden, told him that she suspected an inmate to have contraband in his cell. Told him she believed the man had phoned someone a few nights before. Rooker added a favor. He wanted it done his way. Wanted the cell tossed, and if the phone were recovered, he asked to speak to the inmate. The warden, knowing who the man was and what he'd done to Rooker's son, obliged. But he also told him how unlikely it was that Meachum had gained access to a phone.

They would raid his cell, and Rooker hoped for a call back within minutes. He didn't want to talk to him; he didn't know if Meachum would even comply. But he desperately needed the person who had called him to be Meachum. If it wasn't him, Rooker was in more trouble than he'd thought.

Two thousand and twenty-four miles away, Tate Meachum was dressed in his prison whites, humming the blues and whispering to the solid concrete wall. His hair was once unruly, tunnel black. Now his thick waves were buzzed short, to stop him from ripping them out of his own head. His California tan had faded long ago. His skin looked snake-slimy, white as melted candle wax. He raked the dark halo over his crown, the white scar the size of a toothpick down his widow's peak. Months back, he'd throttled his head, with all his might, into the perforated steel door. The doctors had stapled the gash shut. The guards had to babysit him to make sure he didn't dig them out of his skull. He'd tried to assault one of them, filed his fingernail down to jab into the man's wrist through the food port of his door. He left only a scratch.

A raspy shriek bellowed from one of the cells in his pod, echoed like a caged lion's roar. His lips broke out in a smirk.

"Hear that?" He slapped his leg. "It got another one."

Tate Meachum spent twenty-two and a half hours a day in the C-7 block of SHU, Pelican Bay State Prison's security housing unit. It was the term the federal prison system used for solitary confinement. SHU was a prison within a prison: six pods, eight cells per pod, designated for the worst of the worst: killers, gang leaders, threats to national security. This was where he'd be for six life sentences—one for each victim— without the chance for parole.

He was allowed ninety minutes a day in the yard. Prisoners called it the dog run. It was a concrete box the length of three cells, with a higher ceiling. Two cameras watched Meachum while the walls laughed at him. They were bare but stained dark, as if the concrete were bleeding inside. Sometimes he laughed back.

He was locked away in his eight-by-ten cell, a windowless box with a pencil-thin mattress, a built-in steel combination sink/toilet, and walls that seemed to have shrunk little by little each day. He slid his plastic compartment tray away from him. Today's dinner was Nutraloaf—imitation meatloaf with tomato paste—bean slop, and a piece of whole wheat bread. He had chowed it down.

Meachum sat crisscross, mumbling, his hands clutching onto his ankles. He'd rock back and forth. Sometimes slowly. Sometimes fast. He switched his tune and was murmuring either Wilson Pickett's "In the Midnight Hour" or Otis Redding's "I've Been Loving You Too Long." Then he'd stop in a split second, snap-of-the-finger fast. Like a scared child walking through the woods at night. Frozen. And then he'd whisper.

It had been more than a year ago. *Rooker Lindström.* He could see it plain as day, like a projector was playing it on the wall in front of him. Nine miles outside LA, South Pasadena. The two-story California Craftsman he'd put so much time into. The FBI and SWAT broke the door in clean off its hinges. They stormed the house like a wave swallowed a ship. They shouted. Their boots thumped. The smoke alarm cried out from the M84 stun grenade they tossed inside. There was a flash of white. It rang out like a shotgun blast—more than enough decibels to rupture an eardrum. Tate Meachum's whimpering fiancée—her eyes shut tight—was thrown to the ground in a PLNU T-shirt and rose-pink thong. They later discovered the rock she was wearing, a 1.2-carat diamond ring, had been taken off one of the victims. As was her round diamond necklace.

He tried to bolt, escape through the cellar hatch. But they were on him. They dragged him downstairs, where he had just finished framing part of the basement. Drywall was going in. When they tore it all down, that's where they found it. Meachum's six victims, each of their initials, carved into the wall like handprints in wet cement.

He thought about it now, tracing their initials with what was left of his fingertips on the solid concrete.

Warden Hastings followed behind Williams, O'Malley, and Holden. They were three of the larger, more muscular guards. He felt safer following their lead. Williams was tall, young, and Black. He had been a high school football player, defensive end. An injury had turned him from Division 1 college prospect to coach, then prison guard. O'Malley was an Irish tank. His hair was a messy mix of red and brown; a thick, more orange beard hid a fair amount of his pale white face and acne scars. He was army. Holden was the stockiest of the three, but he was someone you didn't want to hit you or get ahold of you.

The three of them lined up at the cell door, the warden behind them. O'Malley tapped his baton against the steel, its loud clank echoing throughout the wing. He opened the slot door for Meachum to get cuffed. The slot, the bean chute, the cuff port. They all had different names for it. But Hastings looked between the two large shoulders and saw no movement toward the door.

"Inmate, let's go!"

Hastings eyed Tate Meachum sitting cross-legged on the floor, rocking back and forth, facing the far wall. He wasn't sure if the prisoner was talking to the wall or himself. Maybe he thought someone was there. Isolation had a way of doing that to a person.

It was like Meachum didn't even hear them. He just kept rocking, murmuring.

"Prisoner, get up!" This time it was Williams. "Last chance!"

Meachum looked toward them, observed them beneath hooded eyes. He pressed his hands against the ground and turned the rest of the way until he was facing them, smiling. He got to one knee, pressed off the ground, and stood still, staring at them.

"You know the drill! Turn around, back up with your hands out."

Meachum did as they said. He backed toward them slowly, said one more thing to the wall. It seemed he would continue his conversation when they left.

Warden Hastings caught sight of his hands extended through the slot, observed his fingertips covered in dry blood, his fingernails nearly gone.

"What's wrong with his hands?"

"He likes to dig at the walls; he writes something. We try to make him stop; he doesn't," Holden said, shrugging his massive shoulders and shaking his cinder-block head.

Hastings watched them slip the cuffs over Tate Meachum's wrists and tighten them. Definitely too tight, though he didn't question it. But the inmate said nothing.

"Forward!"

Meachum moved to take a step, and they pulled the door open. Holden pressed the prisoner up against the wall and searched him, patting him down thoroughly. There was no privacy in a place like this.

"Cough," he commanded. Then, seconds later: "Nothing on him."

Hastings held Meachum up against the wall, letting him watch as the guards searched his cell. There wasn't much to search. O'Malley smiled at Meachum as he started tossing the bed. It was a double bunk built into the wall. Meachum didn't have a cellmate, so the top bunk was empty.

O'Malley threw the small, flat pillow to the ground, tossed the flimsy excuse for a mattress as well. There was nothing there. Nothing on the top bunk. Nothing in the small storage hole beneath the bottom bunk. Williams was checking the sink and toilet; nothing there either. There was nothing in there aside from a photo taped to the wall. It was of Rooker, beside a newspaper clipping of his son's face from the story when he was killed.

"Why does he have that in here?" Warden Hastings scolded.

"Don't know."

"Get it out of here."

Williams tore the items off the wall and handed them to Holden, then continued looking around the room. It appeared there was nothing here. Hastings stepped inside, watching Meachum carefully as he passed. He paused, looking at the wall where most of the skin and nails of Meachum's fingers had gone. There was writing there. Hastings read it to himself. DOES THIS LOOK LIKE MY MOTHER? KILLER. There were tally marks. Seven of them. And then he saw the name large and capitalized, carved into the moon gray. ROOKER.

Williams kept reading until he'd scoured every word on the walls. It must have hurt tremendously to etch into the concrete, deep enough to where the words were legible. Tucked away beside the bed were two more names that were of interest to Hastings. *Jada. Terrence.* They were Hastings's wife and son. He looked Meachum in the eyes, realized what kind of sick human being he shared the air with. He felt tainted, like he would be infected with the same sick that spilled out of Meachum's nose and mouth. He saw a bit of blood at the corner of the bottom bunk, dark marks like jagged jigsaw pieces where paint chipped. There was a mark there, something red.

"What is it?" Holden asked.

Hastings motioned O'Malley over. He put his finger to the bloody mark, felt the structure move a little. He looked at Hastings, then wiggled the concrete back and forth until it loosened. He pulled the piece away from the wall and dug out a small blue-and-black flip phone.

"NO, NO, NO, NO, NO, NO!" Meachum screamed. Saliva sprayed from his curled lips: scabbed and cracked and rabid as his mind. His mouth found Holden's arm; his teeth sank deep into his skin and weren't letting go.

"Fuck!" Holden slammed his arm along with Meachum's head into the wall, and all two hundred and fifty pounds of him collided. Meachum's teeth still bore into him. Blood pooled around Meachum's mouth, dripping rivulets of red down Holden's forearm. He drove Meachum's head back again, this time like an I-10 head-on collision, and the blow separated the two, though a bloody yellow tooth was still lodged in Holden's arm. Meachum fell to the ground, smiling, his overbite grin wide and red, a gap where his tooth was now gone. Holden got the last word in; his meaty leg wound up, his size-twelve-and-a-half steel-toe boot launched into Meachum's stomach. The prisoner howled, coyote-like. A twisted laugh erupted from his mouth before Hastings— two knots bulging in the crooks of his jaw—called a stop to it.

Chapter 15

December 4

An hour crawled past. Rooker's cell still hadn't rung. The numbers moved so slowly, he thought it might be busted. The phone was in his hand, his eyes glancing down at it over and over. What was taking so long? It couldn't be good. Finally, it rang, and he pressed the green button before the second chirp.

"Rooker," he answered.

"We found it. We had a bit of a situation."

"What happened?"

"When we found it, he bit a guard. Got him pretty good."

"Jesus."

"That's nothing. The guy barely has any skin or nails left on his fingers; he digs them into his cell wall, writing. He used them like a damn pen—can't imagine the pain. Your name was there. As were my wife's and son's."

Rooker sat there, imagining his name up on the wall. He pictured it scrawled in blackened blood, menacingly crooked capital letters oozing with nail chunks embedded in the concrete. Meachum was a monster, but the thought of being on the monster's wall was newly sickening, nauseating.

"Good news, your home phone number was found on the phone's recent calls." He paused. "Bad news"—cue a longer pause—"there was someone else, someone other than you he was talking to. He received several calls from a private number. We don't know who gave him the phone, but they must have found your number for him. He wants to talk to you."

"Let's get it over with."

"Oh, one more thing," Hastings said. "He killed six people, right?"

Rooker didn't want to answer. He shut his eyes. Pictured the victims, the ball-peen hammer to the fingernail, the time of death carved into it. "Yeah, six."

"There were seven tally marks drawn in his cell. Not sure if it means anything. I'll go get him."

The detectives stood around him, the phone both on speaker and being recorded. Rooker waited out the silence. For a while, he heard nothing, like the other end was muted, maybe a dead zone in the prison. And then he thought the line went dead. There was an anxious pit in his stomach.

And then he heard the footsteps, the murmurs, the scrape of the chair being pulled out, the metal cuffs clink as they dragged across the top of the table.

"It's on speaker. Go ahead."

Neither end said anything. There was only an eerie quiet. Rooker pulled his head away from the phone to make sure the call hadn't dropped. He knew Meachum wouldn't talk to him on speaker, not with a crowd watching. He believed that he and Rooker were forever linked, that they shared a bond.

"Rooker, he won't talk on speaker." After a minute, the warden was addressing Meachum. "No games, inmate."

There was the sound of the phone moving, like it was scratching up against his cheek. Rooker imagined open sores, lesions where insects slithered and squirmed out from his pores.

"I miss our calls, Rooker."

He shuddered. Five words were all it took to turn the oxygen in the room stale. *A monster dressed in a man's skin.* "So it was you the other night."

"Well, who else would it be?"

Breathe. "There were others who knew about the phone calls. I needed to make sure."

"So how is Minnesota? *The Land of Ten Thousand Lakes.* Is it cold?"

Rooker didn't answer. He tried to breathe slowly, softly, silently.

"What's it like staying where your father killed them?"

"I think our conversation is over. Enjoy solitary without your phone."

"Don't you hang up!"

The words were bone-chilling. They didn't scare him, but they left a low hum ringing in his ears. Rooker could still hear them in the silence that followed.

"Tell me about the North Star State."

For a long moment, he didn't reply. He thought he could hear the slightest hint of a smile in Meachum's tone, the grating voice trapping him like barbed wire. It left Rooker broken. *Damaged.* He did his best to shake the feeling from his mind. "It's freezing."

"Tell me, can you hear their voices? The women he killed. Do you hear the wails, their screams?"

Rooker fought the shiver that boiled up his spine. He wanted to run away. Again. He knew what Meachum was dying to say to him.

"Do you hear voices, Meachum?"

"I hear your son. Britton talks to me."

Bingo. Now I need a drink. The ground beneath him unsteadied. He leaned against the wall for support and let his head droop toward the floor. "I thought you wanted to talk, not play games."

"I hear your wife's snoring, like a pig. *Oink, oink!* Did you know I went to the master bedroom first? I almost chose her. Do you wish that I did?"

Rooker closed his eyes again, told himself to relax. Now that he knew it was Meachum who had called, he didn't need to hear much else.

"Warden Hastings said there's a seventh tally mark you drew. You killed six people. Why a seventh marking, Tate?"

"That's for me to know. If I told you now, you'd never want to chat again."

Even though Meachum wanted to talk, Rooker knew he wouldn't get anything about a seventh victim out of him. At least not by asking. He'd have to give him something.

"Did you make friends with someone? Who told you I was in Minnesota?"

"A little birdie. They call me *the Madman* in here."

"We both know that's bullshit. Everyone's all but forgotten you. I hear you whisper at the wall all day. Maybe you really have gone mad, making up invisible friends like a child. Look, I've got to get going. Enjoy your cell."

"Right, you have a new killer to catch."

Rooker flinched. He was about to hang up. His finger hovered over the red button. But Tate Meachum's words caught him off guard. Everything went silent. The room was buzzing in his ears like a wasp swarm. He thought he could see Meachum's face, his smirk as he spoke the words Rooker was hanging on to.

He leaned forward. "Is that so?"

"He has a thing for blondes, right? Not hard to find there, I bet."

Rooker's body electrified. Meachum knew. Not only was someone feeding him information about the murders, he knew the killer.

"Who is he?"

"You know I can't tell you, Rooker." A grin in Meachum's voice.

"What did you tell him?"

"We talk a lot about you. About how we're alike, how we're different. He talks about how you'll never catch him."

"How do I know you aren't bullshitting me? How do I know he's the one who's been calling you?"

"Who else could know about you and your little crush on the neighbor? He saw you with her; he was watching when I called you that night. He told me how angry it made you. You smashed the phone."

This wasn't a nightmare he'd wake up from. It was real.

"I'm going to find him. He's going to be in a cell just like yours, living out as many life sentences as I damn well please. We're done."

Rooker went to hang up the phone, but then he heard screaming over the other end.

"WE'RE DONE WHEN I SAY WE'RE DONE!"

Rooker ended the call. He watched the screen go black. Meachum's voice had grabbed hold of him, shackled around the forearms where the little hairs rose. If there was a time for a drink, it was now. But first he needed to find Evelyn.

Chapter 16

"Evelyn Holmberg." Rooker swallowed back a feeling of vomit and guilt, a lump in his throat. "Widow, she's my neighbor. She lived next door to my father all those nights he was killing women. I think the killer is after her now."

"You believe Meachum? What he said?"

Rooker let out a deep sigh. "The usual crazy that spews out of his mouth? No. But the rest: that he was the one who called, that he talks to our guy on the phone. I believe him."

"What about visitation?"

Rooker shook his head. "He doesn't get visitors in there."

"We'll get the nearest sirens over there. Let's hope she isn't dead already."

It was exactly what Rooker was thinking.

The Ford Taurus slid to a stop twenty minutes later in the graveled slush. The Holmberg residence was surrounded. At least ten officers stood around outside with their arms crossed or their hands on their duty belts. The door was wide open, and cold panic seeped into every pore of Rooker's goose-pimpled skin. He and Tess got out of the car and walked toward the house side by side.

"Anything?" Tess asked a uniformed officer.

"She isn't here. No sign of forced entry. We checked the cellar door; there's a steel hatch to the basement around back, but it's locked from the inside. We checked the windows too—nothing suspicious."

It didn't mean anything. If she wasn't here, there was a good chance she was dead elsewhere. If so, it would be another body on his tally, another body he'd blame himself for and drink to forget. She didn't have a connection to Gunner the way Sophia Persson did. Evelyn would never have been in the killer's sights if Rooker hadn't called her over that night.

"You guys looked inside?"

"Yeah, front door was locked; we had to bust it. We checked the neighbor's house to see if they'd seen anything, but nothing's there. Looks like shit. Doubt anyone's living there."

"It's mine," Rooker said.

The officer turned to him. "Sorry."

"No worries. You're right: it does look like shit."

A few of the beat cops standing around laughed, but Tess's face was stone. Rooker could see the wheels turning in her detective brain. He walked closer to her. Stared off into the same opening in the woods where her eyes fell.

"What're you thinking?" he said.

"How well do you know these woods?" she asked.

"Not too well. Why?"

She said nothing. And neither did he. Thoughts of Evelyn left him depleted, his gas tank merely running on fumes. He assumed she was thinking the same thing he was, that Evelyn was dead, naked, and left out somewhere for them to find.

Chapter 17

December 4

The floorboards whined as he paced upstairs. The bed was a mess. Water dripped down from the ceiling to the nasty white bucket below. It was filled to where the handle was bolted into the plastic. It would overflow by nightfall.

He thought the place looked even worse than the last time he was here. The wood beams and ceiling were rotting, warping, maybe even caving in on top of him. But when the image caught his eye, his feelings of being cramped and claustrophobic washed away like a tide.

He looked out through the boarded windows. The trim along the windowsill chipped nearly the entire way across; specks and blotches of white were all that remained. The gutter was partially dangling off the roof, frozen and filled with dead leaves and icicles hanging from the side.

But none of that was what transfixed him.

He looked outside, at the lake beautifully frozen over. Snow bordering the ice, swirling a perfect ballroom waltz atop it. The trees in the distance were marvelous, white powder across their shivering branches. He watched them rock gently back and forth. It reminded him of the first time he'd seen it when he was a boy.

The curved bill of his black baseball cap was pulled low, his sunken eyes shadowed beneath. He stood back from the boarded windows, and looked out between the gaps at the police still hanging around Evelyn Holmberg's home. He'd been at Rooker's place for more than an hour, waiting for Evelyn to return. He watched the police break the door down, frantic, maybe expecting to find her dead. That would have been the case had she been home. On the walkway, standing on the shovel-scraped path beneath the light post, he saw him. Rooker was standing by the staircase alongside Detective Tess Harlow and a group of police.

The police would get nothing else out of him. Meachum had served his purpose: it had really fucked with Rooker.

Rooker would know now that he'd been outside the night that he and Evelyn had had their little romance, watching them, watching Rooker get the call from his son's killer. He'd taken it upon himself to make this Rooker's own frozen hell, one he'd never escape. But with the police here, he'd have to wait until darkness before he could fade away into the night.

They were squawking in their little circle. There was truly little to separate the police from the detectives. Detectives asked a few more questions, usually dim-witted ones.

The wind whistled through the walls, its chill plunging past the insulation in his clothing, nosediving into the wound still healing in his chest. It felt like ten thousand ruler slaps on his knuckles. At the sight of Rooker, his brain adjusted like a camera's portrait mode, the crowd around him just unfocused blurs.

And right then, Rooker turned to the house. He stepped back farther from the window, still watching. Rooker was walking toward the cottage, and he knew he had to do something fast. Then he remembered what was down there, below the floorboards, the place where he could hide: Gunner Lindström's killing room.

He eased down the staircase. The steps creaked one by one, like whispers beneath his weight. They were frail like the rest of the place.

Some of them were higher than others, some warped in the center, some with nails not entirely hammered in. When he made it downstairs, he turned the corner and stared at the spot on the floor. The ground was discolored where the freezer used to be. He imagined what Gunner had felt when he stored the heads on ice. He imagined him placing them with a jeweler's touch, positioning them perfectly in his display. It was a long time since he'd seen the freezer. There were the photographs the police had, the heads of women frozen Botox-stiff like mannequins. But that wasn't the first time he'd seen it open.

Though he had been only thirteen then, it fascinated him. He'd snuck peeks at the case files, pored over the photos they confiscated, landscapes Gunner took. His father had spoken about Gunner as a loser, as a man with no real talent, no true artistic ability. If he was anything special, someone would've bought his photos, turned them into a collection. His father called them shit, said his brain was filled with the same manure, and that was why he killed defenseless women. He loved to talk his father's ear off about it, but his mother wouldn't allow it. Several times he'd been scolded by her at the dinner table. *That's no talk for a boy.* His father would tell her, *He'll be a man soon enough. You can't only teach him all the good in the world; he ought to know the evil too.* And that's what he was transfixed by, captivated by, mesmerized by: the evil.

At the bottom of the stairs, he tapped his shoe around, pulled the knife from his jacket pocket. He didn't want to kill Rooker, not yet. He had to suffer first. Rooker was like a spiderweb crack in glass, and he wanted to break the rest of it. And just then, there, he felt it. The hollow sound in the floor beneath his heel. He bent down, pressed his knife between the boards, and pried one upward. He pulled it away, put his legs inside, eased himself down, and hid there in the putrid darkness. He inhaled the airless odor, something like musty earth, dust, mold.

His hands were balled tight. Sweat filled the cracks in his clenched fists, his knuckles probably ghost white beneath his gloves. They were lightweight and black, designed for winter training, mostly runners. He figured they'd keep his hands warm enough and help him blend into the dark, and they wouldn't feel like pillows or couch cushions when he needed to strike someone in the face. And here he was, hiding out in a black abyss where he couldn't see a damn thing. But he'd be able to find the floorboard above him, and that's all that mattered.

Boots squelched in the wet slush just outside. Rooker had gotten to the wood stairs and the landing. The door slammed open. The stomping of the heavy boots sounded angry, though it was probably just the way the flooring was. It was old wood, thin like the walls; nothing in the house seemed to be built right. He heard Rooker strolling around upstairs, his feet getting closer. Then they stopped.

He knew why. Rooker had found his present.

Chapter 18

December 4

Rooker yanked the front door open. "Harlow!" he yelled. She looked at him and knew it was nothing good. Seconds later, she was at the door, her breath thin clouds in the air. They stood in front of the table, looking down at the black purse positioned perfectly in the middle like a floral centerpiece. He knew what it was. They had never found Sofia Persson's purse, and there it was: a black purse with a silver chain strap, just as her mother had described.

Harlow lifted her radio and told Keene to have the cops canvass the area. The woods too. She took her sidearm out of its holster. "Stay here," she told him. Her movements were stealthy. She cleared the downstairs level, then climbed the stairs fast. Silent. In seconds, she was back beside him, putting her pistol away.

"You want to do the honors?" she asked him with faint sarcasm.

"I'm good, thanks."

She pulled on a pair of gloves from her back pocket, opened the flap, and scowled.

"What is it?"

"Her tooth."

"So he leaves me the missing tooth and the purse—why?"

"Maybe to show you he can get to you, get in your home."

"The other cop." Rooker paused. "He said he came over here. He didn't see anyone? Nothing?"

"That's what he said."

Tess had an officer bring over a few evidence bags. She covered the table with them, then poured the contents of the bag out onto the plastic. Two white plastic pieces toppled out together; one stood upright, the other slumped over. It was a chess piece that had been snapped in half: the rook, just like the one needled into Rooker's skin. There was a piece of paper there as well, a note that Tess unfolded. It was in standard Times New Roman font, centered on the paper, which looked a third of a normal sheet.

You think you've suffered all you can, but I promise you will suffer more.

"I don't get it," Tess said. "First he looks like a copycat killer following after Gunner. Now he seems to have a vendetta against you. But he never could have planned for you to be back here."

"Killers evolve. Look at Meachum. At first, he abducted them, took them somewhere remote. Then he'd stalk them and murder them in their homes. Each time he called a tip line, he sounded less agitated when he told them where to find the body. His first kill was sloppy. There was blood everywhere. But he learned. Each one the police found was more precise. The ball-peen hammer to the fingernail. The time of death carved into it with a knife. And his usual selection of women, well, changed."

"Do you think you know him?"

"I . . . I'm not sure. I think it's someone I could've met before. But I don't know." There was a silence that trapped the thought in Rooker's mind. It lingered there, like the smell of a dead rodent. "Is there anything else in it?"

Tess searched the rest of the compartments, mostly coming up empty. Then she pulled out a fraying Polaroid split apart at the corners. It was a photo of a young boy in boxing gloves standing beside the man she knew as Gunner Lindström. A worn, stern look on his face. The two of them stood feet apart side by side. The boy's face had a hole burned through it, like someone had lit a cigarette or a match to it, then extinguished the flame. She could make out the trunks, the boy's skinny white legs, the outline of headgear a halo around the scorch mark, the ring ropes behind them. It looked like a competition. The boy was holding a trophy. "Is that you?" she asked Rooker.

He stared at the photo a few seconds longer. It was probably one of the few photos of the two of them together. "That's me."

Tess eyed the vacant stare of Gunner Lindström, his arms, one across his stomach holding the other that was hanging down at his side. He didn't hold his boy's arm, didn't have a hand on his back or shoulder, not even on the bronzed statue the boy was holding.

Static and a voice played over the two-way police radio clipped at Tess's hip.

"Harlow?"

Rooker stepped toward something lying on the floor just where the stain differed, something small he could see from a distance. When he got closer, he noticed it was also a photograph. He bent down, dug at the corner of it, and lifted it. It was the freezer. He saw the heads sitting there staring back at him. He felt as though he'd seen them before. Maybe he'd dreamed of them; maybe they really did haunt him and the house.

Tess lifted the receiver from her pants and clicked a button.

"What is it?"

Her head cocked in Rooker's direction.

"Ma'am, Evelyn Holmberg just walked in."

Rooker turned the photo for her to see.

"He really left you a gift basket."

◆ ◆ ◆

"Where have you been?" The words left Rooker's mouth cold and chastising. She'd only ever helped him, taken care of him. And here he was ready to scream at her for yet another thing he was responsible for.

"I was in town, running some errands and food shopping."

"From now on, no more," Rooker told her. "You'll have officers here twenty-four seven."

"I don't want officers in my ho—"

"I don't care what you want. If you don't want them here, you need to go stay with a relative. This guy was in my house, waiting for you to come back so he could kill you. I thought you were already dead somewhere."

"What is this about? Your father was never after me."

"Well, this guy is."

"How can you be so sure?"

Rooker looked at her, trying to glare some sort of telepathy to her brain so she'd understand. *Oh, I don't know. Because he watched us fuck.* His teeth were gritted, his jaw clenched. He closed his eyes, told himself to relax, and opened them. "My son's killer told me. That's as much as I can tell you."

All of a sudden, he sounded disengaged, political, like a cop—like one of them. It was the roundabout sort of answer that police would sometimes give him when he needed material for a story. He just needed her not to die because of him; was that too much to ask? Rooker walked out of Evelyn's home and through the crowd of police. Tess was right behind him.

"He's back sooner than we thought."

Sooner than you *thought*, he wanted to say.

"Let's get everyone back to the station. See what we can come up with."

But Rooker had a thought. "Can you call the office now?"

"What for?"

"Call Langston. I want to know who's still there."

Tess looked at Rooker. He could tell she knew what he was thinking. And he could tell she didn't like it.

"For one"—she held up a finger—"I don't take orders from you. I let you into this investigation. Got it?" She held her ground, gave him a long stare. "And second"—another finger raised—"no way. No."

"Come on, Tess," he said.

"You want me to investigate my own team."

"I think it's someone in the cesspool of law enforcement, no offense. Whether it's a cop, medical examiner, maybe a relative of a cop or detective, or a judge, I don't know. But there's no other way for someone to have all that information on Gunner. His photographs, his relationship with Greta Persson, this stuff isn't public record—believe me, I'd know. This guy has the files, or copies of them somehow."

She hesitated. "I can't make waves like this if we don't have anything concrete."

Rooker pleaded, his palms to her like he was warming them by a fire. "I'm not asking for waves." His tone softened. "I'm asking you to call Langston."

"And what if Xander isn't in the office?" He knew where she was going with it before the words flew out of her mouth. "You immediately think he's the killer?"

"That's not what I'm saying."

"And we don't know how long ago the killer was in your home. We don't know how long ago he left. This doesn't prove anything."

"Please call."

Tess pulled out her phone, dialed Langston's extension, and left it on speakerphone. She would be in the office as always, probably glued to her desk or in the research room where the files were kept. Sure enough, Millie answered after a few rings.

"It's Tess. Who's still in the office?"

"Am I getting anyone in trouble?"

"No, I just need to know. I have to get everyone back there soon."

"Right now, it's only me. Sterling left not too long ago. Martin said he was getting lunch with his wife, said he might head over to Evelyn Holmberg's. I haven't heard anything from Elias or Xander."

"Okay, thanks. Can you call those guys, tell them to get there as soon as they can?"

"You got it."

Tess thumbed the red button on the phone and stared at Rooker with a smirk.

"Okay, so that tells us nothing," he said. "But we know the killer is somehow connected to Gunner Lindström." He added his last name like they weren't related. "The only way for that to be possible is for someone to have known Gunner better than anyone—which is highly unlikely—or someone has access to files. Even then, I don't think everything was recorded digitally. Do we have a way of checking who has gone through any files relating to Gunner?"

"The second I do that, the team will find out I'm looking inside the department. That we're looking at a detective. And if it is a detective, we risk them covering tracks, maybe running. I'll get everyone back to the station, and we'll go from there."

When the team was gathered, Rooker couldn't keep his eyes off Xander. Every now and then, his glance would shift to Vic Sterling, a man he imagined kept his cards close to his chest. He could tell Vic was smart, calculated, but there was something mischievous about him. He couldn't place it, but Vic Sterling was on Rooker's radar, his own suspect list. Also on his list, medical examiner Walter Erickson. He seemed like a nice enough guy, not the type to rape and butcher women, but who knows. Keene was supposedly with his wife, but that meant nothing to Rooker. There was Cole too. There were beat cops, other detectives in different areas of Grand Rapids. Rooker didn't like this, not any of it. But someone had too much information. That fact should have narrowed down the suspects more than it did. Someone was connected to the Gunner Lindström case.

While Tess was conducting the chaos symphony, silencing the orchestra, Rooker took a pen and paper from the desk and made a few notes for himself.

Need to know ANYONE connected to Gunner. Old case files, police on case, medical examiner.

He dragged the ballpoint pen in circles, swirling sloppy black lines around ANYONE before he stuffed the folded paper in his coat pocket. Rooker listened absentmindedly to the team briefing. It was white noise, like the droning of windshield wipers beneath hammering rain. He wondered for a moment whether the killing would stop if he just left Deer Lake. He didn't need to search deep down. He knew it wouldn't.

The top priority now was research. He needed Langston's help. He needed her to dig up the old files quietly, wherever they were. He had a bad feeling that some of it—hell, maybe all of it—was gone. Still, he hoped this would be his lucky break, that the files were there, that maybe the killer has duplicates, maybe got his information from a person instead of the files. If he got lucky, he'd have the files and names of those who had taken them out recently. He'd have it all without setting off any alarms. But he didn't feel lucky.

After about twenty minutes of babble, the meeting ended. He took nothing from it other than observing some of his suspects. Keene looked as harmless as ever, but Rooker couldn't cross him off his list. He probably couldn't see his dick when he peed, but he was a good detective—meticulous, careful. Cole sat like a statue behind his desk, aside from the times he contributed to the conversation, the pen weaving between his fingers. Vic Sterling perched with his hands folded against the table like he was a guest on a talk show. Occasionally, he traded glances with Rooker. And then there was Xander . . .

When everyone started putting on their coats and making their way out of the station, Rooker made his way over to Langston. She was still sitting cross-legged in her swivel chair toe-tapping away like she had no intention of leaving. Her head was prayer-bowed to the paperwork on her desk. Frizzy waves of strawberry-blonde ran down just below her chalky collarbone. She wore a pullover striped knit sweater with dark jeans and black boots.

"Can I borrow you for a bit?"

She looked up to see Rooker, her eyes large and surprised anyone was standing there. She poked her glasses up the bridge of her nose. "Hi, yeah, sorry. I'm a bit swamped." She leaned back, and he couldn't help but admire the small bumps at her chest. "I've been looking for some correlation with where and how the women were abducted. So far, not much to go on. But I'll find something. What do you need?"

He thought for a moment how he should ask. She seemed like someone who did everything by the book. What he was asking her to do wasn't wrong, but asking her not to tell anyone would be.

"I need the files on my father, Gunner Lindström."

"It may take some time to find everything. And I'd need Tess to clear it."

He decided to avoid the latter for now. "You know where it all is?"

"Everything should be in the basement. He was here in Itasca County."

"And if it isn't?"

Confusion boiled on her face. "I don't understand."

Rooker debated how much he should tell her. She didn't need to know everything, but she was smart and would probably figure out what he was up to.

"The information this person has on Gunner—some of it had to have come from the files. It can't all be public knowledge."

She knew what he was saying. She even smiled, like she'd just solved the mystery inside an Agatha Christie classic. "You think it's police."

"I think it's someone who would have access to confidential information. It could be the person who cleans the floors for all I know, but I need to see what they have."

"And you want it done quietly."

"No, I need it done quietly. Please. And I can't have anyone knowing that I'm looking at a cop. It might send him underground or make him even more careful than he has been. I need to find this guy."

"Well, I'd still need Tess's okay."

"Let me worry about her."

"Let you—" She stopped. "No offense, but you were a murder suspect not that long ago. She's my boss."

He took a last stab at her. "*You're right—she is your boss.* Don't you want to be the one who finds the connection between the killer and Gunner's case?" He paused. "Sometimes the devil is in the details. You're the best researcher here. I was a damn good crime journalist. If anyone in this place is going to find something in those files, it's going to be one of us."

She let out a sigh. "Do you even know what you're looking for?"

"I have a few things I want to check out."

She stopped. "No one finds out I did this for you."

"Deal."

"I'm serious. And you owe me."

"Anything you want."

She opened a heavy metal filing cabinet, and Rooker heard the jingle of a set of keys before she shoved the drawer back closed. She led him down the hall to a door, opened it, and let him in first. She locked it behind her, flipped a light switch, and went down the stairs. When they got to the bottom, she flicked another, and the basement blinked awake. Rooker watched dust particles float high in the air, the smell old and chalky. There were shelves stacked with bins and boxes sorted in alphabetical order.

"Give me a few minutes."

He followed her anyway, watched her navigate the aisles like a librarian. When they arrived at the correct aisle, she flicked through files, running her fingertip along them until she got closer and closer. She tipped the file down toward her and plucked it like a needle from the haystack.

LINDSTRÖM, GUNNER was written horizontally on the tab. Rooker read the red stamped CLOSED on the outside of it. The file was thick, held together by a massive rubber band. He read the case number at the bottom.

"The file was never entered digitally in the records?"

"Not as far as I know . . . hold on."

Rooker assumed she hadn't been working there too long. She was definitely the youngest on the team. But as he looked at the basement, he was aware how organized the place was, and he assumed she was the one responsible for it all. When she came back, she had a box in her hands with his father's name on it.

"There's a table here," she said. "I don't want the files to leave this room."

Rooker nodded and thanked her. He took the box and carried everything over to the old foldout table. It came with a rusted foldable chair. But it would do the trick. He rolled the band from the file and opened it. Rooker saw photos of his father as he flipped through, but he didn't pay them any mind. He turned to the box, lifted the lid, and saw that it was all evidence logged from the case. He put the lid back on it and moved it out of his way. He went back to the file and saw the birth certificate for Gunner Kjell Lindström, flipping past it. Rooker skimmed pages of receipts and latent fingerprints, descriptions of the capture, transcripts of the trial, newspaper clippings of both. There were pages on the transport to prison. The papers were yellowed, some with blacked-out areas. In places, it was like a blotch of dark ink had been used to redact larger sections.

Rooker's calloused fingers riffled the corners of the papers, leafing through them like a child assessing a homework assignment.

"Langston."

"Yes?" She hadn't yet ascended the stairs.

"Why don't I see the police who caught my father or the psych results anywhere in here? They would have had a psychiatric doctor evaluate him."

"I don't know."

The next two nights, Rooker came into the office when it was clear of everyone except Millie Langston. Each night he brought her a bag from Janicke Bakery. The storefront was partly glass and partly stone that somehow made him think of pecan pie. He had no idea what he was purchasing, but they looked good, so he got two of each. Langston would take him downstairs, give him the same spiel, and leave him alone. And each night, she would stay as long as she had work to do. But eventually, he'd hear her come down the stairs, and he'd wrap it up. Then watch her put everything back just the way it had been.

He spent hours upon hours riffling through the photos: black-and-white snapshots from every angle of the cottage back in the early nineties, photographs of the victims dating back to 1988. He pulled priority requests to search the premises and a request for the use of cadaver dogs. He turned over the case narrative, which noted that the police were searching for human remains. There were initials scribbled—no help there. He went through the newspaper headlines, the stories written on each of the victims, went through all of it. He searched for hours on end, looking for what he couldn't find. Until the third night.

Rooker riffled through the papers again, counting. "Thirteen," he said out loud to himself. "Thirteen." The next time the number came out, it was to Langston.

"Thirteen!" he hollered up the stairs. "Langston, why are there thirteen?"

Her chair squeaked, and he heard her voice at the top of them. "What?"

"Thirteen. There are thirteen women in this file." She was coming down the stairs. "Where's the fourteenth?"

"I don't . . ."

"He killed fourteen women. Why is one missing?"

She didn't have the answer he needed. Rooker flipped a couple of pages back and found something he never expected to find. There were autopsy records for each of the women killed. He followed them one by one, skimming the notes, his focus on the name he read on each of them. Klas Erickson. The medical examiner on the case was Walter Erickson's father.

"Who was the last person to take this out of evidence?"

She stood over his shoulder, and he got a waft of what he assumed was Lady Speed Stick as she flipped the pages all the way back to the beginning. He wasn't sure why or how, but she usually smelled of honeysuckle, but not tonight. There was a printout of dates and times the police had logged the book. The last entry was just weeks before: Tess Harlow. It wasn't what he'd expected to find, though he knew she had been looking at him as a suspect at first. Still, it didn't add up.

"What if someone else had taken it out and didn't write it in?"

"I'm sorry, but there would be no way of knowing. We don't have any cameras installed down here."

"Have you ever seen Erickson come down here?"

"Not that I can remember. Are you saying you think it's him now?"

Rooker knew next to nothing about Walter Erickson. He couldn't say with any certainty what he thought about the man. But the fact that his father had conducted the autopsies on Gunner's victims couldn't be coincidence. *Could it?* "Klas Erickson, Walter's father, was the ME on every one of the murders in here. We need to know if he was the ME on the fourteenth victim, who she is, and why she isn't in here. And I need the police officers who were on the case and the doctor who evaluated Gunner. That might narrow it down."

Finally, we're getting somewhere. Walter Erickson was already a suspect on his list, and this only moved him to the top.

Chapter 19

Rooker slumped down behind Tess Harlow's desk, looking over the mess that covered nearly every square inch of it. He dialed her number and leaned back against the cushion of her office chair.

"Harlow."

"I need you back here," he said as he snooped through her papers. "I may have something."

"I'm only ten minutes away. I can turn around. What is it?"

"The ME on my father's case—Klas Erickson. Father of Walter Erickson."

"Holy shit."

"Don't get biblical on me yet. Shit is right. It could explain a lot. If it is Walter, it would explain how he knows so much about Gunner."

"You think it's him?"

"I don't know. He was on my list, sure. But not at the top."

"And now he is?"

"And now he is."

"His address should be in the directory at my desk. I'll be there in five."

"How do I find it in this mess?"

"It's in the left drawer. Get out of my office."

"You just said ten minutes."

"I'll put the lights on."

◆ ◆ ◆

Six minutes later, Tess was at a slow jog through the double doors. It was either the cold air or the news of Walter Erickson that breathed new life into her. Her cheeks were flushed; she looked like she had some newfound energy.

"Let's go."

Rooker grabbed the piece of paper that he'd torn from the back of Tess's notebook. He'd scribbled Walter's address and triple-checked to make sure he had it right. The two of them hurried into the brisk air and soon enough were inside her Taurus.

"So, when did I tell you it was okay to go through confidential files?"

"I had to see what was there. I figured the killer might've taken the entire book, that there would be nothing. Maybe we finally got lucky."

"You *ask* me. If I have to worry about you interfering with my investigation, then you're out," she said. "So nothing was missing?"

He wondered why she'd ask. Maybe she was following up on his premonition that something would be missing. He remembered her name, neatly written there on the sheet, that she was the last person to look through it. He thought better than to give her too many details.

"I didn't sit with it long, nothing missing as far as I could tell."

The words were fiction, and he wasn't surprised how easy it was to lie to her. Suddenly, he found himself wishing he hadn't told her about Klas Erickson so soon. The old photograph of the freezer he'd found in his home, the photographs his father had taken—it all could have been taken from the file. She would have noticed, wouldn't she? And there clearly were a few other things missing from it, including one of the victims. He didn't want to trust her. And he told himself that he wouldn't, not until the killer was found. Not until he could put his father behind him, back in the cell his mind rotted away in, back in the cold hard ground where he belonged.

He wasn't sure whether she bought it, but he didn't need her to. She needed him, *didn't she?* Was that really why she came to his door asking for help? Now he wasn't certain. But he *was* helping. How he did it might be a different story.

She turned the key in the ignition, the engine roaring to life in the blustery frozen hell. That's what it was for him. Even before he'd returned, he decided this would be his purgatory. This would be the place he'd live out his days in suffering. It was what he had to do for his dead son.

The sky looked cold. Any time he looked up, he thought of Britton. He remembered building the mobile, hanging it over his son's crib. He'd watch him look up at the stars and planets spinning overhead. He bought his son a telescope for his seventh birthday—an at-home model that came with its own tripod. His son would sit there with it for hours, looking out his bedroom window up at the stars. At first, he'd just point to things and give them made-up names. But it wasn't long before he knew what everything up there was called. When Rooker had found him dead, it was as if every planet in the sky, every star, and the sky itself came crashing down.

"Rooker?"

He turned his head and saw her staring at him. He figured it wasn't the first time she had said his name.

"Hmm?"

"You okay?"

"Yeah, fine."

"His house is out a ways, maybe twenty-five more minutes."

He didn't say anything. Instead he wondered how much of Gunner's file Tess had gone through. Had she seen Walter's father as the ME? If she did, why didn't she say anything? Maybe she thought nothing of it, that Walter was just following in his father's footsteps. But it didn't add up.

The more turns she made, the farther out in the boonies they went. Rooker watched the roads and houses turning more rural, suburban neighborhoods with open land. Eventually, they pulled up to a large two-story contemporary, one of the few modern homes on the street. It had to be at least three thousand square feet. Years ago, Rooker had googled how much the average medical examiner makes—thinking surely it had to be more than a journalist. He was right. Between $75,000 and $150,000 put the earning potential at more than double of what Rooker ever saw. And now, as they sat in the driveway, he couldn't help but think that Walter must be one hell of a medical examiner because the house looked to be worth anywhere from $1.5 to $3 million.

Rooker and Tess stepped out of the car. The driveway was long, flanked by a rock wall bordering the home. The exterior was seamless, white-painted walls with dark wood accents. Walter had a modern, contemporary style. Rooker figured it had to do with how pristine and neat everything needed to be for a medical examiner: he assumed they were all obsessive-compulsive freaks. That would explain the seemingly sterile nature of the home—large, open steel railings, matching steel shutters.

Rooker followed Tess, who made her way beneath a roof covering between the garage and a tall rectangular stone pillar. She led him to the door, rapped her knuckles, and called out.

"Walter? It's Tess Harlow."

Nothing.

She tried again. Still nothing.

Harlow peered through one of the windows, and what she saw was enough for her to lift her pistol from its holster and try the handle of the door. It clicked open.

As he followed her inside, he saw what had spooked her: a mangled black ball of feathers. Talons like tiny twigs sticking up. Two dead eyes. Belly up, its neck twisted ninety degrees to the side. Staring down at the dead bird, he shuddered the way he did when driving past some creature crushed on the road.

"Stay behind me," she said.

The inside was nicer than Rooker had imagined. The wall to the left was enormous and white, lined with golden mahogany storage where a couple of wool suits and blazers were spaced out. The adjacent alarm panel was disabled. They followed the hallway's enormous slabs of gray marble tile offset with shimmering wood floors and passed a room with two large white sofas, an enormous slate fireplace, and a wall of floor-to-ceiling windows that overlooked the trees and water.

They turned and stepped into the largest kitchen Rooker had ever seen: an enormous white island with chrome stool seats that looked like they belonged in a morgue. Matching white cabinets with chrome fixtures stretched along the wall to the stainless-steel fridge.

A large wood table with eight chairs sat in the dining area, but they looked unused. Beside it was a massive staircase bordered by glass and matching wood railings. Rooker followed close behind Harlow, and at the top, they found yet another view down to the water. The hallway was lined with art pieces bordered in dark frames that all had to do with the human anatomy. Toward the end of the hallway on the right was where they located the master bedroom. The bed wasn't made, which struck him as odd. As Tess cleared a couple of empty bedrooms, he wandered to the last door at the end of the hall. It was open a crack. Though he knew he should wait for Tess, Rooker nudged the door open and peeked inside.

And that's when he found Walter Erickson.

Walter was stiff, hanging still as could be from a rope strung around his throat. A horrid line, deep purple-black, spread across his neck. Rooker assumed by the smell that he'd been hanging there awhile. He did his best to recall Erickson's appearance the last time he'd seen him— at the meeting with the chief only three days ago?

"Tess," he yelled to her. He heard her rushing down the hall as he plunked down in the leather chair behind a large desk. There were two ragged paperbacks on Erickson's desk, novels by Stieg Larsson and Jo Nesbø. The books were dog-eared—like they'd been read a thousand times or purchased used at a bookstore. The text was fading in some places, the covers like riddles with missing letters and creases and folds in the corners.

"Fuck."

Rooker looked up at Tess, who was staring at Erickson and fumbling for her handheld radio. He heard her call in for an ambulance and her team and then start to move around the room. He stared at the walls and saw Erickson's medical degree hanging in a frame. He had received other achievements and recognitions. He saw that Walter Erickson had written his own text—*Autopsy: Living Life in the Lab*—it was placed upside down on a chair and looked to be the only book in the room never opened.

Rooker felt drawn to the desk drawers. He went to grab one of the brass handles and saw Tess waving frantically out of his peripheral. He looked up at her, confused.

"Don't touch anything without gloves."

Tess handed him a pair of dark Nitrile gloves from one of her pockets. Rooker slid his fingers in and wiggled his hand as far as it would go, trying to pull the glove down without tearing it. He used that hand to pull open the drawers of the desk. Everything in the left-hand drawers looked normal. But then he opened the top right drawer and saw photos of himself.

"We have to canvass the house."

He responded without looking at her. "What's the point?"

"The point is that this is a crime scene."

"Oh, but look how clear it is," he said, his tone petulant. "Our killer found that we were onto him, and he hanged himself. Look at the photos here, our proof."

Rooker tossed the photos onto the desk. They slid down in a winning solitaire pile, photos of him, photos of Tess, photos of the dead women while they were less dead.

"You don't think it's Walter."

"Of course it isn't fucking him." He was wound tight, too tight, ready to unravel. Right about now, he could go for a shot of vodka and a cold beer to chase it. He thought about doing one of those *Price Is Right* model hand flourishes. *A brand-new car!* "You think this killer goes through all this"—he pointed at one of the dead women—"just to hang himself in a room filled with photos of us and his victims? Jesus Christ."

"We still need to search the entire house; maybe there's something else. Maybe there are fingerprints we can—"

His mocking laugh was like an incision, her words caught cold in her throat. "Please stop. The only fingerprints we'll find here are Erickson's, yours, and mine."

"Do you know a single thing about how a case works? A medical examiner is found hanged in his study with photos linking him to a crime. We have to go through procedure, have the place canvassed even if we doubt anything will turn up."

"What a waste of time."

"He was a nice man. He's right there, dead, and you're calling his death a waste of our time."

"Not a complete waste. He did help eliminate someone from the suspect list."

She shot him a cold look. It was repulsion mixed with sorrow for someone who could sink so low.

"Leave," she said. "The team was right: this was a mistake. If I need you, I know where to find you, probably wasted."

"You're my ride."

"Find a new one."

Chapter 20

December 9

For fuck's sake! He woke from a ten-hour drunken slumber thinking that someone was pissing on his head. He muttered a curse word or two, unfurled one eyelid, and realized he was in his living room. Even though he was still lying down, the room was spinning, twisting, the ground crooked and moving. He felt like he was inside a snow globe someone was shaking. Through one narrow slit, the other eye still completely closed, he looked up. The water was coming down fast in thin globules, teardrops falling from different areas of the ceiling. He thought for a second and remembered the bucket. It must have overflowed. He pulled a blanket from the floor beside his chair and tucked it beneath himself. It would catch whatever water would fall until he was able to get upstairs to the bedroom.

The recliner snapped shut, and he pushed off the armrest to his feet, swayed over to one of the old wood cabinets and knocked something off the shelf. It slammed hard on top of his bare foot. The eighty-proof fluid coursing hot through his blood dulled the sting, though he knew he'd feel it again when he sobered up. While he wobbled a few paces to the bottom step, he heard Geralt howling outside the door. Sweat guttered in the cracks of his hands. One palm pressed against the wall to steady his climb. When he made it to the top, he tottered to the overflowed pail, drops of water careening over the lip. He lifted the handle, water pouring down the sides. He staggered to the window, ready to launch the water out of it. But the window didn't budge. He set the bucket down and tried with two hands, but still nothing.

Instead, he lifted the bucket, went to the other side of the room, and launched the water at the boarded windows. It was like a tsunami wave. Half of it found its way out through the areas that weren't sealed; the rest splashed off the boards and fell right down. But the bucket was empty. He put it back in its spot, sauntered to the bed, and fell on top of it. He turned his head and watched the water drip from the boarded window. His eyes closed, and he passed out.

Hours later, Rooker woke up freezing. In his drunken state, he'd never gotten the blankets over him. But it wasn't the cold that woke him. It was Tess's voice.

"Hmm?" he muttered, barely conscious.

"I need you to wake up."

"I'm not awake," he mumbled with his mouth nearly closed.

"I can see that."

"So go away."

"You're a child."

"Please, Mom, ten more minutes."

"Do you recognize this? Your prints are on it, but they're old."

At that, Rooker lifted his face from the mattress, turned his head toward her. He felt his neck pop, and his foot was in pain, but he couldn't for the life of him remember why. He opened his sleep-blurred eyes, shocked at what she was holding in front of him. He was suddenly more awake, pushing himself up on his elbows.

"That was at Erickson's?"

"Yeah."

"That's my fish and tackle box from when I was a kid." He yawned and scratched at his bed head, then rubbed his eyes. "My dad would take me out on the lake."

"How would Erickson have it?"

"The real question is how the killer would have it. What was in it?"

"I need you awake. We have work to do."

"Harlow," he said. "What was in it?"

She showed him a photo. "It's you and the neighbor." The photo wasn't perfect, but it was clear enough. He saw himself, pressed up against Evelyn Holmberg. The person who took the photo hadn't been very far away. Rooker's chest capsized. It felt like it was filled with ice water. Then she showed him a torn yellow page, most of the black text scratched over in dark pen. It looked satanic; the only thing missing were actual pentagrams. She read it to him. "Prepare slaughter for his sons because of the guilt of their fathers." Her words hung in the air, almost the same as when he'd found Walter Erickson. She turned it over, and there was another word on the back. *LIAR.* "What does it mean?"

He shut his eyes. "Hell if I know. That he's a psychopath?"

"When were you going to tell me you slept with the neighbor?"

"She has a name, you know," he muttered.

"I think you're lying."

"Yeah? Why's that?"

"Why would he call you a liar?"

"Already told you, I don't know."

She didn't say anything. She stood, arms crossed, looking down at him. "Get up. We have work to do."

Chapter 21

December 9

Tess felt Rooker's shame as he rolled out of bed. At his best, he was sharp, witty, even attractive. But now, watching him was a cover-your-eyes movie flop. It was a geriatric rise; she pictured loose skin like raisins or crinkled paper. It reminded her of where her mother was—that distinct old-person smell. He slid his legs over the edge of the bed, the soles of his feet sinking slowly, sadly to the ground.

"You should invest in some pillows, might spruce the place up."

"I don't do pillows." He shielded the light from his bloodshot eyes. "The only sprucing would be a lit match." He mimed a fiery explosion with his drunken hands. She found it slightly amusing.

"Why don't you start writing again?"

"I'm done with that bullshit. My masterpiece is collecting dust on the mantel downstairs. Haven't touched it since I put it there. I'm getting in the shower."

"Hurry up."

Tess sidled down the stairs first, nervous that they might not hold her, also afraid that Rooker might fall down them and break several bones in his current state. But he made it to the bottom fine, and his sly smile with closed eyes was a nice touch. Grabbing a towel off a bench, he pressed his face into it and apparently decided it smelled clean enough to use.

Tess roamed until she found the mantel and discovered a thick stack of stapled paper. Rooker was right. It looked like it had survived a Saharan dust cloud. Nor did it smell great. It was musty, damp to the touch. Nonetheless, she brushed away the thin layer of grime it was caked in and read the top page.

THE KILLER IN ME
By Rooker Lindström

She flipped the top page; there was no dedication there. She wondered whom he had left to dedicate it to if it were ever published. Then she began reading. Before long, she realized it was all in first person, about a boy whose father was a monster. It was different to see him through his writing, the thing he did so well.

She skimmed the beginning about a father who hated his boy, despised the name the boy's mother had given him. She heard the water turn off, figured the hot water only lasted maybe a couple of minutes. She stuffed the manuscript into her bag before she heard him call out to her.

"Can you grab me some clothes from my dresser?"

"Yeah, sure."

She walked upstairs to his bedroom, opened the drawers, pulled out underwear, thick wool socks, a sweater, and grabbed the pair of pants from the floor. She started folding them, then looked up at the dresser mirror. There was a gold necklace with Saint Michael on it. She'd never seen him wear it.

She found her footing on the stairs carefully, made it to the bottom, and turned the corner. Rooker was standing there in a towel. His chest was scarred, as was the left side of his neck. She assumed it was something he wouldn't talk about, but maybe she'd find it in the book he wrote. She looked down at his foot welted purple in the center.

"What the hell happened to you?"

He followed her eyes down to his foot.

"That's a good question, can't remember. But it hurts like hell. Thank you." He took the pile of clothes from her and turned back to the bathroom. She saw the tattoo on his shoulder blade, a bird with a chess piece.

"That's beautiful."

"You should see it without the towel."

"You're an asshole."

He laughed and shut the door behind him. She waited.

"It's the rook. Often mistaken for the crow, same family—Corvidae. It was my mother's favorite bird. She thought Rooker sounded California-movie-star-esque. She'd call me her Rook, tell me to never leave her nest."

"And the Saint Michael?"

"Typical detective, snooping around."

"I've never seen it on you."

"I'm too far gone to believe in such stories. But he wasn't a saint. He was an angel, the patron of warriors. My mother never wanted me to box, knew it would probably give Gunner excuses to discipline me, which meant beat the shit out of me. But she always called me her warrior."

"She sounds incredible."

"She was. It was her father's. She gave it to me, and then I passed it down to my son."

The door opened, and Rooker finished putting on his sweater in front of her.

"How do I look?"

"A little better than ten minutes ago."

"Ouch, I must still look like dog shit."

She watched him struggle to get the second boot—he saved the hurt one for last—onto his foot. Once the top of his foot was pulling against the inside of the boot, snug up against it, she watched the wince on his face. He laced his boots loosely and stood. Then he threw on his heavy jacket and followed Tess out to the car.

"It might be time to start locking that door, you know," she told him. "With a killer watching you and all."

"He doesn't want to kill me yet, remember? He wants to see me suffer first. But you're right, I should lock it."

When they were inside the car, Tess found herself questioning why the killer would call Rooker a liar. Intuition told her that he was still hiding things from her. But what? What was he lying about?

Just then, her phone rang. It was Isaiah Hayes, the ME on Walter's case, in the same matter-of-fact voice as always. She listened to him rattle off the gruesome details of Walter's last moments, muttered her thanks, and hung up.

Walter wasn't a cop, but it still felt like they'd lost one of their own. "Fuck."

"What is it?" Rooker looked genuinely concerned for once.

"That was fast . . . Walter's death," she said. "Ruled a homicide. The bruises on his neck weren't consistent with the rope or the amount of time he'd been strung up. He was already dead."

When Rooker didn't reply, the two of them started bouncing questions and theories off one another.

"How could he have your tackle box? We know he was in your house; could it have been there?"

"If it was, that's news to me. I haven't seen it in at least twenty-something years. My question is, who did Walter know? Who did he let into the house? The alarm was off."

"You don't think the killer could have disabled it?"

"It's possible, but I doubt it. I think Walter was home or the killer was waiting for him outside. I think Walter knew him. Probably let him in."

"But why Walter? Why kill him?"

"You took out Gunner's file a couple of weeks ago—your name was written in the log. You tell me."

"I did take it out. I wanted to see if there was anything in there about you."

"Well, you should've paid more attention to the medical examiner. To the number of victims in the file."

"So when you said you didn't find anything missing, you lied to me."

"I did."

"What the fuck is wrong with you? You can't hide information relevant to the case. You're supposed to be helping me."

Tess wasn't someone who asked for help. After graduating from the academy, even though her father was a police officer, she never once asked him for a favor. But unfortunately, she trusted too easily, which she was kicking herself for now.

"You brought me in to see if I was your killer—to see if I'd make a mistake."

"I brought you in because you've caught a killer."

"Bullshit."

"You're bullshit. You don't trust anyone."

"How can I? I've been a suspect since I got here."

Tess didn't answer. She knew he was right. Even though she'd cleared him on at least two murders, she still couldn't shake the feeling that he might be involved. That he was lying to her face.

"I need to find the detectives who were on my father's case." Rooker's words broke through the silence. "I've only found initials of the lead detective, PS. I was able to identify the fourteenth victim: Astrid Thompson. She was twenty-eight years old. Her body was dumped, and her head was missing. But why is she missing from the file? There should be more information in the archives somewhere, however deep. Also, who was the medical examiner for the last victim? Can you get Langston on that?"

"I can."

"Will you take me back to the department? I want to help her out."

"I'll drop you off."

"Where are you going?"

She thought about Rooker's novel tucked away in her bag. "I have plans."

Chapter 22

Tess sat up in bed that night wrapped in Rooker's novel. She read on and on about the father's scare tactics, about the ways he was trying to raise a man. About the boy's crush on the new girl who moved from Wisconsin named McKenna. And then there was the story about hunting.

The boy was only nine. His father made him lug the old Remington hunting rifle, which was pretty much the size of the boy. He had a backpack on that neared his entire body weight. The father made him trek into the woods with him, a two-mile hike of rocky hills, river-banks, and winding woods. The boy couldn't bear his father's smell, the god-awful amount of musk cologne, gut churning paired with stale cigarette tobacco.

His father had pointed out a buck, white above the nose, on the tail, and under its chest. He didn't help the boy get the rifle ready. He watched. But before the boy was about to shoot, his father said one thing. "Behind the shoulder, the heart and lungs." The boy took aim, his father standing behind him. He considered missing the shot on purpose; he didn't want to kill the buck. But he knew what his father would do to him if he missed. His father gave a final "yep" of approval before the shot was fired. It felt like a cannon blast, the shock and force sending the boy flying to the ground. A high-pitched ringing looped in his ears, and then he couldn't hear a thing. He had fallen flat and hard on his back, hit a rock somewhere, and thought his head might be bleeding. He might be concussed.

When he rolled over, slipped to his knees, and pushed off the ground, he saw the deer lying on his side. He was still breathing, but barely. The boy picked up the rifle, stumped toward him. He emptied the cartridge from the chamber like he'd watched his father do, slid a new round into the bolt action, locked it in place, and fired. The deer was dead. He turned around with tears in his eyes. His father didn't look the slightest bit proud.

"Don't be a pussy."

He tried everything he could to keep the tears from running down his face. He bit down so hard on his bottom lip that it bled. It felt like he couldn't breathe, his throat burning trying to keep the tears at bay. But when his father watched one tear slowly trickle down, he said something the boy would never forget.

"Get it home or don't bother coming back."

And he left him there alone to do the job.

The boy dragged the dead animal by the antlers, sobbing through the two-mile stretch. By the time he reached the house, it was midnight. His shoulders and arms and back were screaming. His legs no longer felt like they were attached to his body, though they kept moving. When he walked through the door, his father came from upstairs and said, "Now we have to skin it. Hopefully you didn't ruin it dragging it here."

Tess read on and on. There were more stories about the father's teachings, his beatings. But when she got to a story about when the boy was fourteen, it changed everything. She read the words in horror, and her body turned hot. The father had felt his boy needed to toughen up. He'd become a pretty good boxer, but he'd never get his father's approval. His father wasn't satisfied unless the other boy was knocked unconscious by the end of the fight. If the boy won on points, it was worse than losing. His father would rather watch him get his ass kicked than let judges decide that he'd done enough to win.

Tess read about the woman. She was twenty-four years old, just graduated from university. His father wanted the boy to kill her. She was already bound to the bed with belts. She was wearing white underwear. Her skin was fair. She looked cold, the light, nearly invisible hairs standing up along her stomach. The father threw the pillow at the boy; he caught it against his chest. She cried out, "Please don't!" before he lifted it and held it against her face. He pressed down, but he knew it wasn't hard enough to suffocate her.

"If you don't kill her, I'll kill the both of you."

The boy knew that if his father killed her, she'd only be in that much more pain, maybe even tortured. And the boy didn't want to die. He got up onto the bed, put his knees beside her, and pressed down with all his force into the pillow. She shook violently beneath him. After a while, he felt her stop, felt her body go limp. One of his tears hit the pillow, and he wiped it away before his father could see.

Tess read the final excerpt slowly. And then she reread it. Both times, her hands were clenched, shaking.

I can still feel the blood on the crook of my head. It'll be dark soon, but I lie here, still, against the red rock. The wind whistles low over a thicket, and the wind creeps back into my chest. Water runs down into the ankles of my dirty white Nike Cortez sneakers. The black swoosh drips like a wet rag twist. But the knot on the back of my head, the crimson on my fingertips, the blur in my eyes, it's still so clear two decades later.

The woods whisper to me between the trees. But I can't tell what it is they want from me. I roll over onto my side, and I see the dead deer staring back. Her eyes are like black glass. My knee scrapes on the rock when I get to my feet. And when I push off to stand, my clothes cling sopping-cold wetness to my skin. I can taste the cigarette on my tongue, smell my father's musk cologne I sprayed myself with like a hose. And when I get to my feet, the rifle still heavy in my hands, I close my eyes and let the breeze dance around me. It leaps and twirls and spins like the women my father shared his nights with. I feel a drop of rain on my face. The clouds roll in dark.

The woods whisper to me again. But this time, I hear them. And I smile. My eyes flick open like a lighter spark. And when I look around, the only ones living, breathing, are the woods and me. It's always been me. I look down at her. She was always so beautiful. She looked almost the same as the day she was introduced to the class. Her hair was straight and honeycomb blonde, like waves of sticky syrup. But now the ends are matted, reddened. Her brown Converse Chuck Taylor All Stars are covered in mud where she ran and fell. Her sweatshirt torn from the pricker bushes. Her eyes are like black glass. And when I take her by the hand, most of the leaves part to make way for our path. The rest of the leaves, the twigs, crunch beneath her. And when I drag her home, McKenna was her name, my father rocks back and forth on the porch. And for the first time in my life, I make him smile.

Was the story about the deer . . . this girl . . . the woman he smothered—was any of it real? She looked at the clock and saw that it was past four in the morning. She felt like she couldn't breathe. And then she picked up the phone.

◆ ◆ ◆

After a few rings, Harlow heard an angry mumble.

"Langston."

"It's Tess," she said as her fingers clicked away on the keyboard. "I need you to wake up."

Tess knew that Millie was an excellent researcher and a wiz with computer systems. In fact, Tess had paid for her to attend training courses in data science and cybersecurity.

Millie let out a long yawn and replied: "I just went to bed . . . an hour ago. I was trying to dig up everything you and Rooker needed."

"Change of plans." Tess put the phone between her cheek and shoulder. "I need access to Rooker's computer, his emails, whatever you can get me."

"What?"

"Look," Tess said, using quotations and an asterisk to filter her search for a girl named McKenna who'd gone missing or been murdered. "I'm asking if you can hack into his computer."

"What you're talking about is illegal. Boss, if you don't mind, I think you should—"

"Should anything go wrong, I'll take full responsibility."

Langston took a long, long pause. "I would need his IP address or . . ."

"What is it?"

"I'd need you to plug something into his USB port. It's a device I made in a cybersecurity course. It would override passwords, get into all his files, email, everything. I could even access his microphone and webcam, see what he's doing every time he logs into the computer."

"Is it ready now?"

"Yeah, but—"

"I'll be there in fifteen."

Tess hung up and closed her laptop. She'd found nothing on a "McKenna murdered in woods," despite trying all sorts of methods, different keywords. A few minutes later, she was in the car, the leather interior icy on her skin. She started the car, and a frosty-looking icon displayed on the dashboard let her know the engine was cold.

Even with the ice on the road, she was driving faster than the marker limit as she thought about what Rooker was. He seemed too smart to come back here and follow in his father's footsteps, knowing they'd lead police directly to him. Right? Either way, she would find out what he was soon enough. She inched forward in her seat. The seat belt started to feel like straps binding her to a gurney. She would lose her job; there was no doubt about it. She put the window down, and the rush of the wind made her feel reckless. Her foot pressed harder on the pedal. She was pushing ninety, the engine like a roar in the calm dark of morning. The sky had aged since she'd left, the pitch-black surroundings turning a dark gray.

She eased off the gas as the road curved. But when her headlights shined bright on a tall, skinny deer, she slammed on the brakes. The deer stood perfectly still, staring at her. The car spun out, the tires screeching like a wounded animal. It echoed in her ears long after the car had managed to stop, only a foot from the guardrail. The deer was standing on the opposite side of it, looking right at her. It trotted off into the woods, and Tess sat there gasping, watching it until it disappeared out of sight, the smell of burning rubber clogging her nostrils.

She turned the car around and drove as safely as she could, turning the final ten minutes of her drive to Millie's into fifteen.

Chapter 23

December 10

Just as the digital clock on the Taurus's dash rolled to 4:51, Tess drove through a thick fog that resembled something out of a horror film. She pictured Freddy Krueger's burned face in a red-and-green knitted sweater waiting for her on the other side. As she started up the road to Rooker's cottage, the Ford packed down what was left of the frozen snow. She drove past two squad cars, an older-model Ford Taurus, and a Ford Interceptor parked outside Evelyn Holmberg's house. One of the officers leaned against the hood of the Interceptor, the orange glow of his cigarette casting a violet hue around his lips and fingers in the black of night. He stubbed out the stick at the sight of her and waved. She raised a curt hand back.

Tess steered the car through the same slush that she'd driven through last time she was here. She stopped short of where the tracks ended and put the car in park, then shut it off. She tiptoed up the front stairs of Rooker's cottage, hoping the door wouldn't be locked. The handle turned. She nudged the door, but it didn't move. She put her body weight behind it, and the door budged, but it was stuck. She did it one more time with her hip, and it creaked open. The farther the door opened, the more ghastly its wailing. She held it perfectly still, slid her body into the thin passage, and pressed it closed as silently as possible.

She walked in, turned the corner, and saw the laptop open on the table. The recliner chair was opened. She figured Rooker had sat up and gone to bed at some point. She walked over to the table, ready to take the USB drive out of her back pocket.

"What are you doing?"

The deep rasp of his voice scared the living shit out of her. She jumped and turned around, her heart pulsing. She saw him leaning against the wall she'd passed.

"Jesus Christ, you scared me!" Her words nearly lodged in her throat. They fell like a whispered scream.

"You didn't answer."

She thought quickly. "I just spoke to Langston. She said you might still be up. I wanted to see if you'd gotten anywhere."

He studied her. She figured he was suspicious, but it was a good answer. Hell, it was the best answer she could have possibly given him. Driving over here, she remembered how her blood was boiling, how she was furious with the man she had started to trust. Now she felt herself growing nervous, rubbing her goose bumps down, scratching at the back of her hand.

"The initials, Langston found the name," he said. "Peter Sundgren. He was the lead detective on the case. There wasn't much to find, a lot of useless stuff in archives, but we were able to find that. We got an address—I was going to tell you about it at a reasonable time when people should be awake."

Langston had already told her about Peter Sundgren when she recovered the drive.

"Sorry, I thought you might be up."

"You could've called."

He was right. It didn't make a ton of sense for her to drive over before five in the morning and let herself in. Unless she had a different reason.

She lied. "I couldn't sleep. Had a nightmare."

He didn't reply.

She thought of the photos in the drawer at Erickson's. It wasn't the best, but it would do.

"The photos of us in Erickson's office, Sofia Persson's purse here. It makes my skin crawl to think that he's watching me."

"He is. He's watching both of us."

"And it doesn't bother you?"

"I wouldn't be human if it didn't."

"Do you have anything to drink?"

"Tap water. Hold on."

Rooker shuffled out of the room toward the kitchen, and it was her chance. She slid the drive into the computer's USB port. Langston explained how the hack was already installed and was designed to execute once the drive was in place, meaning Tess didn't have to open any programs. She tried to explain preprogrammed keystrokes and disabling firewalls and whatever else, but Tess needed whatever was on the computer. And this would give it to her. But it wasn't going to work. The screen glowed a blinding white. She heard the faucet cough, hiss, and run. She heard Rooker rummaging for a clean glass in the cupboard. Meanwhile, Langston had said to leave the drive in place for at least a couple of minutes. Tess hit a few buttons until she found the brightness and lowered it. The white light disappeared.

He walked around the corner, and Tess stood to take the tall glass from him.

"Thanks."

Something caught her eye. She held it up away from her like she was checking the authenticity of a Ben Franklin. There in the water, she saw the tiny flakes, black particles floating around like fish behind aquarium glass.

"Something wrong with your water too?"

"Ah, shit, sorry. I haven't been drinking from it. Probably rusted out. Maybe it will add flavor."

She set it down on the table. "I'm good, thanks." She needed to distract him. "So, is there only one bedroom? Where would you stay when you were here as a kid?"

"I was only here with Gunner a handful of times. I'd sleep on the couch."

"What are you hoping to find when you talk to Sundgren?"

"His insight. I want to know what he thought. I need to know about Astrid Thompson and who the examiner was."

"He may be an old man by now. The case was over twenty years ago; maybe he doesn't remember."

"I'm willing to bet he remembers; he probably wishes he didn't."

Tess felt like an idiot for coming here when she did. In the moment, reading Rooker's novel made her so furious that she needed to act. But now that she was here without backup, all that made her feel safe were the other police stationed hundreds of feet away outside the Holmberg residence and her sidearm.

"How do you think the killer knows so much about this place? How can he know so much about Gunner, about you?"

"Those are the questions I keep asking myself."

"Do you think you know him?" It was the second time she'd asked him that now.

"I've only been here a handful of times. I never really knew anyone. My father only brought me here to make a man out of me."

"Do you mind if I use your bathroom?"

"Sure. Did you think you'd be needing that?"

She followed his gaze to the pistol holstered at her hip.

"Didn't plan on it." She smiled weakly.

She walked into the tiny bathroom and closed the door behind her. The shower was barely large enough for one. Tess noticed a few pieces missing from the mirror; a crack running the width of it warped her face like a fun-house reflection. She gave it thirty seconds, flushed the toilet, and ran the faucet. Next, she pulled the medicine cabinet open. Paco

Rabanne cologne, Degree antiperspirant, a tube of Crest toothpaste, and a frayed toothbrush. Behind all of it, she saw a prescription box, moved the other items aside, and read it.

Ziprasidone. 60 mg. The box intact. It had never been opened. She put everything back.

When she returned, Rooker was standing with his back to her, staring out the window. She stood beside him and peered into the darkness. The lights were out at Evelyn Holmberg's home. An officer was patrolling the perimeter of the house, the other ass-pressed against the side of the squad car. Smoky gray clouds blew from his mouth—she guessed a freshly lit cigarette.

They stood in silence a little longer. Outside, everything was perfectly still. The only sounds she could hear were her own heart beating and the wind's heavy breathing, whistling through the walls and the upstairs windows.

"I'd better get home."

She found herself wondering about a girl named McKenna.

"I was going to help Langston at the station in the morning, try to track down more of the detective team that worked Gunner's case," he said. "If that's all right."

"That's fine. I have a few things to get done. Get some sleep."

"Hey," he said to her. It took only one word, the way it hung there, like he knew something. It made her feel as if she'd fallen through the ice, was clawing at it, trying to find the surface.

Her heart thumped. "Yeah?" she asked.

"The two books in Erickson's office, can I borrow them?"

Relieved, she said, "They're evidence. Just buy them."

"No, I need those copies."

"I'll get them to you when forensics clears them. It might be a while."

"Thanks."

"And thanks for the water," she said as she turned her back to him to block his view. In one motion she lifted the glass, and with the other hand snatched the drive and slipped it into her pocket. She handed the glass to him.

Tess pulled the door open and shut it behind her. Outside, she shivered, and her hands trembled, but not from the cold. She was between a speedy fear walk and a jog when her foot slipped deep in the slush, but she caught herself. She opened the car door and locked it quickly. She jabbed the key at the ignition multiple times until it caught. All the time she could feel his eyes on her.

She turned the car around, made her way back out to the road, and dialed Langston.

"Yep."

"You're still up."

"Figured you'd need me."

"Did we get anything?"

"I've got it. Accounts, passwords, and limited access to his computer, but we can see what he's looking at in real time. Do you need me on this ASAP?"

Tess could hear the sleep in her voice.

"Sorry, I do. Let me know what you get. I'm going to put surveillance on him."

Langston let out a long yawn. "You got it."

"And find out what Ziprasidone is."

Chapter 24

December 10

Liar. Just after 8:00 a.m., the white Volvo pulled up outside the address Rooker had penned on his hand. It reminded him of the way life once was—times when as a reporter, there was never a day that ink wasn't smeared on his hand. He handed the driver the cab fare, got out, and shut the door. He'd lied to Tess's face about helping Langston at the station, but he didn't have time to follow "procedure." The home was one level and sat on a half acre of land. He walked the broken brick pavers, up three cracked cement steps to the front landing, knocked twice on a door that looked like it had chipped and been painted over. Moments later, an elderly woman answered.

"I'm looking for Peter Sundgren."

"I'm Helen, his wife. Peter," she called out. A few moments later, Rooker heard a screen door swing shut and watched the man step into the doorway. The man stared at him, squinted almost in disbelief, though maybe Rooker was reading him wrong. Then again, he looked familiar.

"Holy hell." Sundgren scratched the windswept hairs at his temple. He searched Rooker's face for a few long seconds until he looked certain. "Rooker Lindström."

Maybe he had come to the right place after all. He figured maybe Sundgren had seen him in the newspaper when his son was killed. They probably ran a "Son of Minnesota Serial Killer's Boy Murdered" clickbait headline.

"How do you know who I am?"

"I remember you as a boy. You never forget the eyes of the devil— pardon me, or eyes that've seen too much. Frankly, even as a boy, you had both. Still don't look much like him, though, do you?"

"My mother always said I got her genes."

"Well, then, I'd say you're quite lucky. What on earth brings you back here?"

"To be honest, I lost a lot back home. I figured I'd come hide here. Hasn't worked so well yet."

"That so? What is it I can do for you?"

"It's a bit complicated . . . Mr. Sundgren, how is it that I've had such a tough time tracking you down? I couldn't find a name for the detectives on the case when my father was caught. There was nothing in the file."

"Cases like your father's"—he breathed out heavily—"can bring the wackjobs out. The last thing I wanted was my name in the papers or to put my wife in danger. But as far as it being in the files, I couldn't tell you, I'm sorry. I think the better question is, why are you looking into your father's file?"

"Because I think the past is coming back to haunt me." Rooker sighed. He looked Sundgren in the eyes, two circles like warm blue water. He was readying himself to talk about this new killer, but he stopped short.

"A case can do things to you. That one"—Peter looked down into his hands like his next words were written there—"was my last as a detective. Turned in the badge the morning after we got him. Sixteen years as a detective, but you open a freezer box to human heads, that was enough for me. When I looked him in the eyes—Gunner—it still gives me the willies to this day. I have a feeling you have more questions. Come in. Tea or coffee?"

"Coffee, please."

"Helen," he called out. "Can you put some coffee on, please?"

The man shambled over to a large recliner that could use a reupholster, inched down, and flopped his behind into the cushion. Rooker was still standing, looking into the smiling, tired face of Peter Sundgren. Dark liver spots were like dalmatian markings on his head surrounded by thin white slicks of hair. His face was aging but cheerful, cleanly shaven aside from a few long, dark whiskers of hair in his nose. His eyebrows were pencil thin and a shade darker than the snow-white and slush-gray hair on his head. They were colors he was growing sick of. Helen stirred in the kitchen, the fridge opened and shut, and a few cabinets did the same.

"Take a seat." Sundgren motioned for Rooker to sit on the couch, and he did. He leaned forward.

"Someone is out there, killing women. Again. My father is somehow connected. My son"—he pulled the wallet-size photo from his back pocket and faced it toward Sundgren—"was taken from me by someone like my father. And it was my fault." He watched the former detective's face. Rooker didn't so much as glance at the photo, or even the back of it, out of fear of seeing the outline of his son. Sundgren nodded. "What can you tell me about the Lindström case?"

While Rooker slid the photo back in his pocket, Sundgren fumbled with the topmost button on his heavy flannel shirt, a mash of McIntosh red, faded blue, and cinnamon brown. He wore pleated khaki corduroy pants and brown steel-toe boots.

"I can tell you everything. I certainly have the time, but I'm not sure that you do." He smiled.

"Please, I need to know."

Helen nipped into the room a moment later with a mug of steaming coffee in hand. She set it down on the end table beside Rooker.

"Dear, I'd like you to meet Rooker. He was a boy when I last saw him."

"Nice to meet you, ma'am." Rooker shook her hand. It was delicate, wilting in his hand. But her smile was radiant. "I hope you don't mind if I steal your husband for a little."

"Oh, please do. It'll keep him out of my hair." She beamed and left the room.

Rooker could see the wheels turning in the old man's mind. Once Sundgren got going, though, he went over the details like a bulldozer.

"Gunner's first kill was a woman named Marijeta Danielsson in . . . November of 1988. You have to understand, we didn't have the technology you do now. It took us quite a while to identify the victims when all we had was a body. The heads we found later. She was reported missing by her mother, Harriet. The hounds found her body dumped in the woods a few miles north on the MN-38. Bruising to what remained of the throat and her head cut off." Rooker watched the man go back all those years, back to when he was on the case. He was sharp. Rooker was impressed. It didn't surprise him that he had been one of the men to catch his father.

"What can you tell me about the victims? And I want your insight, your analysis."

"Well, they were all attractive women, the youngest in her midtwenties, the oldest maybe forty. All single. I believe the women were seduced by Gunner. He was a ladies' man. Tall, lean muscle, dark hair, charismatic—Ted Bundy type. It seemed they had consensual intercourse—no signs of drugs in their system, no physical damage to the vaginal wall or anal cavity, pardon my saying. No signs of bruising aside from the lower portion of the neck consistent with asphyxiation. No dislocated or broken bones. Then the cut across the throat."

"You don't think any of them were taken by force? All went willingly?"

"That's what I believe. In fourteen victims, drugs or alcohol were never found in their systems. There were never markings on the skin consistent with bindings. They were all single women."

"And you think he killed them during or after sex?"

"That I can't be sure of. Having intercourse with them, knowing what he would do to them—I think that's what got the sick bastard off. No offense."

"None taken. How well did you know Klas Erickson?"

"The medical examiner? Not well, just the professional-courtesy level. Strange man . . . soft-spoken when he opted to speak, never the joking type. Figured maybe it came with the profession."

Rooker was starting to like Peter Sundgren.

"Have you ever met his son, Walter Erickson?"

"Not that I can remember."

"Who was your partner on the case?"

"William Sadler. He's dead now. Died years ago, pancreatic cancer. There were a few other detectives we had—Jensen, the crazy prick . . . Davies . . . Schultz was bright-eyed and bushy-tailed, rookie kid; and Meltzer—but I was lead, and William was second."

"Did you keep any of the files? Anything related to the murders or your team that could help me?"

Sundgren's eyes narrowed slightly. The corner of his mouth, his cheek indented like a crescent moon. "Why are you really here, Rooker? Why dig up your father's murders?"

"I came back here to die." It was the first time he'd said it out loud. But it wasn't like a weight on his shoulders suddenly fell to the floor. His words only polluted the air. "Then I got here, and women started dying. Maybe if I catch this guy, it's a chance to do right by my son; maybe it's my chance to catch someone like my father. Maybe it's just something to keep me from drinking. I don't know. But I need this."

Sundgren gave a wry smile. "'We are each our own devil, and we make this world our hell.' Don't know many quotes, but that one—Oscar Wilde—stuck with me after your father. Once you know that a certain kind of evil is living and breathing, it makes it difficult to turn a blind eye to it." He paused. "I still have some things in the attic you can take a look at. Helen's been yelling at me to get rid of them for years. It's been an ongoing battle. If you take them with you, I may lose the war."

"Thank you. I mean it. I'll get them back to you."

"I know you will."

Rooker stopped his leg bouncing with his hand and tried to get back on track. "You said fourteen victims? Was there anything you found that just didn't sit right with you?"

"Yes, fourteen confirmed. There was something odd about a fifteenth girl who went missing; she wasn't found, body or head. But I think she was related."

"What makes you think so?"

"She disappeared around the same time as the others. To me it just fit. But we never found her."

"What was her name?"

"Olivia Campbell. She was"—he paused and scratched his head, his eyes closed—"I want to say she was twenty-four, maybe turning twenty-five. She lived here on Deer Lake, same as your father's cottage. Middle school math teacher, I think grade eight. The missing person's report and her photo should be in the boxes I kept. The family taped Lost signs all over the county for a couple of years, like a puppy they hoped would find its way back. With the ongoing case, we took it seriously. We investigated it, but nothing ever turned up. The family finally stopped, figured she was dead."

"And the fourteen confirmed, do you have something on each of the victims? The file for one of them is missing, along with a few other things. I was hoping you'd be able to help me with that."

Peter made a peculiar face.

"What is it?" Rooker said.

"Did you happen to find the victim's name?"

"Astrid Thompson."

Peter's face scrunched. "That one's been on my mind for decades."

"Why?"

"I'll show you. I have some trouble getting up there now." He pointed to the attic door in the hallway. "The stairs come down, just watch out for the top step. Above them, there'll be a cord to pull for the light. I hope you don't mind a few spiderwebs."

Peter rocked his chair and scooted forward to the edge of his seat. He pushed off the armrest and stood. Rooker watched him struggle to get his flannel off and decided to help him out.

"I was doing some work outside. The legs tend to lock up. The wife yells at me, tells me I'm too old. I have no idea what she's talking about." He smiled. Rooker followed as the man shuffled in the direction of the hallway, where a thin white string hung from a rectangular outline. With a good yank, the attic door shrieked open a sliver. Dust mizzled down from the opening over Sundgren's head. He pulled at the wool collar of his sweater and hacked a dry cough. "Don't tell my wife." He laughed. The staircase let out a haunting metallic cry the entire way down.

"Are you boys okay?" Helen called from the other room.

"Never better, hon," Peter lied.

Rooker scaled the stairs slowly. They reminded him of the ones at home, not to be trusted. He popped his head up into the airless square, a black hole. Darkness breathed cold, damp air in his face. He waved his hand around blindly until it snagged on the metal cord—an ungodly chill and what felt like years' worth of grime—and pulled. The single dim bulb blinked to life a few times, went out, came back, and then stayed on. Peter had said, *A few spiderwebs.* This looked like it was a tarantula farm, maybe a metropolis. Cobweb silk intersected like city streets.

Rooker listened to Sundgren's instructions once more, found two large boxes stacked on top of each other, and carried them back down carefully. The top box sagged beneath a layer of mildew. Once he brought the boxes back into the den, he dropped them to the floor and wiped his fingers on his pants. He knelt over the two boxes and lifted the lids from both, the sight of at least twenty spiders making him shiver. Luckily, they were dead.

Before he lifted any of the files from the box, he paused. It wasn't the spiders. It was his curiosity.

"When's the last time someone has seen these?"

"I haven't taken them down in at least fifteen years. No one knows I have any of it."

"And you haven't talked about the case to anyone?"

"No . . ."

"I'm sorry. I don't mean to sound—"

"Son, don't apologize. If I were in your shoes, I'd ask me too."

They spent the next two hours going over the files. Rooker could see the old detective coming back to life, but he wasn't here to give the man another case, a purpose, something to do. He needed this chapter of his life gone. When it was closed, he'd put it on the shelf next to his failure of a manuscript.

The two of them started with the victims. Rooker wanted to find the file on Astrid Thompson, the fourteenth victim missing from the file. Sundgren thumbed through the files; they were in the order that the victims had been killed. His hand stopped on the fourteenth victim.

Sundgren held the manila folder shakily, reaching to hand it to Rooker.

He opened the file. Astrid Thompson was twenty-eight at the time of her death. Her head was missing from the scene. She was identified by the scarring that ran down the length of her hip from surgery as well as a series of distinct freckles. She'd graduated from college five years earlier and had been in a serious relationship with her boyfriend. He was one of the people police had asked to identify her. Her boyfriend was positive. It was her.

"She's the one who, for more than two decades, I've thought of."

"Why is that?"

"For one, she was in a long-standing, committed relationship. None of the other victims were. For two, take a look at the photographs. The incision across her throat. Do you see how jagged it is? Your father was precise. It's one of the reasons I thought maybe he was in the early stages of Parkinson's. Maybe the disease was causing his hand to shake, or maybe he was losing strength? But he hadn't. Maybe he was in a hurry? To this day, I think about Astrid Thompson."

Rooker heard Sundgren foraging through the other box, watched him grab ahold of a piece of paper and stare at it.

"This is the girl." He handed the paper to Rooker. "The fifteenth. The one I was sure was a victim of Gunner's."

It was a missing person's report. One that left Rooker mortified. The blood rushed from his face. It was a large black-and-white photo of Olivia Campbell. "Olivia Campbell. She disappeared at the same time of the murders. But we never found any remains."

His stomach twisted. Rooker looked down at Olivia Campbell for the second time in his life. The last time he had seen her, he had been sitting on top of her, holding a pillow over her face, his father standing behind him watching, waiting.

Chapter 25

December 10

Shortly after 9:00 a.m.—two hours late, as she was usually the first one in around 6:45—Tess marched into the office, bit down to fight back a yawn, her cheeks ballooning like a puffer fish. She had slept on and off for only an hour, the cold sun high in the sky before she finally dozed off. Keene and Cole were sitting at their desks, mulling over something together; she didn't bother to ask what. She sauntered past them as if they were invisible. Langston was already sitting.

"Where's Rooker?" Tess said.

Langston's eyes had reddened. Tess could tell she was wired, running off caffeine and zero sleep. "What?"

"I thought Rooker was coming in to help you track down the other detectives who caught Gunner."

"No, haven't seen him."

Tess assumed he was drunk again, maybe sleeping the booze off. Regardless, she needed to be sure. She stepped out of her office toward the cubicles and yelled to Sterling.

"Vic. You and Xander are on van duty. I want you two on Rooker. Now." When the two of them didn't question her decision, she stepped into her office and threw her coat over the chair. "What do you have?" she asked.

"A few things," Langston responded, holding back a yawn of her own.

"After this, you can take the rest of the day off."

Langston didn't say a thing about it. Instead, she got right to business. "So," she said. "He did a search on you in late November. It looks like he read a few articles on you, a few of your cases that made the papers."

"Must've been after I went to see him the first time."

"But then he started researching the murders. Again."

"What do you mean, '*again*'?"

"His search history showed that he researched murders in Itasca County. He pulled up the murders two weeks earlier. I think he linked the murders—made the connection that there was a serial killer before you went to see him."

"Well, he's clever. We know that."

"But that's not what concerns you."

"What do you mean?"

"I'm not stupid. You think it's him. Our guy."

"Look, I don't know what I think."

"You're seeing him again as a suspect. Why? You said you cleared him, that you were watching him when a victim was killed."

It was true. She had cleared him on the murder of Charlotte Johnson, the third victim. She knew for a fact that he was home at the time she was killed. But it was also true that he was never cleared for the first two victims. Choosing to dodge the question with her own, Tess said, "What else is there?"

"Ziprasidone, the drug you told me to check out. It's an antipsychotic. There are a lot of things it can treat—schizophrenia, bipolar disorder, dementia, hallucinations, nightmares, agitation, paranoia, the list goes on." Tess said nothing. "Other than that, some porn searches, nothing that stands out. Just standard male/female and lesbian porn."

"That's it?" she asked and immediately felt awful. She knew that Millie had probably been working on this since she'd spoken to her last.

But now she felt like the stunt she'd pulled earlier this morning was for nothing. "Sorry."

"Tell me what you found that makes him a suspect."

"He wrote a book. I took it. I know we can't use it. But there're things in it, things that his father did to him, things he made him do. I think Rooker killed a woman here in Minnesota—when he was fourteen. There's a story in it that the boy suffocated a woman with a pillow, that his father made him do it. There's not a single pillow in the house"—she held up a lone finger—"not one."

"But it's a story. Who's to say it's an autobiography?"

"Right. And then there's another story, about a girl named McKenna whose body he dragged through the woods."

Langston stopped her. "I did find this."

She ran a program on her own PC, opened up Firefox, and logged in to Rooker's email. As she did everything, she told Tess how she'd gained access to the passwords for all his accounts, how she'd found this in the drafts of his email.

"He never sent it."

Tess read the subject line.

FUCK YOU, YOU FUCKING FUCK.

Langston opened it and let Tess read it for herself.

> You piece of shit. You said you'd represent me and that we had a bestseller. That's what you said. "Hook, line, and sinker," your words. You sold me on horseshit. You said to give it a rewrite, that you'd be able to sell it to a publisher without a doubt. I spent countless hours on the rewrite. And now you tell me that you can't represent me anymore. I should fucking kill you.

Tess felt hot as she read the words.

"So this is his agent."

"Was. He didn't send it. But . . ." Langston paused.

"What?"

"Get this. His agent, Danny Ross, was on life support a year ago. He's recovering now, but he nearly died."

"What happened?"

"Hit-and-run." Langston opened a new tab in Firefox, searched the web, and pulled up the article in the *Los Angeles Times*. The vehicle was totaled: the agent's black Mercedes GLS rolled twice off the road, glass all around it. "A few days later, Rooker Lindström signed papers to take over his father's house."

Chapter 26

"Do you mind if I take this?" Rooker held a sheet of paper up for Peter Sundgren to see. It was a list of his old team members on Gunner's case. Sadler was dead, and Peter believed one more to be. Dead or not, Rooker needed to find some connection between one of them and a possible suspect.

"Go right ahead."

Rooker was able to confirm that the medical examiner on Astrid Thompson's case was in fact Klas Erickson. Though Peter Sundgren didn't have any kids, Rooker thought maybe he'd still look into nephews and nieces. But he didn't believe the man to be lying. Those boxes looked like they hadn't been opened in a century.

While he stacked everything Sundgren had on the case and said his thanks, he put the lid back on the box and carried it under his arm.

"If you think of anything, please call me." Rooker found a pen on the table next to a crossword puzzle and jotted down his number. "I may need to come by again and pick your brain—would you mind?"

"Not at all. Good luck with the case."

Rooker thanked Helen Sundgren for the coffee and closed the front door behind him. He stood on the concrete steps and slid on his jacket.

And then he saw it.

Parked on the south side of the street, more than half a block away: the van. A navy-blue Ford Transit, unmarked, decal-less, with blacked-out windows. He'd noticed the vehicle on the cab ride over, but it had turned off the main road long before Sundgren's street.

The wind chilled him to his core. But his anger, his adrenaline, they would warm him. He started down the street a ways before he thought to call Tess. He pulled his phone out and turned ever so slightly in time to see the van pulling away from the curb. Rooker turned right at the end of the street and followed the sidewalk. His steps sped up, pitter-patter slapping off the pavement.

He started to make way for an old woman taking her afternoon stroll, her ankle-biter Maltese hooked on a short blue cord. She smiled at him and waved her plastic-bagged hand. But he stopped her.

Rooker smiled at the elderly woman and thanked her. She was pleasant as could be. He patted the little rat on the head and walked away. Once he turned right down the next street and knew he was out of view of the van, he slipped to the right between the third and fourth house and hunched down behind the trash cans. His fondness for spy novels, Tom Clancy mostly, was suddenly coming to use. He was partial to Matt Damon's Jason Bourne as well. He waited for the van. It didn't take long for it to come into view and to drive past where he was hiding. He waited. When he saw it, it brought a smile to his face. The van doubled back.

Out of the driver seat stepped Xander Whitlock, the passenger seat Vic Sterling. Rooker watched them from afar as they spoke to the old woman. Sterling wiped crumbs from the chest of his gray hooded jacket. The old woman lifted the piece of paper and handed it to him, and once he unfolded it, he smiled. Vic handed it to Xander, who was fuming.

A simple handwritten *FUCK YOU* was all it took to make Xander heave a thrashing kick into the van's bumper.

Rooker dialed Harlow and brought the phone to his ear.

"Harlow."

"Hey, it's Rooker."

"Hey. I thought you were helping Millie out this morning?"

Rooker could tell. She knew he hadn't met with Langston. "Something came up. How'd your errands go?"

"Why do you sound out of breath? And what errands?"

"You said you had to get some things done this morning."

"Oh, right. Actually, I have another call . . . mind if I—"

"It's probably Xander or Sterling. I just lost them."

Rooker ended the call and turned off the phone. If they traced it, the GPS would only come back to this spot, where it was last switched on. He started jogging down the street, and before long he found an intersection and another white taxi. Rooker opened the rear door and got inside.

Tess spent most of her day wondering how Rooker could've gone off the grid. She tried to locate his cell phone, but it wasn't working. He must've shut it off or taken it apart. She'd put Xander and Sterling on the streets, and Keene and Cole had gone to Rooker's cottage but couldn't find him. There was no word back from anyone, at least no good word. She'd told Langston to keep an eye on the phone. If it came back on, she'd want to know about it first.

Tess was sitting at her desk thumbing through the file on Rooker, tapping her pen like a seesaw against the edge. She pulled up Rooker's Word documents on his computer.

TAP-TAP-TAP-TAP-TAP.

She saw the dashed line of ink she was making and rubbed it away, then closed the file and searched for Danny Ross on his literary agency's site. Ross was fortyish with a blocky head and boyish, even mousy features. His dark eyes drooped beneath short jet-black hair like they were beginning to melt, his grin goofy and tight. Under his biography was the press release celebrating a six-figure book deal for one of his clients. The contact info listed was the same email address she'd found in Rooker's correspondence, so she dialed the agency's main number.

"Hi, this is Detective Tess Harlow, of the Itasca County Sheriff's Department in Minnesota," she told the receptionist. "I need to speak with Danny Ross; it's about an ongoing investigation."

"Yes, ma'am, one moment."

After being on hold for two minutes, a man's voice stopped her drumming in its tracks.

"Danny Ross," the man said, his tone a mix of suspicion and curiosity.

"Hi, Mr. Ross, I'm sorry to get ahold of you like this. My name is Detective Tess Harlow; I'm with the Itasca County Sheriff's Department. I'm investigating an ongoing case. I was hoping you could help me out. What can you tell me about Rooker Lindström?"

"Rooker Lindström?" His voice rose like he hadn't heard the name in years. "He's an old client. Look, I'm a busy man. I can't just—"

"I'm sure you are, Mr. Ross. This will only take a minute. Did Rooker Lindström ever threaten you?"

"No, what? Rooker was always nice. I could tell he was upset when I decided to part ways with him . . . I just don't think this business was for him."

"You didn't think he was good enough?"

"I took him on because of his reputation as a journalist. He's talented. But I didn't think he would break through with what he had. What is all this about?"

"When did you last see him?"

"We're talking . . . at least two years ago—when I cut him loose. I took him to coffee, and I told him straight. I figured it's how he would've wanted it."

"And how'd he take it?"

There was a pause. "At first, I thought he took it well. But when I looked at his hand . . . it was clenched so hard, his knuckles turned white. And when he grabbed his cup of coffee, it was shaking."

"In your hit-and-run accident, did they ever find the driver?"

"No, they never did."

"Did you see the driver or the vehicle?"

"No, it was just a blur, and then I was unconscious, woke up in the hospital weeks later."

"Thank you for your time."

Tess hung up. Another dead end, mostly. While she wondered if Rooker had it in him to plow through someone in a car, she zoned out. It was a while before she glanced up at the clock hands to see them inching toward 10:00 p.m. She let her head hang and massaged the nape of her neck, her hair falling in front of her face, and pushed the keyboard away like a plate of food that had gone cold. She would've rather slammed it until not a single key was left. She draped her coat over her and clipped her holster to the hip of her jeans.

She only ever needed to fire her service weapon once, the SIG Sauer P226. It was reliable, used by the Navy SEALs. Carrying her pistol made her feel safer. Still, the thought of the photographs, the killer watching her and Rooker, it made the little peach hairs on the back of her neck stand tall. She'd even gone as far as to stash a gun in her bedside table.

Tess strolled through the empty office, flipped the light switch, and pushed past the double doors. The cold was paralyzing. A wind flew at her hard, whizzing by like a family of bats.

The garage was empty aside from a few vehicles. It was a single-level parking structure, nothing special. Large concrete pillars stood scattered. Old LED lights hummed and flickered like bug zappers. Some of them had gone out entirely, only to leave gaps of darkness.

She usually handled the cold well, but not tonight.

Her car was parked nearby. Twenty steps from the double doors. The smell of old rainwater flooded the garage, along with puddle spots. Her steps clicked and clacked, echoed toward her Taurus. She pressed the button on her key fob. The lights flashed, and she saw something. A figure. Her hand inched down her side to her holster. She wasn't sure what it was she was seeing.

A man? A woman? Maybe eighty, ninety feet from her.

She unlatched her holster, slid the SIG Sauer up by her side. She decided to trust her mind, that it wasn't playing tricks on her. Sweat trailed cold down her forehead. She let out a cool, shaky breath.

Then it moved. The shape bent down, crouched low, and something rattled, ricocheted off the ground. She heard a woman scream.

Tess was in a shooter's stance with her pistol before she could even process what had happened. The figure bolted, and she chased. She was speedy. But so was whomever she was after. She was getting closer to where she first saw the shape, closer to the screams. Just as she made it behind the concrete pillar, there were two earsplitting cracks. She saw the two flashes, the gunshots blistering. They sparked only feet from her.

She thought she could hear the steps sprinting away toward the exit through the high-pitched ringing. Her hand reached around blindly; her palm clapped in a puddle, then cold concrete, more water, the ground. She finally felt it, grabbed hold of it, and pulled it around to her side. It was a microcassette player. She switched it off, and the screams disappeared.

Tess cornered the edge of the pillar, popped her head out not even a few inches, fast, and another bullet whipped into the pillar. She thought she could hear where it came from. She peeked fast, fired three rounds, and got back behind cover. She slid down on her butt, looked beneath the parked cars—but there was nothing. She waited again, ready for the slightest movement. Her ears were ringing like church bells inside her skull. She was listening for something. Anything. But there was nothing. It was gone.

Tess learned that four minutes feels like an eternity when you're waiting to be shot at. That's what she told forensics and the team when they flooded the garage minutes later, barraging her with questions. When they cleared the garage, they found nothing aside from the microcassette player—which played only the screaming voice of a woman, potentially one of the victims—and impact points where the bullets had hit. One of the shots she fired had shattered the back window of one of the squad cars. No blood.

An hour after that, Tess wrapped up giving Martin her statement. She told him she had called it quits for the day, was walking to her car, and saw a figure. There was nothing else she could identify. The moment she was done, Keene told her to go home and get some rest. He'd brought over a thermos of hot chocolate, as ordered by his wife. She'd wanted to hurl it at the wall when he handed it to her, but by the time she was ready to leave, she'd emptied it.

Almost everyone on her task force offered to drive her home or to let her crash at their place. She was far too stubborn, far too angry to take any one of them up on it.

On her way home, her hands were still shaking. She only gripped the steering wheel harder to make it stop.

The heat blasted from every vent in the car, all aimed at her. The windows were down too, the gust prying the tears free. They felt good on her skin. She pulled into her place, got out, and walked like the living dead past the concierge.

She listened to the cables in the elevator up to her floor. She pulled her keys from her pocket, her hand trembling, shaking as she tried the door.

"Need help?" The deep, eerily calm voice nearly gave her a heart attack. Her hand went to her sidearm, and she saw Rooker slumped on the floor, his back against the wall across from her door. Before she even realized, her gun was firm in her hand, the P226 sights pointed square at his chest. The safety was off. She thought about firing her gun for the third time in her career.

Chapter 27

December 11

"Whoa. Was it something I said?"

"Don't move. I swear I'll shoot you."

He hesitated. "What's wrong?"

"I was in the garage at the station. Some asshole shot at me. They left a tape recorder of a woman screaming."

"And you think it's me. That's why you're having me tailed; you think I'm your killer."

"Prove you aren't. You *are* a killer, aren't you?"

Just then, one of the doors on the same floor opened. A sleepy, irritated man with rumpled-feather bed head was ready to yell at whoever woke him up. When he saw Tess pointing a gun at Rooker, he started to back into his room.

"Police business," Rooker said from the ground.

"Have a good night, Tess," the man said, closing his door, the lock clicking behind him.

"I've been here for almost two hours—check with the concierge man downstairs. He let me in," Rooker said. "Call down to him if you don't believe me."

Tess phoned down to the desk. The concierge picked up within seconds.

"Anders, it's Tess. Did you let a man in who said he was here to see me?"

"Yes, Rooker Lindström. The man you brought here days ago. He said he had information for you."

"What time did you let him in?" The phone was against her cheek between her shoulder and her head, the pistol still on Rooker.

"I wrote it in. He was in . . ." Anders was checking his books. "Eleven twenty p.m."

"And he hasn't left?"

"Hasn't left. Not unless he scaled down your balcony and jumped. Would've seen him if he took the stairs or the elevator down."

"*Never again*, Anders. I don't care how well you think I know someone—never let anyone up to my apartment again."

Tess hung up, still staring at Rooker.

"Are you okay?" he asked. He knew the answer.

"No, I'm sure as shit not."

"I'll tell you what you want to know."

Tess tossed Rooker the keys and let him unlock the door. He opened it and put the lights on. The cushion of the couch barely budged beneath his weight.

"Don't move," she said. Tess walked into the bedroom, found what she needed, and tossed it to him. He caught his manuscript and looked down at it.

"I've read it," he said.

The P226 was still in her hand. "Did you kill her?"

"It's a story. Same as any other story. A little truth and mostly lies. That's why they call it fiction."

"I need to believe you."

"What else do you want to know?"

"Danny Ross. Did you try to kill him?"

"What? No."

"What about the email you typed up, saying how you wanted to kill him."

Rooker paused, looking at her.

"You hacked into my computer?" He smiled. "Langston, I should say. You had her do it."

"I did."

"That's against the law."

"Sue me. Did you try to kill him?"

"No. Never. I had to go to therapy as a kid. They all wanted to see if little Rooker Lindström had Daddy's genes. They wanted to see if I'd become like him. They told me to express my feelings; the email, that was me expressing. The story was meant to be just that: a story. Danny jerked me around, said we had a *New York Times* bestseller in our midst, big book deal, big payday, and then he dumped me. That's it."

"So why are there no pillows? Are you worried you'll kill someone with them?"

He hesitated again. "My father . . . I had just won a tournament, was feeling my oats. Same night, he was screaming at my mother. I clocked him hard behind the ear. It was a good shot, not a glancing blow. Hard. Everything I had. The son of a bitch didn't even stagger. He turned toward me like the Terminator. I can still smell the alcohol on his breath. He pulled a pillowcase over my head, cinched it closed with something, tight around my neck. Then he started walloping me. I blacked out. When I woke up, my ear was still bleeding."

He opened his phone and showed Tess a photo of Astrid Thompson. "She's our missing victim. And this"—he pulled a folded paper from his pocket—"this is a list of the other detectives on my father's case."

"What good does that do us?"

"I think someone on this list is linked to these killings."

"Do me a favor?" Tess put her gun back in its holster, unclipped it all from her waist.

"Yeah."

"Go to the station. Or go home."

"Got it."

Chapter 28

No one was at the station. Not even Langston. Rooker settled into an empty desk and kicked his feet up on a chair. He opened a new tab and put the list of the six detectives on top of the numeric pad on the far right. He wasn't sure yet how he'd find a list of all their living male relatives, but he started by trying to find a current address for each of the surviving team members. He even looked up William Sadler, hoping to find a widow or kids still in the area.

In an hour and a half, Rooker was able to dig up three of the addresses. He wanted to ask Langston for help, but knowing she hacked into his computer made him feel betrayed—even if she was just doing her job. He'd get to the rest of the detectives on his own. Still, he sat there, pulling up each of the recent murders, cycling through them one at a time, reading the newspaper articles on each, trying to find something that maybe he'd overlooked. He'd profiled the killer initially as someone who didn't care for theatrics, someone calculated and efficient. But things had changed, or maybe he'd been mistaken all along. The killer was taunting Rooker—he'd shown them he was watching them. He'd been inside Rooker's home and left him a nice little gift basket. He wanted them to find the bodies just the way he'd left them. Rooker knew there would be another one to find soon.

There was something there, the artwork angle. The BTK Killer would draw women in bondage. The police found his illustrations when he was captured. In prison, he'd mail drawings to his followers like they were postcards, until the prison put a stop to it. Rooker researched other serial murderers who in some form made art. He closed out of everything when they made him queasy.

When he couldn't think of anything to type, the blinking cursor roared laughter in his face.

The morning crept along, the station quiet as a library, and by eight thirty, Rooker was in and out of consciousness. His head drooped and bobbed—but it jerked upward when he heard Xander clear his throat. He took that as his cue, walked outside where the wind crept through his jacket, and called a cab.

"Where to?" the driver said without turning his head.

Rooker consulted his list of surviving detectives and gave him the address of the nearest house. It was Oscar Jensen's. Jensen had left the department a few years prior at sixty-one. There was a newspaper article about his retirement. He'd apparently never pushed to move up the chain. When asked if in all his years as a detective he'd ever seen anything similar to the Gunner Lindström case, he didn't comment. Rooker thought this one would be a waste of his time, but he couldn't rule it out.

The taxi dropped him off at a traditional two-story house. It was small, barnyard-red with white trim, a front porch big enough to fit a couple of chairs, but there was only the one. The rock foundation was cracking, same as the steps he climbed. Rooker knocked on the door; no one came to it. He tried the doorbell, but it must've been broken or disconnected. He went to bang on the door a few more times, but it slivered open before his knuckles rapped a second time.

"What is it?" the old man snorted. His brow furrowed in curiosity. Oscar Jensen reeked of old tobacco and boiled eggs. Below a wrinkled scowl, white and gray stubble looked like it had been left a few five o'clocks ago. Dark circles stained the underarms and hem of his plain white T-shirt, which was smeared with oil or grease. Rooker glanced around the cracked door and saw the man was holding the end of a pump-action shotgun.

"I'm sorry to bother you," Rooker said.

"Then why bother me?" He stared into Rooker's eyes like he hated him, but Rooker figured it was the world he hated.

"Mr. Jensen, Oscar Jensen?"

"Who's asking?"

"I'm sort of consulting with the Itasca County police. I wanted to ask you a couple of questions if you don't mind. It shouldn't take long."

"I've been retired three years; what could I possibly answer?"

"It's a new case, similar to one you worked in the nineties." Rooker paused. He was leading him, something the old man had probably done to suspects a hundred times during interrogations. Rooker noticed the sour in his face, and the man's hand start to ball into a fist before it stopped and opened.

"You'll be leaving now." He started to push the door shut, but Rooker's foot slipped between the crack.

"I'll shoot your fucking foot off if you don't move it."

Rooker kept his foot there for a second before he pulled it back. He believed the old man would do it. The door slammed shut. It didn't lock. The man probably would've liked him to walk in and give him an excuse to shoot. He'd plead self-defense after he riddled Rooker's body full of twelve-gauge rounds.

"I need to know about the Gunner Lindström case," Rooker shouted through the door. "I need help catching this guy!" He watched the old man through the glass in the door walk away, shotgun down at his side. He never turned around, just disappeared into another room. Rooker walked back down the steps to the taxi.

"That was fast," the driver said.

"Thanks," Rooker said sarcastically. *This is going to be an expensive day,* he thought. He was basically renting out a taxi driver. He'd get the money back from Tess or the department. He recited the next address, and the driver typed it in.

"If you want to sit up front, you can," he said.

Rooker looked at him in the mirror. "Just drive," he told him before turning his head to look at Oscar Jensen's home.

Rooker felt like he'd already struck out. His day had just begun, and the very first one would rather shoot him in the foot than talk about Gunner Lindström.

The car started and pulled away from the curb. Rooker left his seat belt unbuckled, pushed his back up against the door, and slid his legs up on the seat. He opened what he had on Billy Schultz—saw an old, pixelated photo of him from when he was working Gunner's case. Rooker lifted his head, stared at the gray upholstery, sighed, and shut his eyes.

If this second visit was another bust, he was looking for the nearest pub.

PART II

Chapter 29

December 14

Stay in bed, or Mommy will end up dead.

Ines Claesson's big brown eyes nearly leaped out of her tiny skull. She was having another bad dream. There was a man watching her. His voice was scary. She couldn't see his face, just the black baseball cap pulled low and something shiny, pointy in his hand. But that wasn't what woke her. It was the crack, like a tree branch snapping outside her second-story window.

Her lips parted, but her throat went bone-dry. Nothing. Not a word, not a single peep. There were no car engines buzzing by, no wind batting at the shutters.

"Mommy?"

There was no answer.

Fear rose in the pit of her chest, colored her pale cheeks. For what felt like an eternity, she stared at the shadow huddled in the corner of her room, then looked to the window and back. When nothing happened, Ines slipped out of her twin bed, her feet cold the instant they grazed the floor. Pink and purple stars spun around the room and now across her blue-striped pajamas. *Night-lights are for babies.* She'd pleaded that she was too old for one. Now she was happy her mother hadn't listened.

She snuck out into the hallway, a dash of yellow light seeping from the living room. She was eight and much too old, she knew, to be afraid of the dark.

She walked downstairs, her small feet taking up not even half of each step, the soles of her feet like ice against the hardwood. Emma Claesson, her mother, was fast asleep in the recliner; she often fell asleep like that. Her snores were boisterous and long, very little silence filling in the gaps. Her head was turned awkwardly. You'd think her neck had been snapped if not for the noise coming from her throat and the teakettle piping from her nose. It was only the two of them in the house, and her mommy was a night owl. She'd stay up late after putting Ines to bed and watch television until she crashed. She'd often awaken to the sounds of Ines in the morning, to her daughter tugging on her clothing wanting breakfast. Usually, it was just a microwaved Jimmy Dean breakfast biscuit or a warm Toaster Strudel on a paper towel.

Ines tiptoed her way to the kitchen and reached up as high as she could on the counter for a clean glass, which she filled halfway with tap water. Loud gulps rushed cold down her throat until the glass emptied, her feet ready to be back beneath the warmth of her sheets. As she walked, the living room came into view. But her feet stopped suddenly. There was something outside. Her eyes opened wider, like they were saying *ahh*, but she couldn't make anything out. It was near the big tree in the front yard. She walked over to the door and stopped. Her little fingers flicked the porch light on, and she stared out the window. The bulb needed to be replaced; all it did was enhance the silhouette of what looked like a woman, long hair and a petite frame sitting on the tree swing.

Her fingertips touched the doorknob but stopped short of turning it. Instead, Ines approached her mother, tugged on the sleeve of her shirt.

"Mommy," she whispered a step away from her ear.

"Hmm . . . ," her mother murmured.

"There's a woman outside."

"What does she want?" Her eyes were still closed. She figured it was a solicitor or something. They'd go away when no one came to the door.

"She's out there on the swing; I think she's cold. But she isn't really moving."

Her mother opened her eyes and looked at her, confused.

Emma Claesson cleared her throat. "She's on the swing?"

"Yes, look."

◆　◆　◆

Emma looked at the digital clock on the cable box. It was four in the morning. Why was a woman in her yard? She looked up at the wall clock. It was a traditional solid wood and veneer case with a walnut finish. It was old; she'd gotten it from her mother when she passed away. She grew up with it and by now she never even heard the chime that rung out every hour. Nor was she aware of the pendulum swing. But she looked at it, ignored the dust caked along the carved accents. She read the metal hands and saw the same time.

She closed the recliner and stood up, rubbed at her eyes, and looked outside. There was someone there. She walked over by the door, pulled her heavy jacket from the coatrack, and zipped it up. She stood her toppled boots upright, and she slipped her feet into them.

"Stay here, sweetie."

She unlocked the door and turned the handle. The night was numbing. White flakes were still coming down. Her feet sank ankle-deep into the snow.

"Excuse me, miss," she said, crossing her arms over her chest to burrow in some warmth. She had no idea what this woman was doing. But she shivered as she trekked on toward the tree, toward the woman sitting there. "It's freezing—you need to get inside." The woman either didn't hear her or was ignoring her. She didn't want the woman in her house, but she said it anyway. As her feet sank closer and closer, she realized the woman wasn't wearing any clothing.

Jesus!

She started undoing her jacket as quickly as possible, started jogging with staggered steps, nearly falling into the snow. She got in front of her, ready to sprawl the jacket over her, and looked up into her face. The woman was dead.

"Oh my God!" She turned to the doorway and saw her daughter standing behind the glass. "Stay there!" Running back to the house, she stumbled forward and caught herself with a handful of snow. When she made it inside, she slammed the door shut behind her and locked everything.

"What's wrong, Mommy? Who is she?"

"Come with me, hurry!" She grabbed her daughter's hand and ran to the bathroom, only stopping to grab the telephone. She dialed the police and got the dispatcher. Then she turned the light on and locked the door behind them.

"There's a woman in my yard! My daughter saw her through the window."

"Slow down, ma'am. What state is she in?"

"Mommy, I have to pee!"

"Shh, hold on, baby." She turned away from her daughter; her voice trembled to a low, frightened whisper. "I have my daughter with me, so I can't say. Please just hurry." She gave her address and was instructed to stay inside the bathroom with the door locked, not to come out until police arrived. "It's okay, honey, go ahead."

But Ines had already started going.

Chapter 30

December 14

The siren cried two lamenting tones, high-pitched howls that bled into the dark morning. While Tess cruised through an intersection, she thought she could see Rooker stomp down on his imaginary brake. Shadows conquered the world above and hovered over them, watching.

They'd all been ripped from sleep when the call came in. But the team had scrambled in record time. Even the patrolmen guarding Evelyn's house had had some excitement: getting Rooker up, dressed, and to the station to rendezvous with Tess.

The killer had staged victim seven in a suburban yard. When they'd all assembled, Keene had voiced Tess's worst fear: there would be media everywhere by first light. They had limited time to secure the scene before neighbors started stirring, kids headed out to school.

When they pulled up to a cookie-cutter street, Tess caught a glimpse of a blue tent in the front yard that read POLICE in white letters. Her hand shielded her eyes from what looked like an EDM rave. Blurring red and blue lights flashed bright in the darkness. There were at least six or seven squad cars, their roofs lit like barrel fires. It was as if a matchbook had struck the whole block.

Police taped off the street. Detectives milled around and tried to keep everyone inside. All of it silent.

The snow climbed at least a foot high. Tess got out of the car. The morning held a strong winter smell laced with exhaust fumes. She inhaled both. Her fingers trapped the jacket zipper, pulled it up to where it caught the skin of her throat. As she walked up, the cold writhed around her ankles. The white was drawing her down nearly shin-deep. There were two sets of similar footprints: one going from the house to the body and a messier set going from the body back to the house.

Where part of the street was taped off, a few cameramen and reporters tried to push their way as close as they could.

"Back," she told them. "Not past the tape."

Nosy neighbors stood on their porches, peeked through window blinds. They all wanted to see the main attraction: the dead woman.

"Wait here," she told Rooker before she disappeared inside the tent.

The victim was sitting slumped over on the swing, the snow like pier water bobbing inches from her bare toes. The nails were painted coral blue.

She was paler than white, with long hair like a grungy black cat. Tess couldn't see her face. The victim's head drooped toward the ground. When the tent opening shifted, shadows danced across her wide-set breasts. Black zip ties dug into her wrists and bound her to the swing's ropes. The rope was black and tattered, each end met by a stainless-steel quick link and a strong hitch knot, or at least she thought that's the knot it was. The wooden board she sat on was long and thick. Tess looked up and saw the rope high in the air fastened over a chunky tree limb.

Tess gloved up and knelt in front of her, looking into her face. When she saw her, Tess's knees went weak, plunging her deeper into the cold. She steeled herself, or else she would have stumbled backward into the snow. A fistful of its cold crunched in her palm, the knuckles of her gloves coated in it. The woman's eyes were still open, her eyelashes frozen. Her blue lips parted like she was trying to speak to Tess.

"Same MO?" she asked Martin.

"Aside from the change in hair color—to a T," he said. "Knife to the sternum. Pulled the calling card from her mouth already, got it bagged." He handed the landscape photo to her in its evidence bag. She held it up to the light—an old black-and-white photograph of what seemed to be the house she was currently standing outside.

"Don't tell me no one saw anything," she said.

"Then I guess I won't tell you."

"*Christ.* In this neighborhood? No one—not one person—sees a *goddamn thing*?"

"I dunno what to tell you, boss."

"What about the homeowner?"

"Mother's name is Emma Claesson, daughter Ines." He pronounced it *ee-nez.* "The kid saw a shape on the swing outside. She woke her mother up, and the mother came out here, freaked out, and ran back"— he pointed to the two sets of prints—"and then locked her and the kid in the bathroom and called 911."

"Get Xander and Sterling on missing persons, see if we have anyone who fits the vic's description," said Tess. "We need to ID her."

She poked her head out and was relieved that Rooker had listened to her for once. He was down by the street, bouncing on his toes and blowing air into his hands. Tess performed a balancing act on her way down the yard.

"Well?" she said. He looked confused and didn't answer right away. "I brought you along so you could tell me why the killer would put a dead girl here. Any ideas?"

"It's the house Gunner grew up in," he said after a minute.

The front porch light was still on. She looked in the windows and saw a woman speaking to Sterling. As she lifted her head higher, she noticed a little girl watching her from the upstairs window. Tess forced a smile and waved at her. A small hand lifted, and she waved back. Tess went to the house and opened the door. She said, "Excuse me," and she ushered Rooker along with her.

"How are you with kids?" she asked him.

"Well, I had one."

They went up the wooden staircase, turned left, and found the little girl still gazing outside.

"You don't need to see that," Tess said, trying to steer her attention away from the police and the tent.

"She's dead," the girl said.

"Yes, she is," Tess said sadly. The sadness was more for Ines, for having to witness the dead woman, than for the dead woman herself. "I like your room."

"Thanks," Ines said.

Tess sat on the edge of her tiny bed, glancing around the room. It was a lot like the room she had grown up in. Soft whites and pinks, polka dots, a miniature dollhouse. On the rug, stuffed animals sat in a circle like they were waiting for someone to sit in the center. Judging by her reaction to the scene outside, she figured Ines had outgrown the girlish touches—much like Tess had at her age. She saw the girl's name in big block letters across her wall.

"Ines? Pretty name."

"Thank you."

"You're the one who saw her outside, right?"

"Yes."

"Wasn't it dark out?" Rooker asked. "You must have some very good eyes."

"I saw a shape. Near the tree."

Tess followed up. "Was it moving?"

"No. When I turned on the light, I saw her. She was sitting on the swing."

"Did you see anything else? Did you hear anything outside? Is that why you woke up?" Rooker asked.

The girl's voice was soft, her shoulder up against the windowsill. "I thought I heard something, like a branch. And then a man's voice. I went downstairs because I was thirsty."

"Was your dad home?"

"It's just Mommy and me."

Suddenly, Tess felt a rush of cold run through her.

"This man's voice," she said, leaning closer to Ines. "What did it sound like?"

"Like his," she said, pointing at Rooker. "But softer."

"Did you hear anything the man said?"

"Stay in bed, or Mommy will end up dead."

Tess looked over at Rooker, then back to Ines. Her face looked sad. Scared. *Was the killer in the house?* No little girl would make that rhyme up—she was certain.

Tess looked out the window at the police. The ground was a frothy wave of sea-foam white, an enormous sheet of printer paper three-hole-punched by dirt-smudged boots.

"Ines," Tess said to her. "Why don't you come downstairs with us for a bit. Okay?"

On the way back downstairs, Tess saw Sterling standing over a coffee table talking to the mother. She pulled him aside for a moment and walked back out into the cold. Looked past all the moving parts: Xander, Cole, and Martin, gloved, setting down markers.

"Did we clear the house?" she asked Sterling.

"No, we didn't have reason—"

"Do it. Get everyone in here to clear it, but don't scare the mother and daughter."

"What's going on?"

"The daughter heard a man's voice: *'Stay in bed, or Mommy will end up dead.'* I think the killer might have been in her bedroom."

At that, Tess watched Vic Sterling gather the rest of the team along with the other officers standing by. They moved inside the house.

◆ ◆ ◆

Rooker watched about eight figures move like a quiet storm inside the home. Tess brought him over to see the victim. *Finally.* But the moment the flap opened and he ducked inside, he felt sick.

Her head twisted toward him. Slowly. She looked at him behind eyes of murky black water. Tears ran like oil beneath them. And then her hand broke free from the rope, and she pointed at Rooker. He shut his eyes. His heart turned to ice. The cold spread through him like an infection. His eyes snapped open. And she was back to normal. Frozen. Dead. A shaky breath clouded weakly in front of him. He twitched like he had been jerked awake by Tess's shoulder against his.

"We'll get everyone out of here fast," she said. "Shit."

"What?"

"We need another ME now."

She was right. Rooker hadn't thought about it. He suddenly remembered Walter Erickson strung up like a marionette.

"I'll have to call Isaiah," she groaned.

"What's wrong with him?"

"Isaiah Hayes? Nothing. Just gives me the heebie-jeebies. Talks to the bodies."

"So he qualifies as a suspect," Rooker said as a joke. Tess didn't find it funny.

Chapter 31

December 14

Rooker and Tess were the first two to pull back into the station garage. They made their way into the office and through the detective desks, only to find Langston taking her jacket off, ready to perch down in her chair.

Millie Langston's head turned so fast, her ponytail whipped the corner of her eye.

Rooker watched the team start to file in one by one, first Keene, followed by Sterling, Cole, and last, and in Rooker's mind least, Xander. Xander's eyes trailed Rooker like he was a spider he was waiting to squash with one blood-bursting blow. Eventually he sat down behind his desk and turned away. Xander was too hotheaded, too impulsive, too dense to be on the list. Yet for some reason, he was still there.

When everyone was in, Tess commanded the floor. "Xander and Vic, let me know if you find an MP that ID's our girl. Martin and Cole, see if you can find a working camera near the Claesson home—convenience stores, bars, traffic cameras—look for anything suspicious, check license plates and make and models around the time we think the victim was staged. Langston, you're on the phones. I have to go see Isaiah."

"Hayes?" Xander chirped. "Why do we need that freak?"

"Well, if you hadn't noticed, Walter Erickson is dead. We need someone experienced to examine the body. Isaiah works fast."

"Can we be certain he won't have sex with the body?" Xander pelvic thrusted in his office chair.

If Tess's look could kill, Xander would be dead on the floor. Rooker thought he saw Sterling and Keene crack smiles. He couldn't see Cole's face.

"Is any of this funny to you?" She paused but didn't expect an answer. Instead, she waited for his expression to change, and suddenly he looked a bit nervous. "There's a guy out here killing women. Walter Erickson's death—*thanks to Isaiah*—has been ruled a homicide. So we can assume he killed our medical examiner. He's probably the one who shot at me. What part of that is funny to you?"

Xander didn't say a word. No one did. Rooker could see Tess's face burning pinkish red.

"I'm headed to see Isaiah, hear what he has to say. He said he'd take a look at the body today, so maybe his autopsy report gives us something that helps us ID her. Rooker," Tess said.

He looked at her and realized it meant that she wanted him to go with. He caught up beside her, and the two of them walked out the doors to her car.

They drove to Hibbing, nearly thirty-five minutes with light traffic. The stench of rich leather and old coffee lingered. Tess bit the upper portion of her bottom lip, her eyes distant, deep in thought. She didn't speak. Rooker tried to focus on the soothing whoosh of oncoming cars. It seemed so long ago that she had appeared at his doorstep. Now Rooker had started to measure time in bodies, the women piling up like minutes and days and weeks.

The car stopped outside a short skyscraper. Aegir Security was a stone-beige tower, more jailhouse-gray now with the dark tear streaks crying down it. Massive picture windows bordered the building. Isaiah Hayes worked on the bottom level, privately contracted by some organization that dealt with forensic pathology.

Rooker followed Tess's lead around the back, down a ramp to an entrance, and into a private elevator that looked like it would transport you to your worst nightmare. The chrome panel had warped. The metal button engravings were all scratched off. Black Sharpie numbers and letters were scribbled beside them. She pressed the button for the basement level of the building, and they went down a floor before it stopped. The doors pig-slaughter-squealed open.

Rooker and Tess stepped out of the elevator into a flickering corridor. Rooker followed her down the hall to the right, large square windows overlooking an autopsy room. A man stood hunched inside wearing a white overcoat, hovering over a body. A pair of oversize bifocals with an elastic strap wrapped around snug to the back of his mostly bald crown. Isaiah Hayes resembled a cadaver meant for his table; gaunt, discolored complexion; a strong jawline above a pencil-thin, deathly white neck; and an enormous Adam's apple that looked like part of his skeleton was poking through his skin. Rooker could see his lips move. Then the man stopped. His head didn't turn, but Rooker could see him looking at him out of his peripheral. The man stood still for what felt like a very long ten seconds. Then he turned, peered down over the top of his glasses, and forced a human smile.

He walked over to the double doors and backed into them, poked his head out, and said, "Tess Harlow. Welcome. Please come in." Then went back inside. Rooker and Tess glanced at each other and followed suit.

"Please put on a pair of gloves," he said robotically. Rooker and Tess did as they were told. He was standing over a body that wasn't their victim. It was lying on a stainless-steel rectangle, a table built for autopsies. Rooker moved to the next table, where a white sheet was tucked pristinely over a body. Isaiah took the end of the sheet in his fingertips, fattened and pale as grubs, and gently pulled it back like he was trying not to wake the dead.

He stared at her.

When the sheet was down far enough, Rooker could see the ligature marks on her wrists, the discoloration on her neck. She'd been strangled.

"Asphyxiation?" Rooker asked.

Isaiah glimpsed over his shoulder at him and paused. Rooker couldn't read the expression on his face. "Good eye. She was bound; you can see here and here." Isaiah pointed to the markings on her wrists. "Where she tried to pull herself free. Standard zip ties. The thin indentations on the skin, rectangular and flat, not any sort of rope or cable."

"What about her throat?" Tess asked.

"No sign of a rope or anything. No garrote. I believe he did it with his hands."

"He did *that* with his hands?" Tess sounded put off.

"If you look here—" Isaiah ran his finger along her neck, along the throat. "The carotid arteries, meaning the major blood vessels that would carry blood to her brain, they've collapsed. Not only that"—he ran his finger along her again—"her trachea, or her windpipe, where our air travels from the throat to the lungs, is crushed.

"It's possible that the trachea was broken while she was still alive; it's also possible the victim was either unconscious or deceased before it was broken. If she was still alive when it happened, she wouldn't have been able to resist her attacker anymore. In a lot of cases, the victim will begin to convulse, so that's a possibility. But what is most fascinating"—he opened the victim's eyelid—"is the petechial hemorrhaging in the eye. Though petechiae don't necessarily prove or disprove strangulation, the severity in this instance is what was concerning."

"How so?" asked Tess.

"Well, constant pressure, in this case strangulation for thirty seconds, would produce petechiae. But due to the severity, see the red and brown, the purple, I think your victim was strangled for several minutes."

"So even after she was dead," Tess said.

"Correct. He strangled her long after she was dead."

Chapter 32

December 14

Rooker and Tess left Isaiah with the body, hoping that his final report would help them find clues to ID her. But the chances weren't looking good. It would take somewhere in the ballpark of four to eight weeks to get DNA or dental records. The hope now was that someone reported the woman missing—maybe they could find out where the killer had taken her from. It could help them narrow down their grid a little bit, but that wasn't likely to happen. There were too many bodies now, piling up like trash in winter city streets. Rooker was sure that's how the killer probably thought of them, as trash. Until he stripped them naked and put them on display in his sick and twisted artwork.

The day was getting late. The streetlights and window lamps started going on. Among the trees and their bare branches, the lights began to cast sinuous gray shadows all around. Rooker unfolded the list in his pocket, studied the names again. He opened his phone and dialed Peter Sundgren.

"Hello." It was Helen again.

"Does Peter ever get up and answer the phone?"

She laughed. "Hi, Rooker. No, his butt is mostly glued to that chair unless he's outside. Let me get him."

Rooker waited, walking back and forth as the gray sky blackened. A minute later, he heard Peter.

"Yello."

"Peter, it's Rooker."

"I have some things I've written down. Ready?"

Rooker had a thought. "Actually, can I come by? I'd like you to meet someone." He knew Tess wasn't going to like it.

"Sure, I'll see you soon."

Tess was sitting in the car waiting for Rooker to get in. The window was rolled down, and she stared at him with eyes that needed him to hurry up.

"Can you get in already? Jesus."

Rooker got in and shut the door behind him. "I want you to come meet Sundgren with me."

"What, right now?"

"It'll be quick. Maybe he'll see a connection; maybe there's something similar to when he worked Gunner's case. You trusted me, sort of: a washed-up crime reporter in his underwear who caught one killer. This guy is overqualified if you ask me."

"Just give me the address." She exhaled an annoyed sigh.

An hour later, they pulled up to Sundgren's house, a box of files in tow. Rooker could see that Tess felt he was wasting her time, that this was the wildest goose they'd chased yet. He led her up the walkway, and Helen opened the door. Her face was bright and charming with crow's-feet at the corners of her eyes and a few wrinkles like permanent dimples around her mouth.

She welcomed them into her home and took Rooker's hand like she'd known him for years. They made their way over to Peter, still seated in his chair, and saw a handwritten list on the end table beside him.

"Shall we?"

"Peter, this is Detective Tess Harlow; she's running lead on the case."

"Very nice to meet you, Detective." He shook her hand, and Tess and Rooker sat side by side on the sofa.

"Where do you want to start?" Sundgren asked Rooker.

"Let's go down the list, starting with Oscar Jensen—guy threatened to shoot my foot off if I didn't move it."

Peter smiled. "Jensen was the pit bull of the team—you're lucky to still have your foot. He was honorably discharged from the army. Surprising, because he had zero regard for rules or chain of command, was contemptuous as could be—would take a grudge to the grave with him if he could. Despite that, he was a damn good detective. He never married, never had kids.

"Jeff Davies was the opposite: a stickler for rules."

"Davies had a stroke," Rooker said.

"*I heard.* He was a good man . . . sad, what happened. Davies did everything by procedure, possibly to the degree of being obsessive-compulsive. I heard he fell in the kitchen, and his daughter, Ruth, found him a day later. Now she takes care of him, along with a caregiver."

"When I tried to ask him about the Gunner case, it was the only time his face changed; his eyes bulged. I think he was surprised anyone still cared."

"There's Billy Schultz—he was a rookie. He was twentysomething, barely finished puberty. He was tall and lanky, never saw him eat a bite of food. Jensen would mess with him, call him Zit or Pimple, sometimes Billy 'the Boil' Schultz. He was a nice kid, worked usually with Davies, followed him around like a dog."

"He's working security at Woodland Bank. He's married now, no children."

"And then William Sadler." Sundgren paused. "William was my number two. One of my closest friends. He died from pancreatic cancer. He was married to Selma; they had two boys. Haven't seen them in years."

"How old would you guess the boys are now?"

"Well, they would be somewhere around thirty or thirty-five. The younger boy passed away, tragic. Helen and I went to the funeral."

Rooker knew he'd have to check it out.

"What about Carl Meltzer?"

Peter stalled before he spoke. "So, this is where it gets odd."

"How so?"

"You think your killer is somehow connected to one of these people, correct?"

Rooker said, "Yes," before Tess could cut in and give the spiel about it being an ongoing investigation.

"Carl was always a nice man, great colleague. He was friendly and outgoing. His wife couldn't conceive; I remember him telling me early on. And one day, a boy came to the station with Carl. The boy was an orphan, had apparently witnessed things no boy should see, Carl never said what. But he became the boy's foster parent. He said the boy wouldn't say much, mostly one-word answers. But when Carl talked to him about his cases, specifically Gunner's case, the boy wouldn't stop talking. He was fascinated by it."

"We need to find Carl Meltzer," Rooker said. "I actually wanted to show you something; we made copies. Would you mind taking a look at these? Tell me if you see anything, anything at all. Whether it relates to the old case, whether you think it has any sort of significance."

"Sure, gives me more reason to stay in my chair."

Rooker and Tess rocked forward from where they'd sunken into the cushions and stood. "Thanks. You have my number if you find anything."

He and Tess walked out onto the street, the air even colder after sitting in a room sweltering like a summer California day. They scurried to the road and sat in her car. While Rooker put off touching the metal of the seat belt—what he would call the Siberian subarctic—he listened in on Tess's call.

There was only one ring before he heard Millie Langston's voice answer, "Hey, boss."

"Millie, I need the address you found for Carl Meltzer." As she waited on the line, she blew warm air into the doughnut hole of her fist. Rooker watched her as she turned the heat dial to the farthest red notch. A few moments later, Millie came back over the line with the address.

"Thanks, Millie." Tess hung up and took the car out of park.

◆ ◆ ◆

They pulled up to a split-level on a dead-end street. The Meltzer house was quaint, white siding with a screened-in porch and a bit of dead vine draped over the siding. A two-car garage attached on the right, bordered by dead hedges and telephone wires running to the house just below a tree's branches. The two of them got out and walked up to the house. Tess knocked on the screen door, what sounded like a tin rattling, her badge digging tight in her hand.

"Carl Meltzer?"

"Yes?" His figure was dark, shadowed by the black netting in the screen door. They could feel his eyes watching.

"Detective Tess Harlow." She held the badge up for him to see. "May we come in?"

"What is this about?"

"It's an ongoing investigation. We need to speak with you."

Meltzer opened the door, moved aside, and let them in. When Rooker stepped into the living area, he was met with several tiny faces hanging on the wall. A woman, whom he assumed to be Meltzer's wife, was watching warily from a distance.

"Are they all foster kids?" Rooker asked as he stared at the wall of photos.

"Yes, they're children we've taken in over the years."

"That's actually why we're here. We're looking for someone. He was a boy when you fostered him—it was during the Gunner Lindström case."

He watched the man's eyes light up. Rooker wondered why. He glanced over to the man's wife, an expression more like shock on her face.

"You've found Henry?" the man said, hopeful.

"I don't understand," Tess said. "Is that his name? Do you have his full name?"

"I never knew his full name. There was an incident when he was young that kept his records sealed. And the boy never said. But you've found him?"

"Mr. Meltzer, when's the last time you saw Henry?"

"Right after we caught Gunner, he disappeared. He didn't have many things, but what he did have was gone one night. He never came back."

"It's why we've never moved out of this godforsaken house," the woman said bitterly. "He always thought that boy might come back."

"He was troubled," the man said firmly.

"Troubled? That boy was the devil reincarnated." She walked closer, showed the two visitors her right hand. Rooker saw a deep, heavy scar running at least four, maybe five inches along the inside.

"He did that? Why?"

"He did that because I took his drawings away from him. The boy would draw the darkest things, dead people, dead women. One of them was me. And then when I grabbed the drawing from him, he bit into my hand, clawed at it like a damn wolf. Eight stitches. They said if he bit any deeper, he would have gotten a nerve."

"The boy had seen things when he was younger," Meltzer interjected. "He only knew how to respond with violence. It was something I was trying to help him with. Henry didn't talk much. I was trying to get him to open up—to talk to me."

"He was Carl's charity case," the wife scoffed.

"He wasn't my charity case. I wanted to help him."

Tess spoke up. "So the boy was more talkative when you discussed the case with him, correct?"

"Yes, but—"

"What would he say? What would he talk to you about?"

"He would ask me how a man was capable of so much evil. He would ask me if it were possible for someone to keep the evil inside, not let it out. If the evil would take over eventually, consume you. Things like that. I was trying to help him."

Mrs. Meltzer muttered, "The only thing that could help him was a psych ward. The day that boy went missing was the best and scariest day of my life. I prayed he'd never come back."

Rooker broke his silence. "You thought he'd kill you?"

"Sure as hell did."

"When did the boy go missing?" Tess asked.

"It was the winter," Mrs. Meltzer said. "It had to be—"

"February," Carl Meltzer interrupted. "February 1997."

"So you don't have a full name on the boy? No way for us to find him?"

"All they ever told us was that his name was Henry and that he'd witnessed his mother's death."

"Do you think he killed her?" asked Rooker.

Mrs. Meltzer's answer was immediate. "Yes. Drowned that poor boy too, I tell you."

Carl glowered at her, displeased. "No, I don't think so."

"What? What boy?" Tess asked.

"Selma's boy," she said.

"Sadler?" asked Tess.

"She's been saying that shit for years," Carl said. "She thinks aliens abducted her brother Adam too."

"Did you ever discuss the confidential details of the Gunner Lindström case with Henry? Stuff that wouldn't have been on the news?" Tess asked.

Rooker knew the answer to Tess's question based on Carl Meltzer's sheepish expression.

"Not in great detail, only basics. But I did find him reading through the files I'd brought home. I'd woken up in the middle of the night, saw the light on in his room. He was reading them."

"Just some light reading before bed, the little murderer." Mrs. Meltzer had had enough. She folded her arms beneath her chest and walked out of the room.

"The boy wasn't all bad, just troubled."

"I'm sure people still say the same thing about Ted Bundy," Mrs. Meltzer thundered from the other room.

Rooker and Tess left Meltzer's home thinking the couple probably wouldn't be speaking to each other for the rest of the night. Now the most important thing—they needed to find a boy named Henry who had gone through the foster system.

"Where do we go from here?" Rooker said as he settled into the passenger seat. "We have a real suspect now and no way to find him."

"We'll find him. He can't have stayed off the grid for more than twenty years. But we'll check out Sadler too just to be safe. Maybe the wife or older son has something."

An hour later, they pulled up to the Sadler residence. It had been a long day. All Rooker wanted was to go home and sleep. But his day was only about to get longer.

It was a two-story Craftsman on a corner lot with dark-brown vinyl siding; Rooker could only imagine it appeared invisible in the dead of night. He and Tess walked up to the door, stood on the mat before it, and rang the bell. Maybe thirty seconds later, he could see movement in the entrance's glass cutout. The porch light came on, the buzzing glass bulb lit, followed by the smell of burned flies and gnats, like they were immolated by fire. It opened slowly.

"Yes," a fairly tall woman said. Selma Sadler didn't seem old aside from slightly graying hair. Her voice sounded young, suspicious.

"Ma'am, I'm Detective Tess Harlow. This is my colleague Rooker. May we come in?"

He wasn't surprised that she didn't use his last name. He wouldn't say it either, if he didn't have to.

"Is this about the break-in?"

"The break-in?" Tess repeated.

"A few nights ago, the back door was busted. Someone broke the glass and came in."

"Right," she said. "Could you show us?"

Rooker and Tess followed the woman through her home. The inside was cozy; it had a homey feel to it. It was the kind of place that made you want hot cocoa, wrapped fireside in a blanket. The woman led them to the back door, where she'd put a piece of cardboard over the missing glass and taped it tightly against the door.

"I noticed the glass inside and saw the window broken. Then I called the police."

"Did they take anything?"

"Everything was a mess in the storage closet—I found it wide open. That's where my husband kept his old case files. He was a detective, like you. When he passed, they boxed his things up, and my son and I put the rest of the junk there too."

"Do you mind if we take a look?"

"Not at all."

Rooker and Tess followed her upstairs to a room with a small storage closet in the corner. She turned and pulled the bolt that locked the door. The latch was flimsy, nearly falling off. She gave a good pull on the door a few times, and it pried loose. The boxes were old, not in very good shape after they'd been tossed around.

"So everything of his should be here from when he was a detective?"

"As far as I know. I stored everything in here, never took anything out of it."

Rooker grabbed the pair of gloves Tess handed him and struggled to get them over his fingers. The glove snapped short of his wrist. He dragged the boxes out hunchbacked, slapped webs from his arms, and coughed up dust. When he finished pulling them out, the boxes sat in the center of the room. He lifted the cardboard lids one by one. Each time there was a scratchy pop and papers inside in disarray. It looked like a child had splashed around in the boxes and stuffed everything back inside when a parent was coming. Rooker started pulling things out; he wasn't sure yet what it was he was searching for. After twenty minutes of sifting through papers, he thought about what he'd seen in the boxes at Sundgren's home.

"His service weapon," Rooker said out loud.

"Yes, I never wanted a gun in the house. Even when my son told me to keep it because it was William's. But I left it in there, never touched it."

"No, it isn't here."

"What? It has to be—"

Rooker cut her off. "Who else knows about this, the storage closet? Who knew your husband kept his things here?"

"Well, my boys did. But—"

"Did they ever have a boy named Henry over?"

Rooker stared into the oval of her face, the lines in it creasing like she was aging before his eyes. She held his gaze. *"That boy."* Her mood darkened like soot-black clouds falling from the sky. "He was all sorts of trouble. My younger, Gregory, got along with him well, had taken a liking to him. I told Gregory not to hang around with him, but one day I found them together in the house. Sometimes I'd come home and hear doors shut, and I'd think he was hiding here, or that my boy had snuck him out of the house. Erik was older by two years. He never liked Henry. Even gave him a bit of a beating once, though I couldn't tell you why."

Though Rooker already knew the answer to his next question, he pressed anyway. "Do you know if Gregory has had any contact with him?"

Her eyes dimmed, and now she looked tired, older, sadder than when Rooker had first seen her in the doorway.

"There was an accident; Gregory passed away a few years before my husband did."

"I'm so sorry," Tess told Mrs. Sadler. "How did it happen?"

"The boys in the neighborhood were on the ice. It was getting dark. Gregory was never a great swimmer. The ice broke, and he fell in. I think he panicked or went into shock. The boys said he never came back up. He was small and thin for his age, but his father had been too."

Neither Tess nor Rooker said anything.

"I held on to hope that he'd walk in the front door soaked and wet. But the police said they couldn't search the water with how frozen it was. That's when they told me even if he'd managed to climb out, he'd be dead from hypothermia or whatever animals were out. They said he wouldn't have suffered too much—he'd drift asleep and stay at the bottom of the water. At least they gave it to me straight. When the ice thawed, William hired a private investigator, who hired a couple of guys who owned diving gear, who never found anything but our money. And yet here I am, every morning, drinking my tea, staring at that door." She paused, beaming at a photo of the boy on the mantel next to the front door. "The worst part, they turned him into an urban legend. I overheard them in the grocery aisle, some kids talking about *the boy in the lake*. They said he'd climb out of the lake at night and walk the woods. If he touched you, your body would turn to ice. I left my cart in the store, hurried to my car, and just sat there. I cried my eyes out.

Anna always said it was Henry. She said he was pure evil, that he killed my son."

"Anna Meltzer?"

"That's right. She would say it every time I spoke to her, which is why we no longer speak. She just kept reminding me how dead my child was."

Rooker had it easier, in a way. He knew that his son was gone. This poor woman would sit and stare at that door every morning until the day she died.

"You think Henry came back, after all these years, to take my husband's gun?"

"I don't think so, Mrs. Sadler," said Tess. "We'll get someone over here to keep an eye on the house, make sure no one is coming or going without us knowing. Thanks for talking to us; you've been helpful."

Rooker stood to leave and paused a moment. "Mrs. Sadler, where is Erik now?"

."He's an executive at a firm in Minneapolis. Doing well for himself— he sends money now and then. I wish he'd visit more."

"Thank you for your time."

Tess called and arranged for a squad car with two officers to be posted outside Mrs. Sadler's home.

"You think it was the gun? In the garage at the station?" Tess asked when they were out of earshot.

"I'm sure it was."

Chapter 33

December 15

She was model tall, thin with winding-road curves that would make the catcallers hoot and holler. *Give me a smile, honey! Where you been all my life? How you doin', sweetheart?*

It was a little after eight. The white lights on the seventh floor—her floor—went out like a birthday-candle blow.

He'd shrunk in his seat, slouched shoulders, body slumped forward. The second he saw the lights go out, he scooted back. His body tensed. He sat straighter. The wound at his chest throbbed with every movement. The engine had gone cold long ago, but his forehead was fever-hot, his hair moist beneath the black cap.

He eyed the lobby behind dark window tints for the third night that week. He'd spread his visits out so they wouldn't seem suspicious.

The downstairs was encased in massive paneled glass, like a high-end storefront. Marble tile gleamed throughout. A young blonde receptionist sat behind the desk between two monstrous elevator doors.

A few minutes later, the woman peacocked out of the open door like someone pulled back the stage curtain. Her billable hours, her six-figure salary, none of that changed what she was to him.

She chatted up the receptionist, finished with a pageant smile and a wave to the security guard. She sauntered out into the cold, into his grasp. In his mind, she was putting on a show for him. Her Marilyn Monroe shiver, her dainty fingers slipping into her leather gloves, the cloud from her lips for both her and him to see. He could feel her breath hot on his.

She was dressed like something out of a business-formal catalog. A lapel shirt wrapped around her neck like a slack noose. Her sweater, black with a white grid design, clung tight to her body beneath a coffee-creamer-beige overcoat that fell to her thighs.

She shifted back and forth on her black pointed heels and lifted her phone out of her handbag. While she made a call, her hand shook the dark waves of hair that rippled in the wind. She wore it down, part of it to her midchest. Her quivering in the cold made him smile. He pictured her skin pimpling, goose-fleshed, her nipples swollen like a cow for slaughter.

It was only a minute before her driver pulled to the curb in a luxury black and chrome-accented Jaguar XJ, rushed to her door, apologizing like he'd just made roadkill of her pet dog. She manufactured a smile and got in. He closed her door and ran back to the driver side, slid in, and drove away.

She would be his masterpiece.

PART III

Chapter 34

Rooker felt grim. They had struck out weeks ago.

For Tess, this would be it—the end of her career as lead detective. Between pressure from the media and the chief and the threat of the FBI swooping in—she'd be demoted or fired.

They'd gotten nowhere with the Meltzers. Carl and Anna didn't know a thing about Henry or where he'd gone. When they followed up with the happy couple, they learned that the principal would call on nearly a daily basis saying the boy had disappeared from school, had never showed. Whenever he would turn up late to the dinner table, he'd sit in silence covered in grime and sweat while he shoveled forkfuls of food into his mouth. Anna Meltzer swore to them it was blackened blood under his fingernails, not dirt. When Henry finished with his plate, he'd ask to be excused before scurrying off to the spare bedroom he was staying in.

Nor had they gotten anywhere with Selma Sadler, the widow of William Sadler. They tried to get ahold of her son Erik, but he was never in the office, supposedly. They were told to give a call back later. Tess left her number with the secretary but figured he wouldn't be returning her call.

No missing person's report. No ID. Sundgren was stumped—nothing in the files they'd left for him jogged his memory further.

Rooker was clicking away on the Lenovo keyboard so faintly that no letters were appearing on the white page. He just kept the constant *tap-tap-tap* going, his index finger phantom drumming on whatever key was beneath it. He didn't care to look. His eyes were unfocused, blank as the page in front of him. His focus was elsewhere. He reopened the box from Sundgren's, thumbed through the files on Astrid Thompson.

Astrid Thompson was unlucky number fourteen. *Why her?* he thought. Why was she different from the rest of his father's victims? Why was she missing from the file? He didn't find anything.

Rooker sat deep in thought about the boy named Henry. He played back the conversation with the Meltzers in his mind, how Carl could get the boy to talk only if it had to do with something as dark as the Gunner Lindström case. The boy was obsessed. Whether he wanted to hurt anyone as a youth, Rooker wasn't sure. But what was certain in Rooker's mind now was that the boy was never able to suppress the evil within him. He'd unshackled it. It was free. And now there was no going back.

His thoughts wandered to Anna Meltzer, a woman who had grown to hate and fear the orphaned boy she took in. The mere mention of Henry made her clutch onto the white scar from all those years ago, the gash that it took eight stitches to close. Rooker kept picturing the drawings. He thought to call Anna Meltzer, but he eyed the clock. It was late. He didn't want to bother her, and he had a feeling she'd keep him on the phone longer than he wanted to be.

What about the drawings Mrs. Meltzer mentioned? What were those about? There was something artistic about the way the killer was positioning the bodies. It might not mean anything, but he thought it did. Maybe there was a connection between the drawings and his father's photographs. That was the problem with being sent on a wild fucking goose chase. You never know what's truly important and what's insignificant. He pictured the boy who drew dead women in his bed-room, imagined him all grown up now.

Again, he stared at the bright-white empty page. He watched the cursor blink in one-second intervals. It was gone. It was back. Gone. Back. He tried to think of anything that would help him, but he had nothing. When he finally passed out from fatigue, he was still mulling over the files and the photos on his phone.

◆ ◆ ◆

There was a storm traveling north. The smell of rain tiptoed in through the window. The aroma made Tess feel comfortably warm, weightless. But as she peered down into the face of her father's watch, she felt like a prisoner of war. A Longines Le Grande Classique. Gold face, brown leather band. Retail was somewhere in the ballpark of $1,600. It was a fake, but that did not matter to her. What mattered was that it was her father's. What mattered to her was the glass broken like a shattered window, the date and time fixed forever. She would look at it every day, at the very same moment the car had hit him. Or the moment he'd stepped in front of it.

She pricked her finger with a piece of the glass and dragged it over one of the lines already there. Red bubbled on her fingertip. Beneath was the white scar—not a shattered window or a web; it was a single snowflake. It was for her mother.

She placed the watch back in the nightstand drawer and shut it like a coffin. It reminded her of how powerless she'd felt when her mother was raped and how she could do nothing to save her father from taking his own life. But nights like this gave her that power back.

Tess parked half a block away from the AWAK∃N nightclub next to a rusted-out '81 Pontiac Firebird Trans Am. Even beneath the streetlight's bright polish, a burning glaze, the black paint and corroded orange were matte and dull. It was the closest she had ever parked to him. It belonged to Clyde Miller, petty criminal: DUI, assault, robbery, and a couple of Ponzi schemes. Some guy once called him Bonnie—get it, Bonnie and Clyde? Suffice to say, he had to get his mouth wired shut. Clyde had to pay his hospital bills. She saw him standing out front of the club. The man beside him was the more dangerous of the two. Jan Cullen. They called him the Janitor, meaning he was good for cleaning up a mess. If someone owed you money, you paid Jan to smack him around. He enjoyed it. His rap sheet was the length of a shopping list and more violent than Miller's: DUI, animal cruelty, assault, assault with a deadly weapon, grand larceny, and arson.

Jan Cullen nudged Clyde Miller in the arm outside AWAK∃N and stubbed out a cigarette beneath his boot. Cullen's muscles rippled beneath a black dress shirt open at the collar. Gold and silver rings were around nearly every one of his fingers. Miller, on the other hand, was lean, bordering on wiry. He wore his long blond hair in a bun and a roll-neck sweater that made him resemble a skinny eggplant. Rays of neon light strobed out onto the walkway and flooded the street. The two of them started walking back to the car, each with a matching right-side limp. But this was no faux-gangster limp. They were very much real. The shallow back of Clyde Miller's knee had exploded one night, and it was only seconds later that a second bullet tore a hole through the center of Jan Cullen's meaty foot. Tess knew all too well. She was the shooter.

That night seemed so distant now. Tess dressed in all gothic black, her face shielded by a sweatshirt hood. Her blood was like a broken faucet; it couldn't decide whether to run hot or cold. When the police showed up, it was Cullen who said it was a woman who shot them. He said she had a nice body; *tight* was the word he used. He was able to see a bit of dark hair beneath the hood too.

Tonight, Tess wore mascara that made her lashes full and carbon-black. She had foundation and light blush on that made her cheekbones glisten, not because she was worried about them ID'ing her but because she wanted their attention. She wasn't Detective Tess Harlow tonight. She had left her badge buried in the gym bag in the back seat. Tonight, she was a dolled-up damsel in distress.

Weak. Vulnerable. Prey.

Miller and Cullen were getting closer to the car when Tess rolled down her window. The crisp night air carried along the stench of cigarette smoke and cognac. When Miller noticed Tess, he slapped Cullen on the arm. And when Cullen noticed Tess, he smacked him back. It was time to play ball. Cullen raked his dark, straight hair with his fingers and pulled at the long strands of his patchy beard. Tess hid the pistol beneath her purse on the passenger seat.

Jan Cullen pigeon-toe hobbled over. "Hey, snowflake." He smiled and leaned his powerful forearms against the open window.

Tess frowned down at the scar on her finger, then smiled back. "Hi, boys."

"How come we didn't see you inside?" he said. He was staring down the front of her backless black dress. She let him.

"I just walked out."

"I would've remembered you," he said.

"Is that what you tell all the girls?"

He smiled and did what was probably his party trick: blew a cigar-style ring of smoke into the air. "Only the ones I want to break my heart."

That was not the only thing she wanted to break. She looked at Clyde Miller. "Is he your boyfriend?"

Cullen's mouth turned upside down. "Don't think so, *snowflake.*" His hand shot out and locked around her wrist. He pulled it out of the window, and she did her best to hide the scar on her fingertip. The whiskers above his lip rubbed against her knuckles. And he kissed them. While he did, Tess slid the pistol to her side and concealed it between her legs. His touch was like a wet spider. She wanted to squirm beneath it. The spaghetti straps of her dress felt tighter. Tess should have expected what happened next. Jan "the Janitor" Cullen put her hand on the front of his black jeans. And Tess played along. Her fingers pinched the clasp of his pants and pulled the zipper down. Her other hand closed around the pistol grip. She wanted to shove the gun right through the hole of his pants and fire. And just then, her phone rang. She grabbed the phone with her right hand. It was Langston.

"Hey, boss," Millie Langston said. "We just got a call, a strange one. He asked for you by name. Can I transfer it?"

She took her hand off Jan Cullen's crotch and held a finger up. "Who is it?"

"A priest, at Saint Andrew's."

She muted the phone and turned to Cullen. "Sorry, boys." She reached out and gave a hard squeeze to his testicles. "Maybe next time." Tess let go and drove off, then unmuted the phone.

She almost wanted to say, *Forgive me, Father, for I have sinned.* Then again, what did a priest want with her?

"He says he has someone at the church; they broke in. He thinks it's someone we're looking for."

"Who?"

Tess waited on the line. When it stopped ringing, she answered. "Hello?"

"Yes, Ms. Harlow? I'm Father Alan."

She said, "Detective. What can I do for you, *Father*?"

"I've been watching the news," he said. His voice wavered, soft, and his phlegmy whoop did nothing to help. "This man, the one killing women. The church sometimes shelters the homeless and abused. If they stay the night on the streets, the cold will kill them. There's a man staying here who's not one of these people. I found his things; he's squatting in a room downstairs. He has newspaper clippings of the victims. He paints them."

Tess pulled over, grabbed her duffel bag from the back seat, and changed her clothes.

◆ ◆ ◆

Rooker's eyes were fastened shut, his neck twisted to the side. The laptop had slid down between his thigh and the corner of the recliner. His pectoral muscles twitched, and his feet untangled when the phone buzzed again on his chest. Finally, he opened his eyes and looked down at the phone's display. It was Harlow.

"We may have him."

"Who?"

"Henry. I just got a call from a priest at Saint Andrew's, says a man has been breaking in downstairs, set up a little room for himself. The church sometimes houses people whether they're abused or homeless, right. But this guy isn't one of them. And there's a room downstairs that is usually locked. He found a way in." She paused. "He has the newspaper clippings. And he paints."

Rooker's eyes opened wider as she spoke. "When do we check it out?"

"We?" she said. "There's no we this time, Rooker."

"Come on, Tess. Without me, your investigation would be nowhere." He regretted the last part instantly. "I'll stay way back, far behind you guys."

"The answer is no." The line went silent.

Chapter 35

January 11

The van tires splashed to the curb half a block away from the cathedral. Rain was pouring down, the whirring of the wipers on high. Tess could make out the short stone wall along the front of the building by the street. An onyx-black wrought iron railing sat atop it. Just beyond it were five or six trees that had seen better days. The reflection of the stained glass twinkled in the moonlight, surrounded by old stone architecture. Reaching toward the clouds like a dagger, the spire stood tall with a cross at the peak. The streetlamp out front was dim. Faintly looming over the dark mist the wind carried, thousands of black and gray hay needles fell from the sky.

The wipers stopped. Keene killed the engine. Tess watched him stuff the keys into his back pants pocket. They watched the church for a few minutes, going over their plan.

Tess would be inside along with Keene and Xander. There were three exits, one being the main entrance and their way in. Cole would take the left exit, Sterling on the rear. If anything went wrong, Sterling had an extra set of keys to the van and would pull it around. If Henry escaped, he or Cole would be on him.

The doors opened, and everyone piled out of the van. Keene turned to Sterling and Cole and slapped the two of them hard on their vests. "If the suspect is armed and tries to flee, you take the shot," he said. While water flowed down his head, he said, "Let's go."

The doors shut quietly, and the five of them hustled down the street. They stood together out of the rain. A few of the homeless were huddled together beneath tattered blankets and clothing. The rest were probably somewhere inside fast asleep.

Tess counted Keene down, and on her go he opened the door a few inches. It was just enough for her to squeeze by, and then he followed. As the door shut, cold, damp air clung to the back of her neck. A shiver shot down her spine. Tess and Xander drew their handguns. Keene carried a Mossberg 590 pump-action shotgun that seemed small in his thick, gargantuan hands. They advanced as a unit. Moving silently and cornering the walls, they were alert, focused.

The three of them moved down the dark-walnut pews, clearing the nave. They knelt, checked underneath seating, looked up to make sure nothing was there. The three of them cleared the altar. There was nothing. Xander was beginning his descent, heading down a staircase lined by candles that were no longer lit. She watched him flip on his flashlight, which attached to his pistol. A small, steady stream of light illuminated enough of the staircase for them to see where they were going.

The windows hazed like sheets of ice. His head turned up at the church. Rooker never liked going, had never forced his son to go either. He felt like he and the big man, if he existed, never saw eye to eye.

He shut the cab's door quietly behind him and stepped up the sidewalk. The church entrance was a gothic set of double doors. He stepped over the outstretched legs of a woman asleep beneath a torn blanket and pulled one of the doors open.

It was the moment the door closed behind him that he felt like an idiot. Why had he come here unarmed? Why was he so stubborn?

He saw something—a shadow and a circle of light—moving down a staircase. He followed.

As he rounded the railing and peered down the staircase, he saw Martin Keene trailing Tess and Xander. Quietly, he began to take the stairs one by one.

When Tess and her team reached the bottom, there were more rooms. Candle flames stood at the end of the hall. They cleared each room one by one. Nothing. Until they ended up in a much larger room filled with tables and chairs and piles of labeled boxes and storage bins. Xander's whispered voice said, "Boss, got something."

He had to fight the urge to head in their direction. Instead, he sat back, crouched low, and waited for the three of them to take each room one at a time. He watched them going one by one, turn the knob, push the door open, and clear it. He hadn't expected them to be this good, especially Keene. He figured Xander would get off on this type of thing, probably thought of himself as the macho, big-testicled detective. He knew that if anyone was going to shoot Henry dead before he could talk, it would be Xander Whitlock. When the rooms were pronounced clear, he followed the three detectives down the hall to where the candle flames waved them by. Rooker's steps came faster. He was right behind Keene's enormous Kevlar-plated back when he said in his softest voice, "Don't shoot."

Tess entered the room lit by candles and mustard-tinted recessed lighting. Then she saw it. There were two standing wood easels and paint and brushes scattered on top of a mahogany table. On the floor, leaned up against the wall, were squares of something, whatever it was hidden beneath filthy pieces of cloth.

"Boss," Martin Keene whispered.

When Tess turned to see Rooker standing behind Martin, she gritted her teeth so hard, they could break. *What the hell are you doing here?*

"I had to see for myse—"

"*Never mind!* Stay out of sight. Martin," she ordered.

"I got it. Don't worry."

Tess skulked to the easels, pulled out the farthest, and lifted the fabric from it. She was stunned. She saw the strokes of white and gray and black. The tree was dark; different shades against it made the snow glisten, some branches nearly devoured by it. The house in the background was a bit blurred, like the light on the front porch had been the culprit. Confectionary-white sparkled beneath the swing—which hung at a morbid angle, a bit darker, as did she. It was the woman. The Claesson house. Gunner's childhood home. Her head sagged down, her chin tucked to her clavicle, her body bare and nearly as pale as the ground. The painting was beautiful. But the moment Tess realized what the image was, her eyes were drawn to the rest—the other canvases cloaked in dirty white veils like dead brides—all of them leaning upright against the wall.

"Jesus Christ."

"It's him," Martin said. "It has to be."

Xander walked to the far left and started pulling the pieces of cloth from the paintings. Victim. Victim. Victim. Each sheet he pulled off was another.

"*Stop!*" Tess whispered to Xander. She could suddenly hear the faintest sound of rain, like a sprinkle from an open window. Seconds later, a door creaked farther down the hall.

"Put them back!" she whispered at him again.

Xander rushed matador flourishes of cloth back over the paintings. Tess did the same with the most recent victim. The sheet snapped down over her naked skin, like a tarp over a muscle car. They took their places like they were film-set X'd on the ground. Each of them had a position of cover, ready for Henry to appear. Tess cornered a wall that was out of the sight line of anyone entering the room. So did Xander. Keene sight-aimed down the twelve-gauge barrel.

They heard the squelching thud of heavy steps. And soon enough, they stopped. Tess still had a view of the paintings. She noticed the one on the far left that wasn't entirely covered, the painting itself tilted to the side.

She peeked around the wall just enough for one eye to focus on the figure cloaked in the shadows; a dark hood was pulled down over the person's head. Rain was dripping off them to the ground. Tess could vaguely make out two sunken, frozen eyes. The figure took a step back.

The steps turned and started running; the first one to chase was Xander.

"Stop!" he yelled at the figure, but the hallway erupted. Jarring cracks like cheap fireworks—that hollow hiss ringing in her skull. Just as Tess turned and saw Xander's body, her throat tightened. She ran beside him, knelt down, and checked the wound. Blood soaked through Xander's shoulder, dark red running down between his fingers. "Rooker! Come here and put pressure on it! You'll be all right," she told Xander confidently before she got up and ran after Keene.

Another shot blasted toward her. She saw the hallway flash.

Tess moved faster down the hall when she heard the steps dimming. The side door burst open, and there were three gunshots maybe ten seconds later. *Pop. Pop-pop.* Tess kept going. At the door, Keene slammed it open and hid behind cover. *Quiet.* Then, in one motion, he swung out with his shotgun ready to shoot, and Tess with her pistol. They stepped out into the rain to find Cole on his knees clutching his arm, and a man dead with two red holes seeping from his chest, only an inch or two apart.

"Fuck!" Keene yelled.

Cole was hunched down over him, panting, checking for a pulse, but there was nothing. The rain was pouring down his face. Tess called in an ambulance, letting them know that two officers had been shot, one badly. A POI was dead as well.

◆ ◆ ◆

Rooker thought the pain had formed tears in Cole's eyes that he couldn't fight.

Keene slid the handgun away from the suspect's body with his foot. Rooker looked down at it and saw that it was the old Glock model from the photo forensics showed him. There was no doubt it would match the slugs they'd found the night Tess was shot at in the parking garage. The same gun Rooker believed was stolen from the box at the Sadlers'. Vic Sterling rounded the corner in a sprint.

While Tess and Keene went back to check on Xander and clear the rest of the cathedral, Rooker and Sterling waited with Cole and the dead man. Rooker couldn't help but wonder how Henry had been living, whether he was sleeping here, where he would eat. The man was such a mystery. And now Rooker might never find out.

"How is it?" Rooker asked stupidly.

"Burns like hell." The words were shaky, his mouth tight. Rooker watched the pain in Cole's watery eyes as they reddened. Two orbs like white pavement, cracked, blood filled.

Soon enough, distant blue lights flickered in the rain. It took only minutes for the official vehicles to pull up after Rooker first heard their wailing. One ambulance took Cole and Xander. Xander was too stubborn to get onto the stretcher; he hobbled up into the back without assistance aside from Cole's hand pressed into his back. Cole told them to just cut his shirtsleeve and stitch it and he'd be fine. Sterling bumped fists with each of them before the doors closed. Rooker watched the other ambulance bag the dead body and put it into the back. They'd transport him to Isaiah via Tess's orders. The night was nearly over. Rooker was wound so tight that he felt the need to get shitfaced.

He was left standing curbside with Tess and Keene. He wanted to search the place, see if any of his father's old photographs or files were here. He knew Henry must have had some of them. But he was tired. He figured the crime scene people would come in and do all the work. That almost made him smile. He was tired, too tired to do any more of this today. The rain was still coming down. Rooker was drenched and in need of a shower or just enough alcohol to where he'd forget how soaked he was.

"Anyone care for a drink?" he asked the two of them.

Keene's mouth clicked when his phone call went unanswered. "Boss," he said. "Mind if I get home? If Lynn finds out about this before I get there, she'll be worried sick and I'll be sleeping on the couch."

"Sure, Martin. Give her a hug for me."

"Will do."

Tess let out a heavy sigh. Rooker could tell she was relieved. He didn't know if she should be just yet, though he wasn't sure why.

"I need to finish up here and stop in and see Xander. Have to brief Larsson too. Then I'll take you up on that drink."

"Sure."

It was after one in the morning when Rooker was glancing at Tess beside him. She wore a distant smile. Even heading up the elevator in her apartment complex, he was wondering what was going through her head. He thought about her bare skin on one of Isaiah's tables, a saw cutting through her skull and poking around inside.

The smell of cold rain lingered on the clothes Tess still had on. Rooker had left a sopping trail with his hours ago, and even after each piece was thrown to the floor of the cottage, the chill pierced his skin until he rinsed it from his body.

While Tess showered, he poured himself a drink and her a glass of wine. Half his glass he downed in a single loud gulp. The liquid burned, but it went down smoothly.

While he stared at the photo of her and Martin Keene, Rooker called out. "So," he said. "Did you find anything?"

Rooker listened to the sound of the water change as she shifted beneath it. "There was an old Polaroid of two boys. And there was a black-and-white photograph; not one of Gunner's. It was the woman dead on the swing."

"Nothing else? No ID? No weapon, zip ties, gloves?"

"Look," she said. "It's him."

"How could you know?"

"What?" she called out over the water.

"How could you know it's him? Henry."

"Rooker," she said. "It's him."

"He disappeared years ago without a trace. He hasn't got any ID on him. There's no way of knowing—"

"It's *him*, Rooker." The words came out firm. "Isaiah has the body now. We'll show the picture to the Meltzers and Mrs. Sadler, Erik too. But it's him."

Rooker dropped it. "How's Xander?"

"What?"

He walked closer and spoke through the bathroom door, which was open an inch or two. "How's Xander?"

"What, are you guys buddies now? He's fine. The nurses are already complaining. He'll be out in a day or two."

"And Cole?"

"Already discharged. They stitched him up, and he said he felt good as new."

"And you?"

"Just dandy."

"You know." He couldn't help himself. "When I did that search on your father . . ."

"Yeah?"

Rooker walked past the door, over to the dusty gold-accented frame that held her father's black-and-white portrait. He caught a glimpse of Tess's blurred silhouette behind the shower glass. The door fogged over, water drops trickling down in streaks, but the curves and lines of her body forced his chest to hurdle. He turned away. "All I could find were a couple of puff pieces. Years in law enforcement, his role in the community, that sort of stuff. There was barely any mention of a traffic stop and no mention of the car that hit him."

"What are you asking me?"

"I know how these articles work." He used his headline voice. "'Police officer dies in routine traffic stop.' I didn't find a single story like that. Everything I found was like a written memorial."

When Tess went silent, Rooker couldn't help but gaze at her. She stood still. Her head hung down beneath the showerhead. And then she turned the water off. "The car that hit him, it was a family. Mother, father, and a little boy in the back seat. They aren't mentioned anywhere because they did nothing wrong. They even pulled over and did what they could to save him. My father wasn't hit by the car; he stepped in front of it."

The words gripped Rooker like a hand around his throat. "I'm sorry."

"Yeah," she said into a towel. "Me too."

Tess came out of the bathroom in a gray tank top, all but one button done, and a pair of jogger sweats. Her hair was still wet down one side of her shoulders. There was something sexy about it, the way it fell like waves, the other side of her petite neck bare. She brushed past him, the subtle smells of vanilla and almond warming his face.

"Larsson's holding a press conference in the morning. The prick says the public needs it."

"Won't you be there?"

She laughed and took a sip of wine, her eyes hanging on Rooker over the edge of the glass. "Some of us still have work to do. Maybe one day if I make chief, I can stop working like Larsson. For now, maybe I won't be fired just yet after all." Tess held up her glass.

Suddenly Rooker understood the pressure she had been dealing with. "I'll drink to that."

The two of them passed a bottle of cabernet sauvignon back and forth in the kitchen like it was a blacktop game of Horse. They sat side by side on the counter. She liked her wine. He wasn't a fan, too fruity. But it was doing the trick. And they confided in each other. She told him about moving up the ranks as a woman, how she never thought she'd work a case like this one—that she hoped she never would again.

"What happened with your wife, exactly?"

"I gave up." He smiled sadly. "I was the one beaten as a kid—raised to fight. She grew up with the dog, the picket fence, the loving parents. Yet when my son died, she was the fighter. I locked myself in his bedroom and cried and drank. She put on a brave face—then makeup and went to work. When I started investigating my son's killer, I obsessed to the point that I was lost. Laura tried her best to grieve while dealing with my shit. But when I looked at her, it only reminded me of our son—how I got him killed . . . I ran. Haven't spoken to her since I left."

Rooker eyed the fullness of her lips as they pressed against the bottle. She held it there, and her lips stained deep red like cherry pie. When she handed it back to him, he found himself closing his eyes, pressing his lips as hers had been, like he was stealing a kiss. They emptied the bottle between the two of them and got started on another. When it was half-empty, Tess corked the bottle and slid it back on the counter against the subway tile. Rooker felt her leaning into him, and he leaned right back.

She slid off the counter, took him by the hand to the bedroom, and kissed him. Her lips were soft, magnetic. "Mmm," he muttered and managed to pull away. He said, peering into her face, "Probably a bad idea—" but the words even he didn't believe were cut short.

She kissed him long on the mouth and sealed it with a bite on his bottom lip. And he gave in. Her hands ran through his hair. He could taste the wine from her mouth like he was drinking it. Before long, she sat astride him, her hair hanging in his face, his sweatpants down around his thighs.

When it was over, she wrapped herself in his arms like he was a blanket, brushed her finger along his scar like a loose thread. It wasn't long before he felt her hand stop, felt her drift to sleep against his chest.

Chapter 36

Rooker woke up to Tess fast asleep. He pulled the sheet off himself and covered her bare chest. Over the edge of the bed, he saw the pillow he'd thrown to the floor. His hand went to the television remote. He pressed the red button and watched it brighten. The news was on. He saw Jim Larsson, the police chief, giving a press conference. The makeup on his face made him appear far more alive than Rooker had seen him last. He imagined this was how he'd look in an open casket. He channel surfed, but it played on all the news channels. There was a crowd of people hurling questions at him, the bottom of the broadcast playing BREAKING NEWS.

Larsson told them about the killer, about the man his team had caught last night and gunned down in self-defense. He told them that two brave officers were wounded and recovering, but they couldn't save the man who could give them answers. Larsson said he was positive they had found the killer and credited the team he'd put together. Rooker turned off the TV and went back to sleep.

In his dream, he was surrounded by beautiful women, the women the killer had taken from this world. They were mostly nude, some half-naked, their heads intact, their bodies uninjured. Some of the women his father had killed were there too. He saw Olivia Campbell, the woman Rooker had lied to Tess about. She often haunted his dreams. He figured she was here to remind him what he'd done to her. The pillow pulled tight over her face, him pressing down with all his might. But now, her hand was on his leg, moving slowly up it. It felt so real. He could feel her fingertips light against the hair on his thighs. And then they were all there, their heads rotting, falling from their bodies like trees chopped down. He felt something, and his eyes flashed open.

Tess was sitting there, dressed, shaking him. "Bad dream?"

"Something like that."

Rooker got dressed and left the apartment, grabbing a cab back to his place. He wondered whether he would hear from Tess again now that the case was over. But when the cab was maybe halfway to the cottage, he changed his mind and had the driver take him to the cathedral instead. There were media outlets and vans and cameras outside, standard three-inch barricade tape surrounding the perimeter of the building.

Rooker thanked the driver and got out, shut the door, and walked past the cameras and under the tape. Someone tried to stop him, but Vic Sterling waved him through.

"What are you doing here?" Sterling asked him in surprise.

"There're a few things I wanted to check out, if you don't mind."

"Not at all. What are you thinking?"

Rooker walked through the doors alongside Sterling. "Did you find anything yet, any files, any supplies like zip ties, knives, weapons, any of the photos, anything like that?"

"Aside from the two photos, nothing yet. It doesn't mean he didn't store them elsewhere, though, or maybe they're here somewhere. He did have the gun."

"What about a cot? Do we know if he was sleeping here?"

"There was something in back, in one of the rooms."

Something seemed off to Rooker. It wasn't that It was easy, because it wasn't. Two cops had taken bullets in the process of capturing the man they assumed to be Henry. But it hadn't left Rooker with the same feeling he'd gotten when he caught his son's killer. It didn't fill the hole in his heart. Maybe it was the fact that their man was dead, that Rooker couldn't talk to him. He didn't know. But his mind was a mouse trapped in a maze; he didn't know what to think or where to go. It's what led him back here.

"Mind showing me what you've got?"

"Sure thing."

Rooker walked in and saw all the paintings lined up on the wall, the cloth from them removed. He eyed each one, studied them. They were in order of the first victim to the latest.

"They're beautiful, aren't they?" Sterling said.

Rooker looked at him out of the corner of his eye, then back to the paintings. "That was my first thought as well last night. They're remarkable. Sick but remarkable. He was talented."

Sterling nodded. "A lot of the talented ones are—sick. Most of the truly gifted ones have some kind of vice, whether it's drugs, sex, maybe they hear voices, maybe they're doing the work of God. Who the hell knows."

"I think there's crazy in all of us. It's just a matter of if we suppress it or if we embrace it."

Sterling walked over with a bagged photo and handed it to Rooker. "Found this in here."

Rooker's eyes dipped down to the photograph. It was the girl on the swing. It looked like it was taken from the sidewalk outside the home. Her head hung there, just as he remembered her. "So he used Gunner's portraits, location's important to him. Then he kills the women, stages them, photographs them so he can paint them."

"Sounds about right, doesn't it?"

Sterling led Rooker into a small room with a tiny military cot against the left wall. A thin, unfolded blanket and throw pillow sat on top of it. The blanket would never cover him entirely and he could picture Henry curled up beneath it trying to stay warm. There were a few changes of clothing folded on a wooden chair beside the cot. There wasn't a single color in the mix. There was a black hooded sweatshirt; two pairs of pants, one black and one dark gray; a couple of old dark T-shirts; and gray socks. They were the outfits of a man who wanted to go unnoticed. Rooker picked up on something else. Not a single pair of gloves. There wasn't anything that was warm. He couldn't envision Henry waiting outside to abduct a victim or staging one of the bodies the way they had been with this little clothing on. It didn't mean he didn't have things stored somewhere, but Rooker was not convinced that this man was the killer.

He scouted around the room; there was nothing else. "This is it?" Rooker hadn't seen any of the tools used on the women, not a single knife, nothing. If it weren't for the paintings and the gun, they wouldn't have anything.

"We did find this." Sterling grabbed a sealed bag with something thin inside it. He put it in Rooker's hand. It was a small black-and-white Polaroid, old and hanging on by a thread by the looks of it. He stared at the two boys standing arm in arm, bundled up, the lake behind them. That's about all he could make out. The photo was old and a bit blurred at this point. The bottom read M 18:6. The numbers were old, the ink ran and faded, but it was there.

"If I had to guess," Rooker said, "I think it's Henry and Gregory Sadler, the boy who drowned years ago in the lake. They were friends. I'm not sure what changed. Mrs. Meltzer, she and her husband fostered Henry, and she swears he killed the boy. Selma Sadler doesn't seem to disagree."

"Then it would go with the verse," Sterling told him.

"What?"

"Matthew 18:6. It's a bible verse. 'But whoever shall offend one of these little ones—those who believe in me—it would be better for him that a millstone were hanged about his neck and that he were drowned in the depth of the sea.'"

"Didn't take him for the bible-fearing type."

"Well, it wouldn't be the first time someone used the bible to justify their mission. I wouldn't doubt that he held the boy's head underwater and drowned him. Look at the first victim, slammed her head against the ice and drowned her too," he said matter-of-factly.

Rooker took a deep breath while Sterling continued.

"Look at how he was living. Who can live with so little?"

It was true. Rooker figured the foster system made Henry the way he was. He was a kid who likely never experienced luxury. Carl Meltzer probably treated the boy better than anyone. But bouncing around in different homes, it was clear he never had much. Never needed much either.

When Rooker didn't respond, Sterling asked if there was any news on Cole or Whitlock. Rooker told him Cole was already home and stitched up, that Xander had to stay overnight and was probably being taught by the nurses that he wasn't bulletproof. Sterling got a kick out of that.

Rooker sat with the paintings. He perched there at a distance, his legs crossed and his chin resting against his knuckles, studying the details, the victims painted so clearly. They were beautiful. There was nothing gruesome about the paintings. Rooker never had artistic ability, not really. He'd drawn the image for his tattoo, but it was only good enough for the artist to see what he'd wanted. He'd always yearned to be able to draw or paint or sing or play guitar. Instead, he was given a pair of boxing gloves and no choice. He'd had a decent amateur record and some trophies he'd lost track of years before. That was all he had to show for it.

He sat there nearly an hour in the same position, his eyes going from painting to painting. He thought of the families of the victims, how they probably wouldn't find the paintings to be beautiful. It made

Rooker feel a little guilty, a little dirty for thinking so highly of them. But he couldn't help but admire them. He looked up and suddenly remembered where he was. He hated churches. He could still see the day clearly when he'd helped carry his son's casket down the aisle between the pews. The blue steel exterior had been cold to the touch. He thought about his son dead, even colder inside. Finally, he pushed himself up off the ground; his ass was cold, and his legs had gone stiff and numb. As he walked outside into the cool biting air, he figured the taxi he'd told to wait at the curb wouldn't be there. It wasn't.

Chapter 37

"I've got him," Langston yelled.

Tess was in a daze in her office, staring blindly at the case file she needed to finish when Langston appeared in her doorway.

"Henry Frederick Hult. I just got a call from my friend. There was an arson case when the boy was eight years old. He said it was an accident. The house burned down with his parents inside, killing them. The neighbors found him standing on the grass in his pajamas and shoes; they called the police."

"Well good for him," Tess said. "No one is coming to bury him, so he'll go into the oven. He'll end up the same way his parents did. What good does that do us?"

She didn't care what his middle initial or last name was. And she didn't care if he'd burned his parents alive on purpose or by accident. She assumed he'd meant to. What mattered now was that he was gone and that there wouldn't be another victim. She was happy the bastard was dead. At the moment, she didn't even care about the publicity she'd get for catching the killer, what it would do for her career. She was just happy she'd still have her job.

◆ ◆ ◆

Rooker was lights-out, sleep cradled by a handle of vodka and a bottle of lemon-lime soda. He'd spent the night tossing different amounts of each into his mouth, then sloshing the concoction around and taking a big gulp. He had been hit with an epiphany last night as he was considering whether he would stay here in Minnesota. He thought about places where he could be as close to happy as possible. He wasn't sure yet. The TV was on, flickering the only light in the room like a dull fire. He had fallen asleep watching one of those shows where people buy homes, trying to find a place that looked nice to him. But he had drunk himself to sleep in a T-shirt, gray sweatpants, and socks filled with holes. His hairy middle toe stuck out through one of them, the long nail split and jaundiced. He tucked his feet beneath the blanket and wrapped himself in it like a burrito.

Before he fell asleep, before he started drinking, Rooker had been typing away. He had opened a document and started writing about two kinds of evil. One was the evil that lived inside Henry. Here was an individual whose mind worked differently from everyone else's. There was evil in him as a youth. There were the drawings. Rooker thought that some evil had to be born that way.

The other kind of evil had to be bred. Whether someone experienced trauma that turned them evil, whether society had a hand in it or a person had a hand in it. That's the evil Rooker had been subjected to. Somehow he had been able to withstand it, though Gunner had worked hard to create evil within his son. So there were two kinds of evil, born and then bred. Rooker wasn't sure what he'd do with what he was writing; he was nearly positive he'd never attempt to publish it. Maybe it was still his way of venting, expressing his thoughts. After he'd written a few pages, he closed the document. He considered deleting it but decided to save it to his hard drive.

He was dreaming. He saw his boy again. He saw him there hovering over him, felt him pulling at his shirtsleeve. He flicked one eye half-open, saw him through his drunken view. He could see the golden pendant before his face, hanging from his son's thin neck. Saint Michael. He tried to clear his vision, but his eyes turned misty, teary. He wanted his boy back more than anything in the world. He'd kill in the blink of an eye to have him back. He felt his son reach over him, could hear the clink of the bottle again, then his son pulling the blanket tight over him. Rooker's arm fell over the side of the chair, hooked his fingers like talons into his son's shirt. He couldn't let go, wouldn't let go. Not this time. But he felt his son wrestle his hand free.

"Daddy, it's okay. Go back to sleep." The voice was hushed, soothing like a lullaby. He could picture his son's mouth moving. It sounded just like him.

But Rooker snatched at the boy's slender wrist. His fingernails bore into him. He could feel bone just beneath the skin. When Rooker's eyes tilted down, he could see dirt beneath his nail, a ring above his son's limp hand, the skin turning raw, pale.

"Ouch! Dad, you're hurting me," he whispered louder, trying to yank his arm free.

Rooker loosened his grip and saw the broken skin, an orange peel dug too deep. It folded back. Red droplets bubbled. Splotches sprouted up from the cuts. Blood smeared his wrist, the side of his hand.

"I'm so sorry," he slurred. When he closed his eyes and opened them, his son was gone. He stared at his hand, but there was nothing. There was no blood beneath his nails. They were like almonds, chewed short, jagged and grimy.

The phone buzzed. His neck turned. One eye cracked open, but the light from the television blinded him. When he was able to focus, he saw the digital clock on the cable box. The blue letters read 11:37. Rooker lifted the phone, the one Tess had given him. He hesitated to answer, but his curiosity got the best of him. He pressed the green button.

He waited. There was nothing. Yet. He couldn't hear anyone breathing. That was the MO.

"Meachum," he said to clear the silence. But there was no response. Now Rooker's eyes were open. He was wide awake. The call ended. Rooker dialed Warden Hastings; he'd been given his cell phone number. Rooker knew with the time difference that he should be answering—it was 9:37 p.m. The phone rang a few times, and he heard Hastings's voice on the other end.

"Warden Hastings, it's Rooker Lindström. I need to know where Tate Meachum is. I just got another call."

"He's in the box, Rooker. We moved him. That isn't possible."

"Can you check?"

"He wouldn't even get service in there."

"Can you *please* check anyway."

"Fine, fine. All right. I'm not at the prison—let me make a call."

Rooker waited on the line. He sat frozen to the chair.

A couple of minutes later, Rooker heard Hastings's clear voice.

"There's no phone, Rooker."

"Shit! I'm sorry."

Before Rooker could hang up, there was another incoming call from a restricted number. His blood froze like liquid nitrogen injected into his veins. He answered the phone and stood up.

"So you aren't Meachum," Rooker said angrily.

He waited. The silence was going to make him sick. A few seconds later, he heard a deep voice. It only breathed one word. "No."

A thunderous crack rang out deep in the woods, and in that split second, everything went south. The window exploded. Rooker crumpled to the floor. He heard a low whisper out in the trees that seemed to travel for miles. Worst of all, he knew someone was coming to execute him.

A second shot rang out like a cannon blast and tore through something only a foot or so above him. Rooker went down face-first, his nose and mouth caked in floorboard dust. It took everything in him not to scream out in pain. His lips tremored. The pain in his chest was unearthly. The bullet had ripped through him, searing like a cattle iron. He could picture his skin blackening like scorched earth beneath his shirt. And when he touched a finger to it, he could feel flames engulfing him.

Rooker's best army crawl quickly turned into an infant on all fours. Deep wheezes and soft moans made him sound like an amateur porn star. One of his shaky hands reached back and clutched onto the cell phone.

He wondered if he was going into shock, if he was going to die.

He stayed low and managed to drag his weight to the kitchen. Each time he clawed and pulled, it felt like his muscles tore from bone. He grabbed on to the countertop and pulled himself to his feet, his back to the wall. It took an eternity for him to open the phone, but he could hear everything. He heard the ticking of the clock on the kitchen wall. He heard his own heart, could feel his pulse ringing in his ears. He was waiting to hear footsteps. Not yet.

He dialed Tess.

"Harlow."

"I need help!" Rooker tried to whisper through gritted teeth. "Please!"

"Rooker?"

"I'm shot . . . my chest. The killer is here. Please!"

"I'm calling it in now." She was off the line for maybe twenty seconds, and he could hear rustling, drawers slamming shut. He wished the police were still on their detail outside Evelyn's home. But they thought they'd gotten the killer, that they'd caught the right guy. Rooker couldn't help but picture Evelyn dead inside. He figured she had to be. Suddenly, he heard Tess's voice again.

"Rooker?"

"Mm-hmm." His jaw was clenched tight. He struggled to get that much out of his mouth. He could hear his own pain so clearly.

"How bad is it?"

"I'm bleeding a lot."

"I'm going to hang up. Turn your ringer off. I don't want him to hear it."

There was a pair of old boots nested with spiders by the door. He moved to them, slid them on his feet, and grabbed a scarf that was hanging there. He tied the scarf at an angle tight around his chest and under his arm. He could see the temperature gauge blinking by the door. It was 17 degrees Fahrenheit. He cracked open the door that went out the kitchen. He thought he heard the whistling from the broken window inside stop. The next thing he heard was the crunch of broken glass. Rooker slipped out the door and held it still. He pushed his phone into the snow next to him and tried to move as silently as possible. His back was against the house now. He heard light steps creeping around inside; he'd be found soon enough. The boot prints would lead the killer right to him. He decided it was now or never.

Rooker took off toward the lake. There was a shack a couple hundred yards away that he used to run to when his father was hunting for him. Now it was his only real hope. He couldn't tell how much blood he was losing as he tried to make his way, but he could feel the scarf sticking to him, which meant there was probably a good amount. He gave himself twenty minutes. He had to survive for twenty minutes. That was the internal clock he set, how long he gave himself to either bleed out or succumb to hypothermia.

He moved low, as fast as he could, slipping, catching himself with his arm, which sent more pain through his chest. He crept close to a tree, and then a high-powered crack whistled. Smoke and bark flew into the air. He started running as fast as he could. Seconds later, another bullet ripped into a tree nearby. The whistled hiss, the bullet less than a foot from his head sent him face-first, flat in the snow. The shots were close enough to make his ears ring. In other words, *too close*.

Bolt action. He could tell by the sound of the rifle and the time between shots. Probably a scoped hunting rifle. He got up and took off.

He couldn't take in a deep breath and felt his face grimacing from the pain. He was nearly at the shack. Wind tears blurred his vision, and he rubbed them away. The shack was dark. The glass windowpanes were still intact. He ran into the door, and it flew open, causing him to fall to the ground. But he scurried up to the door and shut it. He dragged a bulky dresser in front of it and huddled in the corner. His hand was to his chest. His knees were tucked up, and his legs and stomach were cramping, but he didn't budge. He sat there in pain, listened for movement. Still, all he heard was the howl of the wind. His feet felt frozen. The backs of his ears, his earlobes, his nose too. Tears were freezing to his cheeks.

And then he heard it. Footsteps. At first they were delicate, ice crunching beneath a shoe. By the time they were close, they crackled like twigs snapping in half. It was his own fault; he should have kept running, used the trees for cover. Instead, his tracks had led the killer right to him. Then he heard the voice, one he could trust.

"Rooker," Tess called out.

He stood up and saw her standing there, with Keene behind her and out of breath from the run and the climb.

"You okay?" Keene asked.

Rooker was scared out of his mind. He opened his mouth, but the words struggled to come out. When they did, his teeth chattering, his jaw clicking, he mustered out a simple, "Yeah." He took a shallow breath. "Honestly . . . even . . . if it were Xander, I'd probably . . . be the happiest fuck who ever lived."

"Let's get you out of there."

Rooker was shivering, and it felt like the icy ground beneath him was unsteady. He sensed Keene on his left arm, more or less dragging him. He stumbled a few times, but Keene held him upright. His eyes were too heavy to keep open. He let them close.

When they made it back to the house, police cars were pulling in. Rooker could hear the sirens and an ambulance closing in. It looked like

Tess had gotten every cop in the area over here practically at warp speed. It made his heart feel warm, even as the rest of his body was frozen.

Tess wrapped blankets around him. "If you want, we can just set the place on fire. Might warm you up faster."

Rooker tried to force a smile, but it didn't work. All he could think about while he was waiting to die was his son and how much of a coward Rooker had been lately. He had come to this place to cheat life, to die. He'd wanted nothing more in this world than to have his son back with him, even if it was in the afterlife. Now, things had changed. Rooker didn't feel so ready anymore. There was something he needed to do. He needed to catch this guy. He needed to live for his boy, even if it were only a little longer.

"It was him." Rooker coughed. "Henry wasn't the killer."

"You don't know that," Keene said. "Henry still looks like our killer. Maybe this is someone out to get you, revenge against your father maybe."

"11:37." Rooker said the numbers and opened his eyes, then turned to glance at Tess. Cold sweat beaded across his forehead. "It wasn't Meachum. I called the warden and had them check on him. I got a call back before I could hang up with the warden." Rooker replayed the words in his mind.

So you aren't Meachum.

No.

"It was a man, deep voice. All he said was the word *no*. And then I heard a crack. It happened so fast." He started taking in deeper gulps of air, was struggling to breathe. "I feel like I was on the ground and my chest was on fire before I even heard the window explode."

"Stop talking," Tess pleaded.

"He's a good shot." Rooker pointed to his chest, and a medic started cutting his shirt.

Rooker hadn't noticed Keene leave the room, but now the detective hurried back into the cottage and said to Tess, "The neighbor is dead. Her throat is slit."

Rooker's eyes shut again. His heart sank. He wanted to cry, scream, squeal, but he couldn't. Here was another person he had killed. Rooker had always wondered why she wasn't dead already, why Evelyn Holmberg hadn't been one of his father's victims. It was a sorry excuse, but maybe she had been living on borrowed time all along. Maybe he had been too.

Chapter 38

January 15

Their hushed voices didn't wake him. It was the pain. Excruciating, empty-stomached, nauseating pain. His chest was throbbing like he'd been shot all over again. It forced his stomach to flip, to churn on empty. The morphine drip was no longer helping.

He kept his eyes closed tight, his face relaxed like a child playing sleep. He listened through agony.

"Rest and rehabilitation," a doctor urged. "We had to operate in order to remove some bullet fragments. No organ damage, but there was heavy swelling and fluid buildup due to the force of the bullet. We were able to drain it, clean him up, and stitch it closed. He'll have a scar front and back, but he'll likely recover all function. I've seen some lucky people come through here, and he's at the head of the pack. Lucky to be alive."

"Thank you," he heard. It was Tess.

"But he needs to do the rehab. And two more things."

"What are they?"

"The ultrasound showed early stages of liver damage. If he keeps it up—the drinking—you're talking cirrhosis of the liver."

No shit, Rooker thought.

"And the second?"

"Do you happen to know if he takes any medications or heavier drugs?"

"There was something in his home, a prescription for Ziprasidone. It wasn't opened."

"Ziprasidone can be used to treat a range of things," he said. "Schizophrenia, bipolar disorder, hallucinations . . ."

Rooker wondered what other tests they'd run on him. He wondered what the EKG read, if it was just broken lines, the fragments of what remained of his heart, much like the bullet fragments they had to pull out of him. He imagined them playing a game of Operation. He tried to muster up the strength to talk, but he couldn't.

The rest of the conversation blurred, like the droning lull of someone talking into a fan. His head started to feel empty again. And then it went blank.

Chapter 39

The media staked out the station. Outside, Tess drove past vans for WCCO, FOX 9, and KSPT-TV. Camera crews were setting up. Her teeth broke into the first thing she'd eaten in close to ten hours—a protein bar that tasted like a mixture of nougat and chalk. She watched a portly, suited man squash an ember bug-like beneath his sneaker. Another man dressed in jeans and a hooded sweatshirt wrangled wires and untangled himself. A woman and her Pomeranian eavesdropped from the sidewalk; she donned gray pajamas beneath a black winter coat, with fur slippers on her feet and a dark leather handbag around her wrist. There were boom microphones attached to poles like fishing rods, cameras and cell phones held high overhead. And then she saw vans with satellites on their rooftops and the logos for ABC, CNN, FOX, and CBS.

I'm fucked, she thought. That meant it was receiving national news coverage. Larsson wasn't taking her calls. He had hung her out to dry.

A hammering ache blazed behind her eyes.

The parking garage wasn't blocked off. Still, she parked at the curb and watched the news anchors through the glass preparing to go live, one brushing her silky hair, another applying lipstick. A man with a graying mane adjusted his periwinkle paisley tie, as well as the place where he stood. Nearly all of them plunged forward for a better spot, as close to the station as they could get.

Bastards. She scowled and pinched the scar on her fingertip, picking at the rigid white skin, muttering under her breath as though the horde might hear her otherwise.

Tess was dressed in what she'd worn last night—dark jeans, a navy sweatshirt, and zippered blue jacket. She exited the cruiser and hurried toward the front entrance. Her ponytail swayed. She kept her head down. But sure enough, someone saw her. And then they were all moving toward her, a loud crowd banging shoulders and equipment, cutting her off from the entryway. In her peripheral, she caught someone receiving a shoulder check before they shoved someone backward with the palms of their hands. She watched the woman from CNN trip over someone else's leg. A couple of vehicles stopped at a green light to see what the commotion was about.

"Detective Harlow! What's Rooker Lindström's status? Do you care to comment on Evelyn Holmberg?"

Tess waded through the flood of them. Pushed and shoved her way past.

"Did you shoot an innocent man? Where's Chief Larsson?"

She ignored them. But as she considered the latter, she thought to herself again—*fuck Larsson.* While more questions hurled her way, she marched farther away from them and saw three people step outside. Sampson and Wood—two muscular guys who worked the drug task force—pushed the mob back, while one of the dispatchers, Molly Hughes, stood watch from the stairs. Tess turned back and said pettily, "Chief Larsson will be giving a press conference later today. You can direct your questions to him."

When Tess made it past Molly into the building, she tried her best to breathe. The door slammed shut behind her, and the shouts dimmed to whispers.

She made it into the detective room, where the tired eyes of her team looked up at her. She knew they'd spent most of the night canvassing the area around Rooker's home. But there was nothing to find. No shell casings. Nothing aside from the broken glass and Evelyn Holmberg's body.

"It's crazy out there, boss," Sterling said.

"Yeah?" she quipped. "Couldn't tell."

"How's he doing?" Cole asked.

"He just got out of surgery." She blew a long breath of air, tucked a few stray strands of hair behind her ear, and plopped down into a seat. "If the shot hit any closer to his artery, he'd be dead. The doctor said he's one of the luckiest patients he's ever seen, said he's expected to make a full recovery."

Sterling put on the television.

"Right now, we are following that breaking news in Itasca County. Rooker Lindström—the son of the infamous serial killer Gunner Lindström—was shot last evening in his Deer Lake home." Tess read the news ticker at the bottom of the screen: ROOKER LINDSTRÖM SHOT, NEIGHBOR MURDERED.

How sweet, she thought. *"Neighbor." They couldn't even put Evelyn's name.*

A wavy line distorted the center of the TV. Xander got up from his seat and gave the side of the television a good whack. But nothing happened.

"Don't think that works anymore." Sterling smiled. He changed the channel while Xander sat back down.

"So what are we thinking?" Martin Keene asked. "Do we think Henry had an accomplice? That *they* shot Rooker and killed Evelyn?"

Tess poured a cup of coffee, popped two ibuprofen capsules in her mouth, and swallowed hard. A small tremor seized her hand from caffeine and lack of sleep. "I think we have to."

"We are at the Itasca County Sheriff's Department, where if you look behind me, we just watched Detective Tess Harlow enter the station without comment. Detective Harlow headed the investigation that led to the death of Henry Hult, the suspect in the murder of seven women. We have not learned anything of the shooter in this incident."

"It's every channel," Sterling said, while he switched to another.

". . . as you see behind me, it's a grim scene out here at the Lindström cottage, also known as Lindström Manor. Tape has bordered off the perimeter of the home." The camera panned to what was left of the window. Broken glass covered the ground. *"Mr. Lindström is said to have survived the shooting and has made it out of surgery, but the neighbor"*—the video panned to the home a few hundred feet away, to Evelyn's home— *"Evelyn Holmberg, was murdered."*

He changed it again.

". . . where Rooker Lindström was taken by ambulance to—"

"Turn it off," Tess snapped.

Chapter 40

He wasn't dead.

It was a good shot. He'd known it the moment the glass shattered and Rooker collapsed. Running through the cold with a bleeding wound—knowing what a bullet could do to organs and tissue—Rooker was sure to die. But he hadn't. The fucker was tough. He thought about how easy it would be to kill him now—lying there in a gown in his little hospital bed. If it weren't for the police outside the room, he could just wring Rooker's neck and be done with it.

When Henry was killed, the guard dogs keeping watch outside Evelyn Holmberg's home had been called off. And for good reason. With the killer dead, why would they stay?

Only, I wasn't dead.

Since that night, he hadn't slept. He even tried the pills he had been prescribed, the blue-and-pink ones. They only left him jittery and paranoid. He could feel his mind fighting to stay conscious. He'd lie awake, picturing himself the hunter, taking his spot two hundred feet out in the snow. The fog of his breath. The sweat collecting in the pits of his arms. The revitalizing cold against the inseam of his pants. And behind the scope, the smile across his face and the tears in his eyes from the adrenaline and the wintry gust. And then the whip crack and the power of the rifle in his hands. His prey bleeding out, fleeing futilely from him. Even though Rooker was still alive, he felt electrified.

He'd waited there in the dark, pencil sketching the signature Henry left at the bottom of the paintings. It was just a bleeding tear. It looked so simple. Yet every time he tried one, his hand smudged over it, and it came out blotchy, runny like a burst egg yolk. Still, he scribbled the signature over and over in the notepad on his lap.

Lena.

He could picture them calling out to her. Over their crunching steps in the snow and the roaring wind through the trees—shouting. Pleading. Lena. Lena.

Call her name, but you won't find her.

Chapter 41

Rooker spent the last few days of his hospital stay cursing the physical therapist they'd sent him. *Hans.* Rooker thought he was just as evil as that other Hans. Hans Gruber. The villain in the greatest Christmas classic ever made—*Die Hard*. Rooker pictured himself as John McClane, sending Hans out a window of the thirty-five-story Nakatomi Plaza.

The new Hans would poke and prod and pull and each time leave Rooker in more pain than the last. Tess walked in just as they were finishing up, Rooker's grimace and squinted eyes making her smile. He was cursing at Hans through gritted teeth.

"It's not funny," Rooker growled.

"Not at all," she replied, the smile only growing. "Once you're done, you can get out of here."

Rooker managed to slip his jacket on, and he made his way out of the room with Tess. He never looked back.

"Thank God," Rooker said as he made it out of earshot. "Any news?"

Tess knew he was talking about the case. "No news."

"They say no news is good news, but I'm not so sure in this case."

"Me either."

Rooker thought about that. Why would the killer come after him, shoot him, then wait to kill again? He should have been out there racking up more victims, leaving more women dead on display. Maybe the killer was waiting for Rooker to get back on his feet, to play this cat and mouse game a little longer.

"I want a gun," he said. He waited for the scrutiny, for her to say that he wasn't a cop.

"I can't give a civilian a loaded weapon."

"I thought I was a consultant on the case."

"You are. I still can't give you a gun."

"If I'd had one that night, you might have your killer."

"Or I might have a dead consultant."

"I'm a good shot, believe it or not."

"Yeah? You aren't even fully healed. You can't fire a gun."

"I'll shoot lefty. I bet you I'm a better shot lefty than you righty."

What Rooker didn't tell her was that he had been a lefty, until his father forced him to do everything with his right hand. It's the reason he was so good at fighting orthodox.

"Not happening, sorry. Why don't you tell me about the Ziprasidone?"

Rooker smirked and watched her. "Typical detective. It's for psychotic symptoms in PTSD. After my boy died, I started seeing stuff that wasn't there. Hallucinations. Dark things. They usually go away."

"So why was the pill box unopened?"

"Don't want to be medicated if I don't need to be. I have it under control." He didn't know if it was the truth or a lie.

Once outside, he winced as the cold air invaded his shirt. His hand covered his bandaged chest to block the icy gusts. Tess opened her car door and eyed Rooker standing there.

"Well? Get in."

"I have to do something."

"No chance." She shook her head like she was his mother. "You were shot. You could have died. You don't leave my sight."

"It's about Evelyn," Rooker lied. "She had a daughter. I'd like to speak to her and pay my respects."

Tess stared at him. "I'll give you a ride."

"No, I need to clear my head."

Tess bit her cheek and let out a heavy sigh. "You get back to the department within the hour. Got it?"

"Yep."

"If you aren't back within the hour . . ." She paused, unsure what to threaten him with. Instead, she said nothing and shot him a look.

Rooker waited for the cab to pull up. When it did, he sat inside and gave the address for Peter Sundgren's house. He needed a gun.

Twenty minutes later, the cab pulled up to Sundgren's. Rooker got out and asked the driver to stay. He said he'd be maybe twenty minutes at most. He walked up the steps, knocked, and waited for Helen to come to the door. She greeted him with a warm smile, took his hand, and patted it as she walked him inside. Peter was watching an old black-and-white film. It was a fuzzy detective picture. Rooker recognized Jimmy Stewart but no one else. He could see that Peter had been dozing off, but now he came awake.

"Rooker," he said, rubbing his eyes. "What brings you here?"

"I hope you don't mind. I need your service weapon."

Rooker took in the look Helen suddenly gave him. "Can I get you some food, dear? You look hungry."

"Yes," Sundgren said. "Eat something."

Helen whisked away to the kitchen, and Rooker could hear her open the refrigerator door.

Peter was staring at him, looking stunned. "It was in the papers; Helen and I sent flowers. I hope you got them." Rooker nodded. "We visited too. But still . . . I was a detective. I can't just give you my gun and send you after this guy."

"I won't be going after him. It's for protection. If I'd had one that night, I might have done a lot better."

A crease cornered Sundgren's mouth, skeptical to say the least. "You know how to use one?"

"Yeah."

"Then show me."

The next part came easily.

Rooker went back up to the attic, pulled the box down, and lifted the lid. He took the gun out and turned the lid of the box over. He released the mag, racked the slide, and checked the chamber within twenty seconds. It was empty, no bullet in the chamber. Then he pointed the gun away, pulled the trigger, and pulled the slide back to release it. He detached the spring and barrel next, rubbed away at it with the bottom of his undershirt, and reassembled it. He was fast. Sundgren was surprised.

"How'd you learn to do that?"

"There was one in the house growing up. I considered blowing the old man's brains out plenty of times. Why do you still have it?"

"Sometimes a detective retires, the gun retires too. I holstered this pistol for twelve years. It kept me safe. Helen doesn't want one in the house, so the attic is our compromise." He paused, looking Rooker in the eyes. "Eat something."

"Look, Peter—"

"*Now.* And if you have to use it, you make damn sure you get him first. And it doesn't come back on me."

Peter got up from the chair and grabbed a box of ammunition down from the top of a cupboard. Helen brought over a sandwich on a dish: thick pieces of dark rye loaded with roast beef, hard-boiled egg, pickled cucumber, radish, and some sort of mustard topped with capers. Rooker scarfed it down. He handed the plate back to Helen, said his thanks, and shook Peter's hand. He promised to stay out of trouble, but he knew it wasn't possible. He kissed Helen on the cheek and received Peter's ruffian act, though the two of them smiled from beginning to end.

He ambled out onto the street and took the cab back to the station. When he arrived, he walked through the doors and knocked on the wall of the room where everyone was sitting. Tess had the team working weekends. Keene waved him over. Whitlock was back, the same scowl across his face aimed like a shotgun at Rooker's eyes. He stared back, straight down the twin barrels.

Cole was sitting behind his desk, spinning an antique pen like he'd never been shot. Rooker gazed at the board; it was new. Henry's dead face was at the top with a large red X drawn through it like he was a target in a spy film. It meant that he was a suspect, and now he was dead. There was a question mark above his face. To the right was a separate board, a map of Minnesota with small photos of the dead women in Itasca County. And now Evelyn Holmberg was up there. He turned away. The corner of the room he happened to turn his gaze to was lined with photographs of the paintings.

Tess was leaning back against Langston's desk. She looked up and noticed him. Almost seemed surprised that he was there this soon or maybe that he'd come back at all. But her expression changed little.

"Good to have you back." Keene clapped a firm, beastly hand on his shoulder. The force almost sent Rooker forward, but he planted his feet to steady himself. It didn't feel the best on his chest either. There were a few heads nodding around the room, and he indicated his thanks.

"We're too late in the game not to have a suspect," Tess said, staring at the board. Rooker knew she was looking above Henry at the question mark. "If this man indeed is Henry, then he's connected to the killer. Maybe the two worked together. But if we don't find him soon, we'll be knocking on more doors, letting their next of kin know that they've lost someone they love."

Rooker eyed the brown bakery bags and coffee. The bag crinkled as he plucked a raspberry cave cookie and a Punsch-roll. He poured himself a cup and sat down sipping it, crumbling powdered sugar and chocolate flakes everywhere.

"If I'm the killer and I know two cops are down and I hurt this guy bad, I'd feel invincible," Xander said. "So why don't we have another victim yet?"

Tess appeared to choose her words carefully. Even as she said them, they seemed distasteful to her. "Rooker thinks things have become more personal. He thinks the killer's mission has changed."

"Changed how?" It was Vic Sterling, clearly intrigued.

"I don't know." Rooker bit into the cave. "Things feel different, like he wants to punish me."

"No shit—he put a hole through your chest." Xander snickered.

"But the waiting, there not being another victim yet. It feels like he was waiting for me."

"Mighty presumptuous of you," Xander said.

"Knock it off," Tess said. "Right now, people don't feel safe, and they shouldn't. The chief put it out there that we'd caught the killer, and maybe we thought so too. Now the public knows we were wrong. We need to catch this guy."

Xander shrugged. "So what do you want to do? Set a trap? And who's to say there isn't another victim, and maybe we just haven't found her yet?"

Rooker was already tired of hearing Xander speak. "Setting a trap won't work with this guy," he said. "He's smart. Calculated. Patient. Putting a girl out there on the street for him to take would never work."

"Maybe we could get it out there in a magazine that he's a homo, that maybe his mommy used to touch him."

Rooker's face went hot. It burned the way his chest had when the bullet went through him.

"Out," Tess said. Xander gaped at her in disbelief.

"What?"

Rooker stood up, ready to dismantle Xander Whitlock. The office was filled, everyone was there, but he promised himself he wouldn't let anyone pull him off. He didn't care about the stitches in his chest. He'd cave his fucking head in, make his face resemble a different person.

"You heard me," Tess said. "Get out."

Xander got up, pulled the jacket from the back of his desk chair, and stormed off. He was lucky Rooker hadn't gotten a crack at him; Xander had alluded to the article that got his son killed. Eduardo Arroyave was more friend than source. They both had sons around the same age; Rooker had even taken Britton to a backyard birthday party at the Arroyaves' one year.

In the murder case, Arroyave had been on the front line. Rooker trusted him.

The two of them had met at Angie's Diner on West Florida Avenue. Rooker was always the earlier of the two. Arroyave would slide into the booth like he was right on time, even if he was ten minutes late. "Evidence points to sexual abuse," Arroyave had told him. A glob of runny egg yolk dribbled off his lip. As he wiped it, he said, "We think by his mother. Can't really spill the details—let's just say it's 'Mommy's little secret' kinda shit. We think it went on for *years*—it's why he hates women. Explains the violence toward them. Our profilers think he's a homosexual."

It was a lie. The same lie Rooker typed up that evening and ran a day later—and the story caught like wildfire.

Even with Xander out of sight, Rooker could barely control himself. He wanted nothing more than to go after him. He was still standing, staring at the doors Xander left through.

"It's not worth it," Keene told him.

The meeting dragged on, but Rooker didn't hear much of it. They had nothing new. The potential suspect Erickson wound up dead; the clear suspect Henry was equally dead.

He walked into Tess's office, where she was typing something up. He sat on the carpet and talked to her for a few minutes before he fell asleep right there on the floor.

Chapter 42

Rooker was lying beside Tess's desk, throwing a mock-Earth stress ball into the air and catching it. His hair was getting long; he raked a few strands from in front of his eyes. Tess had told him she'd cut it, but he hadn't given in just yet. She'd also told him if he kept it up with the ball, she'd cut it in half.

For three weeks, he'd visit her office and offer whatever assistance he could. It wasn't much. But now, thanks to the Meltzers, they had a positive ID on the dead man: Henry Frederick Hult. He had suffered a second-degree burn on his left wrist and forearm at a young age. The scar was still there. Anna Meltzer breathed a sigh of relief when she knew the boy—the man—was dead.

"I just got a call from an old friend. Nils went through the exams the same time as me. He's part of the detective squad for Minneapolis PD First Precinct. A woman asked for you by name. Her name is Elaine Warrington. Her daughter Lena is missing."

Tess put the call on speakerphone, and Rooker gave her a what-do-I-say expression.

"This is Rooker Lindström," he said.

"My daughter is missing. I got a call; he said he'd kill Lena if I didn't phone you."

Rooker looked at Tess. "How long has she been missing?"

"She was supposed to call me last night when she got home from the office. Her driver said that she wasn't there when he went to pick her up. Her glove was on the ground. He figured her fiancé picked her up."

"Mrs. Warrington, I'm only a consultant on the case. I'm not a policeman. But I am working with them, and we're going to do our absolute best to find her. I can't make any promises. And I won't lie to you; she is in danger." Rooker hadn't exactly worked on his bedside manner. He knew what she wanted to hear, and this wasn't even close. He'd much rather someone had been honest with him, like he was being now.

"Please find my daughter."

"The police are already on it," he assured her. "What's the number I can reach you at?"

He asked for a few details as far as height, weight, hair color, and clothing. He watched Tess grab a notepad and pen and scribble everything down. He told her he'd be calling soon.

Before she could hang up, he had one more thing.

"Mrs. Warrington?"

"Yes?"

"What's her fiancé's name?"

"I know what you're thinking. Erik wouldn't lay a hand on her."

"It's standard—it's what they'll ask you. What's his last name?"

"Sadler."

He froze. His hand started to shake. "Thank you, ma'am. We'll be in touch." He hung up.

"Jesus Christ," said Tess.

"What the hell is going on here? Are we sure the man we have is Henry?"

"The Meltzers positively ID'd him. Why would they lie? Anna Meltzer looked like she was going to throw a party."

Rooker watched as Tess dialed Nils. She spoke quickly but clearly. She told him about their situation, that the killer was still out there and about Erik Sadler's fiancée. She asked if he could get access to cameras outside Lena's office.

Rooker's first thought was to perform a basic search on his laptop. "Lena Warrington, thirty-one years old, bigwig executive at a law office in Central Minneapolis," he told Tess. Rooker pulled up her bio when he typed her name into the computer. In her photo, she wore her hair down. Long black waves flowed down the left and right edges of her face, where a manufactured smile and professional eyes made her look artificial. His second thought was that she might already be dead.

Tess went to the doorway and yelled out to the team. "Lena Warrington—Erik Sadler's fiancée—is missing. Everyone, pack a bag; we're getting on a plane to Minneapolis within the hour."

Tess called in some favors and was able to get the seven of them chartered on a private jet to Minneapolis. It took them an hour, compared to a three-hour drive. They didn't even need to go through screening, so they all carried their holstered weapons. Even Rooker, whose pistol was tucked away and hidden by his jacket. Tess sat beside him; Millie and Cole were across the aisle; and Keene, Xander, and Sterling argued over the window seat. The three of them were stuck next to each other. Keene won but somehow got talked out of it by Sterling, who sat with the window shade down the entire flight. Rooker had dozed off once or twice and woke up when turbulence made his head fall off his hand. When he stood up, his arm hurt from pressing down into the armrest, and his legs barely moved.

When the plane landed, they were escorted down to the ground with their bags and driven away in two vehicles. Nils Peterson was waiting for them beside a blacked-out Dodge Charger. A different man was waiting beside an unmarked SUV. Langston got into the front seat; Keene, Cole, and Sterling squeezed into the back. Nils Peterson had a skin-fade military haircut and a thicker beard. His eyes were light, but his eyebrows loomed over them like hurricane clouds. He shook Tess's hand and gave a hint of a smile, then shook Rooker's without it. Rooker thought he could see Nils's hand constrict a bit more around his hand than he did Tess's, but he didn't mind.

"I'm taking you both to the department. We're on short notice, but things are mostly up and running. Just let me know what you need, and I'll do my best. We're currently trying to get the video off those surveillance cameras outside the office. We found three cameras that overlook it, one camera inside that faces the door. We should be able to go through that soon."

Tess nodded. "I want Millie Langston on that with whoever you have. She's our best when it comes to that sort of thing."

"You got it. Do we have any leads; do we know any places where he'd take her?"

The car pulled out and before long, Rooker could see the airport in the distance. He sat in the back seat, occasionally looking at Nils. Rooker would catch one side of his face; every now and then the two would make eye contact in the rearview mirror. Rooker had seen plenty of military types with all the bases in California. He couldn't help but wonder if this guy hated him or if it was just his natural disposition. It was too soon to tell.

"Why Lena Warrington?" Nils asked.

"The more important question is, why Erik Sadler?" Rooker said this from the back and watched Peterson's reaction.

"So you're more concerned with him than with the woman whose life is in danger."

Rooker's eyes narrowed. "Am I missing something? Why does it sound so personal?"

Nils didn't say anything at first. His lip tightened to a crack. Then: "If you have one bone in your body like your old man's, I'll arrest you and make some shit up to lock you away."

"Sounds perfectly legal," Rooker said.

Nils continued to drive but seemed to be sulking beneath that thick beard. After fifteen minutes, the car pulled into a lot lined with police cars. The three of them got out. They walked into the building, and a minute later, Langston, Cole, Sterling, Xander, and Keene were bustling through to catch up.

The place was more official, probably twice if not triple the size of the department in Itasca County. Nils commanded the attention of the room much like Tess usually did.

"All right, everyone, listen up. This is Detective Tess Harlow; we went through the academy together. This is her team. We're looking for a man who took this woman"—Nils directed their attention to a large photo on a projector screen—"Lena Warrington." He paused. "Tess told me they have reason to believe she was targeted because of her fiancé, Erik Sadler."

Tess jumped in. "Erik Sadler is connected to Henry Frederick Hult, a suspect my team shot and killed in self-defense. The two of them were boys in the same neighborhood; we think Henry was responsible for the death of Erik's brother, Gregory. We believed Henry to be the serial killer, but now we know he can't be based on the disappearance of Ms. Warrington and the attempted murder of Rooker Lindström. The killer went after him about five weeks ago, after Henry was killed."

"So we think it's Erik? Right?" one of the men on Peterson's team said. "He didn't even report his fiancée missing. And he's lawyered up."

Rooker had leaped to the same conclusion when he was on the phone with Lena's mother. He wasn't sure it made sense, though. Yes, Erik Sadler was connected to the case, would have potentially had access to the files through his father, and knew Henry. But Erik Sadler believed Henry killed his brother, didn't he? Rooker imagined the two wouldn't be working together.

"It's a possibility," Tess said, to Rooker's surprise. "We have to consider all possibilities. So we'll look at him while trying to find any leads and the whereabouts of Lena Warrington."

The meeting continued for another ten minutes. Langston was put on the surveillance; Cole said he'd help her. Peterson's men would be dispersed to Lena's offices to question her colleagues as well as her driver. Keene went with them. That left Sterling, Xander, Rooker, and Tess. Tess told Xander and Sterling to check on Lena's family. Rooker wanted to see where Erik and Lena lived. He asked Tess if he could go with her to the house, and she said yes.

Unfortunately for Rooker, their escort was Nils Peterson. He sat in silence and pretended Nils didn't exist, while Nils and Tess weren't speaking much either. Parts of the city reminded him of the buildings he'd seen in California and New York City, but then there were colorful buildings that made him think of castles.

They pulled up to a three-level house with brick that resembled milk chocolate or marble. The roof looked brand-new and was a dark metal sheet. The garage doors were open, and a white Land Rover sat beside a black one.

"His and hers," Tess said.

Rooker looked up at the multimillion-dollar house. He'd seen places like it on his drives to La Jolla, Coronado, and Del Mar. To the right was a beautiful pool surrounded by large, square gray tile. Rooker could see through the floor-to-ceiling glass that went from the garage into the downstairs living space. A moment later, he watched a man come to the door and open it toward him.

"Please come in," he said.

Rooker was last to shake the man's hand, and what it looked like surprised him. The nails looked manicured, but the palms were calloused, with cracked straw-yellow bubbles lifted at the base of each finger. A few of the knuckles were split and ash-white. Rooker thought about asking what had made them that way, but it would only give Sadler the perception that he was a suspect.

Otherwise, Erik Sadler looked the part of the primped attorney on sabbatical. A powder-blue striped dress shirt tailored perfectly to his physique, the top two white buttons undone. It sat pristinely ironed, untucked above dark-blue pants and brown shoes. He was chiseled with dark, wavy hair parted to the left and a well-kept beard. To Rooker, the guy looked more like a male model than a businessman.

Sadler walked them up a wooden floating staircase with a glass railing and small circular lighting to the right of each step. They walked past a room with a sectional sofa and a large flat-screen TV mounted on the wall with what looked like a surround system built in. There was art positioned on the walls, and Rooker figured all the pieces were expensive based on the rest of the home.

Erik Sadler walked the three of them into a kitchen and living area that looked like it was out of a catalog. There was an entire wall of gold snakeskin. The room was more futuristic than modern.

"I want to remind you that I do have a lawyer," he said to them.

"If you feel uncomfortable answering anything we ask, you don't need to answer," Nils said.

"Tea or coffee?" Erik asked the three of them.

Rooker ignored the question and continued walking, looking out the windows.

"Do you have a maid? Anyone who cleans the house?" Rooker heard Tess ask. Of course, she must have known the answer so was using the question to get him talking.

"Yes, we do; she's here three days a week."

"Can you think of anyone who might've wanted to do Lena harm? Do you think the maid could've been in on your fiancée's disappearance?"

Rooker watched Tess. So far, she had in no way let it be known that he was a suspect. By doing this, they would see exactly how cool, calm, and collected Erik Sadler was. Rooker noticed the man pause, but his eyes didn't linger.

"Excuse me?"

"The disappearance, can you think of anyone who might be in on it?" she asked. "You're worth a lot of money, Mr. Sadler. Have you been contacted about a ransom?"

"At the moment, no. I can't think of anyone who would kidnap my fiancée." The last bit came out sharp. "And no. I haven't been contacted about a ransom."

This time, Nils Peterson spoke up. "Mr. Sadler, why didn't you report your fiancée missing?"

Rooker almost wanted to like Nils for asking the question he wanted an answer to.

"Well, I didn't know she was missing. Not until her mother called. I thought maybe she had been working late or had driven to her mother's."

"Isn't that her car in the garage?"

"Well, yes. I meant maybe her driver took her over."

Rooker backpedaled out of the room. While he eavesdropped on their conversation, he snuck around to do a little investigating of his own. Just as he turned a corner, he saw it. It was the same size as the others. The canvas hung inches from the wall. The paint was white, gray, and black. The trees in the distance were dark aside from the snow that covered them. The water shimmered like glass. He stared—as he did many mornings—at the view out of his second-story window, at his bedroom's view of the lake. He was staring at one of Henry's paintings, only this one was meant for him.

Rooker snatched it from the wall and stormed back into the room. "How did you get this?"

"A man sold it to me. He told me it would look perfect in my home."

"Who?"

"I don't know; I never got his name—"

"Was it this man?" Tess said. She showed Erik Sadler a photo of Henry.

"No—isn't that Henry? His photo was released in the papers. Still had those baggy eyes and that rat face."

"You two didn't see eye to eye," Tess said.

"No, never. He was the black sheep."

"Black sheep?" Nils repeated.

"He was a problem child. If you ask me, he was the type to cut up animals in a sink. The other kids said he had a disorder and that he killed someone. They said he heard voices, things like that. He would always give them this menacing look back, like he was thinking about killing them. They called him Handjob Henry, said he was gay for my brother. Probably why he drowned him."

Rooker listened to all of it. He was fixated on the painting, but his ears were tuned in to every word. He wondered what the painting being in Erik Sadler's home meant. Was Rooker supposed to find the painting? Did Erik Sadler want him to see it, to show he was the killer and that Rooker was going to die? And then he thought about the night he was shot—sprinting through the woods. Maybe it was meant to symbolize Rooker's death that night—but he lived.

"What happened after Gregory died? Henry just disappeared?" Rooker said.

"No, I saw him one more time, weeks later. I was walking home, and he was standing there by a tree, staring at me. I ran at him and tackled him, started hitting him in the face. But he had something, slugged me across the front of my temple with it. I don't know what it was, but it felt like a damn baseball bat, and then blood was gushing down my head. I felt him scurry out from under me. He told me I was lucky he let me live; then I heard his feet as he ran away. That's the last time I saw him."

"You're positive it's the last time?"

"Yes."

"Mr. Sadler, how did you come by the painting? Did the man approach you with it?"

"I was headed to the office. Same route I always take. At a stoplight, this guy walks right up to the window like a panhandler. But then he shows me this painting and tells me how I need to take it."

"When was this? Did you see his face?"

"Maybe two months ago? And no, it was starting to get dark."

"Did you see him approach any other vehicles before yours?"

"No." Sadler scratched his manicured nails at his forehead. "I don't think so. I just wanted him to go away, so I pulled a few bills out of my wallet and handed them to him. Lena ended up thinking it was pretty, so she hung it up."

Rooker knew that Erik Sadler would become the newest suspect in the case. He figured Sadler knew it too. Was he playing them? He seemed too calm, too calculated for a person whose fiancée was missing. Rooker wondered how clean a shot he was, if he owned a rifle. Rooker turned from the painting and searched Sadler's frostbite-blue eyes. He was staring, trying to conceal his scowl, to put on a neutral mask.

"Do you have any reason to believe your fiancée would leave you?" Tess asked.

"What did you just say?" The words were like fire seething from Sadler's lips.

"I'm sorry, but I have to ask—"

"You have to ask? Of course she didn't *leave* me. Is this an interrogation? I thought I was helping you people."

"And you are," Tess said.

"Do you own a rifle, by any chance?" Rooker said.

"That's enough, Rooker," Tess said.

"Keep your dog leashed, Harlow," Nils said.

"Or what?" Rooker looked Nils dead in the eye and hoped he'd swing at him. But he didn't move.

Tess cut in. "Thank you for your time, Mr. Sadler. I apologize, and we'll do everything we can to find her. If you think of anything, you have my number. I'll do my best to keep you in the loop."

When they shut the door behind them, Tess started wringing him out on the spot.

"What the fuck was that?"

"The painting, didn't you see it? It's the view out my bedroom window, Tess. You think he got it by chance? Henry painted that."

"I don't know how he got it. But right now, we're looking for his fiancée."

"Oh please, how do we know she isn't tied up in his basement or already dead somewhere?"

"We *don't* know. But we look for her while we consider him as a suspect. We don't antagonize him and compare dick sizes."

"That's not what it was. I wanted to see the true Erik Sadler, not the pretty-boy facade he puts on. I wanted to see him squirm a little, know that we're watching him."

"*We?* If it is him, now he'll be that much more careful. Thanks to you and your ego."

Rooker decided to let the conversation end. He got in the back of the car and sulked like a child waiting for his parents to sit up front. Every now and then, he'd rub subconsciously at the spot where someone, maybe Erik Sadler, had shot him. Nils started the car while Tess buckled her seat belt. He turned his head when he put the car in reverse but paid no attention to Rooker. His eyes looked right through him like he wasn't even there. The entire ride back was spent in silence. At one point, Rooker heard the splash of the tires, felt the burning sensation in his chest when the tires hit a pothole. He winced, then told himself he was fine.

Back in the department lot, Nils shut off the SUV and got out of the car. Rooker expected him to wait for Tess, but Peterson walked back through the double doors alone. He looked over at Tess. She stared back at him in the rearview mirror, then turned her head to peer into his eyes.

"You think it's him," she said. "You think Erik Sadler is our guy."

"I think he's far too clever, far too calm for someone in his expensive loafers with his beautiful fiancée missing. Everything he does, everything he says, it all seems premeditated. He could be our guy. I'm not saying he is, but he could be."

"I don't think you're wrong, but you seemed to be looking for a reason to stamp 'murderer' across his head."

"What about the painting? You think someone mapped out his trip to his office and targeted him?"

"Maybe it really was Henry. I don't know. But having the painting doesn't make him a killer."

Bullshit, it doesn't, Rooker thought. But she was right. For now, they'd keep a constant, unblinking eye on him. Sadler would know he was a suspect. In the meantime, they'd try to locate the fiancée.

"Ready?"

She opened her door, and Rooker slid out into the brisk chill. At least he was out of the back seat. He no longer felt like a toddler who'd been scolded. He followed behind Tess, admiring her curves. One of the guys held the door open for her, then for Rooker by the sheer fact that he was only two strides behind. Based on the look Rooker was given, he figured the man wanted to shut the door in his face but didn't dare. He followed Tess into a room where Langston's voice beckoned her.

"Boss, we got something."

"What is it?"

"So, we've been going through the camera footage of the building. Take a look at this." Langston pressed a few buttons and clicked the mouse. Rooker was peering over Tess's shoulder like a spectator from nosebleed seats. He watched the footage in fast forward come to a stop and begin to play in real time.

"Here." Langston pointed to a vehicle that parallel parked outside the building not even half a block from the front of it. "The vehicle sits here for the next hour and twenty-seven minutes. The driver waits in the spot even after our girl leaves, about twenty minutes after, then drives away."

"Do we have anything on the vehicle? Plates?"

"No plates. The vehicle has no markings, and we can't pull up a VIN number. We narrowed it down to an early 2000s Ford F-150, two-door, dark navy, gray, or black. Tinted windows and the grille emblem missing. Even the back of the truck looks like he scraped or pried everything off and painted over it to throw us off."

"So how do we find it?"

"Well, there's the issue. We tried to track it with the cameras, but we lose it a few minutes down the road. The vehicle turns onto side roads, and we can't locate it. Another issue . . ." Langston paused.

"What is it?"

"The top-five selling car models in Minnesota, he picked the most common. He knew it would be hard for us to find the truck."

"Wait, you said he picked it. Do you think he bought it or stole it?"

"That we don't know yet. We're looking into it, but either way, it would take time. If he stole it, we don't know where he stole it from. If he bought it, same thing. We'll try to find it, but he made it damn hard for us. We'll keep trying to find something on the cameras."

"Thanks, nice work," Tess said. "Let me know if you see anything else."

Tess walked out of the room, and Rooker followed.

"How many people do we have watching Sadler?" he asked.

"We have Keene and Sterling in a car, and two of Peterson's guys are in a Suburban on the other side. He won't be able to leave the house without us knowing."

They got into the car Nils Peterson was lending them. It was a black unmarked Dodge Charger, a few models old but sharp. Tess drove to the Hewing Hotel where they would be staying. They picked up their room keys, stepped into the elevator, and Tess pressed the button for their floor. When the doors opened, Rooker followed her out.

"What's the story with you and Peterson?"

She turned toward him. "What are you asking?"

"Were you two a thing?"

She smiled. "Would that make you jealous?"

Rooker didn't answer.

Chapter 43

Rooker thought to follow her back to her room but decided against it. He expected she had chalked their night up to a onetime, drunken fling. He wasn't sure how he felt.

He stepped inside his own room, threw the key card on a small table, and fell face-first onto the bed. It was uncomfortably soft. He always liked his mattress firm, nearly as firm as the floor. Which was where he imagined he'd be sleeping tonight.

He pushed up from his stomach and felt a tingling in his chest. When his fingertips massaged the spot that was freshly healed, the skin felt foreign, like it didn't belong. Rooker stood up and slipped off his jacket and his shirt. In the mirror, his eyes locked on to the pale dash where the stitches had sewn his chest shut. To his journalist eye, it was like an em dash.

He was lucky. He had been meant to die that night, and he didn't yet know exactly how to feel now that he hadn't.

As he turned away from the mirror, he caught a glimpse of the Glock handle. It had been clawing into his hip. He slid the pistol out and checked the chamber and the slide. No one else had touched it. No one other than Sundgren knew he had it. Still, he had a compulsive need to check it. He set the pistol down and lay on the floor, looking up at the ceiling. The design overhead was foreign to him. He found himself almost missing the hypothermic chill of his bedroom, the dripping of water from the roof to his bucket. Almost missed the feeling of playing the lottery, wondering what his odds were of the roof caving in on him by morning. In the shadows on the ceiling, he could see Sadler's smug face. The raspy ticktocks of the bedside alarm were wicked chimes of laughter taunting him.

He stood once again, grabbed the pistol, and tucked it in the back of his pants. It was time to check in on Erik Sadler. In his mind's eye, he pictured the man: tie undone, face convulsing, eyes bulging wide while he strangled a poor woman long after her breath was gone.

Rooker pulled his shirt back on, grabbed his key card, and swiped his jacket in one swift motion, then took the elevator to the ground level. The doors opened, and he surveyed the lobby. He thought he saw someone resembling one of Peterson's men, but he kept his head down and walked as nonchalantly as he could. Outside, the night was cool under a dark-gray sky. The earth's ceiling would be turning black soon enough, which Rooker was hoping for. When he was far enough from the hotel, he hailed a cab and gave the driver the address.

A few turns into the drive, Rooker spotted a sedan four cars back, following them. It had been keeping its distance since he had gotten into the cab. Only a mindless idiot like Nils would consider him a killer, after being shot and nearly killed—maybe Peterson thought he'd run off and do something stupid. Nonetheless, the car was there, and Rooker didn't want anyone to see him. Not tonight.

Getaway plans ran through his mind. He wondered whether Tess would help Nils track him down. Pulling the phone out of his pocket, he powered it down and slid it back inside. He looked up front to see the estimated time left on the GPS. Thought about the turns he needed to take to get to the house. Then he gave the driver a proposition. He'd pay him the same amount and he wouldn't have to drive nearly as far. Instead, he'd have the driver make a right turn instead of a left, get out of the car, and wait for Peterson's men to follow in the wrong direction. He would walk the rest of the way to Sadler's.

He dropped the money on the passenger seat and told the driver where to turn. The steering wheel swiveled sharply, which gave Rooker even more time than he needed. He opened the door and sprang out, slamming the door shut as he took off and ducking down behind a concrete staircase. He could swear he heard his ticker thumping in his chest as he waited. The cab continued down the street and, sure enough, four cars back was the black sedan. The windows were tinted dark enough to mask their faces, but he could see the outline of two men. Once the car was out of sight, Rooker let out a long breath of air. He zipped his jacket all the way up and tucked his chin into his chest. An icy shiver escaped him as he pulled the gloves out of his back pocket and slid them on. He had decided to take them in case he needed to fire the Glock 17 Sundgren had given him. If his hands were frozen, he'd struggle to get the safety off—hell, he'd struggle to get the gun from the back of his pants. There was a flutter in his chest that almost worried him. He told himself it was just the adrenaline taking over.

Rooker turned left and headed straight across the street. He felt like a child playing a game of hide-and-seek. He steered clear of the streetlights, lampposts, and cameras and walked with his head down not just to avoid any attention but to leave less skin exposed to the wind. He trudged uphill. The streets weren't busy. Now and then, he would pass someone walking a dog.

The chill forced Rooker's arms to tighten across his chest and his head to shrink into his turtleneck. The temperature was dropping by the minute, but when he reached the street and spotted a dark SUV parked down the block from Sadler's home, he suddenly felt a little warmer.

He started heading toward the back of the house and saw the other blacked-out vehicle. Rooker stayed low, kneeling between the fence and the house. He was out of view of the surveillance team in the car, and if Sadler looked out the window, he'd see only pitch-black. Rooker didn't remember seeing any outdoor lights during his daytime visit, but if they came on and he was noticed, he'd take off running.

As he sat there in the dark, his ass wet and cold, he wondered what the hell he was doing here. The house, the painting, Erik Sadler, all of it had some kind of magnetic pull on him. Every now and then, he'd shift uncomfortably, put his arms between his legs, lean back against the hard fence, or try to scrape the snow out from under him. Nothing worked. He wished for the comfort of his hard bed or the old recliner that was falling apart in his living room. He hadn't gone back since the night he nearly died. Really, the hospital wouldn't discharge him. He assumed there would still be yellow tape all over the cottage and only hoped the place hadn't finally come crashing down.

There were lights on in Sadler's house, but the downstairs was pitch-dark. Rooker remembered seeing an alarm system beside the door. He also remembered Tess telling him that Peterson's men were in the Suburban, which left Sterling and Keene in the other car. He wondered what the two of them were talking about. A bitter shiver went through him; it wouldn't be long before he had enough of the cold. He started an internal debate about whether he should get up and go sit in the car with the two of them or continue to wait it out on the cold ground. He decided to stick it out a little longer.

Twenty minutes later, he watched a room turn black directly in front of him on the west side of the house. He watched Sadler calmly walk down a hall. He still donned the same dress shirt, only now the sleeves had been rolled up and cuffed just below the joint in his elbow. To Rooker, there seemed to be something off, though it could just have been the fact that he wanted all of this gone, to be left alone. But right now, he needed to find the killer. And he needed it to be Sadler.

Rooker's eyes were focused like the lens of a camera, steady and unblinking. He stood, brushed the snow from the back of his pants, and started moving. Looping around the fence, he walked slowly for about thirty seconds toward the blacked-out sedan. He could not stop staring at Erik Sadler. When Rooker was only steps from the vehicle, he snuck up to the passenger side and knocked hard on the passenger glass. The window came down a bit, and he cocked his head to the side to see Martin Keene busting a gut in the driver's seat, Vic Sterling beside him with a look of perplexed amusement.

When Keene stopped laughing, he asked, "What the hell are you doing?"

Rooker smiled through the cracked window. "Thought I'd go for a walk. Let me in—I'm freezing my ass off out here."

He heard the doors click and went to open the rear passenger door. It didn't budge.

"You're lucky Sterling didn't shoot you. He jumped like a little girl."

"Did not," Sterling said. "If it were Whitlock, you would've taken a bullet."

"Yeah, yeah. Just let me in."

The locks clicked again, and Rooker pulled the door open, slid inside. His teeth were chattering from the cold. He slid to the middle so he had the same view as the two of them. Martin Keene was sitting back like he was in a recliner, a thermos resting on his belly. Vic Sterling sat with his legs crossed. Not a care in the world.

"Does anyone know you're here?" Keene asked him like he was Rooker's parent, but he didn't mind. He knew Keene was looking out for him.

"Just you two."

"I've got to let Harlow know."

"You can, but not yet. Wait a little bit."

"Why?"

"I want to see for myself what Erik Sadler is really like."

"Yeah, Peterson said you had a hard-on for this guy." Sterling sounded robotic, like he was merely stating a fact.

The car got silent for a very long minute before Sterling spoke up again.

"Why don't you like this guy?" he said, staring up at the house. "You really think he's our killer?"

Rooker shook his head. "There's something about him I don't think is right. His hands, the calluses, the cuts on his knuckles. He's too calm. And he never reported Lena missing. The painting. I'm not saying he's the guy, but there's something wrong here."

They sat there for the next couple of hours, shooting the shit and watching the house. The two detectives had thermoses of coffee. A few times, Harlow and Peterson radioed for updates. Each time, Keene would look in the rearview mirror and see Rooker, but, clearly against his better judgment, he said nothing about him being there.

"If she finds out you were here, she'll kick my ass."

"I'll protect you," Rooker said, cracking a smile.

"Oh yeah. How did he explain having the painting?"

"Said a guy gave it to him. Told him it would be perfect in his house. He didn't ID Henry as the man who sold him the painting. But when he saw Henry's photo, he said his face hadn't changed much. Still looked like a rat. His words." Rooker stopped. "And even when he saw the photo, he didn't seem all that upset. Or surprised. You'd think that seeing the person who drowned your brother, or who clocked you silly once upon a time, would bring up some pretty dark memories."

"Do we know how much this guy is worth?" Sterling asked.

Keene smiled. "Close to forty million."

Sterling's eyebrows rose. "And we're sure it's our guy who took her?"

"If it wasn't, we'd be dealing with a ransom, don't you think?"

Rooker listened to the two of them talk. It wasn't long before the radio came over again.

He listened to his own name come out of Nils Peterson's mouth. "Have the two of you seen Lindström? I had men tailing him. They lost him."

Sterling turned and looked at Rooker. Keene caught his eye again through the rearview mirror, concern plastered across his face. Rooker shook his head side to side. Keene picked up the radio and pressed down on the button.

"Haven't seen him; will let you know if we do." He put the radio back down, and Rooker gave a nod.

"Why does it matter if he knows you're here?" Sterling asked.

"Because he hates me. He'd probably rather convict me than put the right guy behind bars."

"That seems like a stretch," Keene said. "Besides, if something happens, you might be better off if he knows you were with us. You'd have an alibi."

It made sense, but Rooker did not want Peterson to know his location. For now, he felt like he was above the law, he was free, he could disappear. What he really longed for was the freedom to use the weapon he was carrying. If it was never recovered, anything he did would never come back to him. Tess would have her suspicion, but nothing would stick if he played everything right.

Eight minutes had passed since 11:37 p.m. Rooker thought maybe he should turn his phone back on, see if there was a missed call. Instead, he kept looking up and down at the different levels of the home. Lights were on in various areas of each level; he knew Sadler was still on the second level somewhere past the kitchen. He suddenly regretted not poking around, not getting a feel for where everything was. He figured the master bedroom was on that level, but he couldn't be positive.

"Do we have the blueprint for the house?" Rooker asked.

"We don't," Keene said, clearly curious.

"Floor plans, building permits, that should all be public record here, right?"

"What are you thinking?"

"I want to know what room he's in, if he's added on to the home, stuff like that."

"We could get all of it, not sure about at this time at night. Might take a little while."

"Can you put in a request?"

"Will do."

Keene's phone looked like a toy in his massive furry-bear hands. He was opening a text and typing in letters, but something happened that grabbed the attention of all three of them. The lights flickered once more, and then every light in the Sadler home went black.

"Shit," Keene breathed out. His eyes were fixed on the windows, but none of them could see a thing.

"What do you think?" Sterling said.

Rooker looked around at the surrounding houses. The ones that had lights on were still lit. Erik Sadler's was the only one that had gone pitch-black.

"Let's move," Keene ordered. He opened his car door, holding his hand over the automatic light. Then he turned to Rooker. "Stay put—don't leave the car."

Rooker knew he wouldn't be listening to that. Keene and Sterling moved to the back of the car; Keene keyed the trunk lock and lifted it. Rooker was out of the car now, as quiet as a mouse, beside them. He watched Keene toss a vest to Sterling.

"Do we have one more?"

The two of them looked at Rooker. Keene knew it went against every protocol to let the civilian go with them, and he was a man who followed the rules. Seldom in his detective years could he remember going over the line. "I don't want to cuff you to the car, Rooker."

"Then don't," he said. He weaseled between the two men and pulled another vest from the back. Keene secured the straps, the Velcro so tight that Rooker struggled to breathe for a second.

"Do me a favor—don't get shot. And don't engage."

"You got it."

The three of them moved low and fast, becoming smaller targets, a little harder to see. They moved to the back door, and Rooker thought about whether the alarm was off because of the power. He hesitated for a moment. Again, something was not right.

"Wait," he whispered.

"What," Keene responded, his pistol in his hand as he got to the side of the door. Sterling was positioned on the opposite side, pistol in hand as well.

"Something's wrong. If the power were shut off outside, the other houses should've lost power, right?"

Rooker watched his thought come to fruition in Sterling's brain.

"You think it was shut off from inside," he said.

"It could be Sadler playing us. Or he could be in trouble."

"Can't risk it," said Keene. "We go in."

Keene spoke quickly and quietly into the radio. "We have a situation over here at the Sadler home. Lights went out, only house to lose power. Something possibly wrong, no location on the target, requesting backup or roadblocks. We're going in—radio silence for now."

The radio powered down, and Keene clipped it back onto his pants. He tried the door. It was locked, so he tapped the glass paneling beside it.

"It's tempered," he said. "It'll take a few swings." Keene got ready, and Rooker and Sterling stayed out of the big man's way. He pulled his sidearm upward and hurled his weight behind the butt of the pistol into the glass. Nothing. Rooker could've sworn he felt the ground tremble beneath them. Keene took another swing at it, and this time the glass burst into tiny particles. Martin reached his burly arm through the opening and patted the back of the door blindly for the lock. He found it, and the three of them heard a click. Keene turned the handle and opened the door. As the three men moved in, Rooker could feel the crunch of glass against the soles of his boots. Keene and Sterling took the lead while Rooker hung back as ordered. The two detectives took the stairs, waving to Rooker to stay put. When the two of them were about halfway up, he followed behind with his hand on the Glock. He scurried along behind them, pulled the pistol upward, and wrapped his fingers around the grip.

With Keene and Sterling in front, they swept the level they'd come in on and found nothing. The last Rooker had seen, Erik Sadler was on that level. *He should be right here,* he thought. But he wasn't. They scoured every inch of the house. Sirens suddenly came into range. Rooker could see flashing lights approach off in the distance.

Erik Sadler was gone.

Chapter 44

February 19

"What do you mean he's gone?" Tess did not mask her anger. "He's our lead suspect." She stopped talking, glared at her team and at Peterson's men who had been positioned on the other side of the house. "And what about you?" Her eyes were on Rooker now. "Why were you here?"

He didn't care. "To be honest, I'm not a fan of being tailed," he said and turned toward Nils. Rooker looked back at Tess. "Did you know about that? That he was watching me?" He took in her expression. It said enough.

Tess tilted her head toward Peterson. "No, I didn't. But when he called to tell me that you'd disappeared from the hotel"—she turned back to Rooker—"I tried to have Langston track your phone. What were you doing out here?"

"I wanted to get a better look at him."

"A better look," she repeated, shaking her head. She turned her attention back to the others. "I want you all tracking down Erik Sadler. Run a trace on his phone. Check his office. We need to find him now." The meeting ended, and Rooker walked away by himself. He was ready to head back to the hotel, but Tess yelled to him, saying she would give him a ride.

"You really did scare me," she said. "When Langston couldn't track the phone, I was worried."

"I'm sorry."

"Look, I get it. You want this to be over. Just try not to run off and scare the shit out of me."

"Okay." It was all he could say. Two lines between her brows arched. She rubbed at her forehead like she was fighting a migraine. Rooker didn't think it was the time to be witty or sarcastic. He watched her and didn't try to hide it. She knew his eyes were on her, but she didn't say a word. It was only a few minutes before they were back. Rooker left her on the ground floor and went up to his room. The door blinked green, and he went inside. In the center of the bed were the two books from Walter Erickson's study that he'd tossed there before he left. Stieg Larsson. Jo Nesbø. Both copies looked like they'd been read a hundred times, and Rooker was nearly certain they didn't belong to Walter Erickson. Yet there they had been, sitting on his desk. He turned the lights on and sat on the bed, his back up against the headboard. He opened the books, shook them, but nothing fell out. He was hoping it would be like a pair of pants, green bills and change seeping from the pockets.

He was tapping their covers as he tried to think. There was something here, though he didn't know what it was. The way they were left out, it was like they were a message, possibly for Rooker, one he didn't know how to decipher. He put one book down and kept the other open, searching the inside of the cover, then turning the pages slowly to see if he'd find anything there.

It took him a while to find it, but there was a page missing. It wasn't torn out. It had been cut out with precision, with a scalpel or a razor blade so it looked like it wasn't even gone. He dialed Tess.

"Harlow," she said.

"Tess, did they notice any pages missing from the books?"

"What?"

"The books," he said, feeling frantic. "The two books we found at Erickson's. When they checked for prints, did they find anything, pages missing, things underlined or circled? Anything like that?"

There was a pause on her end. "They found your fingerprints and a page missing in one of them. A few circles or markings here and there, but that was all."

He hung up on her and looked down at the page missing from the Larsson book. It was page 245/246. He found a pen in the nightstand and wrote 245/246 on the palm of his hand. He flipped several pages forward and saw Chapter 13 intact and the dates beneath it, "Thursday, February 20—Friday, March 7" above where the chapter began. He flipped backward and found Chapter 11, which read, "Saturday, February 1—Tuesday, February 18." He went through the rest of the book, looking for missing pages or markings. He found nothing else.

He opened his ThinkPad and typed the book title and chapter into the browser search bar. The missing page was in the chapter marked February 19. He found the year in the Nesbø book. He opened it and scoured it the same way, like he was reading the fine print in a contract. He came across page 19 and page 97, both numbers underlined in black pen. He typed in the date, searched records and newspaper archives. He located an article published on the day his father was caught. There was the photo of Gunner in handcuffs at the center of the page. He didn't know why the killer would go through the trouble of doing something like this. He dragged the page down farther, skimming the rest of the paper, starting to think that maybe this was nothing after all. Maybe the killer was just giving glory to his father.

But as he scrolled down, he knew why.

Local Boy Drowns in Lake

The day the police captured Gunner Lindström, the day the boy drowned in the lake, they were one and the same. Now Rooker understood. Anna Meltzer was wrong. It wasn't Henry who'd killed the boy. Rooker powered on the phone and noticed a missed voice mail. He held it to his ear, heard scratching, and then Erik Sadler's voice came over clear as day.

"You'll find her where Mrs. Persson should have died." And then a text message came through, one he wouldn't show Tess. Rooker rose from the bed and went to the door.

Chapter 45

February 19

Rooker knocked on Tess's door. When she opened it, he made his way inside.

"We need to leave," he said.

"What?"

"Chippewa National Forest," Rooker said. He played her Erik Sadler's message. Then: "Mrs. Persson told us about the spot. Lena must be there. There were pages missing from the books that were at Erickson's. I found a date. February 19, 1997. It's the date they arrested Gunner. It's also the day Gregory Sadler drowned. I don't think Henry killed him."

"You think it was Erik?"

"I think we need to leave."

"Get your stuff together." Rooker listened to her call in for a search party. "That's a lot of ground to cover. We're going back."

◆ ◆ ◆

By the time they returned to Itasca County, darkness stretched the length of the sky. Massive lights and a search party were already underway deep in the woods. The search was mostly locals, along with canines outfitted with orange vests and police. He listened to the shouts, each one a different voice but the same long-winded pitch.

Lena. Lena.

Dead thickets and groves rose like stalagmites from the frozen earth. All that was left was icy trees and snowy rock. Rooker got out of the Interceptor and surveyed a map of the area. The forest was more than 298 miles. And they didn't know where to start. There were hiking trails, places designated for hunting and camping. And numerous cabins. To top it all off, there was heavy, packed snow. If Lena Warrington was alive when the killer brought her here, she'd be dead by the time they found her. Tess tossed Rooker a flashlight, and the two started walking, the frozen ground giving little way.

It wasn't long before he stopped.

"*Shit,*" he said. "I left my phone back there. Can I have the keys? I'll run right back."

She handed them over and told him to hurry. But he wouldn't be back. Before he returned to the car, he pulled the phone from his pocket and read the message again. Come home. Alone.

Now he responded. On my way.

Just try not to run off and scare the shit out of me. He heard Tess's voice in his head. But he was going to do exactly what she'd told him not to. He knew where Sadler was.

As he got in the car, put the pistol on the passenger seat, and pulled out, a few eyes were on him, but it didn't matter now. He was off like a rocket, thirty over the limit as soon as he'd turned onto the road.

It could have been the cold or the anticipation making his body tremble. Either way, there was a tingling shiver in every muscle. He started playing out scenarios in his mind. None of them was promising. Why, he suddenly wondered, was he so stupid, so stubborn? Why was he unable to ask for help? Maybe his death would be penance for the people he'd gotten killed. Atonement was something he had never believed in, not until he lost his son and needed a morsel of hope that he'd see him again someday.

He weaved between the cars that were on the road this time of night. The blinding streams of white from oncoming traffic sent his eyes into a squinting, watery mess. He was fifteen minutes away now. Rooker watched one white circle float in front of the windshield and melt against it. Then another and another. They soared in the wind like miniature birds. After a couple of minutes, they were falling faster, larger and heavier. The lever by the steering wheel twisted in his hand, and he watched the wipers erase the droplets of snow that had already begun to freeze. The low, steady drum of the wipers going back and forth usually made him relax. Not tonight.

He pulled off the freeway and slowed down on the side roads. The snow was beginning to stick. Soon the ground would be coated in white. The roads would be more slippery, and he didn't want to risk crashing Tess's car, especially after he'd stolen it. About a quarter mile from the cottage, he pulled to a stop, turned the lights off, and parked. The engine went silent. He sat perfectly still, peering out into the darkness. He could hear the light wind and the drops of snow falling to the windshield.

Rooker picked up the pistol and nudged the door shut quietly. At a steady trot, he made his way toward the house.

He was dressed entirely in black; he would let the night hide him, conceal him in its belly. The squalls and whispers of the wind masked his footsteps. He knew how close he had been to death the night he was shot with a rifle, how good a shot the killer was. This time he needed to shoot first. He needed to end this, whether he fired one bullet or the entire clip into the killer. It didn't matter as long as it was done.

Rooker steadied himself against the base of a tree he could barely see amid all the precipitation. He took a deep breath and held it there, exhaling through pursed lips. Then he did it again, his rapid, shallow breaths slowing down. He figured it was the surgery, the exercise he hadn't done since it was over. He peeked out from the edge of the tree. There was a strange light, a flickering yellow at the back of the house. He had no idea what it was. And the light switch for the back hadn't worked since he'd been there. He had tried flicking the switch, and nothing ever happened. Now there was something out there.

Chapter 46

"Boss!"

Tess Harlow stopped in her tracks. Millie Langston's voice shrilled over the receiver. She bounced on her toes, burrowed deeper into her jacket, observing thin strobes of white light scatter across the earth floor. As much as she didn't want Lena Warrington to be dead, in the back of her mind she thought she already was and hoped they'd find the body soon. It was freezing out. She knew it was wrong to think that way. But this case had led her to think the worst. If she ever encountered another case like this one, she had a new mantra to operate by: *Prepare for the worst and expect the unexpected.*

Lena. Lena.

She knew what she'd be hearing, over and over again, as she tried to get some sleep—whenever that would be.

Despite the presence of the search party, there was something spooky about these woods—the way the trees juddered wildly and stilled to their clamoring for Lena. Their shadows contorted, inhumanly pointing the way. Or maybe not. Because Tess didn't think they were going to find her here. Not tonight. Maybe not ever. Her throat went dry. "I'm with the search party, Mil."

"I know." Grumbled hoots and hollers rang out, their voices spiraling all around her. Between the shouts, it was like the wind spoke—an unsettling whisper caressed the lobe of her ear and made the invisible hairs on her arm rise.

Millie Langston's voice climbed higher. "I found something you're gonna wanna hear. Something about this case—Henry, I don't know. It didn't sit right."

"Millie," she said before the call cut out. Tess imagined bloody handprints in the snow somewhere, leading to the body of Lena Warrington. She pictured matted hair, clumps of twig and blood and brain tangled in a net of snow. It reminded Tess of how her mother would brush her hair in the mornings before school, raking away at her messy curls, and she'd jerk her head away from the hairbrush.

WHAT HAVE YOU DONE?

As she looked around, she caught the large back of Martin Keene walking cautiously away from her. "Martin, where's Rooker?"

Martin twisted toward her, the flashlight beam in her face. She squinted to see his overcoat collar upturned to shield his neck, and he hollered back, "Sorry, boss." He aimed the flashlight down. "Haven't seen him."

"Millie," Tess said again.

Millie's voice came over the phone. "I've been digging and digging. Looking through old missing persons reports—"

"Hey!" Tess yelled as she witnessed a man launch his boot into a layer of underbrush reaching out from the ground. "Watch your step, guys."

"Cross-referencing anything near Itasca County. Searching for anything on the whereabouts of Henry Frederick Hult after he vanished."

Tess sighed. A shock wave of wind rushed through the trees. Shielding her face, her cold finger pressed into the hollow of her ear. "He's dead, Millie."

"I know. Just listen! I found something else. Annie Redmond. She kept her last name. Lived in Coleraine all her life. She said they never found her son. Get this, he went missing in the spring of 1997."

"Okay . . . same year Henry vanished . . . and the Sadler boy drowned."

"Right. But, Tess . . . the boy's name: Elias. The father's last name was Cole."

Chapter 47

Rooker wrapped around to the west, keeping the same distance from the house. He was moving slowly, quietly. Ducking low, he shuffled, packing down thicker, softer snow behind the veil of trees. Some places, it felt like he was sinking. Others, it was like a sheet of ice his boots skated over. But the farther he moved, the more the yellow glow came into focus—blinking, not like a firefly but like a momentary power outage. A howl on the far side of the lake startled him. It reminded him of that feeling, climbing through the ropes all alone. It was only him in there, his sole means of survival. Since his boy was killed, he'd felt that same way—a perpetual, never-ending state of it. He had isolated himself from the world. It was for the best. The world without his boy was a vile, evil place.

Rooker kept moving. He'd come too far to go back now. His phone was turned on, but he'd left it in the car. He told himself it was because he didn't want it to attract attention in case it rang. Really, he didn't want any interference. Win or lose, he needed to settle this. Then again, maybe this time he did want to be saved. Maybe he was hoping that Tess would come and save him.

Advancing around a bend, his foot slid where the ground dipped to a small hill, but he caught himself. He held the back of a tree, pushed off it, and bark flaked in his hand. He moved to the next tree. Finally, he got a full view of the cottage. A string of murky lights dangled out back, trembling like coal embers. When for a second the lights were all intact, Rooker saw her bound to the chair, tape tight across her mouth. He thought he could see a red gash on her forehead and the same color at her cheek. Her head drooped, hanging like an insect caught in a web. His eyes focused on her. He could see her move. She was breathing. But why?

As he watched her, he understood. She was bait. Rooker turned to head back the way he came, took a couple of steps, and a branch snapped beneath him. Echoed in the quiet night. *FUCK.* He got back behind the tree just in time. Almost. He winced as sections of wood splintered off and hit him hard in the face. He touched the pain above his eye, dribbling blood. At first, he thought he was going into shock, that he had been shot.

CRACK. Another blast sent tree bark exploding all around him. Same high-powered rifle. Semiautomatic. Right after the shot belted the tree, Rooker turned and fired three shots in the direction of the woods where he thought the bullets were coming from. At a dead sprint, he dove behind a different tree and heard another shot farther from where he was. He crouched. Scurried on his ass. Cold, pebbled snow found its way under the back of his shirt. Mucus dripped from his nose. His heart was pounding.

He waited. But he couldn't wait long. The killer didn't care about the woman. She was nothing to him.

Rooker pressed his back up against the tree. Pushed off the ground to where he was standing upright. His legs were burning. *Now or never,* he told himself. He took off toward the tree closest to the back of the cottage. It was barely standing and had begun to topple over the house. One day, he'd probably wake up to it crashing through his bedroom, but tonight he needed it. He got to it and grabbed hold of it to stop his momentum. The woman was squirming in the chair.

He squinted at the lights and fired four shots. When one connected, they all went out simultaneously. Breathless, legs shaking, Rooker bolted from his unsteady spot and grabbed the chair by the arms. He lifted the woman off the ground and ran. Pulling her to the back door, he turned the knob and slammed all his weight into it. The door burst open, and a loud crack whizzed by over Rooker's left shoulder. Something exploded in the darkness. He dragged the chair through the door and kicked it shut. Freezing sweat raced down every pore of his face and neck, soaking the hem of his collar, cleaving it to his skin. The woman groaned, her sounds all he could hear beneath the tape across her lips. Smears of dirt and blood coated her face. He pulled the tape from her mouth, and she hurled curses at him.

"My hand! You ripped it open!"

Rooker did not answer. He was gasping, trying to get air back into his lungs. His chest burned from lifting the chair with her in it, but that was the least of his worries. He peered down at her hand. She was right. A dark stream of blood trickled between her fingers. When she tilted it, the blood smeared over her wrist and forearm.

"Why the fu—"

Rooker pulled the tape back across her mouth, patted it down just in case. "If he hears you, we're both dead."

He had to keep count now; it might save his life. Three shots before he ran, then pop-pop-pop-pop. Four at the lights. He'd taken seven shots. The pistol held twelve. He crouched on the ground, trying to catch his breath. It wasn't working. The adrenaline was coursing through his body like electricity. He tried to focus, to think of anything that could give him the upper hand. There was nothing except the fact that he should know the landscape better than his adversary. But a pistol against a sniper rifle wasn't exactly fair.

"Come out, Sadler!" he yelled into the night sky. The words echoed loudly; it was like the trees and the moon screamed the words back at him. Rooker waited there, sitting with his back against the wall. The soles of his boots were against the floor, his knees up, the pistol ready.

"I won't shoot if you won't," he hollered again, laughing maniacally to himself. As if that would ever work. He was starting to wish he had brought the phone with him. But still, he had five shots left in the clip. He only needed to make one count. He thought back to the deer he'd shot as a boy, how it was still alive when he'd walked over to it. He heard his father's words in his ear: *"Don't be a pussy."*

Rooker assumed Sadler was moving through the trees right now, closing in on the house. The problem was he had no way of knowing which direction he would come from. If Rooker popped up to check, he might be seen. Plus, the chances of him seeing any movement out there were slim to none. He could wait, but what good did that do him? He suddenly thought of something. He slid over to the cupboard and yanked a drawer open, reached up and started pulling out silverware. He could feel prongs and blades and the round back of a spoon. He grabbed them all in his hand, then crept to the door. He stood the fork upright against the bottom of it. Hauled ass on all fours to the front door and leaned a spoon up against it. Then he hurried to the side door to the kitchen, where he'd narrowly escaped death last time. He leaned another fork upright and got into position with his back to the wall. At least now he had all the entrances covered. And if Sadler somehow scaled the roof and came through the bedroom, it would be no secret. The floor would whine beneath every step.

Rooker sat stock-still. He could hear his own heart beating, imagined he could hear the sweat drip from his face to the wood floor. The woman in the chair had finally stopped trying to talk, so he was left in complete silence. But the silence turned to a constant low humming. He almost wished for any other noise. Anything but another bullet intended for him.

Rooker did not move. It felt like he'd been sitting for thirty minutes, maybe an hour. He knew it wasn't even close. It was the deafening silence, the waiting. But suddenly he heard it. A metal clank as one of the utensils hit the floor. It was to his left, the door that he had slammed his way through. Once he heard the noise, he turned and fired three shots. A blast was fired back in his direction but missed. He ran toward the door and two lower-decibel, smaller-caliber shots fired his way. Rooker swung the door open, peeked out, and pulled his head back before bullets rained into the doorframe. He got low and fired twice. Raising his head for a millisecond, he saw the pistol on the ground, the man standing there in dark clothes and a black cap. He was starting to pull a glove from his hand, and Rooker watched as the man began to shake and convulse. His glove was stuck to his skin, like it had woven into the torn flesh. Pain painted his face while he tugged it all the way off. A dime-size hole in his knuckle dripped blood to the snow. Rooker had grown used to watching a pen twirl between the fingers of that same hand.

"Sadler, right? Gregory Sadler."

The man Rooker had come to know as somewhat of a colleague craned his neck to the sky, breathing in the fresh air. He smiled as if the pain of being shot was nothing. "I haven't heard that name in years." There was a hole in the man's shoulder as well, dark liquid against torn black fabric. Rooker must have hit him when he'd shot toward the door. "How did you know?"

"The books—clever touch. Your brother hated Henry. When Lena was taken and Erik disappeared, I couldn't help but picture your mother. Every morning she stares at the door, waiting for you . . . it kept reminding me how they never found your body. But it was when I saw the article: the day you disappeared, one and the same as the day Gunner was caught. You used the chaos of that day to vanish."

He had been right. All along he'd said it was either a cop or someone connected to his father's case. It turned out it was both.

"I even made Henry call me Elias."

"The boy in the lake, I don't understand."

"The urban legend." Elias Cole closed his eyes again like he was reminiscing. A sinister line formed in his face. He breathed in the cold air. "I loved it out here." His eyes were closed, his hand dangling with blood pooling against the snow beneath it. He took a step toward the pistol on the ground.

"Don't," Rooker said. Shit. Suddenly it dawned on him. Three shots in the woods. Four at the lights. Three at the door. Two more. It was empty.

Cole was smart, and he was a cop. He might even know that Rooker's magazine had run dry. If Rooker ran at him, he might be able to get there before Cole could grab the gun. But Rooker would take at least one bullet in the process.

He didn't want to be shot again. Instead, he inched closer to the man, stalling. If Cole saw an opening, he'd move. It was ending just as Rooker always knew it would: only the two of them, him and the killer.

"Tell me about the legend."

"Henry had a hand in spreading it. He was my true brother."

"And yet you killed him."

"I *saved* him," Cole said sharply. "I saved him from dying at the hands of someone like you. The goddamned priest"—his mouth contorted, clenched in anger—"I kept a burner phone, but I never brought it to the station. I couldn't tell him to run."

"So you let him wing you in the shoulder, and then you shot him." Rooker smiled, understanding something as he thought out loud. "Explains the tears. And the reason you had them cut your shirt to stitch you. The cut in the cottage. The woman who stabbed you with your knife before you shot her in the head."

"You're clever enough, Rooker. You just saw it too late."

"And what about Erik?"

"Sharing the same blood with Erik means nothing."

"Where is he?"

"He's still alive, not for long probably." Cole paused. "It was Gunner, believe it or not. The legend." He winced and gritted his teeth. "One night, I was off playing in the woods alone. I saw this figure drag something out of his car and drop it in the woods. But when I went to see for myself what it was, I saw her head missing . . . he snuck up on me and lifted me by the throat. Slammed me against a tree. But I didn't flinch. I think he sensed something in me, which made him take me under his wing rather than kill me.

"Weeks later, he baptized me—held me underwater in the ice. Said it would make me his disciple."

"How?" Rooker said. "How does a boy vanish—how does Gregory Sadler become Elias Cole?" He was stalling for time, knowing Cole was doing the same.

"We spent years running, Henry and me. It was only weeks after the night Gunner was caught, the night I drowned." The word seemed to evoke a smile. "For fifteen miles, we walked the tracks in pelting rain. We reeked—body odor, Marlboro 100's, and gin. The two of us walked the ballasts until we saw a boy up ahead through the haze of rain. Still remember his sneakers. Dirty white Adidas. High-tops. He was our age, even sort of looked like me. I hit him, cracked him over the head with an aluminum bat. He was already dead after the second blow, his eyeball dangling from the socket. We left him there on the tracks, his face in a black puddle of bloody water. The best part: he had his ID on him. I mean, how perfect? One day we got caught, and someone asked my name. When I didn't answer, they found the ID. Elias Cole. So that's who I became."

"Where's Erik?"

"Oh, please. You didn't even like him. Why save him? Why not let him die?"

"I think enough people have died."

"Your precious boy." He laughed. "That was good, admit it. The phone call, Tate Meachum. That idiot."

"So you're the son Gunner always wanted. Bravo." Rooker clapped with the gun in hand. He wanted to change the subject from his son. For Cole to keep on talking. "A guy who cut heads off liked you and he didn't like me."

Cole took a step closer to the gun. Then he smiled. "I sense some jealousy."

"Delusions of grandeur," Rooker said. "Commonly associated with psychopaths."

"Ouch, Rooker. You're hurting my feelings." Cole, Gregory Sadler, whoever the hell he was, took another step toward the gun.

"Astrid Thompson," Rooker said. "Why wasn't she in the file?"

Cole grinned.

"I can still smell her, you know. She wasn't your father's. She was mine—my first. She was a teacher's aide in school, studying to be a teacher herself. I'd stare at her all through class. They gave Gunner the credit. But she was mine all along." He took another step forward.

It exhumed the horror . . . Olivia Campbell. He'd had to live with what he'd done to her. The terrors of *that day* haunted him even now. But that was the difference between him and Sadler. Sadler had a choice. Rooker didn't.

"If you move another inch, I'll shoot you."

Sadler eyed Rooker's Glock and grinned at the stance he had taken: his feet shoulder width apart, his arms slightly bent, the sight of the pistol just below eye level. In shooting position. "Glock 17. What is that, Sundgren's?" He laughed. "You're empty."

Cole dove for the gun. Just as his hand wrapped around the weapon, Rooker tackled him into the snow, managing to turn Cole's hand at the instant he fired. Rooker pressed into the hole in Cole's hand, causing the man to screech like a wounded animal.

He ripped the gun free, dropping it into the snow. Cole was not finished. He pulled a knife from his pants and jabbed it at Rooker's chest. He caught the serrated blade with the padded edge of his hand;

it was the only thing he could do to stop it. Cole put all his weight into it, and Rooker felt the blade slide in his hand. Screaming, he brought his knee up hard into Cole's groin. He followed it up with a headbutt right to the bridge of Cole's nose, causing a loud crack. The man who was Gregory Sadler lay on his back, still holding the knife. Rooker's hand was on fire, but the threat of death was an effective distraction.

While Sadler struggled to find his footing, Rooker punched him hard in the jaw. Then he grabbed the knife and launched it out onto the ice. He found the pistol, picked it up, stood, and aimed down.

"It's over." Rooker watched Gregory Sadler on the ground, only feet from where it all began. Steps from the ice where the boy disappeared all those years ago. It was where Gunner Lindström had turned him into a killer. Rooker glared at him, and for a moment, all he could see was his father. He was about to squeeze the trigger and rid the world of Gregory Sadler forever.

"No!" He heard someone screaming. "Do not shoot, Rooker."

Tess was running alongside Martin Keene. *Perfect timing,* Rooker thought. They had to show up now. Now, when he was ready to end it all. When he was finally ready for a win.

"We take him in," she said as she closed in on him. She inched toward Rooker like he was a dangerous animal that had escaped captivity.

Of course, she was right. A monster lay in front of him, a man who tortured and killed women, who'd tried to kill Rooker, had almost killed Tess.

But it was Tess's duty to reel Rooker back in, just as it was her job to bring Sadler to justice.

"Please." She was pleading now, and Rooker was ready to give in.

"Where's your brother?" he asked the man. Sadler wiped the blood from his nose, but it only came right back.

"He isn't my brother."

"Where is Erik Sadler?" Rooker asked again.

He didn't respond. Just grinned through bloodied teeth.

Rooker turned to Tess. "Search the house. I think he's some-where—" In that moment, Gregory went for him. He leaped from the ground and grabbed hold of Rooker for dear life. Rooker couldn't pry him loose. He dropped the gun and put everything he had into fighting Sadler off. The two men slammed hard into the ice, and it gave way. Rooker grabbed for the surface, but a chunk of it broke off into his hand. He swung it at Gregory's head and connected. The two were fighting underwater, Gregory grabbing at Rooker's throat, Rooker grabbing back at Sadler. He squeezed with everything he had, digging his thumbs into the man's windpipe. Eventually Gregory Sadler's grip loosened, and then he wasn't there at all.

Martin Keene was about ready to dive into the freezing water when Rooker's hand and face came to the surface. Keene dragged him up onto the ice, Rooker shivering, his body seizing uncontrollably.

"Get divers out here," he managed to say. "This time, make sure the boy in the lake is dead."

Chapter 48

Within the hour, the cavalry had shown up. First the ambulances, the rest of the detective team, a few cop cars, then the divers. They were trying to get Rooker into the back of the ambulance.

He was outside when a team went into his house and pulled the tape from the woman's mouth. She was screaming that Erik Sadler was under the floor. *Gunner's kill room.* They found Erik Sadler badly beaten, handcuffed to the table. Purple knots and dirt and dry blood splotched the orbital bone on his right eye. His lip was split. Blotches of red stained the lapels of his dress shirt, the top buttons ripped from it. When he found out it was his brother who had taken him, had killed all these women, had kidnapped his fiancée, he was speechless. Selma Sadler was called. She'd have to look at the body of the boy she'd lost decades before.

Rooker drank hot chocolate from a steel thermos alongside Keene and Tess. He changed inside the house, and they bagged his clothes for evidence. They draped a few blankets over him while a medic stitched the side of his hand. They inspected his chest, but it was nothing more than a long, gross cut. It didn't need to be stitched, but they applied surgical glue and bandages to it. Vic Sterling, Millie Langston, and Xander Whitlock came out to the scene. Rooker realized he appreciated having them there. Even Xander, who clapped Rooker on the back and walked away in silence without ever looking at him.

He sat and waited once again. The snow had stopped falling. His eyes trailed off into the woods, and he could have sworn he saw a wolf take off when all the bright lights and sirens were driving in. Nearly forty minutes later, he watched the team pull a body up onto the ice. They carried it over, put it in a black bag, and he looked down at the face. It was Gregory Sadler, or the detective Elias Cole. Rooker might be able to sleep tonight knowing it was over. Or maybe this would just add another nightmare to his collection. Keene stood to talk to one of the cops, which left Rooker and Tess. She scooted over beside him and pressed her shoulder into one of his blankets.

"Want one?" he asked, his teeth still clicking.

"No, it's okay. How's the hand?"

"I'll live." He turned it over and perused the bandaging. He was sure it would scar. "Anyway, if you need me, you know where to find me."

"So you're staying," she said.

"As of right now." A yawn leaped from his mouth. "But that could change any day. I'm freezing my balls off in this place."

The next morning, Rooker trudged downstairs and saw the dishes that Evelyn had brought him. They were still piled up in the sink. Though he had eaten everything on them, a putrid, rotten-corpse odor remained. It all felt so long ago, Evelyn delivering her home cooking. And now the house next door was empty because of him. He grabbed the sponge and washed all the dishes, toweled them dry, and took them over to her house. He turned the door handle still wrapped in flimsy yellow tape and made his way inside. Opening the cupboard, he stacked the dishes in their proper places. Then went back out the door and closed it behind him.

He stepped back into his kitchen and opened a drawer. He had thought about this drawer quite often. There were a few matches left inside a matchbook. It was the first time in a long while that he considered burning the place to the ground. He tapped the book against his hand, went over to where the picture of his boy was, lay down on the floor, and smiled up at him. He had done something the boy could be proud of. He gazed into his son's smiling green eyes. Man, did he miss the hell out of him. After a few minutes, he sat up and stared at the picture frame. For the first time, he thought to turn the photo upright, even held the frame in his fingers. When he heard a vehicle approaching, his fingers stopped. He pocketed the matches and went to the door. A white delivery van sputtered in the wet sludge. A man sat in front, straight as a board. And then a boy got out of the van. Rooker opened the door to see what was going on. The boy made his way over toward the cottage, a package in tow almost as large as he was.

"Delivery for Rooker Lindström," the boy squeaked, bustling over, struggling to carry it.

"Yeah," Rooker said, curious. The package was wrapped in brown kraft paper and thin rope, the boy holding it overhead like he was shielding himself from torrential rain.

"We were told to deliver this today; it's from a . . ." He paused and read the name written on the tag. "Gregory Sadler."

Rooker's heart skipped a beat. "Thanks," he said and took it from the kid.

He walked inside with it, set it down on the table, hesitant to open it. He was too anxious to pry at the rope knots, instead going to the kitchen and pulling a knife from the cupboard. He tore the paper off, pulled the canvas out, and placed it on top of the table. It was a painting of Rooker. His own jacketed back, standing there looking out over the frozen water behind his home. It was darker, more sinister than Henry's other paintings. Still, it was beautiful. The kid stood in the doorway, admiring it. Rooker dug around the inside of the paper and pulled out a note.

> Rooker,
> To you, living in your frozen hell. I hope they write stories about me for years to come.
> —The rightful son
> G.S.

Rooker couldn't help but picture Gregory and Gunner side by side, couldn't help but wonder at the things they talked about. What was it that made Gunner take Gregory Sadler under his wing? There were so many unanswered questions. He would never fully know how Elias Cole came to be. What he did understand was that Gregory Sadler was more the son of Gunner Lindström than Rooker could ever have been.

He turned, and the boy was still hovering in the doorway. The kid must be waiting for a tip. He didn't look like he had much money. He wore a hand-me-down long-sleeve sweatshirt, loose and ragged and old, along with tattered jeans with boots probably a size too big for his feet. Rooker riffled through the pockets of a pair of pants that lay on the floor, found a few dollars, and took them over to the kid. The boy reached out, an odd smile on his face. When he stretched his arm out, his sleeve pulled back. Rooker regarded the boy in horror. They were there. There, on his wrist, the skin still healing from where Rooker had dug his nails into him. He hadn't been dreaming it. It was real. He backed away, his eyes glued to the boy.

In an instant, the boy's face changed. Rooker backed far enough into the kitchen to where he'd stashed the Glock 17. They had let him keep it after last night, even gave him rounds to go with it. He had reloaded it this morning, intending to return it to Peter Sundgren in the same condition it had been in when it had been given to him. He slid the drawer open, grabbed the pistol, and took aim. The boy had entered the house now, a knife in his hand.

"Don't, kid." Rooker took the safety off; his finger tapped and rested on the side of the trigger guard.

The boy dropped the knife, turned on his heel, and ran.

Once the boy was gone, Rooker phoned Tess.

The cycle had continued—almost. A boy, manipulated by a psychopath, sent to do the bidding of Gregory Sadler. Rooker went up to one of the rusted nails jutting out from the ceiling and hung the painting there. He looked around the cottage. It brought back so many memories. He was standing on the very spot, there beneath the floorboards. The police never found her. The dogs never picked up her scent. It was where he'd put Olivia Campbell.

Rooker walked outside. Closed his eyes. Letting out a shaky breath, he stared up to the milky gray sky. The smoky winter cold invaded his lungs. He felt like it was choking him. And then the tears came.

Rooker went back inside and closed his eyes for what felt like an eternity. Then he pulled the matchbook from his pocket, stood in the doorway watching the siren lights flicker in the distance, like the fireflies when he was just a boy—and lit it.

ACKNOWLEDGMENTS

Thank you, first of all, to the friends and family who supported me in the pursuit of my dream. You are appreciated more than you know.

To the extraordinary writers that inspired me to become an author, I wouldn't be here without you.

I would like to thank my lovely agent, Victoria Skurnick at Levine Greenberg and Rostan Literary Agency. Thank you for taking a chance on me. I promise this is only the beginning.

Thank you to Jessica Tribble at Thomas & Mercer for loving this story as much as I do.

Thanks to a dear friend, Tom Giustino, PhD in neuroscience and semipro sportswriter, for your continued support and your expertise in anything brain-y.

To Minnesota, and specifically Itasca County, thank you for being the perfect setting to place Rooker Lindström. I'm sorry for the serial killer thing. Again, this is a work of fiction.

To Rooker, thank you for carrying the burdens I've placed on you so ungracefully. I'll see you soon.

ABOUT THE AUTHOR

Pete Zacharias received a BA in English with a concentration in creative writing. He is a lover of Nordic noir, dark thrillers, and anything spy, and credits Michael Connelly's *The Poet* as the novel that inspired him to become a writer. *The Man Burned by Winter* is Pete's first novel.